CW00421182

FYNODEREE

Alexander Caine Duncan

1

Alexander Caine Duncan was born and brought up in the Isle of Man. What began as a mild interest in his homeland's folklore soon turned into an obsession, taking up most of his spare time and a lot of time when he should have been doing other things.

Alexander is an actor and lives in London.

Author note

This story takes place on the Isle of Man, Ellan Vannin as it is sometimes known or at least the island of my childhood dreams. It is not dissimilar from the Isle of Man I grew up on, but like dreams, sometimes unfamiliar, strange and fantastic.

There are several people I'd like to thank who joined me on the journey. To those dear friends who offered me their help and guidance whenever and wherever they could, Matthew Faulds, Clare Glynn-Riley, Tom Peters and Angie Greenhalgh. Thank you to William Faulds for his wonderful art work and enthusiasm and to Roy Tilleard without whom you wouldn't be holding this book right now. And lastly to Mum, Dad and my brother, Rob, this book is dedicated to you.

First Edition November 2006
Second Edition January 2007

Published by Lily Publications
      PO Box 33, Ramsey, Isle of Man, British Isles, IM99 4LP
      Tel: +44(0)1624 898446.
      E: lilypubs@manx.net
      W: lilypublications.co.uk

Copyright: © Fynoderee Ltd

ISBN 1 899602 97 6

All rights reserved. No part of this book may be reproduced in any form or by any means without permission in writing from the publisher, except by a reviewer who may quote brief passages in a review.

Publishers Note:
1. On the Isle of Man, Ellan Vannin, it is bad luck to say the word "r a t", and so in this book they are known as "long-tails"

FYNODEREE

"O land of our birth ....

O island so strong and so fair…"

(an extract from the Manx national anthem)

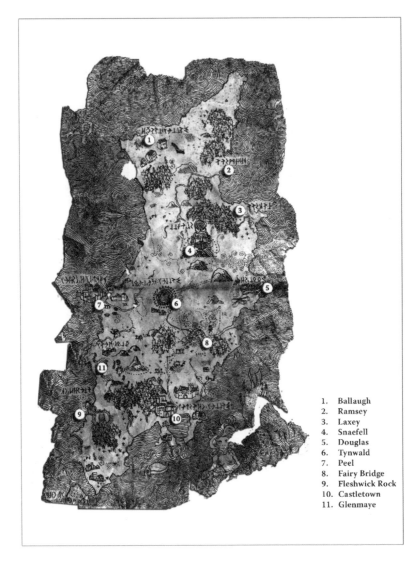

1. Ballaugh
2. Ramsey
3. Laxey
4. Snaefell
5. Douglas
6. Tynwald
7. Peel
8. Fairy Bridge
9. Fleshwick Rock
10. Castletown
11. Glenmaye

The Isle of Man, or Ellan Vannin

ONE

Bea waited behind the dry stone wall, sheltering from the late autumn winds. The gusts blowing in off the sea were strong and shrewd for the time of year, even penetrating his thick fur, and bringing with them whispers of change. The whispers whistled down through the valleys, rattling the windows and shaking the trees, and in his shelter Bea pricked his ears up high to listen. The change was coming soon, that much he could tell, and leaning back against the rough stone he sniffed the chill night air stinging his wet nostrils. The air smelt old and churned his stomach, like rotting meat. It was the smell of fear.

Bea closed his eyes and offered his thanks to the spirit of the island, Manannin, that no man had yet heard the whispers on the wind. That was the way he prayed it to stay. He knew they wouldn't understand and a whole world they never believed in would be put in danger.

Yet where there was fear, there was also resilience. Life didn't stop, but continued nonetheless. Owls were still out, hunting for stray voles and field mice, and Bea could see two Manx cats spying each other suspiciously through the undergrowth of the nearby trees. He also needed to continue. He had no other choice.

He had been out all night searching for answers to the questions that wouldn't stop spinning through his mind, but they kept themselves well hidden, and out of reach. Like every other night since the leaves began to turn, he would return home with nothing. Loath to give up as he was, he knew that it would be moondown before long. He had to be safely out of sight by then and besides, he was too weak to stay out any longer. He feared he was too weak to get back home to Fleshwick Rock. He needed food. Otherwise he was certain his journey, though short, would be futile. He would be dust before sunrise.

He lifted his head up and over the wall and looked down the

slopes of South Barrule. Towards the foot was a quiet sleeping cottage glowing in and out of view, like a beacon, as the moon shone through the breaks in the cloudy night sky. He sighed. Being so close to men didn't feel right. His parents had taught him early on to either keep his distance from them or use his strength to move in the shadows and shift with the land, in *arraghey*, as they called it in the ancient tongue. His kind depended on it.

'We must remain a myth, it's better for everyone,' his father, Dane, had told him numerous times. And so an instinct for stealth had been bred into him, an instinct he would have to rely on wholly, as he certainly lacked the strength needed to *arraghey*. He would have to be as cautious as he had ever been if he was to go in and out of the cottage unnoticed.

Bea hated the thought of stealing but sadly knew that guilt wasn't going to feed him. He would only take enough to give him the strength to return home and not a crumb more. Shamefully resolved, he climbed over the wall, neglecting his natural ways, and paced down towards the cottage.

His hard feet crunched on the gravel of the path but could barely be heard over the blustering sounds of the wind as he made his way to the back door. Once there, he slowly turned the handle to see if it was open. It wasn't. So he quietly placed the sharp nail of his index finger into the small keyhole and twisted it until he felt a definite click.

Inside the house, up the stairs and down the landing, Derrick Kermode stirred. He was usually a heavy sleeper but a force far beyond his control, like a loose spring in his mattress, had become unbearable and interrupted his slumber. Hunger had woken him.

Derrick's dribbling had spread into a grey patch over his pillow, his eyes stung and felt crusty, and there was a growing pain on his left side. His gaunt features wrinkled up as he carefully eased his wife's large arm from on top of his and sat up, shaking it several times to ease the stiffness.

He slipped out from underneath the covers and jumped when the bare soles of his feet felt how cold the wooden floor was. He quickly pulled on his slippers and, rubbing his eyes with the back of his hand, looked at his wife, her mouth wide open, all her teeth proudly on display, and gave a small smile.

Though Joyce was continuing to snore as though her life depended on it, Derrick was still very conscious of his empty stomach and held it with both hands to muffle its grumbling. Pulling his gaze away from her, he breathed in, and carefully set off for the kitchen. As he passed the bed he didn't pick up the faint click of the back door lock being picked and the tentative squeak of the rusty hinges as the door was opened and shut with skilled caution.

Derrick's Labrador, Duke, jolted to attention in his basket when the bolt of the door snapped back in place, and padded across the floor to investigate. He paused beneath the kitchen table before moving into the pantry where the back door was, and froze. His wet nose, shining like mother of pearl, picked up a scent of burnt wood in the cold air and through the dark he could see the bulky silhouette of a stranger only a few paces in front of him. Its shape was not unlike that of a man, though broader with strong, defined muscles on its arms and chest, but what was most unusual was the wild, thick fur covering its whole figure. So different was this *thing* from his master, or any other man he'd ever seen, that Duke drew back from it in wonder.

It was too dark to make out its features in detail but as it twisted its huge shoulders its deeply set eyes fell upon him. Duke could easily see that the irises were a deep penetrating green and in the low light they seemed to glow.

As the green eyes moved closer to his and the *thing* raised its thunderous arm above its head, Duke let out a quiet whimper and squeezed his own eyes shut, preparing to be struck. After the moment passed and the strike hadn't come, Duke cautiously opened one eye in time to see the huge hand of the *thing* come down and softly pat the hair on the top of his head. Bea tried to show the dog he should fear no harm, and stroking him, gave him a wink.

Duke's tongue fell out in relief and he nodded his head in

understanding. He knew that it was no time for running around chasing his tail and when Bea's hand did a small brushing movement, he was quick to pick up its meaning. He turned around and crept back towards his basket, pausing only once to turn to the *thing* and nod in farewell. Bea nodded back in reply and Duke curled up into his basket and within a moment returned to sleep.

Bea let out a slow breath and anxiously waited until the silence stretched out through the house. When he was sure he was alone, his muscles eased and he took a few further steps towards the pantry. It seemed that not even the night registered his movement as his long toes quietly gripped the kitchen floor with each step before uncurling and lifting from the smooth tiles. He had been born hiding in such shadows.

When he reached the pantry, his mouth was wet with hunger and all he could hear was the pulse of blood thumping and quickening inside his head. He gently reached out his hand and took hold of the faint outline of the fridge door. He hated himself in that moment; he was no better than a thief, and let his head drop in disgust. His thoughts were so far away that he failed to hear the soft sound of slippers on the carpet of the stairs, as Derrick made his own way down to the kitchen and towards the pantry.

The night wrapped around Bea, hiding him from Derrick, who was sniffing the air trying to decipher what the new smell, tickling his nose was. Bea's stomach growled, but he ignored it; all other matters had been eclipsed by his hunger. But then a hissing sound came from close by as Derrick stifled a sneeze and Bea realised he wasn't alone.

In a blink all his instincts flushed back to him with a sobering slap across the face. For someone so used to feeling like a ghost, he could sense Derrick's presence only a few paces away. Without turning to him and revealing the bright green glow of his eyes shining through the light-less air, he jumped with an effortless spring and grabbed onto the frame at the top of the door. He gripped with both his hands and feet and held his breath just as

Derrick passed directly beneath him.

As the fridge door opened Bea was struck with the new light flooding the room. Suddenly everything shone with its own renewed colour and distinction. Derrick was so pale he seemed to reflect the light and shivered with the cold air hitting his face. Bea was still not breathing and squeezed his eyes shut, unable to *arraghey*, praying to Manannin that he might go unnoticed. How childish it would be to be seen by man for little more than a slab of cheese.

Beneath him Derrick began to mumble quietly, moving plates of meats and bowls of fruit. He sniffed the air once more and shook his head. Bea grimaced, knowing the odour came from his unwashed matted hair only a foot or so above Derrick's head.

Clamped onto the doorframe, his muscles began to tire and his lungs were burning, but after some time Derrick gave a little sigh of pleasure and excitement. He drew out a plate carrying a dark pudding and kicked the fridge door closed with the back of his foot as he began fervently spooning the cake into his mouth and leaving the pantry.

He continued through the kitchen and was about to shut the door when he felt an unpleasant backward chill. A shudder ran through him and he felt the hairs on the back of his neck lift up. He looked back into the room to check if he'd accidentally left the fridge door ajar but there was no light coming from the pantry. He would never be that careless. But the draught, now stronger, was coming from the very back of the house. He strode over to the back door, only to discover that it was wide open and banging noisily against the outside wall. He began to pull the door closed when something caught his eye up ahead, a dark shape crossing his sight at some speed. His first thought was that it might be a fox but concluded that a stray dog looking for scraps was more likely and quickly dismissed it. Taking a deep breath, he closed his eyes for a moment, feeling the breeze on his face, and caught the sweet smell of the grass from the fields sloping up behind the house. He then shut the door, picked the fallen key off the floor and locked it, shaking it once or twice to check it was secure.

'Did *you* see anything old boy?' he asked Duke, again awake and not too pleased about it. Duke replied with an expression suggesting both innocence and ignorance.

'Useless,' Derrick muttered, spitting out a few cake crumbs and returning upstairs to bed. Duke huffed, knowing that if Derrick had seen the dark *thing* that darted out the backdoor he would have retreated to the nearest basket too.

After a brief dash to cover, Bea was at a safe distance from view and, panting, he gazed back down towards the cottage carved into the landscape. His panting wasn't from exhaustion, although his hunger was tugging on his strength more and more, but from fear of discovery. That had been too close for comfort. Men hadn't seen his kind for many centuries now, and it was no time to lift the darkness clouding their eyes.

He looked down at his badly scarred hands and the booty nestling guiltily in his palms. He had snatched a handful of cheeses and fruit in one hand and several cuttings of cold meat in the other. He frowned. This couldn't go on for much longer.

Crouching down behind the wall in the cruel wind he began to eat, gratefully wolfing down the food, groaning as his stomach was filled and life returned to his muscles. After a short rest he felt far more himself again and climbed onto the wall to get a clearer view of the fastest way home.

The rising of the sun was not far off; he didn't have long. It was such a pity though, he thought, stretching his neck skyward and tasting the air. He knew it would be a fine day. He longed to roam around the hills and lakes on such a day, as he was told his kind once had in the ancient stories. Just to walk in the day.

To the north lay the thick forests of Ballaugh; a perfect cloak in the gloom of night, but too risky during daylight with the constant stream of heavy footed ramblers. To the east and the south lay towns of men, many men. Although he'd never set foot there, the plethora of lights and smoke were enough to keep him away. He leapt off the rock and began to run west, with the wind behind him and getting stronger with every step.

He bounded onto his path with a graceful ease and followed

the journey of a narrow river, as the moon lowered in the overcast night sky. What light there was tumbled down and reflected its blue-silver glow on the river leading towards the harbour at the village of Peel. Bea would usually take this route, following the water to the coast, then make his way round in the cover of the rocks. But it was now too early and he knew men in boats would already be preparing for their daily catch. Instead he headed south at the next small waterfall, bubbling beneath his wet feet.

Speeding past an old mill, he jumped over the small stretch of man-made road. He didn't want to feel the smooth, unnatural surface under his feet, and let the strengthening wind quicken his pace. Through the next barren headland he ran, and the thick overgrown fields of heath and gorse sped past him as he made his way up hill towards the long-standing folly at its summit.

He slowed to a walk and, closing his eyes, dragged his hand over the ruined out-house of the folly. He gently circled it, feeling its coarseness and age on his fingertips, before continuing on the steep descent towards the gateway at Eairnyerey.

A smile drew across his face as he caught up with the speed of the wind and then passed it, moving so swiftly his feet barely had time to touch the ground. The wind was an old friend, and they played together whenever he was out in the open. He bounded from the earth and let it carry his weight a short way, circling his fur, before dropping him rather crudely in front of a brittle stile that led to a footpath lined with dried bracken and heather. Bea knew the wind was teasing him and let out a small puff of misty air as he climbed over. He recoiled suddenly when some of the fur on his ankle was snagged and pulled off by a loose string of barbed wire. He looked at the thin gash on his skin as it closed up, and the torn hair instantly turned white, crumbled to a dust and then fell onto the earth, disappearing into the muddy path. He rubbed the barely visible mark that remained and without another thought, continued on his way.

The coastline flew past him as he moved on through the moor-land, staying just off the path and feeling the long grass under his feet. He passed down the steep, slippery slope of

Eairnyerey and the noise of the sea erupted as he arrived in the bay at Fleshwick Rock, stretching out like a secluded horseshoe in the coast. The crashing waves clawed at the pebbles of the bay, pulling on them as though they were trying to reclaim them for their own.

Bea took three enormous steps and fell from the cliff. Refusing help from the wind, he landed with both feet flat on a large, rocky ledge protruding from the rough face of the precipice, narrowly avoiding the wet seaweed a few steps away. The ledge was etched into the rock and high above the waves where no man would risk venturing.

He took one final look out towards the sea and the bruised early morning sky. It was impossible to catch sight of the horizon. He couldn't tell where the sea stopped and the sky began. Spreading his arms wide, he felt the caress of the wind and the salty air wash over him before he turned his back on the onset of day and faced the cliff.

With the sharp nail of his index finger, he touched the rock in front of him and drew his hand down in a gentle curved line. As if he was only pushing his hand through grain, the rock obediently parted in silence at his touch, leaving room enough for him to pass through. He patted the cold surface in thanks and stepped into the quiet windless space of the cave.

TWO

Bea gave a weighty groan as the rocks sealed together behind him, seamless to prying eyes. He no longer had to keep a tense wariness with every step, ready to hide from the dangers beyond his control. He was home.

Inside the cave it was as black as pitch, and the air was stale and warm after the stinging cold of the coastline a few feet behind the rock. There was only one noise to break the silence around him; the brief but constant dripping of water onto stone. Its echo seemed to make the cave stretch on forever, as though there was a whole world behind the rock that man had either missed or forgotten. That was its purpose.

Beneath Bea's feet were many small smooth pebbles, wet from the spray of the sea and scraping together under his weight. He crouched down onto one knee, still looking straight ahead with his eyes forced wide, and put his hand flat on the ground. It was so dark that even he struggled to make out any definition of the shapes around him. He picked up the first pebble he came to and rolled it around his hand, feeling its roughness against his scarred and leathery skin. It wasn't smooth or strong enough for what he needed, and squeezing his palm, he crushed the pebble into dust, which blew away, and he began to feel the ground for another.

His hands may have calloused to be as hard as bone but that hadn't lessened any of their sensitivities. After all, touch was sight when his eyes couldn't see. He shortly found a pebble so smooth it was hard to keep hold of, like a fish trying to escape the clutches of its captor. Again he squeezed his palm, but this time the rock stayed intact. It was just what he needed.

Still in the night of the cave, he stood up. His legs were stiff and sore from the exertion and cold of the night, but he ignored them and put his hand in front of him, pointing to a spot in the darkness beyond. He couldn't see his arm extended but knew he pointed to the right place. This was mere routine for him. He tossed the pebble in his right hand, like a coin, sucked a breath in hard and with the great power of his enormous shoulder, flung the rock into the cloak of black before him and waited, his eyebrows expectantly raised.

The moments of silence stretched out. Even the clock-like ticking of the water seemed to pause, waiting for contact. Then, with a crack, the pebble reached its target. It scraped along the rock of the far wall, lit a fierce blue spark that broke through the dark, and hit a pile of dry bracken, kindling and logs collected in a gaping mouth of rock at the far end of the cave.

The dry wood instantly set ablaze, flooding the cavernous space with the yellows and reds of the flames, and every shadow seemed to dance in celebration at being given light and heat once more.

'*Bolgan Glenney!*' Bea cheered, in the elder tongue of his kin, as the warmth of the fire struck his face and washed off the cold from outside.

He was standing on the lip of a ledge looking out over the, now lit, vast inner domain. It was no cave he was in, but a Great Hall cut into the rock. From where he stood, there was a long drop down to the floor of the hall, which shone like black marble. With the light against it, it gave the appearance of a shimmering black lake beneath him.

The Great Hall had been carved into a perfect dome, the rock tamed and smoothed down to a polished surface, and along the whole length of the circumference were statues struck into the side. Statues of figures like him, stern and imposing, standing proud and noble, gazing down on those living with a solid assurance. Only in their watchful eyes did Bea now feel safe.

From the ceiling of the dome hung countless pieces of glass, dangling down like transparent bats, catching every spark of light and throwing it elsewhere in the hall. There seemed to be never a moment of stillness, everything was moving with the array of colours, bouncing and forever dancing, bringing life to the dull air. Even the eyes of the statues came alive, reflecting the light and staring all about for any intruders.

Yet all the splendour of the dome was draped in long silky cobwebs, like ragged lace from an old dining room table. They hung from everything, camouflaging the hall's true opulence. In truth, Bea knew it had seen greater days. The dome was an image of gradual decay; where once there swung hanging baskets of flowers, bursting with life and scent, only dust and mould remained. And the roof resembled an antique chandelier crawling with spiders and mites. Neglect hung in the air.

A little way from where he stood, a great staircase began its sweeping arc to the floor. Each step was well trodden and faded and the banister was perfectly carved into the form of a long vine winding its way all the way down to the floor.

Bea hadn't walked on the steps for some time, not for as long as he could remember. Even with his aching and tired legs he still stood up onto the vine and, with a kick of his heel, slid down. He whipped round the length of it, leaning into its curves and banking its turns. At the bottom he flew off and landed with a slap on the surface of the hall, a small wave of dust splaying from his feet.

The Great Hall was filthy. Dust was evenly spread as though it had fallen from the ceiling of the dome. But this didn't concern Bea, who nonchalantly kicked away the half-finished skeleton of a long-tail[1] slumped near his foot without much thought. The corpse slid into a dark corner where a crunch immediately told him that the meal was gladly being finished by something else.

He stopped in the centre of the hall and turned with purpose to the wall of statues. All the figures, their eyes gleaming with light from the fire, stared down at him with a calm and regal authority; all but one. At the far end of the line was an unfinished statue. Its brow and eyes were deeply furrowed with lines of worry and deep thought. In its incomplete state the figure seemed to be fighting to release itself from the trappings of the rock, caught in the agony of being only half made up.

Although the eyes of the figure were dead, and the roughly chiselled rock reflected none of the light shining through the cave, Bea turned towards it and lowered his head. Raising his arm, he faced his palm at the figure in salutation, whispering a short prayer under his breath.

Slowly, Bea lifted his eyes and turned around to look past the long, plain and empty stone table in the centre of the hall, to the other side of the spherical wall.

One part of the wall was a smudge of colour; a mess of browns, greens, blues and greys of all shades dragged together and pulled into a distorted, almost horrific image. Bea could hardly recognize what was originally the likeness of his family underneath the swamp of colour. The painting of his face remained relatively complete, with the peaceful eyes gazing back at his own solemn expression. But the three figures surrounding him were an amalgamated filthy palette of their former selves.

Bea walked over to the image, light dust lifting from the floor with every step he took. He reached out to the mess of colour and with his finger, scooped up a shade of white that had mixed with an earth brown and sun yellow, making a dirty golden blonde, and walked to the beginnings of a new unspoilt likeness. It was just beyond a set of shelves stacked with simple wooden bowls and cups, now a resting-place for a farm of spiders and ants.

He carefully drew his finger over the likeness of a young female figure, like him, leaving another hair on the brow of her sun-kissed mane, draping over her narrow slight shoulders. He felt his heart tighten as he looked into her soft blue eyes, shaped like almonds, staring longingly back at him. A tear escaped from his eye and rolled slowly down his cheek as he stroked a finger across her face, smoothing her skin. He took a few steps back to get a clearer look at his work and was satisfied he'd captured her beauty on the face of the cold stone.

Weariness had caught up with him and his legs were burning just from carrying his own weight. He fell onto his side and took one last look at the vision painted on the wall before letting his eyelids drop shut. His head hit the floor of the Great Hall, and he slumped into a heavy dreamless sleep.

Outside the cave the winds passing through Fleshwick Rock scattered the clouds in the overcast sky like a wolf in a flock of sheep. The faint light of the dawn, rising at the very tip of Maghauld, in the far east of the island, let itself in and hit the wet rocks of the shore.

Mr. Boyde and his son, Ewan, were already up and breakfasting on kippers. Ewan hurried through his meal, not wanting to be late for his early morning rounds, and laughed as his father grumbled whilst reading the newspaper of the day before. His father had only got up to see his son off to work on time, not wanting him to taint the family name. But Ewan didn't mind. He was thankful for the company.

Soon after, the sun illuminated the great whites and reds of the Lady Isabella, the towering water wheel of Laxey. Curphey the fisherman had already been out at sea for several hours and was drawing in his first catch of the day.

Bea lay on the floor of the Great Hall, unmoving, brief flashes of scarlet sweeping over his thick fur in the dimming light of the fire.

A few miles south, in Port Erin, Mrs. Quilliam was busy preparing her weekly, and highly regarded, coffee morning. Port Erin was a town of coffee mornings. It seemed to pulse with ladies' chatter and deliberation, and Eileen Quilliam was widely celebrated as having the best cakes to encourage an air of gossip. Whilst she was busy baking in the kitchen, her husband, Hugh, had made himself scarce. Too many women in one room made him nervous, and so he had taken a walk down to the local bookshop and was dreamily flicking through a new trashy romance.

At the stroke of mid-day, the island's capital, Douglas, broke for lunch. Every door of every office swung open, and swarms of suits and well pressed skirts poured out into the main street. Business was on everyone's lips and all were in scarves, hats, gloves and overcoats, wrapped up against the cold.

Inside the Great Hall the fire had mostly gone out. The only light was coming from its glowing embers spreading a low orange hue through the dark. Bea was still motionless, but for his heavy breathing, and was undisturbed by the gentle chiming of the glass hanging from the ceiling.

For the children at Marown Primary School it was home time. Class three cheered as Mrs. Cowley dismissed them for the day, and they darted through the playground and into their patient parents' arms. Johnny and Sarah walked out behind the crowd holding hands, not caring what the others thought. And Richard Gill walked back home, alone, along the disused railway line running behind the school, his shoelaces untied and tripping him every two or three steps.

It was a short afternoon and already dark by the time the working day had finished. The clear, still, star-less sky was even colder than the night before. There would certainly be a frost by morning, and soon people returned to their homes and families, and fires were lit and supper was being served.

Stuart Skelly met some friends for a game of dominoes over a pint of ale in the local pub, as he had done for over forty years. Although the group was smaller of late, the laughter was still loud. And his wife, Gene, was at the farm next door, playing cards and daydreaming of matinee idols.

The sea around Fleshwick Rock mirrored the light of the night sky once more and stars appeared one by one, as the lights of the houses clicked on.

Yet things were also appearing not from out of the sky, but from under the earth. Not moles or mice, but things long forgotten, lurking in the shadows waiting for the right moment to pounce, like a cat crouching in long grass. Creatures of stories barely remembered and of a time not known. The land itself felt their presence, and still whispered the threat through the branches of the trees and the swaying of the grass.

Bea's nose twitched. His eyelids flickered and his ears sprung up. Something was wrong. He lay still. The glow of the fire was faint, but with his eyes wide he could see the lines of the wall and the staircase curving up alongside it to the mouth of the entrance. The place was empty. The fire quietly crackled and the water gently dripped, but there was another sound beyond that. Bea blocked out the familiar noises and there, not too far away, was a scratching, a scratching of claws against stone. Then a rock was picked up and thrown. He jumped to his feet and leapt up the stairs, two sometimes three at a time before reaching the rock at the top and pressing his ear to it.

'Brother. Brother Ivor! Are you sure there's no easier way there?' came a raspy voice from not five paces away.

'Brother Steal, if you want to be seen you can go any way you choose as far as I'm concerned. Knowing what Mother did to the last Brother who got himself seen, I suggest you take my advice and stick to the less trodden path,' the second voice said, with a deeper croak, like that of a frog.

'It'll be an easy take tonight Brother Steal; trust me. It's only a family of four, and two of them are little ones, no problem.'

Bea tried to suppress his anger at hearing them. It was a fight not to open the rock and tear them limb from bony limb, after what they had once done to him. But luck was shining down on him. This was what he had been waiting and searching for night after lonely night out on the headlands, and so he held himself back. This was his chance to learn why they were now coming over ground after so long. Perhaps the whispers were true, and the stories in the stars had been right all along. Perhaps they were seeking the mysterious *key-per*: the one who would bring a message from where no man could tread and finally put an end to the timeworn struggles. Or perhaps that was just the stuff of legend and nonsense.

'We've been waiting for this lot Brother Steal, and we've finally found them. Mother says they have the one prize she wants above all others. You know what that means? We'll be land dwellers in mere days!' They both burst into uncontrollable manic laughter.

'But how will we know when we've found this prize?'

'Oh, we'll know Brother. Mother told me everything. She said bring them back unharmed, especially the boy. Those were her very words.'

'A boy? This is getting better and better.'

Sounds of laughter again broke out, and drifted away as the

creatures moved off along the coast. Bea waited until it seemed safe to open the cave wall and step out onto the cliffs. Looking out, he could see the prickly, scaly silhouettes of the two Brothers in the distance. They were moving very fast, but Bea knew they mustn't see him. He was rested enough and now had the strength to *arraghey*.

He closed his eyes and focused his mind on the sound of the wind and the smell of the sea. They flowed over him and through him and finally became one within him. Slowly each hair on his skin shifted colour until it resembled the nearest thing to it, whether it was the grey of the rock or the shaded blue and green of the sea. He was all but invisible, and knew the land so well he didn't need his sight but could rely instead on his other senses to pursue the two Brothers without the fear of being seen. All he had to do was follow the stench of burnt flesh and bone the two creatures, scampering in front of him, gave off.

He ran along behind them for what seemed like many miles, stopping when they did and holding his breath so as not to make a sound. Although he was able to tread in the dark with confidence, after time he lost track of where they were heading. It was more inland, but the fatigue of keeping covered had taken their exact whereabouts from his mind's eye.

When the smell of the Brothers ceased to go any further, Bea felt for the nearest tree and sat down behind it. The instant he opened his eyes his head span and he began to pant loudly. He had forgotten how *arraghey* sapped his strength and would need to take a moment to pause. He looked around him and recognized the place to be a stretch of headland just north of Peel, close to where he had been the night before. He sniffed the air and knew they were again near the coast. Carefully he peered around the side of the tree.

About fifty paces away stood a modest lonely house. All the lights were on, and its upstairs windows were open with the curtains blowing out into the night. What could they want here? Bea asked himself. What did they want with more people? Was this how they hunted for the *key-per*?

He bolted upright and stared in confusion when the high scream of a female tore out from the house. It was violently quelled and followed by the noise of a struggle and glass smashing, then the shout of a male. Both were cut short by a heavy thud, the shrill cackle of one of the Brothers, and a young child's cries splitting through the night. The cries didn't stop, they only faded as the child was dragged further off, and in that moment Bea knew the threat whispered in the wind was real.

The tumult of screaming and smashing had shaken him terribly. The Brothers were capable of horrors, he knew that well, but his mind couldn't make sense of this new evil. He held back his rage and looked out over the surrounding headland where they had all disappeared. There was nothing. The night had swallowed them up.

He stayed behind the tree, feeling his strength slowly return, when a sound nearby made him start. He ducked down low and looked back towards the house. A boy, no more than half his height, let himself in through the gate and shut it behind him. Bea tried to get a better look at him, but he was so squashed into his clothes, shielding himself from the cold, that it was impossible see his face.

The boy shook the gate, checking it was properly shut, then skipped across the driveway, oblivious to what had just happened. Bea watched him go and felt his heart ache. He knew the Brothers would return for him. What they could want with an innocent boy eluded him, but no one should be treated in such a way. It wasn't natural, and tipped the very balance of the island.

Hardly thinking it through, he made a resolute choice. He refused to let the Brothers take another soul. He knew his father would have done the same, even if it meant being seen, and he stood up in gritty defiance as the boy stepped through the front door of the house and his kind young voice called from inside.

'Mum, Dad, I'm back!'

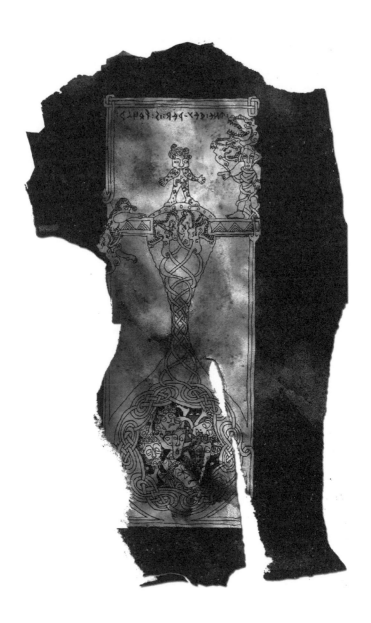

THREE

Long before the moon rose on that very same day, Juan Kerruish was grabbed by his school tie and pulled into the senior boys locker room. He was having a bad day, and it was about to get even worse. Kieran Creeses and Colyn Cairney despised Juan. He had become the most recent object of their displeasure. Juan couldn't understand why. Barely anyone else even noticed him and that was the way he preferred it. It hardly seemed fair that he only attracted the attention of two of the school's most notorious bullies. He wanted to yell out in protest so that someone might help him, but his tie was choking him and he could only manage a feeble splutter. He tried to yank himself free and run, but their grip on him was too tight and he fumbled onwards, like a dog on a leash, trying not to fall over his own feet.

His spirits fell further when Cairney and Creeses began laughing and boasting that senior boys had been flushing junior boys' heads down toilets at the school for over two centuries, or so they had read. Juan was surprised that either of them could read at all. He desperately tried again to wriggle free, but Creeses planted a sharp blow into his stomach and, winded, he fell hard onto his knees in front of an old porcelain toilet bowl.

'Nice to see a lad who respects tradition, isn't it Cairney?' asked Creeses, the larger of the two boys. He had only become a senior that year, but his hair had already begun to recede and there were bald patches all over his head, like a worn plot of grass.

'Nice is what it is Creeses, nice,' repeated Cairney, his mouth full of braces. Cairney, a squat youth with a face like a bulldog, had a bad habit of agreeing with and repeating whatever Creeses said. 'Tradition, yeah, tradition,' he sniggered to himself.

Cairney wasn't a bright boy, and Juan was certain that the only reason he was still at school was because of his notorious skills on the sports field. These mainly consisted of biting and scratching members of the opposing team until the referee caught him and sent him off.

'I guess I'm the lucky one today, eh Cairney?' said Creeses, snapping on a pair of pink washing-up gloves.

'Lucky one, yeah.' answered Cairney, now standing over Juan, who didn't dare look higher than his mud stained shoes.

'Are you ready to be a part of the school's fine history, you great lump, Kerruish?' asked Creeses. Juan didn't answer and his knees were now hurting on the rough concrete floor. He just wanted it to be over as quickly as possible.

'I'll take that as a yes. Now remember porky, don't swallow and keep your eyes shut!' How very kind of him, thought Juan bitterly, as he sucked in one last deep breath.

Creeses grabbed the back of Juan's head, and though he tried to resist, Creeses' strength was much greater and he forced his head down into the bowl.

Juan felt the cold water surround his face. He wanted to take a breath but knew it wouldn't be such a good idea. Creeses' pathetic cackling burst out above him, then the brute pulled on the rusty chain and a rush of water began beating down. It was fearfully loud under the torrent and Juan tried hard to picture he was elsewhere, perhaps teaching his younger sister, Aalin, how to play at conkers. He'd been gathering them since the early autumn and now had quite a collection. He wished he was anywhere else but where he was.

His head was starting to spin when a drip of water sneaked behind his eyelid. The instant it began to sting he panicked and pulled both his eyes open wide. Before he knew what was happening he had accidentally swallowed a mouthful of toilet water and was choking loudly. He frantically coughed and waved his body around like a beetle turned over on its back, but Creeses and Cairney found this most amusing, and were both laughing louder than ever.

Creeses finally released the pressure on Juan's head and let him lurch up and gasp for breath.

'If you don't keep out of our way Kerruish, you little pig,' he said in his most threatening voice, glaring down at Juan with his pale beady eyes. 'We *will* see you again, same time, same place, next week! Right Cairney?'

'Yeah! Same week, same time, next place!' laughed Cairney, unaware of his stupidity.

Juan answered with a small nod of his head, still choking on the water he'd swallowed.

Once the two thugs had left, with Cairney congratulating Creeses on his wit and intelligence, Juan pulled on his school cap over his soaking wet dark brown hair and stood up. As he pulled his satchel over his shoulder, he saw his dank reflection in the mirror. He was in a terrible state. His eyes were blood-shot and his shirt and jumper had been bunched up in a wet mess. But that wasn't all. On the skin of his stomach he spotted some new black markings.

Juan passed a finger over the unusual lines, criss-crossing his skin. They had been appearing for several days, and were becoming more and more frequent. Each morning he would wake up hoping that they had disappeared, but instead there would be another one randomly etched across his chest or along his arm, in no order or form whatsoever. He had scratched and scrubbed them until his skin was sore, but they refused to be erased. As if he didn't have trouble enough, he now spent most of his time trying to keep them as well hidden as he could. He hated to think what Cairney and Creeses would make of them. He felt like some sort of freak, and fearing that anyone might see, he tucked in his shirt and quickly headed for the door.

He checked the time on the clock in the locker room and, to his distress, realised that he was nearly late for class. He was sure he wasn't under the flush for that long and, slipping on the toilet water that had splashed onto the floor, ran out of the room and into the senior boys' corridor.

He scampered through the hallway with his eyes down, looking only at the wooden floor. Juan was still a junior and his appearance in the senior corridor would not be greeted with cheer. Few juniors had ventured into these hallowed corridors as it was against school policy and the punishment was thought to be strict. What's more, he knew from his first day at school that he was an easy target for those with less sense and tried his hardest to keep away from any trouble or, more importantly, keep trouble away from him. In the time since, he had become so adept at avoiding unwanted attention that most people passed him by without a second glance, as if he wasn't even there.

The senior corridor was far more sumptuous than the junior corridor. It was lined with beautifully carved dark wood, and gold framed photos of the school's sports teams hung along its walls. Each player in every photo stood as upright and grim as they could with their arms folded proudly in front of them. Juan didn't have much hope of ever appearing in any of the photos. Whenever teams were being picked he always found himself standing alone at the end before one side gave a disgruntled moan that they had to have him playing for them.

Juan knew he was lucky for the moment; the bell for lessons hadn't yet struck, and the hallway was deserted. Seeing he was alone, he slowed down to a walk so he could enjoy his surroundings. He passed a large door on his right with the words **Head of House** embossed into the wood. The door was ever so slightly ajar and Juan couldn't resist taking a peak. He knew his curiosity occasionally got him into bother but he could seldom help himself; the unknown was always too tempting. Looking in, the room had a thick carpet on the floor and two fine leather armchairs either side of a low table piled high with board games, magazines and study books. Both of the chairs were occupied, but he couldn't tell by whom, as they were holding large newspapers in front of their faces. Juan never realised that senior prefects lived a life of such ease and comfort. It hardly seemed fair that they got to relax when he was drenched in toilet water. But it wasn't enough to just see them; he also wanted to hear what they were discussing. He looked up and down the corridor to check if anyone would see him and then put his ear to the small gap.

'That's another family gone then,' said the voice from behind the broadsheet newspaper, matter-of-factly.

'Who is it this time?' asked the concerned voice from behind the tabloid paper.

'The Clagues, the whole lot of them.'

'Blimey! What do you make of it all? It's more than just a bit odd don't you think?'

'Odd? I should say it's odd! This is the sixth time it's happened now,' said the broadsheet, shaking with distress. 'Not a word spoken from them one day and then a single note from them the next, saying they're packing their bags and shipping off to who knows where. I don't believe a word of it. I don't know why, but something very strange is happening. I'm telling you, none of us are safe.'

As he finished, the bell began to sound, resonating loudly through the corridor. The two newspapers slumped down revealing the Head of House, Charlie Colbourn, and his deputy, Jamie Wilson, behind them.

'That'll be another free period then,' laughed Jamie.

'Hey, there's someone spying on us!' exclaimed Charlie, pointing right at Juan's ear on display in the gap of the door. 'You boy, get in here you little toe rag, you know this area's out of bounds!' he shouted.

Juan's eyes flickered for a moment in shock, and then he dashed down to the end of the corridor, through the far door and into the quad.

The quad was a hexagonal room that separated all the corridors and staircases that led to the different areas of the school. The floor was intricately tiled with the colourful school crest and the school motto on a scroll at the bottom, which read **Disce Pati**. Juan always gulped whenever he saw this. 'Learn to Suffer' was hardly an adage to inspire confidence. The words ran through his mind. It was the hardest lesson he knew at school, even harder than history with Mr. Mortis that he was now very late for.

He jumped up the first flight of stairs, making a din in the empty stairwell. His satchel was nearly bursting with every book he needed as he didn't dare keep them in his locker, knowing they would certainly be defaced with doodles and jibes by the morning. The first flight wasn't much trouble, but by the second, he was exhausted and began pulling himself up by the banister.

He shortly reached the top, took a left turn at the trophy cabinet and burst in through the third door on his right, labelled **History Department**.

A class of faces jolted round to look at him. Each one stretched around his or her chair to get a good view, and every face wore a frown as though he alone had ruined all their birthday parties at once.

Juan stood there in the silence. He'd been in this situation several times and always froze like a hedgehog dazzled by headlights. He expected he'd be given detention but, red faced, he could only wait for further instructions.

Perched cross-legged on the large desk at the other end of the classroom was Mr. Mortis. He was wearing his usual uniform of a finely made tweed three-piece suit and old school tie with his yellow socks proudly on display, and held what looked to be a rusty old scythe in his right hand. Mr. Mortis had been a pupil at the school ever since he was a young boy, left for a few short years, and then returned to take up his post in the history department, continuing through the ranks to become its head. He was as much a part of the school as its motto, and just as severe. His lank hair sank over to one side of his head like an oil slick, and he had a most unimpressed expression on his face. Allowing the silence to sit for a few moments longer, he slowly pulled out a silver fob watch from his waistcoat pocket and glanced at it.

'Your lateness Kerruish,' he began, enunciating every word with a military precision 'runs like clockwork.' He snapped the watch face shut and placed it back in his pocket. The class erupted into fits of childish giggles and Mr. Mortis did nothing to suppress them. Juan thought they looked like a pack of animals.

'Sorry I'm late sir. I was…'

'Doing my homework sir, practising my cricket sir, taking a bath with all my clothes on. Sir!' finished Mr. Mortis, in a sly scornful tone.

'Yes sir.'

'Which one Kerruish?'

Juan knew he was in deep water but couldn't think of anything to do but agree with him. ' Er…all of them sir.'

'You look like a beetroot Kerruish, come and sit at this table here.' And with that, Mr. Mortis sliced his scythe through the air and the tip of it stuck in the table in front of him. A gasp came from the rest of the class and all of the faces watched Juan as he slowly walked between the desks and sat down in his place. As soon as he took his cap off the class began giggling again. It didn't take Juan long to realise that his hair was still wet and sticking up in all directions. He quickly patted it down and looked up expectantly at Mr. Mortis. Again, he allowed the murmurs to settle before he spoke.

'One of the too numerous legends about the birth of our enchanted isle, *Ellan Vannin* as it is sometimes known,' he began, 'is that long ago it was nothing more than a mere clump of earth that was pulled from our neighbour, Ireland. The legend speaks of Finn Mac Cooil ripping out the earth and hurling it into the sea in a tremendous battle between himself and his mortal adversary, the red-haired Scottish Titan.'

A loud cough came from behind a textbook further down the classroom. Mr. Mortis, who had a creepy talent for being able to pick out troublemakers, stared in the book's direction.

'What do you make of that young Quinn?'

Quinn, a wide-eyed cocky boy with a permanent grin stuck on his face, looked up in surprise. His mouth dropped open and his chewing gum spilt out onto his desk.

'Do you consider it a sweet old wives' tale to be told around the fire on a winter evening, or something more ominous, more foreboding?'

'I…er…I…' stuttered Quinn.

'Haven't a clue have you?' he asked without a hint of surprise in his voice. Quinn shook his head, still smiling, seemingly pleased with his own ignorance.

'Very well, get back to your chewing gum. How about you Kerruish, any ideas, or do you just have water between your ears?' he asked, smiling at his own joke.

Juan looked at the scythe in front of him, with its red blade, pebbled with rust from age and use.

'Surely if it's true or not doesn't really matter sir, does it?' he said cautiously, not wanting to seem impertinent.

'Go on boy,' mumbled Mr. Mortis, sitting up straighter than before and looking down his nose at Juan.

'I mean sir, if people believed it hundreds of years ago, then isn't that what's important? Not if it's true or false. Don't legends like that give us a chance to see how those people used to think and what beliefs they followed sir?…Sir?' Juan asked, searching for the teacher's agreement. Mr. Mortis was silent. 'Sir?' he asked again.

'That'll do Kerruish, any other suggestions?'

Juan could tell that although Mr. Mortis hadn't congratulated him in any way, he was mildly impressed. Not to be fobbed off for ignorance was an achievement for any one in his class. Juan hoped this may have got him out of detention for his lateness, and he felt suddenly better.

For the rest of the lesson he quietly sat there, listening to Mr. Mortis' excitable voice. He would never admit it, but he loved hearing his teacher's tales of myth and conquest, from a time when heroes always triumphed in the end. Not the screwed up paper ball that hit him on the back of the head nor Doona Kelly, an annoyingly pretty girl with tightly curled black hair, pointing at him then whispering to her group of friends, upset him in the slightest.

He let his eyes wander over the walls of the classroom, covered in worn old maps, charts and lists of unfamiliar names. There were shelves cluttered with what looked to be old farm tools, rusted spears and arrowheads and bits of flint and other rocks. In the corner of one shelf, nearly hidden from his sight, lay two perfectly circular black stone orbs. Although well polished and cared for, they didn't shine or reflect any of the light that shone from the ceiling. They seemed to be feeding off the light around them.

Behind Mr. Mortis, there was a large map Juan often looked at. It was roughly scrawled on what seemed to be a piece of tree bark and was kept in a glass cabinet that hung from the back wall. Two padlocks on both the bottom and the top of the cabinet secured it. The map was obviously of the island, but not the island that was so familiar to Juan. There were no markings of roads or towns or indeed any indications of modern human life at all. Jagged lines denoted the major hills and forest boundaries, and several circles, not contours like on an ordinary map, but inaccurate dotted circles of different colours were scattered all over it. The key was of no help deciphering their meaning as it was written in a form or script he didn't recognise, probably the long-dead old language, he thought. Now that he looked at it a bit closer it was not dissimilar to his own markings, not the same by any means, but somehow related. As he stared at it, all the noise of the class dimmed. It seemed to pull him in and the periphery of everything blurred. He allowed the image of the script to bleed into his mind when…

'Kerruish?' said Mr. Mortis trying to get his attention. Juan didn't hear him. He was still being lured towards the circles.

'Kerruish?!' he said again, this time with a touch more impatience in his voice. Juan quickly turned to him, unaware that he'd been called twice.

'Sir?' he asked, not knowing if he'd been posed another question.

'Turn around Kerruish.'

'Pardon me sir?'

He was suddenly a little nervous. Was he going to be expelled from the class for not listening or just given a harsh clip round the ear?

'Turn around and look at the class.' Mr. Mortis said, being even more pedantic than usual. Juan slowly turned his head, but instead of seeing every face in the class gawping at him in disdain, there were only empty desks and empty chairs. The classroom was deserted.

'But I was only looking at the map sir, I couldn't have missed the bell sir.'

'I'm afraid you have boy,' he said, with a sinister warmth Juan hadn't heard before. 'The map has been known to have that effect on particular people. I've lost hours trying to decipher it, imagining I was walking around those circles, round and round and round.'

Just as Juan found himself being drawn in by Mr. Mortis' words, the high timbre of Miss Owen's voice, familiar to all the wrong doers in the school, rang out from a speaker in the corner of the classroom.

'Would all of those in detention kindly report to the library… immediately.'

Juan turned back to Mr. Mortis and could swear that he saw him blush at the sound of Miss Owen's shrill voice.

'Is the map old sir?' he asked, ignoring the behaviour of his teacher.

'Very old, many years, exactly how many is too hard to tell, but it's still bang up to date though.'

Juan was slightly struck by this.

'How can anything so old be bang up to date sir?'

Mr. Mortis suddenly stifled a fierce cough. Juan realized his teacher was staring at his hand. He looked down to see yet more new markings on his skin, and he quickly pulled the sleeve of his blazer over his hand to conceal them. Mr. Mortis stood straight up and began adjusting his attire, as if he had spoken and reacted out of turn.

'Enough of such nonsense, old and dead, that's all it is, old and dead. Now Kerruish, you've no doubt missed the early school bus home so you had better go down to the library and join the others in detention until the late bus arrives.' He was stumbling over every word he uttered, whilst rummaging through papers, taking books from one pile and putting them just as clumsily on another. 'Run along. We can't have you late for everything.'

Juan was quite taken aback by his behaviour, but reached for his satchel and left in as much of a hurry as he had arrived.

'Sorry sir, thank you sir!' he called back into the classroom at Mr. Mortis, who was busy checking the padlocks on the glass cabinet.

What was all that about? thought Juan, whilst running down the stairs into the quad. His head was still fuzzy and spinning with circles and lines as he crept in through the heavy double doors at the back of the vast library.

'Detention is about penance,' said Miss Owen, the small yet fierce school secretary, from the far side of the room. 'This time is for you all to take a long hard think about why you are here.' Juan carefully pushed the door shut, holding onto the brass handle shaped like a fist, until he was sure he could let go without being heard.

'Lateness and truancy will not be tolerated at this school, and if some of the things on my offenders' list are even halfway to the truth, expulsion in my view would be lenient,' she said, pushing her tortoise shell rimmed glasses up her beak-like nose.

'If you need me, I shall be in the reference room catching up on my…referring to my…references, yes that's it.'

Juan squeezed into the nearest seat and overheard two detention regulars on a desk nearby whispering to each other. 'She's not even going to be in here, this'll be the easiest detention ever.'

'I'll see you again tomorrow Turner. Have you yet to learn the price of silence in my presence?'

'I don't know miss,' mumbled an impatient Turner. 'Why don't you help me with that one later on?' A number of others laughed at his open flirtation.

'And the next day! Would you like to continue your advances all week?'

Turner didn't reply this time. The boy next to him couldn't hold back his amusement, but Turner hit him swiftly in the shoulder and shut him up.

Juan blew air out of his cheeks, and slumped low into his chair. He turned his wrist over and looked at the newest markings just like the ones from the map in Mr. Mortis' classroom. Maybe he had etched them on whilst staring at it, but couldn't for the life of him remember. Too baffled, he decided to ignore them until later. Perhaps he would finally show his mum and dad, he thought, they'd know what to do, and he raised his eyes to look around him.

This was his favourite room in the school. He always felt safe amongst the books; row upon row of them, which would never trip him or embarrass him or hurt him. Huge, dusty leather-bound encyclopaedias stood upright next to bright, shiny new books pleading to be thumbed through. Juan thought they looked like aged professors awkwardly hovering next to the new intake of first years. He chuckled at the thought of it.

'Pssst!' hissed Turner, trying to get Juan's attention and leaning as far off his chair as he could without falling. Juan didn't say anything but anxiously turned to him, biting his lip and trying not to show his fear for a boy whose reputation outstripped all of those who usually picked on him. Turner tended to pick on the teachers, only then could he be assured a good fight.

'Why are you in here Kerruish, thought you were one of them square like kids?' He knew his name. Juan could feel a bead of sweat trickle all the way down his spine.

'Just waiting for the late bus,' he squeaked, trying to sound his most nonchalant. 'How about you Turner, why are you in tonight?'

'Put acid in Egghead's coffee; thought I'd give him a taste of his own medicine like. Smelt it a mile off he did. How was I supposed to know he had a nose like a bleedin' blood-hound? He didn't have me chucked out though; he knows I know where he lives!'

Juan let out a sound, which was half a whimper and half a laugh. Egghead was his science teacher, unimaginatively knick-named due to his quite perfectly polished bald head.

'Here, Kerruish,' Juan realised he was not only looking at his hands but still laughing awkwardly. He stopped and looked up at Turner's mad eyes.

'Why not catch up on your current affairs. Who knows, *you* might be taken next.' And with a laugh, he threw a newspaper across the room and it landed right in Juan's lap. Juan unfolded the paper and read the front-page:

Another Family Gone, What's Going On?

Fellow islanders, it brings me grave sorrow to be the bearer of more bad news. Mr. Clague and his three children also seem to have left us. This means the toll has now risen to six separate incidents. Where these people have gone nobody seems to know. It is as though they have vanished into thin air. We may all occasionally dream of a life outside our small Ellan Vannin, but for families such as the Clagues, whose ancestry you can follow back for centuries, departing without so much as a single wave goodbye is not only rash and unexpected, but extremely out of character. Besides the Clagues, there is also Mr. Tooly the government official, the elderly couple, the Wattersons, Mrs. Loony the primary school teacher, Mr. Dawson with his two daughters and Mr. Godfrey the parish vicar. Would these folk really leave in pursuit of a suntan? The answer poses a darker conclusion, only emphasised by the uncovering of new, previously unseen evidence. Notes have now been discovered at every home of those who left, all are very similar; untidy, rushed and misspelt. Is this not enough fuel for a public and police enquiry? Be vigilant, something is rotten in the Isle of Man.

Juan shook his head. He felt the unease just like everyone else. His dad had told him that he'd known most of the people involved and was awfully upset, and now it had happened yet again. Nobody believed that these people had just upped and left, but it was simply too peculiar to make any sense.

'What do you make of it all?' asked Turner, his tongue stuck to the bottom of his yellow teeth.

'Very…er…informative,' replied Juan, still surprised that the thug had yet to make any mindless threats. He had enough to worry about without another one watching his every move.

Against his better judgement, Juan hunched over his desk so that nobody would see him and slowly drew up his sleeve to look again at the marks on the back of his hand. He passed his index finger over the etchings, following each stroke and line. The symbols didn't appear to be on his skin, but under it, inside him. He licked his finger and rubbed it over them, but there was no change. He tried once more with more force, his skin went slightly red but there was no smudging whatsoever. They remained un-erased. He sat up and pushed his hand into his blazer pocket, looking around to make sure no one was singling him out. Most were asleep, thinking about their poor behaviour no doubt.

'All those escaping on the late school bus may do so now.' bellowed the disembodied voice of Miss Owen, coming from the reference room past the other end of the library. 'Do retain a little of what I've said. I don't wish to see your spotty faces here every evening!'

Juan rose from his seat and pulled his satchel over his shoulder. Two or three other boys also got ready to leave and began cautiously moving towards the door.

'Corkish, Gelling and Creer, kindly return to your places!' yelled the voice, in a tone not to be argued with. The three boys looked around in annoyance of how they could possibly be seen, before slowly walking back to their desks resigned to the full length of their punishment.

'And we shouldn't have to see your face in here again, should we Kerruish?'

'No miss,' answered Juan, feeling somewhat peculiar talking to a bodiless voice echoing through the library.

'Dismissed!'

Juan took one last look back into the library to see Turner give him a knowing wink, before pulling the brass fist doorknob and dashing out.

He rushed through the quad and straight on to the outside of the school buildings. It was already dark and Juan ran close to the wall, letting his hand rub over the uneven cold grey stone and feeling it harden his fingertips. He looked up to the top arches of the main building and at the gargoyles staring down at him. The large squashed nosed heads of the creatures seemed to be on the side of all those mindless thugs that he knew, like greyhounds before a race; so eager to catch him. He quickly stuck out his tongue at the irreverent grotesque stone faces and ran up onto the school bus.

The driver obviously knew that if anyone were to be the last on it would be Juan, as the door immediately shut behind him. There were only a few other boys and girls on the coach, and whilst he walked down the aisle they either scowled at him or ignored him altogether. So he sat himself next to a window at the back of the bus and watched the dark countryside trundle past.

Shortly after leaving, Juan put his nose to the window as they crossed over the Fairy Bridge. It was hardly much to look at, barely noticeable at all really, but everybody knew that when going over the bridge it was traditional to greet the Little People. Not that they believed a word of what they were saying; it was more out of habit than anything else.

As they went up and over the bridge, everyone mumbled their greetings. Juan pressed his hands to the glass and quietly uttered 'Hello Fairies', his breath misting the window. He drew a little pair of eyes through the mist on the window before wiping it away on his sleeve and they travelled on.

From the coast of Castletown, where the school lay, the bus went in and out of the bustle of Douglas before heading round the narrow back roads of the island towards Peel, taking every hedge lined corner a little too close and a little too fast.

Lumbering past small houses and trees, growing like spindly fingers over the road, they soon came to Juan's stop. The light of the moon was hidden as he got out and began to walk up the hill towards his home. He foolishly hadn't worn his winter coat and so pulled his blazer tight around him to shield himself from the biting evening wind. He could feel the glow of his cheeks and the wetness of his nose as he dragged his feet through the thick covering of damp leaves covering the path. He stopped when he saw a heap of fallen conkers, late for the time of year, near his feet and bent down to pick up a handful. He threw away a couple which were no good, until he found ones that were smooth enough and wouldn't break when he squeezed them. He polished them on his sleeve and put them deep into his pockets as he trudged up towards the lights of his house on top of the hill.

The gate was already open and squeaking noisily in the wind.

Strange, thought Juan, the gate was never left open, but he ignored it and let himself through. He slammed it shut, checking it wouldn't blow open again and skipped faster up to the front door to escape from the sea air blowing round the cliffs near by.

Once inside the porch, it was snug and cosy and Juan instantly pulled off his blazer, dropping it next to the coat stand, and kicked off his muddy shoes next to several other pairs caked in dirt. He ran through the hall, feeling the warm carpet under his feet, hopped past the clutter of dolls and games on the stairs and up to his bedroom, calling into the house.

'Mum, Dad, I'm back!'

Juan barged open the door to his bedroom and let his heavy satchel fall to the floor. He gave a sigh of relief and flicked on the light switch. His room was like a battle ground. There wasn't a single area on the floor that was free from piles of books or clothes or even more books. A stack of paperbacks held up his bed, all the spines scrunched up from many readings. His window was propped open with a large hardback and his desk looked precariously close to collapsing under the weight of yet more books. There were ones small enough to fit into his breast pocket to those that he could barely lift without help. He'd forgotten that his mum had asked him to clean up before he left for school that morning. But looking at it, he wouldn't know where to start.

He negotiated the tip, kicking clothes and books aside as he went, and opened a draw. It was empty. He looked to the floor and retrieved a thickly woven woollen jumper and pulled it over his head.

'Mum, Dad, Aalin, I'm back! Where are you?' he yelled again, walking across the landing.

He poked his head past the door and looked into his parent's bedroom. It was also a tip. The bed hadn't been made and the sheets were strewn over the floor. The wardrobe was open and all the clothes thrown haphazardly around the room. Pictures were off the wall. The windows were open and the curtains were flapping like a trapped bird. He had never seen their room in such a mess. He walked over and pulled the windows shut. This wasn't like them, he thought, they wouldn't leave the house like this. It was perfect, now they couldn't question him on the state of his own room.

He slid down the banister and walked through to the kitchen. It was always so busy that he couldn't tell if it was in more of a mess than usual. There was a high pile of washing-up next to the sink, blocking out any moonlight from the window, and a collection of messy paint pots near Aalin's favourite chair. The taps were still running and dripping into an overflowing sink so Juan twisted them off and went to open the fridge. It was shamefully sparse, but he took out a drink and shut the door. In amongst all the family photos and Aalin's early attempts at hand paintings, something else caught his attention. Held up by a fridge magnet was a poorly scribbled note on a scrap of old paper.

Juan pulled it off the fridge door and stared at it, reading it over and over again. The words of the newspaper article rolled through his mind; *notes have now been discovered…untidy, rushed, misspelt.* He felt faint and queasy from a strange burning inside his chest. His head was spinning and he thought he might be sick when all the lights around him suddenly crackled, flashed a blinding spark and went out. He dropped his drink in fright and it began to spill over the floor. His breathing quickened and his heart was beating like a drum in his chest. In the darkness, he erratically moved back into a corner of the room, knocking a few plates off the table, which smashed loudly on the floor.

Beyond the sound of his heavy, frantic breathing, he could hear a squeaking and banging in the distance. It was the outside gate. It was open again. He tried to swallow but his mouth was too dry, so he slowly calmed himself and stared out into the black space of the room. After several long moments a voice came from out of the dark. It was so unlike anything he had ever heard, he thought he might choke from the fear of it.

'I told you we missed the boy you clot!' it said in a raspy lisp, with a horrible screeching sound beneath each word. Juan squinted in every direction trying to catch sight of where the voice came from.

'He's not so little this one. Remember what Mother said, "especially the boy". He's the prize,' came another voice. It was more of a squeal layered with a throaty cackle.

'Who's there? Who said that?' demanded Juan, his own voice trembling in the cold air. His fists were tight in front of him in fear and confusion.

'You can grab his right arm, and I'll grab his left!' said the first voice. Juan retracted his arms behind his back in terror.

'Which sides right?'

'The one next to your left.'

'Which one's left?'

'This one you clot!' Juan was moving his head from side to side trying to follow the two separate voices.

'I can't see.'

'Oh, just grab him!'

Juan saw two pairs of blood red eyes flash through the black hollow of night. They were staring directly at him. Luminous and malevolent, the eyes began to dart straight for him. Juan screamed in shock, put his head down low and ran blind between them. He hit the doorframe and scrambled out of the room, stamping through sheets of paper littered all over the floor. The voices were not far behind him.

'I've got you, you little blighter!'

'You got *me* you great clot, he's heading upstairs!'

Juan felt his way up the banisters, his eyes so open he was afraid they might pop out. All the lights throughout the house had gone out and he tried to find his way without his sight. He managed to avoid the clutter on the stairs, and heard the eyes behind him screaming, swearing and slipping on the rubbish as they tried to snatch at his heels.

Juan burst into his room, sweat trickling down his cheeks. He trod over all the books, pulled open his wardrobe and began throwing boxes out onto the floor. He scrabbled and scraped through all the useless stuff, trying to find his torch. He knew it was in there somewhere. He pushed his hand deep into a box full of junk and, feeling with his fingertips, found something cylindrical. He tugged, and pulled out the torch. But the blessed thing didn't work. He switched it on and off madly before hitting it, and the blade of light sliced through the dark. It was shining straight up into his whimpering face, wet with tears as he pushed himself to the very back of the cupboard and waited.

Everything on the landing had gone quiet. The only sounds were the wind and the gate blowing back and forth. Maybe the eyes couldn't find him? Maybe they had run away not thinking he was worth anything? Juan felt ill his mind was racing so fast. He blinked hard. His eyes stung from the tears and the new light, but his breathing relaxed in the quiet and he shone the torch out in front of him. And there, maybe an arm's length from his face, was something hideous staring back at him. It was another face, dark green and black with rough bone-like scales stretching in every way across it. The red eyes of the face shone straight at him and the creature wore an inane mocking grin of uneven, sharp yellow teeth with saliva dripping off them. Juan thought of the gargoyles that mocked him at school. He screamed as the creature's sharp webbed hand grabbed his leg.

'What are you!?' he shrieked, coughing on the words.

'I'm the nightmares you've never had!' the creature laughed, lunging for him. But Juan was quick and managed to get his free leg in the way and instinctively kicked out hard, catching the creature in its centre. It gave a low groan and Juan kicked out again, this time aiming at its skull, which crunched loudly. He leapt up and ran for the stairs, hearing fierce screams and curses from behind him as he climbed over the other creature, and dashed for the back door.

The sudden rush of sea air blew around him, but no sooner had he taken one step out onto the long uncut grass behind the house than a large hand swamped his face and pulled him hard against the wall. He tried to scream and struggle but was being held by a grip of such strength that his cries sounded muffled and hopeless. He lifted his hand to the one covering his mouth and could feel thick wiry fur under his fingers. He began to feel faint again when Bea spoke to him.

'Don't be afraid. I'll get us out of this,' the voice said. It was deep, calm and honeyed, and Juan could feel it vibrating through his back. A great sense of relief and thanks went through him.

Both Bea and Juan eased their tension. Bea saw the boy's hands trembling and on one of them, scrawled across his skin, were lines of strange black markings. He stared at them dumbstruck. They had found him, somehow the Brothers had found him: the *key-per.* The stars had been right, and the whispers were true. Bea shook himself, he was getting too carried away, he couldn't be sure, nothing was certain. But if he was cradling the *key-per* in his arms, they had to get away from there, fast. He took a deep breath and stepped out into the doorframe.

The two red-eyed Brothers were now facing them, and both looked not angry but ashen and deeply shocked.

'You're still alive! How can that be?' cried one.

'We killed you, I saw you fall!' cried the other.

'Back from the grave,' said Bea, with no malice, or indeed any other emotion but calm serenity. 'Sorry to disappoint you, but…'

His leg kicked out at the speed of a whip and hit one Brother across his face. His jaw broke, dropped and hung limply above his chest and he fell to the floor like a puppet with cut strings. Bea raised his fist to the other, cracking his knuckles in threat. Juan was certain he saw a wave of deep red colour spread quickly over his dark fur and disappear again. The other creature made a short high-pitched whine and ran into the shadows of the house.

Without another hesitation, Bea lifted Juan and guided his hands round the back of his neck. Juan in turn grabbed a clump of his thick fur and flung his legs round Bea's waist, holding on as tight as he could. He suddenly knew he was going to be safe and the warmth of security spread over him like a blanket. That was before he felt the jerk of rapid movement as Bea dashed away from the house and towards the coast.

Juan had thought the school bus was fast, but moving as one over the rough muddy path with such force knocked the air out of him. The legs beneath him were thumping into the surface of the ground and bounding from it like a wild animal.

They came to a sudden stop, and Juan squeezed his fists and legs tight so as not to be flung from his hold. He gasped with exhilaration and sucked in a cold breath of the sea air before looking out behind him. They were standing on the very edge of the coastline. Bea's feet were clawed around a protruding rock, and if Juan let go, he'd be falling straight down into the jagged, teeth-like rocks of the bay.

'They mustn't be able to follow us,' said Bea, his quiet voice laced with warning. 'Hold on tight.'

The last thing Juan saw before his body finally gave in and he blacked out, was the dark countryside and the barely visible path leading up to his home fall away. A glimpse of the grey grainy rock flashed past him as they both dropped towards the sea, and then nothing.

He dropped easily into a dream, far away from the madness. He was sitting in the middle of a small clump of rocks, surrounding him in a perfect circle, deep down on the sea bed, deep down where it was as dark as night and there was little life to speak of. His right hand felt hot and he slowly raised it through the dense water; it was clenched with beams of white light sneaking through his fingers. His hand opened, and in his palm was a globe, only the size of a conker. The globe was entirely blue but for a tiny speck of land. He closed his hand again and felt the globe burst, the illumination ceased and was replaced with blood pouring through his fist, dark syrupy blood congealing with the water, and spreading until everything faded to black.

He awoke with an almighty start and saw that he was back on the coastline not three miles from where they fell, sitting on some ramparts on the ruins of old Peel castle. The rock was sandy and brittle under him and he began to shiver from the sharp night air.

Bea stood with his back to Juan only a few paces from where he sat, the moon lining his fur with silver. Juan could see the definitions and sculptured lines of Bea's strength under his fur, tight against his skin in the wind. He struck an imposing figure, but not an unfamiliar one Juan realised. He was certain he had read and seen paintings of creatures like him in old books. He knew what he was, but he still couldn't believe it.

'You're a F…a F…a Fynoderee aren't you?' he asked, his teeth chattering and hugging himself for warmth.

'Man hasn't seen us in many years. So long. I'm glad it's by you though,' said the Fynoderee in reply, still with his back turned and the wind in his hair.

'Then you *are* a Fynoderee.' Juan quietly concluded to himself. He had only ever read bad stories about the Fynoderees, and pulled his knees up to his chest.

'Yes, that's what you called us, in a time of fear when we had to run from men and hide in the holes of the world. And what's your name boy?' The Fynoderee turned and knelt in front of Juan. The light of the moon shone down and he saw his face for the first time. His hair was scraped back showing his weather beaten skin, and his large green eyes looked sympathetically up at him. Juan thought he had the look of a young man who had to grow up quicker than his years demanded. He was surprised that he felt no fear towards the Fynoderee.

'J…J…' he stuttered, still shivering.

'A touch unusual for your people, but pleased to meet you nonetheless. My names Bea.' The Fynoderee put his large hand on top of Juan's in greeting.

'No, it's Juan, Juan Kerruish.'

'Then you are "well born" Juan. It's a strong name. Are you

frightened?'

'Well, a bit.'

'Don't be, you'll be safe out here. And in case you hadn't figured it out already, your parents haven't left you behind.'

'I know,' said Juan simply.

'You do?'

'Yes, they'd never leave me. They've taken them haven't they, those things?'

'I'm sorry, but don't worry, they're not hurt yet. They're too important. Do you know what those things were?'

Juan shivered more, remembering their red eyes and coarse scaly bodies. 'Were they B…Bugganes?' The question sounded so stupid in his head. These were creatures from the pages of ancient folk tales, not the waking world.

'Bugganes, good. Those two Brothers are hunters; useless ones mind you, we're lucky the duty wasn't handed to…'

Bea span his head around and looked up towards the moon where an owl was silhouetted flying through its arc of light and hooting in warning. He pulled Juan up onto his feet.

'We must get to safe ground.'

'Where's safe?' asked Juan, his mind still spinning.

'Fleshwick Rock,' answered Bea, standing up tall. Juan held on again and could feel Bea's muscles tense like iron under him.

'W…why are you helping me?' he asked.

Bea looked over his shoulder as he began running along the castle wall.

'*Carrey liorts ny share braar foddey jeh.*'

'What does that mean?'

'It means; it's better to have a friend next to you than a brother far off. Oh, and there was something else.'

'What was that?'

'They have my parents as well.'

FOUR

Four matches held together tore down the rough lighter paper on the side of the matchbox. Although damp, the crack of the spark awoke and partly illuminated the new place.

Eamon Kerruish was a man prepared for such eventualities. He always had a small ball of string, some sticky tape, a work knife and matches, as well as a few other bits and pieces, lining the pockets of his worn jacket. But where they were now, such things seemed like cotton when they needed rope.

He held the matches away from his body, into the shadows, and his wife, Grayse, came into view. Her hair seemed more auburn than usual, and her fair cheeks were dirty and wet with tears of exhaustion and fright. She was holding and rocking Aalin, who was fast asleep, close to her chest. She looked at him and managed to force a small smile. Though Eamon could only see the worry knitted in her brow, he still returned the gesture.

Looking upwards, there seemed to be no ceiling to where they had been taken. It rose up until the lack of light prevented them from seeing the top.

The pit was roughly circular, cramped, and although clammy, thankfully wasn't cold. Eamon turned on the hard floor and saw that the wall of smooth rock was covered with tiny lines. As he looked closer he found that they were scratch marks cut into the rock. He shuddered to think how they got there. The whole place must have been carved straight into the earth, and by the looks of it others had tried to get out.

'We're very deep,' he whispered under his breath.

A hushing sound came from behind him and instantly he span around. Huddled together on the opposite side of the pit were a crowd of people cowering and squinting away from the light. The matches reached the end of their short life and he caught his breath as they burnt his fingers and threw them to the ground.

Everything fell to black once more.

When listening for it, he could hear the breathing of the group quite clearly in the dark, only paces away from where he stood. There must be over a dozen of them, he thought. And if he wasn't mistaken he had even recognised a number of the faces underneath all the stains of dirt and fear before the light went out. The presence of others was a sudden comfort but he found their silence unnerving, as though they thought he himself was a threat. He couldn't understand why not one of them had yet spoken a single word.

'You must keep quiet,' hissed a voice from the group. Eamon was now certain he had recognised someone.

'Dermot? Reverend Godfrey, is that you? Reverend what in the name of hell is going on...?'

Dermot Godfrey, a parish priest from the east of the island, brusquely cut him off. 'Hell is right Eamon, hell and damnation. I fear we are being judged for our sins.'

'Please keep quiet!' said another more desperate voice. 'We don't want them to come again.'

'Who, those freaks in masks?' Eamon spoke up, 'They've got some serious answering to do.'

'Eamon you mustn't, you're dealing with things beyond your control. You don't understand.'

It was another voice he knew, his friend Patrick Tooly, the government official. His stomach tensed. Patrick was one of the people to leave the island so unexpectedly, without telling another soul. He then realised that his anxieties had been justified, but before he could ask anything out loud a fierce sound of burning came from far above them. Eamon saw a small blaze of fire getting rapidly larger and falling towards them.

'Too late,' said Patrick, his voice seized with tension.

Holding onto a torch of flaming pitch, Brother Ivor landed without a sound in the centre of the circular pit. He slowly stood up to his full wiry stature and, grim faced, turned to the group.

'Now that most of you are finally present,' he began, his voice low and gurgling, as though he needed to clear his throat. 'We shall begin our questions very soon.'

'What do you want to know? We'll tell you anything.' a frantic looking man said, surrounded by his three children.

'We ask the questions!' screamed the Buggane. Everyone clung together even tighter in response to his outburst, which echoed above him in the smoke of the torch. He cleared his throat in a polite apologetic manner and continued. 'You will all find out soon enough, until then, no noise, understand?' Everyone quickly nodded their heads.

'I'm afraid I don't understand,' said Eamon firmly, 'I don't know who you yobs think you are, dressing up like that in those stupid costumes and running around scaring everyone, but it's just not on!'

The Buggane turned to him, his eyes as red as the fire from the torch, and struck Eamon around the face with the back of his bony webbed hand. Eamon was lifted clean off the ground and flew back into the wall, landing in a heap. His face was left in a bloody mess, but instead of remaining silent he opened his mouth to speak again, only to be pummelled by another blow across the face. He submitted this time, dizzy from the pain and the taste of blood in his mouth. Aalin woke and began to cry as Grayse leant over Eamon and wiped the blood off his face with her sleeve.

'And make that thing stop crying,' the Buggane added. Grayse began rocking Aalin again and stroking her hair to try and calm her down. Aalin snuggled into her mother's chest, hugging the smiling woollen doll that Grayse had made her, and quietly sobbed.

The Buggane leapt into the air and scrabbled up the wall, much like a spider would, taking the light with him. Eamon watched the shape shrink until it was out of sight. He now grasped that he had been wrong: these weren't pranksters in masks, that was certain. They were something altogether different. In the dark he held onto the remainder of his family, squeezing them close in reassurance, praying that his son, Juan, was safe from all the madness.

Brother Ivor pulled himself over the lip of the pit and hung the torch on the wall where Brother Steele stood, clicking his broken jaw back and forth, and they started down the tunnel.

It was not a large tunnel. A Buggane wouldn't be able to stand up straight if he so wished and it was lit, as were all of the tunnels, by torches of burning twigs hung from the walls. This made the already dull air dense and foggy with smoke.

Brother Ivor and Brother Steele crawled on all fours along one side of the wall, behind a long line of other Brothers and Sisters, avoiding those coming the other way. Any one of them would get angry if nudged or pushed and would be likely to start a scrap. Many were carrying the newly born and the very young to and from more secure chambers where they could grow without the threat of scavengers. Some would hunt for any meal to prevent them from starving.

There had not been enough food to go round since last season and hunger was rife in the nest. The family had grown so much and so quickly of late that rations had shrivelled to miserable portions. They were told this was progress. As soon as there were enough Brothers and Sisters the Reclamation would begin, they would be over ground for good, and food would be in abundance. Thousands upon thousands of them were now preparing for that day, when they would finally return to the island that was once theirs. They would reclaim their right over Ellan Vannin and take bitter revenge on those who had beaten them into the tunnels so many centuries ago. Whilst they had been forgotten by man, they had been beneath him, patiently waiting and growing until their prey was no more than a mouse to their owl.

Among the family, Brother Ivor and Brother Steele had been blessed. They were given the privilege of taking one of the families of man-folk from over ground, a privilege many would have fought for. They hoped that the small and unfortunate details of finding Bea the Fynoderee alive and not bringing back the boy would pass Mother by, though this was unlikely. Every Brother and Sister knew that Mother was a truthsayer, and could read lies as though they were written across their eyes.

The two broke off from the line into a near deserted wider tunnel. They both slowed their pace on the now steeper gradient as the footing became less certain and their sudden and shared nervousness grew. They knew that if their news displeased Mother their chances of ever having a good meal again would fall, quickly.

Mother's temper seemed to spread through the tunnels. If a newly born Buggane showed little aggression and only pleaded affection it would either be burned, or more often than not, fed on. She couldn't afford to encourage such petty emotions, that would surely only lead to weakness and reluctance, and ultimately failure. Aggression and venom were expected from very early on, and Mother had discovered the true secret to such breeding: overcrowding. No new tunnels had been built in generations and the less space there was to move, the more cramped and the hotter it got. The blood of the Bugganes had boiled into bitterness and hatred of all living things.

Large and brutishly built guards lined the wide tunnel, each about ten paces apart. Brother Ivor sniggered. Although fiercely strong, the guards were derided amongst the other Brothers and Sisters. They were thought of as little more than moving rocks, and were not exactly dissimilar in appearance, with their thick necks and immovable stares.

The two Brothers passed by the guards until the tunnel finally opened out into a dimly lit cave. Smoke from the torches hid the actual size of the cave from view. The very walls seemed to be made of smog. The Brothers slowly approached the dais at the far end of the room, the haze lifting the closer they got, until their Mother, the Queen Atta, was revealed in her finest ceremonial robes, drumming her fingers against the arm of her grey throne.

Both Brother Ivor and Brother Steele stopped before her, fidgeting and scuffing their feet into the dust on the hard floor. Few were permitted an audience with Mother, and not one of them had reported ever seeing her in such glory. This was an honour indeed.

She was wearing an armoured skin over her pale brittle flesh. Plate upon plate upon plate, each the size of a man's palm, jigsawed together covering her feminine form from top to toe, as though they kept her from spilling out over the earth. Each plate was made of charred bone, old, cracked and a muddy dark green. A few pieces still had gristle hanging off them. She wore jewellery too, but jewellery from a child's nightmares to embellish her fearful form. The necklace that adorned her neck and shoulders was formed from small decayed animals: long-tails and rabbits next to her burnt body. Around her ankles and wrists was wrapped flesh. Like weeping bracelets they hung, raw and red, dripping thick dark blood onto the stone beneath her feet. Brother Ivor licked his lips at the thought of what creatures had been sacrificed so recently to decorate her. And at her chest hung a skull the like of which the Brothers had never seen. It was thin like a fox with several front teeth remaining on its top jaw, but it was so much longer. It hung from her chest down to between her legs, its garish eyes and mindless grin burning into whoever gazed upon it. It could only be something from deep within the caves, Brother Steele thought. Something like that had never smelt the salt of the sea or squinted with the light of the moon in its eyes.

Mother's hands and feet were still exposed and jutted out of her armour like spikes. Her skin resembled curdled milk, brown and pebbled with warts and welts of grey and black. She had five fingers like a man, but as with all Bugganes, no palm. Instead, her fingers were all webbed together right up to her top knuckle forming a mitten of skin where she clung onto her polished bone sceptre.

She gave the appearance of a patchwork of other creatures' pain and death, as though every skull was screaming of its unjust murder. Brother Ivor swallowed hard.

'There, there, there, my children,' her voice was enticing and full of profound sympathy, but still sent a chill through the Brothers. This was the greatest and most terrible moment in their lives.

'The guilt in your eyes tells me volumes: more than your mouths ever could. Not everything has passed as I wished. Am I wrong? You have been unable to complete a simple and honourable mission towards our Reclamation. Am I wrong? There, there, don't look so bleak, I'm sure it's nothing but a minor detour on our path; otherwise you would never have returned. Am I wrong? So, you have taken some of the family, just not all of them. Hmm? Who is missing I wonder? Not the baby girl, I would not insult you with that much carelessness. And if you have her, no doubt both the parents would have followed. I find their senseless compassion for their young both pathetic and endearing. And now if I were to say the boy had escaped, who is, in a word, invaluable to me, to us, would I be wrong? Would I?!'

The Brothers skulked back at her shrill voice, unable to answer her, but bumped into two gruff guards now towering directly behind them.

'He is the one I told you about, in confidence, the one who has haunted my dreams for longer than I care to remember. He is the prize. I see him standing there; a boy with painted skin and marked flesh. I can see him now, he looks so feeble and helpless but, I don't know why, I fear him.' For a moment she looked to be in a trance. 'They watch me fall,' she whispered to herself.

The Brothers were shocked, there was nothing they knew of that could frighten Mother.

'He could be the *key-per* that was spoken of by our kin, and in the stars. The Watcher found him sometime before moonrise and came to us instantly.' She paused knowing too well how much every Buggane despised the Watcher.

'And yet, you dare to come to me, in my private chamber, and tell me that this is not all that has befallen you. You have news that you fear even more to speak of. Am I wrong? You don't want to upset your dear Mother, such considerate children. What could it be? Brother Steele my child, you have the appearance of one that has been in the wars and come out the worse. No human could have broken your face in such a way. And Brother Ivor you have a look in your eyes of one who has seen a ghost. No, I cast off that opinion. You *have* seen a ghost. Someone you believed walked only in the land of the dead. We are now scraping the surface of the truth are we not? Yet there is more still in your eyes, this is someone close to you, someone you thought you saw die? Am I wrong?'

Brother Ivor, now uncontrollably shivering, stared hard at the ground beneath Mother's feet, waiting.

'Silence has a loud and mellifluous voice my children. I must congratulate you on your honesty. Few could come here and tell me of their failures over ground. And even less could tell me that one of those infernal Fynoderees is back from the dead and freely roaming between our shadows! I presume it is Bea, he always had the luck of Manannin at his heels, am I wrong?' She concealed her fear of him well enough for the Brothers not to see. They were too stunned to nod. Brother Steele so wanted to run, cower or even beg, but could do nothing except stare up at her with wide guilt-ridden eyes.

'It has been lovely to talk to you my children and thank you for being so forthcoming, but now you must leave me to my thoughts. I tire of your company and wish to be alone. Goodbye.'

Brother Ivor's and Brother Steele's heads were spun towards each other with a swift crack, and the final thing that either of them saw was the other's helpless red eyes rolling into their sockets before they crumpled to the floor with their dead weight.

Mother closed her eyes tightly against their pain, as every wiry muscle in her frame clenched in spasm. So close was she to her children that she felt every flinch, every scratch and every wound they endured within herself. She lived, waking and sleeping, with their unending hunger, fatigue and hurt gripping her. It was comforting. No pain meant no family. She smiled. There was much pain to come.

Exhaling, she slumped into her dais. Though she had expected this to come, the panic it brought still ran like thorns in her blood, itching all over. She wouldn't let them ruin it for her. She wouldn't let the Fynoderee and the painted boy see her fall. She had come this far. The family had grown so much since she had become their Mother and nothing would stop her going over ground. She was proud, and the tales of her kind fleeing under ground, burrowing deeper into their tunnels to hide from the men who could travel over the sea itself, sickened her. How dare they come with their sharp weapons of iron and force them into the pits of the world! What sickened her more was that her kind obeyed and fled into the depths and into myth without so much as a crossed word. But now the wait was over. The family had swelled and was ready to take the fight to the land dwellers. The date neared and the preparations would soon be complete. Their appetite was wet for flesh.

Mother closed her eyes. She knew her words and actions had easily swayed the family, it didn't take long to realise that hate could grow as fast as hunger. But she also knew they would be nothing without her, a horde with no direction. That was why she couldn't let her nightmares surface in the waking world. She couldn't let the beast and the boy get near her.

She let out a deep, husky sigh. She thought she had rid herself of the Fynoderee, but it seemed nothing was ever so easy. She stretched her arms wide to ease her tension. At least she could see his death another time, scoff at his demise and witness the end of his vile species once more. She smiled. He would be a fly in her web.

This thought tickled her, and she let out a small titter as she glided from her dais, over the two bodies of Brothers Ivor and Steele to the entrance of the cave.

Her smile faded when she saw the painted boy flash across her mind's eye. She rubbed her eyes trying to free herself of the dreadful image and her rigid fear of it and turned towards the two guards.

'Call on the Watcher again. Tell him Mother desires an audience with him once more before the moon is at its peak. Oh, and tidy up in here boys, supper's early for you two.'

As soon as she stepped through the smoke and up the tunnel into the full view of the Brothers and Sisters busy with their duties, every one of them immediately stopped where they stood. Many bumped into the Buggane in front of them before realising their Mother, the Queen Atta, was present. There were a few gasps, but mostly quiet as she walked amongst them. It was time to show pomp and strength to her family. Let them see their Queen, their Mother, in all her war-like glory. She gave them life and they in turn offered their lives to her. It seemed a fair compromise.

Draped in such finery, she could feel every eye on her, wide with awe. She owed her children the pleasure of witnessing her terrifying beauty, proving she was indeed a figurehead worthy of admiration. Not that there were any dissenters; the Bugganes were fiercely loyal to their Queen. She was their symbol for life, and they shared with her the strongest bond, running through them all, the bond of blood. Nothing was stronger than that.

Atta gave the briefest forward gesture with her hand and the two lines of Bugganes on either side of the crowded tunnel began to move once more. She revelled in this power. Where she would point, they would go.

Many quietly and earnestly muttered their thanks under their breath as the lines began to move in time, like a heart beat slapped out on the rock floor by their bare webbed feet. It was the pulse of the family, Mother thought, and the tunnels were its veins. She couldn't help but be cheered by the wonder of it. Men would regret the day their ancestors beat the Bugganes down. But she was also aware that the slightest blemish or clot in the arteries of the family could cause an unaffordable seizure. Knowing she had to be ruthless for the good of them all, she turned to the line running nearest to her.

'You, Brother?'

'Mymer, Brother Mymer, Mother,' said the scrawny Buggane stepping out from the line and falling to his knees before her. She winced at seeing his skinny frame, with shoulder blades jutting out of his back into the air, but let his weakness pass her by. He was obviously loyal and this was no doubt a joyous moment for him.

'Brother Mymer, my dear child, how many young have you so graciously carried to the warmer caves since moonrise?'

'This is my fifteenth already Mother, it is my goal to carry thirty in one day,' he said panting, but smiling through it, 'to honour your greatness,' he added as an afterthought.

'And I shall love you all the more for it my child,' she encouraged, lifting him back to his feet, 'you may continue.'

He disappeared into the line newly enthused, bearing his burden as though it was the Queen's delicate heart.

She then asked the same of a Sister a little further down the line. Sister Lisium, a strong, broad female with sharp tight muscles, stepped out from the line and immediately knelt before her Queen. The secretion from the young she was holding oozed down onto Mothers feet.

'This is my sixth today Mother, I've been working flat out since moonrise, as ordered.'

'As ordered?' Mother questioned. 'You are not ordered Lisium, child, you are encouraged. It is in all our interests that you do this. Not your way of avoiding trouble. How dare you be so selfish as to neglect the needs of your kin, your fellow Brothers and Sisters!'

'But…'

'And six young moved since moonrise! That sounds like laziness to me. The one thing that this family cannot afford is a lazy child not willing to pull her own weight. Am I wrong?'

Sister Lisium's line had stopped and her Brothers and Sisters were staring down at her bawling on the floor, clutching onto her load as protection, waiting for her judgement.

'No Mother, I have betrayed every Brother and every Sister and no longer deserve my place in this family. Use me as you will.' She knew the words by heart, as did every Buggane, but feared more than anything having to utter them. These were words only spoken before death.

Mother lifted her hand and slowly clenched it into a fist. All of those nearest to her pounced like cats and, stretching their jaws wide, bit down into Sister Lisium's hard flesh. She didn't struggle, she didn't even scream as the Brothers and Sisters fed on her. This was her last act of charity. In her failure to do as well as expected, she would sacrifice her body to the good of the family. Her life was not her own, it belonged to them all. There was no freedom, there was only the family. In the pain and the darkness she whispered her thanks to the Queen for giving her the life that she had.

Mother watched her hungry children fight over the final morsels of meat lying around and licking the blood from the floor with their rough tongues until all that was left of Sister Lisium was the smallest of memories, which would quickly fade. The feeling was exquisite, in one hand she had Lisium's abrupt pain and in the other the feasting and pleasure of her starving children. It was a multitude of senses.

Both lines were moving again and there was no sign of disturbance. A clot had been successfully removed.

She continued on her way through the tunnel, taking the path leading further down into the rock. The tunnel walls widened the deeper she went and the Bugganes were fewer. Those still walking alongside her visibly stiffened in her presence as if they were walking on a tightrope and one wrong step would send them falling into oblivion. This sight cheered Atta. They should be fearful of their leader. Fear led to respect and obedience. Fear was control. Previous Mothers had been so weak, accepting their fate and the life of the tunnels, a thing she could never do. If the Mother couldn't bend the hearts and minds of her children to her will she was nothing.

Further and further down she walked, brushing her hand along the dry secretion lining the walls. The only other Bugganes down so deep besides her were two guards, each holding a torch of burning twigs high above them. One of the guards coughed at the near choking stench of faeces around them. It didn't even seem to be air they were breathing, but a rank gas of waste and torment burning their lungs. Mother paid it no heed and ignored the oppressive putrid gas as if it caused her no displeasure at all.

The path of dark green-flecked secretion eventually stopped, leaving the bare rock on show beneath it. As soon as Mother felt the cool naked surface beneath her feet she came to an abrupt halt, lifting her right arm to signal for the guards to do likewise.

The undulating glow of the torches engulfed her as she knelt and brushed the dust and stone chipping from beneath her to reveal the true complexion of the rock and a thin jagged crack running through it. She blew on a sharp claw of her hand and placed it into the crack, drawing it through each angle. Nothing happened. She looked at the two guards, who obediently ignored her annoyance and turned away as she attempted again.

One of the guards, through the corner of his eye, saw the Queen forcing a large grin as she drew her claw through the crack for a second time. He knew his life would be worth little more than a sneeze if he began a rumour that Mother was having trouble parting rocks.

She stepped aside as the crack finally broke apart. A small aperture in the centre expanded into the mouth of a well in the rock floor. Snatching a torch from one of the guards she let it drop through the new opening and watched the ring of light descend until it slapped on the bottom, revealing two figures embracing, and backed as far away from the light as possible.

Mother was just able to make out their bright green eyes as she called down to them.

'Tell me, how does it feel to be so close to extinction?' she laughed, not expecting an answer.

'Atta, are you here just to listen to the ghastly tones of your own voice or is there a purpose to this visit? If not, we would like to get back to enjoying our hole in private.' It was an old defiant voice that came from below, laced with wisdom and experience. Its calm authority enraged Mother.

'Silence. It will not be long until the final breaths of your kind are taken. You will have the privilege of being sacrificed in full view of my entire family. Isn't that fitting? Your total demise shall be at the moment of our greatest strength, when we will rid this land of the thieves who tread the earth above us. We now have all the man-folk we need and are starting our questioning immediately. Before the next moon rises we will know everything about their kind, from what they fear most, to where they are weakest. We cannot fail. Am I wrong?'

'If you think you can learn everything about man from your

tortuous questioning you are far off course. You will never understand their strength of…. But what am I saying? You will discover everything before long and be as we are now, in a cell without doors. So I ask again, is there a reason behind your intrusion?'

He was testing her. Mother knew this. She breathed into her rage, trying to abate any outburst and match his powerful serenity.

'I thought it right to pass on the news that you are less extinct than we thought. It seems that your eldest son, Bea, survived his own murder, though this news has cheered my sons, who look forward to killing him again.'

A small low chuckle rose from the bottom of the cave. Mother, not expecting such a reaction, was unsure she had heard it correctly.

'What was that?' she called down to the two thickly furred creatures.

The chuckle broke into a full bodied rich laugh. The sound sent a chill through Mother's bones.

'Silence,' her voice hardly registered over the sound of resilient joy. How could this news bring joy? Could they not see how close their end was?

'Silence!' she screamed this time. She was reminded of being a young Sister and not getting her own way. She was now shaking with anger and choking on the foul air.

'SILENCE!' The mouth of the cave closed up with a crack and the dust settled on the surface once more as the sound of laughter swamped the tunnel like a wave.

FIVE

'Oh my…!' The sight of the cave springing to life struck Juan across the face like a bucket of ice cold water. The immediate blaze of light blinded his eyes for an instant, before he could see the true spectacle before him.

He didn't know where to look first. There seemed to be colours and light bouncing off every surface of the domed cave. It reminded him of being a young child and staring with innocent wonder into a kaleidoscope. He looked up at Bea and saw the colours reflected in his eyes. The joy and absurdity of it all made him laugh aloud. Bea returned the laugh, understanding how astonishing the place must seem to him compared with his everyday world. It still often surprised him with its ever-changing glow.

Juan blinked several times, so he could endeavour to take in and appreciate the secret palace of lights. It dawned on him that he was probably the first person to ever look upon the unseen world, and as he walked up to the lip of the plateau, a great and unusual privilege beat through him.

Looking around he marvelled at the ceiling of glass chimes, the curve of murals and paint, the man size sculptures and, in front of him, the beginnings of a stone banister, painstakingly carved into the image of a long vine. He touched the stone work and ran his fingers through its details. Everything he saw seemed to add another thousand questions into his already overflowing mind. He turned towards Bea.

'May I?'

Bea, both taken aback and amused by the request, nodded his head in answer. Who wouldn't want to, he asked himself.

Juan climbed over the banister, and with slightly more caution than Bea may have done, lessened his grip and began descending backwards down the spiral. He couldn't help making an excitable guttural noise as he went. Bea smiled to himself, and for the first

time in as long as he could remember walked down the steps to meet him. He'd obviously forgotten how many steps there were, as by the time he had got to the bottom Juan was standing in the centre of the Great Hall staring upwards, hypnotised by the glass ceiling.

'Would it be foolish to ask what you think?' Bea asked the dumbstruck boy.

'This is by far, the most amazing place I have ever seen!' Juan exclaimed, never faltering from looking upwards. 'But just one thing Bea?'

Bea raised an eyebrow, he was a little anxious for the torrent of questions Juan must have for him.

'When was the last time you had this place cleaned?'

Bea let out a sigh of apology.

'I don't mean to be picky, but really, its filthy, it's worse than my bedroom. I bet if I was to…' He drew in a deep breath and blew down on the imposing stone table in the dead centre of the hall and a cloud of thick dust gushed up and filled the air.

Both Bea and Juan were left coughing and waving their arms as the fog cleared.

'See what I mean?'

Bea shrugged as an apology, still spluttering.

Juan's eyes were drawn to the dust settling over the statues on his left. He tentatively walked over to them, wary of their eyes staring down at him. He was so used to being ignored and passing through crowds unnoticed, that this attention was somewhat daunting. He felt very small.

Each figure was an image of profound strength and leadership. Their ages were also evident; the earliest was faded, with its details of armoury crumbled and dull, then onwards each figure was sharper than the last. The expressions in the worn strong jawed face differed also. To Juan, it seemed that the more recent Fynoderees looked more distracted, their stone brows deeper set. And he was sure that behind the reflected sparkle in their eyes, he could see sadness and even helplessness. This was especially true in the final unfinished statue, still locked in the rock face and unable to free itself. These were not the creatures of fireside yarns or the stuff of myths to frighten children, these were people, different people maybe, but people nonetheless. Juan felt suddenly saddened and ashamed of his attraction to the vicious creature he knew from his books at home, with its wild lion-like features and sharp bloodied teeth. He looked away apologetically and saw Bea with his hands outstretched towards him. He was holding a small array of food; fruit, cheeses, potatoes and bread.

'You must be starving,' he said, beckoning him to take from the array before him.

Juan felt his stomach growl. He hadn't noticed that he was indeed very hungry. With all the excitement and flurry of action he had completely ignored how he was feeling, but now standing still, he was not only hungry, but also a little cold.

Gratefully he took some of the food from Bea and went to sit down on the ground closer to the fire at the far end of the cave. He sat there, one side in the cool of the shadows and one side in the heat of the blaze, and quietly ate the bread and the cheese, which tasted surprisingly good and satisfying.

'Where did you get this food from Bea?' he asked the Fynoderee, now sitting cross-legged opposite him in the dust. Bea coughed, as though he wasn't expecting that question.

'Er…from your house actually, I snatched what I could on our way out.'

'I didn't see you take anything.'

'That was the idea. I don't like having to do it, but I'm sure you understand that we have to eat. I thought you'd prefer it this way, it's much better than being forced to feed on three week old long-tail.'

'Do you have to live like this?'

'Live like what, what do you mean?' said Bea, feeling suddenly defensive. He had never had his habits probed before and it felt strange to look on himself objectively.

'Like a scavenger,' said Juan.

'Not for long, I hope.'

They both ate in silence, feeling suddenly self-conscious in the other's company. This was, after all, not a usual meeting of usual people. The food helped to ease the discomfort however, and by the time Juan had laughed whilst watching Bea eat all the raw potatoes, he broke the silence between them.

'I'm sorry Bea. I shouldn't have been so rude. I mean, I can't even begin to imagine how difficult everything must be for you, especially without your family around.'

'No, no, I'm sorry, you've had so much to deal with in just a few hours, and I think you've realised it's not going to be resolved overnight. You have already shown more strength than I ever could. Of course you have questions, but don't worry, the answers will come when they are meant to.'

Bea saw that Juan was shivering, even near the heat of the fire, and stood up.

'I'll fetch something to keep you more warm.'

Bea walked towards a dark area of the dome and disappeared into the shadows. Juan got up and rubbed the woollen arms of his jumper and stamped his feet on the floor as he turned in a circle to take another look at the breathtaking hall.

There were the reverential statues with their eyes still fixed on him, the vine spiralling upwards to the mouth of the cave and then the wall of colours. For a moment, he thought he could see the detail of faces underneath the smudging, as Bea stepped out, as if from nowhere, and again came into view. Juan smiled, thinking his confusion and wonder must be so clearly written over his face.

Bea was holding what looked to be a large fleece, and held it up for Juan to see. It was indeed a large sheepskin, or several, he wasn't sure, cut into a long hooded coat. The white wool was faded into a well-worn rustic grey and was covered with small flecks of black. It couldn't have looked more inviting, Juan thought.

'This was donated to me by a herd of friendly sheep some years ago. They exchanged it for a small favour: politely telling their sheep dog to stop biting them. I used to wear it when I was much younger during the heavier winters as a second skin. Well, come on, we can't have you standing there shivering, let's try it on you.'

Juan stepped up to him and slid his arms into the sleeves. The first thing he noticed was its considerable weight. He likened it to carrying his school satchel on his shoulders. But then, within a moment, he felt its benefit. It cut out any feeling of a cold draft and trapped the warm air of the fire within its skin as he tucked it around him and held it close. It fell down to below his feet and brushed against the dust of the floor, but besides that it fitted him perfectly. The arms were the right length, it hung snugly across his shoulders and as he pulled the hood over his head, he felt not only considerably warmer, but somehow taller as well. It was as though the length and cut of the coat stretched him out and made him want to stand more proudly than ever before. It was a feeling that Bea recognised when he used to wear it.

Just as Juan found himself beginning to laugh again, he saw over Bea's shoulder one of the paintings and the smudged picture of a family staring back at him. It was a family of four, a mother and father, and two sons looking his way. But more than that, he was sure one of them was Bea. His guilt quickly returned. How could he even smile when Bea's family was in such danger? He imagined the faces of his own family up on that wall, smudged, and barely recognisable, just as Bea's family were. His father with his worn jacket and whimsical smile, his mother with her ragged dull auburn hair and soft eyes, and his little sister Aalin happily sticking out her tongue and showing off her paint stained hands.

'You mustn't worry yourself,' said Bea, 'your family are alive, and you should have peace in that fact. Worrying will do no good.'

'How can you be so sure of that?' Juan asked. He could feel the burning pain inside him, leading down towards an unrestrained anger. 'You said those things, the Bugganes, had you're parents as well. How can you be so sure your parents aren't dead and buried in some field somewhere?'

'Do they feel dead to you?' Bea quickly asked back.

'Feel dead?'

'Yes, forget about what you know, or what you fear, I know it's hard but try, and tell me, do your family *feel* dead to you?' Bea spoke in a slow even voice, full of weight and understanding.

Juan tried to do what he asked, and looked within himself. 'Well, I don't know, I guess not.'

'Then you must trust in that feeling. When someone close to you dies, something, a small part of you also dies, only then will you know it to be true. So please, hold onto that and trust me, they are very much alive.'

Juan nodded, but felt a question that had been hanging around his neck finally rise into his throat. He spoke nearly in a whisper, frightened to hear the answer.

'What do they want with them Bea?'

Bea gestured for him to sit down. Juan solemnly did so, and waited patiently for him to begin.

'I'm a very bad liar Juan, my parents could see straight through any fallacies I ever attempted, and I've no doubt you'd also have little trouble. So I won't treat you like a child and hide things from you, I'll only tell you the truth as I know it, alright?'

Juan nodded, his throat becoming ever drier.

'The family of Bugganes have, for a long time, been breeding in numbers more than before, the like of which man-folk has seldom seen, even in your shaded history, and believe me we have been watching you. Certainly tens, and more than likely, hundreds of thousands of those creatures that you saw tonight are patiently waiting in dank and sweaty tunnels beneath this island. They have been sitting, biding their time, for many years, and they don't intend to sit there much longer.' Bea breathed out a heavy sigh and continued.

'You now know we exist, but with that knowledge you are in a most fragile position. The Bugganes cannot afford to have their existence and intentions known. That would give man-folk time to prepare for their Reclamation.'

'Reclamation?' Juan cut in, 'Reclamation of what?'

'The island,' answered Bea, flatly. 'They have been breeding in such numbers to give them the strength to reclaim what they believe is rightfully theirs: Ellan Vannin, the Isle of Man.

'Bugganes have existed here for a thousand years – before a Viking ever stepped onto its shores. After discovering the land could not be shared peacefully, the Bugganes went underground, hiding under rocks and in the deep tunnels of the earth. They quickly began to adapt to their environment, becoming nocturnal cave dwellers, but still they craved the light and earth over ground. It was only when their numbers began to dwindle frighteningly low through starvation that they began breeding within families. Of course the strongest family soon took charge and wiped out the weaker and continued to grow and grow. But they began to change. They became the distorted, hot-blooded creatures you yourself have seen, blindly following their Queen, their Mother, Atta. They don't believe in freedom or sharing power, and once their eyes are set on something they are like hawks. They don't forget things lightly. This grudge has grown in their minds since they were first banished into the depths, and the time has finally come for them to take justice.

'You and others must have surely noticed people going missing recently?' he asked.

'Missing yes, but everyone said they had decided to just leave the island, that's all.'

'They are too frightened to see the truth, and who can blame them, truth is often an ugly beast to face,' said Bea. 'The Bugganes have taken certain people, non too subtly, in order to help them with their plans.'

'Help them?!' Bea raised a hand to stop Juan interrupting.

'I first thought they were taking people at random, but then tonight I realised there was a pattern to it all. They have taken people who deal with all the major areas of life on the island, your learning, your health, your beliefs, and so on. I believe they wish to understand you, to know how best to destroy you. They intend to wipe out life and take back the isle from man.'

For the second time that night Juan found himself unable to breathe. His lungs were empty, and his body refused to work. It was in too much shock. His dad had been right to be suspicious, no one was safe. He couldn't bare the thought of those vile creatures having his family in their grasp, thinking what might happen to them made him feel sick. He wanted to faint, at least that way he could be free from the news, if only for a short time.

'But what do they want with my family? We're not that good at anything, I mean dad can do outdoor stuff and mum cooks the best roast dinner, but not the type of stuff you're talking about, not the stuff that keeps the island going.'

Bea couldn't stop. He knew that to keep anything from Juan would be to open new wounds later on. It would be easier this way. He had to continue, for his sake.

'True,' he said.

'Then why us?' pleaded Juan once more.

'Because,' he said loudly to get back the boy's attention. Juan looked up sharply, his eyes staring helplessly into Bea's as though begging for him to stop, but too afraid not to know.

'We've known this time of change may come for as long as memory lasts, my elders read it in the stars long ago. They told us that someone would bring a message, a key to deliver us from such troubles.

'It was said that Manannin himself, the spirit of Ellan Vannin, would send us a message when man-folk needs it most, a message written in his very hand, a message painted on a boy. He didn't say how the boy would know of his duty, only that he would bear a message of help on his body. We always thought it was some bedtime story, nothing more. I don't think that anymore. I think the elders were right, and the stars spoke truths. Do you know what I'm saying Juan?'

'How do you know about…?' Juan's voice was faint and trailed off into nothing.

'I saw the script on your hand when I first lifted you up. The Bugganes must have had a Watcher find you.'

'A what?'

'A Watcher. A man tied up in their strings, for Queen Atta to command as she wishes. A puppet.'

Juan, his eyes watering, lifted up his woollen jumper to reveal his bare stomach. And there on his skin were markings running all over him. He scratched hard at the script, wishing more than ever that it would rub off. He scratched harder and harder, becoming more frantic as he finally broke down into torrents of tears, no longer able to hold onto any grip of the situation. He wept at the madness of it all, the markings, the myths he'd grown up with, the Reclamation, all merging into one waking nightmare.

Bea held him as he sobbed, holding gently onto his shaking shoulders. He felt awful having placed so much painful truth on him. How would he cope if he were faced with such news? No better he suspected. He never imagined he would be the one passing this dreadful history down to the *key-per*. His only solace was that he could tell Juan little else. His wounds could not be opened further. Saving it until a later time would only have prolonged what he would have to learn before his new journey began.

He felt Juan's pain grow and fill in his own chest, but forced it down with steady strong breaths. He had to be strong for both of them. He needed to be Juan's strength and courage whilst he adjusted, and let the boy cry all he needed to.

As the tears refused to cease in Juan's eyes, he pictured a hundred faces of everyone he knew, no matter how well. From the people he grew up with in his village, always ready with a wave for the son of Mr. Kerruish, to his fellow classmates who wouldn't so much as notice his absence from school.

Bea placed his hand softly on Juan's head. 'Try to sleep now. It's been a hard night. You need to rest.'

Bea's voice felt distant to him as he thought of the day gone by. It was already like looking back on a forgotten dream or peering through frosted glass into another boy's life. He thought of school and Cairney and Creeses dunking his head in the toilet. He thought of sitting in the library and talking to Turner. But most of all he remembered the blissful ignorance he was in, not knowing any of this. He wished he could be free from it all again. How could so much change so quickly?

As the tears slowly dried, his hazy vision fell upon the painting of the female Fynoderee with her crisp sharp features and haunting almond shaped eyes. He snivelled and wiped his wet nose on the sleeve of his new fleece.

'She's beautiful Bea, who is she?'

Bea looked up at his painting.

'Her? I'm sorry but she's no one, she doesn't exist, nothing more than a painted illusion. I'm the last of my kind Juan. I have no mate, our kind could never breed like the Bugganes.

'I once believed there might be someone, another Fynoderee, for me somewhere, but not now. When I'm gone, our kind will truly be a myth, just like your books say we are. You go to sleep now. I'll stay with you tonight. We shall have much to do when you wake.'

Juan laid his head in Bea's lap and pulled his woollen cloak tightly round him. He could tell Bea was uncomfortable talking about the painting and didn't want to upset him further. He gripped onto his thick furry arm and held it tight as his eyes closed and his breathing steadied.

Just before he fell asleep, he felt a droplet of water drip down onto his cheek. He knew it was a tear shed from Bea's eyes, and gently squeezed his arm, feeling the thick warm fur between his fingers, before drifting into a light and fretful sleep.

SIX

The Watcher shivered before Queen Atta, a pool of water gradually spreading at his feet. He didn't want to be there. He neither appreciated being dragged from his study nor forced to be confronted by Mother for the second time in just as many days. What he loathed above all was that he hadn't the power to say 'no'. He was their slave, and it had begun to grate on him. This wasn't what he had agreed to.

After a lifetime of searching for the Bugganes, it was they who had found him. He was important, Mother had told him. His story was to be one of wonder and pride, not mediocrity. Her words were sweet and honeyed and her promises rich. He was goaded into her persuasive embrace and so became their Watcher. It was effortless. He was to do nothing more than keep his eye out for a painted boy that disturbed Mother's dreams, some *key-per* or other.

Though he was sceptical at first, it had been laughably perfect; as the Bugganes had found him, so had the boy. He had walked right into his classroom that very day, the barely noticeable, forever late, Juan Kerruish. He'd had difficulty containing himself when he saw the boy's markings. What a joke, the etchings of Manannin sent on such an unexceptional boy. Mr. Mortis could hardly believe his luck.

And so he had done his duty. He had warned Mother of the boy and left it at that. But it seemed he had not done enough. He crossed his arms tightly into his damp tweed suit to keep them warm and looked into Queen Atta's impatient and angry red eyes.

Before he had a chance to air his misgivings, Atta's arm flew from her side, and with her mittened bony hand, she took Mortis cleanly round the throat and lifted him from the ground. Her webbed fingers fitted tightly around his narrow neck. This was taking things too far.

For a moment Atta thought to quickly squeeze the life out of

Mortis, but she knew that it wasn't his fault that this Kerruish boy had escaped their grasp, she merely wanted her fears confirmed yet again. She wanted her scratch itched.

'Just tell me one more time how you can be so sure that the young boy was the *key-per* we have been warned of.'

Mortis was turning more scarlet with each passing moment, and, being unable to utter a single word with the unbearable pressure on his wind pipe, was waving his arms erratically for Atta to release him. She reluctantly did so and he buckled to the floor fighting to find breath. Not surprised by her temper, it nevertheless perturbed him. He could usually predict how a hot-blooded Buggane would react and it hardly seemed justified of Atta. He had fulfilled his side of the bargain and let them know about the boy and the whereabouts of his family as soon as he could.

'I saw that infernal script on his hand,' he coughed, 'the etchings of Manannin, the ones you described to me from your dreams. I don't think he saw me spot them, but I've never been more certain of anything my Queen. He's probably got them all over his body by now. I'm sure you don't want him out in the open. You must find him.'

Mortis immediately knew he had spoken out of turn. Although desperate, he stared down in shame at Atta's bloody feet, unable to look in those red eyes of hers and see her revolting beauty.

'If it was as easy as you make it sound, do you not think we would have found him long ago? Am I wrong?' she spat out every word as though it disgusted her. 'The boy is no doubt within the Fynoderee's final dwelling by now. We know as much about that place as they do about ours. They have strong, obedient rocks keeping them well hidden. Their stone is loyal to them and will reveal nothing, unlike our stone, which would shout our secrets from the hills if it could.' She slammed her hand down hard onto the arm of the throne and a crack split its way down to the floor.

'The only stone we know of, that is forthcoming to all, is the *Kiarkil voish Ansoor.*' Atta stopped, surprised by Mortis' vacant expression.

'The *Kiarkil voish Ansoor*? You mean you've never…?' she asked. Mortis blankly shook his head.

'It is said that when standing in the *Kiarkil voish Ansoor*, the Circle of Answers, the stones cannot refuse you the answer to any question you ask, anything. A few brief moments within that circle and the fate of the Fynoderees would be secured.

'But again, its whereabouts have been lost by my pitiful predecessors. Their clumsiness has a lot to answer for.' She let out a low sigh, rasping at the back of her throat.

'To tell you the truth, I would not be surprised if the Circle of Answers could only be found on Manannin's Map, and for all I know that is a legend in itself. If we could but find…'

'Manannin's Map?' Mortis asked in great haste, clutched by an instant hope. 'What is Manannin's Map?'

'Oh, you surprise me Mortis. I thought more of you; I was certain that if there was one mortal man who would have known of its existence it would have been you.

'If I must spell it out to you, Manannin was thought to have roughly scrawled a map onto a piece of bark from a Manx oak, solely for the good of man-folk, moments before he passed into the spirit world. The map, as rough as it is meant to be, apparently shows where someone can go to have one's questions answered, to receive help from the unlikeliest of creatures and to burrow into the utmost depths of the island. In short it would save me moons of effort with the knowledge it holds.' Atta let out a small laugh, catching herself describing such myths and uncertainties.

'But I refuse to waste more time…'

Mortis again cut her short, raising his hand in great apology and clenching his teeth against any outburst.

The thin split down Atta's throne slowly sealed together like a zip in the silence. Mortis cleared his throat before speaking. He could hardly stomach interrupting her, but if she was to fulfil her side of the bargain he believed it was for the best.

'My Queen, I think I have your precious map.' He didn't go on, but stood there waiting for some kind of response, any response. Even he couldn't judge what Atta might do.

She sat there, expressionless, staring down at him.

'What?' was all she could bring herself to ask, the burning in her throat too great for anything else. Mortis fell again to his knees before her and began speaking at a great pace, eager to get all the words out before she had time to do anything rash.

'My Queen, by your description I can only conclude that I have the map you seek. Of course I cannot be certain, but I doubt there are many maps scrawled onto the back of the bark of a Manx oak so old we are unable to date it. I thought it would be of no interest, other than historical. I know how you detest history, and live only for what is to come. If I knew it was worth more, I would have surrendered it to you without a moment's thought. You know I would. I can do little more than apologise and bring it to you immediately.' He had managed everything in one breath and finished with a slight whimper of 'sorry'.

Atta closed her eyes and squeezed them shut, as though the anger might burst forth from them. Her tense frame was shaking with the pressure of keeping her fury prisoner. The arms of her dais cracked and chipped beneath her clenched fists, and the flat nostrils on her prickly face shrunk as she inhaled hard. These were tests, she told herself, stepping-stones towards the land above them. Nothing more.

Slowly she opened her eyes and looked down to Mortis' prostrating form beneath her. Again she was without expression and her voice was slow and restrained.

'Do you hold anything else in your possession that you believe may be of help to our cause?'

Mortis looked up at her. 'If I had, do you not think I would have handed them over to you already? With the greatest of respect my Queen, the artefacts I have collected over the years are my business. Many of the objects I have are tremendously valuable…'

No. That was it. Atta didn't care about patience and acceptance anymore. She had bottled up her temper for long enough, and was certainly not going to let a man, a mere man, cross her in such a resilient way. She leapt from her dais, grabbing Mortis around the shoulders, and skidded with him along the length of the rough floor. She then held him by the wrists with her hands and by the ankles with her feet. He was trapped with his back on the floor, Queen Atta like a spider above him. They were nose to nose and he couldn't move even a fraction.

'Do you honestly think the value of things will mean anything in a matter of days?' she snapped. Mortis could feel her spit hit his face as he held his eyes closed against her attack.

'Your people spend their whole lives chasing wealth, like a child chases a butterfly. And what for? The hope of happiness? That will be man-folk's downfall. They are blind to everything else around them. When we are standing in the shadows right behind them, they will still be chasing their precious riches!'

She took Mortis' face in her hands and pried his eyelids open with her bony fingers, forcing him to look at her. The fire in her red eyes surrounded his world and he coughed on the dead stench of her breath.

Atta, already feeling a satisfied release for venting her wrath, gave him a broad grin. She wasn't going to kill him, not today at least, he still had his uses.

'You shall be royalty Mortis,' she pronounced. 'You shall have the true riches of power in your small hands, a far greater wealth than coins and jewels. Wouldn't that have pleased your family? Even those who hated us, those who nightly wished that we were indeed only legend? That's what it's all about Mortis, that's why you have been looking for us for so long isn't it...revenge?'

Mortis paused. How could she know? he thought. He had never spoken of his reasons for seeking out the Bugganes. He didn't know what to say and only nodded in answer.

'Yes, I see Mortis. Don't think I don't. I can see your family, centuries ago. I can see them in your vengeful eyes. I can see your brave ancestor, the tailor of Greeba, Timothy, helping to rid the town of a Buggane destroying the church of St. Trinian. They were all so happy with him weren't they?'

Mortis, now wide eyed and fearful, nodded again.

'And we came back and ruined it all, didn't we. We came to

your people wanting shelter and food. "How dare they, those beasts, how dare they come and beg from such hardworking, honest and godly folk?" Timothy said. "They don't so much as deserve our scraps."

'So your people turned us away, and did so every time we came. Time and time again you turned us away. Until we turned against you, didn't we? We destroyed your beautiful church, and tore your family apart. Am I wrong?'

A single lonely tear ran down Mortis' cheek as he shook his head.

'Your forefathers became beggars didn't they, beggars just like we were, getting work and food wherever they could. From such a well-regarded family to beggars overnight, that must have hurt. But they swore that they would dedicate themselves to destroying every last one of us, no matter how long it would take. They would turn us into nothing more than legend. And they very nearly succeeded.

'Over a thousand of your years, over twelve thousand full moons, is an awfully long time.'

She changed her tone, and became suddenly warmer. 'You and I are so alike, are we not?'

'Yes my Queen. I spent so long looking for you. It has been my life…'

'I know my child. And I thank you for it. Rest well knowing your forgiveness and allegiance shall not go without reward.' She inwardly smiled knowing how easily he had been bought with gilded lies. 'You did well to have found the *key-per*.'

'And it turns out to be that little lump,' said Mortis. They both spluttered into laughter.

'If that is the best Manannin can do, our Reclamation will be brief indeed.' Their laughter grew together as Atta released him from her grasp and lifted him to standing by the lapels of his jacket.

'You are truly all-seeing my Queen,' Mortis said, brushing the dust off his checked trousers.

'Yes, I am,' said Atta, matter-of-factly, putting her hand to the base of his back and leading him through the wall of smoke surrounding her chamber and out towards the exit, leading uphill to the central most tunnels of the nest.

'But are you sure your plans can work Mother?'

Atta kept quiet. Her silence would answer his question well enough. She resented the doubt in his words, but was strangely moved that she had found another son in the weak shape of this man, no matter for how long.

As they walked together between the light and dark of the burning torches hanging from the tunnel wall, Mortis watched Atta's manic terrifying face come in and out of sight; the face that had turned him away from his family's task in search of a much grander prize. His ancestors could not doubt what Atta had said. He would be royalty.

Mortis noted the tunnels they walked up, dank and simple, with no attempt to make anything more appealing. No painting or stonework to display their great culture. Such gaudy art would promote individual thought, he knew, and dissipate their sense of family. To the Bugganes, individuality and freedom were weaknesses, like a disease.

They halted together at the top of the slope and looked out over the wide tunnel ahead of them. Bugganes were crammed into every available space, busy about their work, crawling in all directions and the occasional group surrounded a fight hoping to get a small piece of the loser to quell their gnawing hunger. Mortis stood there, looking out, marvelling at their species; so vicious, so organised, so beautiful. He turned towards Atta.

'And will it be as you said Mother…no survivors but two: myself and another? That was the bargain was it not? You did promise after all…'

'Yes, don't worry my child, you shall be permitted a companion. Did you have any one in mind?'

'Yes indeed, a lady I work with Mother. I've had my eye on her for quite a while now. She is everything I could wish for, fiercely intelligent, shrewd, a brutal sense of order and justice. She works in the library mainly, wears her hair in an a pretty bun and has the most wonderful…'

'Enough! I can't conceive how you ever imagine yourselves, or each other, attractive, with your bland features and limp, soft skin.' Mother held herself and seemed to shudder with repulsion.

'She will make a perfect Queen.'

'I am the only Queen!' bellowed Atta, standing firmer and taller than before. If he did not know better, Mortis could easily mistake her for a male, with her broad strength and masculine grimace.

'Of course Atta, Mother, Queen, I mistook.' He obediently bowed his head in an expression of fear, but already knew that for the moment he was too valuable an asset to be considered expendable. He was important.

Atta raised her hand and Mortis felt the weighty presence of two guards behind him. 'You know what to do my child. I expect you to be back with the map…soon,' she croaked, and Mortis was grabbed by the two guards and dragged away from her.

Atta disappeared from his view as the guards stamped their way down the tunnel, unnoticed by the busy workers. Their steps were wide and heavy, like rock beating against rock, as Mortis' heels scraped along in the dust. Hardly the way to treat royalty, he thought, trying to relax as best he could. By the time the guards dropped him, his wrists felt like they might come out of his forearms, and he rubbed the burning hard as though he had just been released from handcuffs. He turned to the two guards, holding themselves motionless, and stared hard at them for a moment or two, checking to see if they would blink. He waved his hand in front of their faces, trying to garner any sort of reaction to prove their earthliness, but none came. They truly were living rocks.

'When I have some say around here, the first thing I'm going to do is fire the two of you. Now if you don't mind opening the rock for me, I've got a lot to do.'

Both of the guards simultaneously shifted their view to meet his, and, baring their teeth, leant down towards him. Mortis could hear the low gurgling of a growl coming from the backs of their throats and his smile quickly faded.

The guard on his right abruptly took hold of his shoulders with both his hands and spun him away from them, and the other guard pushed him head first towards the floor.

As Mortis was coming face to face with the stone and just as he thought he was about to get a mouthful of dust for yet another time, the stone cracked and parted. In an instant the crack seemed to grow to his exact size and as he dropped through it sealed behind him. He could only imagine that this was what being gulped down whole must feel like.

SEVEN

Back in his dreams, the circle of stones once again surrounded Juan. He lifted his hand to see the globe resting in his palm, all blue but for the tiny spot of land on it, and smiled. It felt good to be so deep down in the sea where nothing could harm him. Transfixed, he stared at the glowing sphere for a short while, but blinked as the current began to grow in the dense water around him, and, looking ahead, saw that it was now rushing his way.

'…unforgivable…' spoke a voice, flowing through the current.

'…didn't need so much sleep…' The deep voice was familiar to him, but it sounded strange. He'd never heard it speak in anger and it made him shiver. He could sense that something was wrong, but as hard as he tried, he couldn't recall what.

'…precious time…'

The current was now punching into him so hard he had to close his eyes, and as soon as he did so the water ceased hitting him. It was now the cold wind. And when he became aware of being jogged up and down, he knew he had woken up.

He slowly opened his eyes and saw a blurred mass speeding past him. His first thought was that he might still be dreaming. It felt like he was being thrown through an oil painting, as though he was separate from the landscape he was moving on.

Though they were madly watering, he kept his eyes open and looked down. He saw the white tense knuckles of his own hands but protruding between his fingers was dark coarse fur. He was clinging onto Bea. He was running with Bea. The previous night flooded back to him; his family, the story written in the stars, the Reclamation. He checked for the markings on the back of his hand, as if it was proof, and saw the formless, jagged lines under his skin.

He looked around him, but couldn't tell where they were. It

looked like a swirl of greys and greens on his left hand side and dark blues and whites on his right. They were moving so fast, the only thing he could tell was that the sun had nearly set, it was evening. He must have slept all day.

Bea leapt between two crags and let the wind lift and carry him to the furthest edge. Juan caught his breath as they rose up in the air and landed with a small jolt on the opposite side. He knew he would never get used to that. Bea felt to check for Juan's hand on his shoulder and softly patted it when he had found it. Juan gave a little squeeze as if to say 'I'm alright' and they set off again.

'Are you awake Juan?' asked Bea, in his low comforting voice. Juan felt its vibration from Bea's back, and was surprised at how unruffled he sounded. He had cursed himself enough, Juan thought.

'Y-y-yes,' answered Juan, his voice shaking from the leap and the jostling of Bea's running.

'Forgive me for my haste, but do you know anything about your markings?'

'N-no. Only that they've been appearing over the past few days. I tried to ignore them at first and keep them hidden, but there have been more of them in the last w-week.'

'You've never seen anything like them before?' Bea asked. That was an easy question, thought Juan.

'It's funny, but I've only seen one other thing that reminded me of them.'

Bea slammed his heels into the earth and came to a most sudden stop. Juan was thrown from his grip on Bea's shoulders and landed with a bump in the mushy dull brown sand of a beach. He instinctively looked to check if anyone was around that could see them. In the distance was a fisherman standing a little way into the still water, his yellow waders immersed up to the knees and his long rod elegantly waving back and forth before he cast his line far into the calm sea.

Juan span back round to warn Bea to take cover, but saw nothing except for the beach stretching away until it turned a corner of rocks and went out of sight.

'Bea?' he whispered.

'I'm right here,' came the reply, so close to his face it made him jump.

He squinted and concentrated, and there, right there in front of him, he could make out Bea's sizeable outline of hair and muscle. He saw that his fur had simply taken on the colours of the background: the sand, the black sea, even the glittering horizon. He jumped again when he saw Bea's undisguised eyes blinking down at him, like two balls hanging in mid-air, and then a glistening set of teeth broke into a smile beneath them.

'Neat trick!' said Juan, clearly impressed. 'I never read a book that said you could do that.'

'It's not easily done. We call it *arraghey*, shifting, it allows us to move in your world without...upsetting anyone,' said Bea, proudly, and led them further towards the cliffs, away from the view of the fisherman, now struggling with a curved rod, rapidly reeling in his catch.

'Where have you seen anything like this before?' he asked, carefully lifting Juan's hand and pointing at the prominent black lines.

'At my school,' said Juan casually, 'in my history teacher's classroom there's this odd, old map...'

'Oh thank Manannin himself! I hoped and prayed it would be so. This may give us the upper hand, but we haven't much time.'

Bea grabbed Juan by the wrist and flung him over his shoulder, as if he was nothing more than a light bag. Juan let out a little grunt as he held on hard again. He had few questions that didn't sound ridiculous in his own head, but as he saw the thick hair between his fingers turn from the colour of the craggy rock to its usual dark muddy brown he couldn't hold his curiosity any longer.

'Is this magic Bea?'

'No. It's not magic,' he said as calm as before. 'It's just...different.'

And with that, he jumped onto the wall and began to climb upwards.

Mortis was spat out into the dark and fell only a short way before plunging into the quickly running, underground stream. The ice cold water took his breath away, but there was no time to try and catch it in the rapids, merely staying afloat took all his effort.

The thin vein of water was hurtling at a tremendous speed through the rock tunnel and, although to begin with, Mortis was aware of travelling most definitely downwards, he couldn't tell which way he was going any longer. If his senses weren't toying with him, it was as though he was travelling upwards.

A white light started to fill the chute, turning the water from the appearance of black oil to a silvery flowing mercury. The walls were also beginning to be covered with greenery. Wet bracken and weeds stuck out from the cracks to the side and above him, stretching down and drinking from the water.

The weeds grew thicker and thicker and Mortis began brushing them out of his way, when he suddenly fell again as the flow of water shot out from the small unseen mouth of the tunnel and tumbled down the smooth rock of Glen Maye waterfall.

Mortis held himself rigid hoping not to fall onto any sharp rocks and waited for his ordeal to finish. He tumbled into one more basin of water and then, feeling a lack of any current, found the pebble covered bottom of the catch pool and stood up.

He brushed the wet leaves, weeds and hair away from his face and opened his eyes. He was greeted with a clear starry night and a surprisingly bright crescent moon shining between the break of the cliffs a mile beyond him, where the water ran down and completed its journey to the sea.

The world seemed metallic in the calm glow of the moon. The water in the final rock pool was like a lightly bubbling mill-pond, only rippling from the tiny fish darting between the pebbles beneath his feet. A profusion of dark green vines fell down the rock walls enclosing the falls in a small alcove before opening out towards the path leading down to the stony beach.

Mortis waded to the edge of the pool and stepped out onto the mossy bank. His leather shoes squelched on the surface as he tried to shake the water from them and he held his hands tightly under his armpits trying to get them warmer and hide them from the chill of the breeze.

When hearing a dog barking and festering in the hedges of the cliff head, further down towards the sea, he set off inland.

The steps leading away from the sea followed alongside the riverbank and waterfall, and were smooth, wet and slippery from the spray of the water. Mortis took extra care and held onto the various trailing plants beside him to ensure he didn't return to the water before it was entirely necessary.

Crossing over the footbridge at the top of the waterfall he looked down into the white foam beneath and the splashing water glistening like precious stones in the moonlight.

He walked the final few yards up the hill to the Waterfall Inn at the entrance to the glen and, in the orange glow coming from the windows of the pub, shook himself like a dog. After the mist of water had settled, he opened the door.

There were never more than a small number of locals in the pub in the evening, and only one or two raised their heads to look at the sodden figure of Mortis framed in the doorway.

The spindly Mrs. Bowen, sitting rigidly on a barstool, gave a quiet 'tut' and returned to her magazine of wedding dresses. The Brown brothers didn't even flinch from their game of dominoes in the corner by the fire. It looked as though both were waiting for the other to take his turn having forgotten who went last, and their cigars were gently burning towards their fingers. And behind the bar, the burly landlord, Mr. Skellig, was dusting a copper tankard and staring straight at Mortis slowly shaking his head.

Mortis walked uncertainly through the room, leaving wet footprints on the well worn, stained carpet and headed for the bar. Mrs. Bowen didn't so much as glance his way, but raised her tweaked eyebrows and pursed her thin lips in reproof.

'Been for a dip again sir?' asked Mr. Skellig, in a nasal murmur through his thick scraggly beard.

Mortis courteously shook his head, picking up the bar mat in front of him to dry his hands and run through his still damp hair. If Mrs. Bowen's eyebrows went any higher they would have floated off her face.

'What'll it be tonight sir, the usual?'

Mortis solemnly nodded and Mr. Skellig turned around and began to pour him a large brandy. Mortis turned and looked to the people in the lounge once more. Most of them were sitting in their own company, staring vacantly at the haze of smoke in front of their faces. Old man Tim, sitting beneath a large framed fish, couldn't even keep his eyes open, but still continued to bring his glass of ale up to his craggy lips and drink from it. Mortis looked at his face, with wrinkles as deep as rivers. It looked to him like his life of labour had been drawn into every line from his brow to his saggy jowls and the crow's feet around his closed eyes. He looked all but dead, save for his drinking.

He turned back to the bar, took the glass filled with its brass coloured liquid and downed the brandy in one gulp, wincing against the burn in his chest, but still pleasuring in its warmth. He banged the glass back on the bar, pulled his sodden wallet from his breast pocket, removed a damp note and handed it to Mr. Skellig.

'Keep the change.' Mr. Skellig looked down at the note as Mortis was walking away towards the door.

'Are you sure sir?'

'Of course,' he said with his back to the door. 'I see a great recession on the way.' And he let the door swing shut behind him.

As soon as he got into his motorcar he turned on the engine and sat back in his unpleasantly soggy suit. The engine purred as the tyres crunched over the road and the headlights sliced through the thin dark night.

Mortis listened to the steady drone of the motor's engine as he went on his way. It settled his mind as he turned out of the narrow winding roads and headed towards the thick forests further east.

Atta had been right. He had been hunting the Bugganes. His father had planted the seed in him early on by taking him out hunting for them across the wilds of Greeba, and would tell him the story of St. Trinian's church whenever he could. "Imagine what we would have been if it wasn't for them," he would say, "we would be ruling the island by now". And so we will, thought Mortis. Surely that was right, surely.

As he drove on, he could feel no regret for the thousands of lives that would soon be taken by the Bugganes, no fear of what was to come. It neither pleased nor upset him. He felt strangely numb to it.

A black bird flew out of the way, dazzled by the motorcar's headlights, as he headed further south. The road surface was icy and unstable in the cold outside, and there were few others out and about even as he travelled down towards the busier Castletown.

He soon pulled into the long drive of the school and slowed down, as the grey ominous turrets of the buildings seemed to grow out of the earth the closer he got. He had spent his life behind those stone walls. The school had nurtured him, and in many ways still did. It gave him work and food and money and room enough to quietly follow his other interests, like sitting up late into the night in his study hunched over old scrolls, trying to decipher the runes on his map. Though years of effort had earned him nothing.

He tidily parked his motor in his usual place in front of the boarding houses and headed indoors through a side entrance.

A pair of seniors sitting on the first step of the stair well jumped to their feet and took their hands out of their pockets the moment they saw him. Mortis scowled at them suspiciously as he jumped up the steps, smiling to himself as they began to nervously chatter once he was out of sight.

All of the juniors would have been in bed by now and there were only a few seniors still up, strolling around the corridors inpairs, checking that the lights had been turned out in all the dormitories and everything had settled down for the night.

'It doesn't look right some how,' said Juan, peering over the top of the low crumbled ruins that rested just beyond the outer walls of the school. Bea wasn't listening, but sat behind the wall looking out over the sea directly behind them. Dark clouds were closing in like curtains, and he was watching the stars slowly disappear behind them. Juan looked down the long straight road that was the back entrance to the school flanked by sports fields he had seldom played on. Stretched over the landscape ahead was the school itself. But for the occasional pinpricks of amber light coming from the windows, the grey building was well camouflaged with the oncoming overcast sky.

'If it's possible, it looks even more unwelcoming than usual,' said Juan, ducking down behind the wall and joining Bea.

'Be that as it may, there's something in there that could save us days searching for the *Kiarkil voish Ansoor.*'

'The what?'

'I'll explain when we get there,' answered Bea. Juan suddenly felt guilty and ignorant for his constant questions and sat quietly looking out over the sea. Bea put a hand on his shoulder. He hadn't meant to be short with him.

'Are you all right Juan? You're doing so well you know.'

'I'm fine,' he answered, not knowing if he was lying or not.

Juan span round when he heard the low rumble of a motorcar's engine pass only a few feet in front of the ruin on the road. He poked his head over the wall so he could just see and fell straight down again as the headlights of the motorcar passed by them. They both then watched the motor descend the drive and casually pull up to the side of the school, and Juan gasped as he watched Mr. Mortis step out from it. He looked like he'd been pulled through a hedge backwards, Juan thought.

'Oh no, it's him, we have to hurry or…'

He hadn't been able to finish speaking; they had already bounded over the low wall and set off towards the lights.

'We can make it,' replied Bea through clenched teeth, leaning closer to the ground and speeding up even more. Juan shut his eyes against the sting of the rushing air for an instant, and when he opened them again he was already face to face with the grainy stone of the school walls.

Passing through the main dinning hall, Mortis let his hand drag over one of the long wooden tables, feeling the polished oak brush under his fingertips. He remembered sitting at that very table as a junior not so very long ago, usually on his own, and the same familiar smell of wood polish, linseed, and burnt toast still hung in the air.

Several groups of seniors were scattered around the tables in the hall. Some were playing board games and some were having late evening snacks before returning to their rooms to continue with their late night studies. There was a low musty ruddiness to the hall and a calm glow came from the light bouncing off the stained glass windows lining the walls on either side of the room. Mortis looked to the centre most windows, which pictured the school crest floating in front of the school buildings, and each tiny little bit of glass throwing light down onto the polished floor. He thought he'd never truly appreciated its complex beauty and craftsmanship, and gazed a while at its shimmering colours.

A group of girls were giggling behind their hands whilst trying to catch his eye in between their game of cards. Mortis sharply turned towards them, opening his mouth as if to question their behaviour and lack of respect and so forth, but then stopped. What did it matter, he thought, they'll be disciplined soon enough. Let them laugh. It will all be over soon. And, closing his mouth, he turned on his heels and continued through the hall to the staircase leading up from the quad, hearing the girls laugh even more behind him as he left.

He bounced up the next flight of stairs and stopped only when reaching the top in front of the glass trophy cabinet. He checked his refection in the glass front of the cabinet; although dry, he looked distinctly shabby and tried to tame the parting in his hair and straighten the lapels of his tweed suit.

He made a small double take when noticing, next to the cabinet, what looked to be a pile of old laundry. His immediate thought was that all the pupils had lost any semblance of regime and order. He peered at it closer and saw that it wasn't a pile of old clothes but a filthy woollen rug that had been balled up and left there. He gave it a kick and was just about to pick it up and take it to the nearest laundry bin when he heard a crash and loud curse behind him.

He turned around and saw Miss Owen on her hands and knees pulling library books towards her and piling them on top of each other on the floor. He went straight to her aid and knelt down next to her collecting the remaining books.

'Oh Brendan!' she exclaimed in her whiny nasal voice. 'It's been one of those days!'

'Don't fret yourself Olivia, it will no doubt be another one of those days tomorrow as well.' They both reached for the same book, and as their fingers brushed, Mortis retorted and felt his face ignite as he blushed. Olivia looked up at him, and he was relieved that she too was blushing. They both began to speak, but interrupted each other.

'Sorry, you first,' he conceded.

'No you, I insist.' Olivia's relaxed yet forceful tone made Mortis tingle. All of a sudden everything felt rather hazy.

'I was just g-going to ask…how…' he stuttered, trying to find anything of interest to ask Olivia inside his misty head, '…how the library is?' He was disappointed with his effort but Olivia smiled nonetheless and adjusted her thickly rimmed tortoiseshell glasses.

'Quiet and solitary,' she answered, 'the way I like it.'

Mortis grinned. She is perfect, he thought. And he wondered at her small quirks; her pale hands with such bright nail vanish playing awkwardly with the faux pearls around her neck, the straggles of dry hair straying from her bun.

'And how are your history classes Brendan? I'm always so impressed with the enthusiasm you show for your subject.' Mortis could feel himself blushing yet again, and pulled at his collar hoping that it might cool him down. 'Why, you often work so hard, if I didn't know you I would think you were obsessed.' She let out a high, breathy laugh, and Mortis self-consciously joined in.

Olivia took a brave step towards him and lightly took hold of his jacket. He began to breathe very deeply, trying to prevent himself from passing out.

'You know, there's little more attractive than a man with such enthusiasm and passion in his life.' They were very close all of a sudden. Mortis could have drowned in her perfume and could see the few fair hairs above her top lip. 'If I didn't have such professional integrity, I might just...' He saw her close her eyes and was waiting in agony for her pursed lips to meet his, when he heard another crash, this time much louder, come from his classroom behind him. The blissful moment was ruined and he exhaled, feeling as though someone was purposefully trying to ruin his day.

'I must have left the window open,' he said apologetically, forcing a smile. Olivia, though obviously disappointed, picked up her books and followed him.

They were already in the empty wood panelled chamber outside the dining hall before Juan could make any decision about what to do. He was too surprised that Bea had thrown any caution to the wind and was apparently unconcerned with being seen. They had so far been fortunate to have not met anyone else in or around the corridors.

'You need to lead the way to his classroom. I'll follow you. Can you do that?'

'Yes, but…'

He didn't have time to object. Bea had already pushed him into the light of the hall, where he froze. The hall was far from full, but there were still plenty of late night stragglers sitting around the long tables.

Juan was surprised that no one had turned around and noticed him standing there, windswept and filthy, in a great big sheepskin coat. But of course they didn't, he realised, nobody ever noticed him. But for Cairney, Creeses and the few others like them, he was all but invisible through the school, able to walk around without so much as a blink of recognition.

With that, he took a deep breath and began walking through the hall, past tables of boys and girls eating toast and quietly playing at cards and dice. They were all so involved in what they were doing that nobody even lifted a head in his direction. At one point he could have sworn Doona Kelly was about to turn his way, but had so vacant an expression it was as though she was looking straight into space. Why are the pretty girls always so nasty? He briefly quizzed himself.

He let out a deep breath when he reached the far doors and, kneeling behind one of them, looked back into the hall through a pane of glass. His eyes went wide as he saw Mortis enter the hall through the door he had just come from. Juan began hastily looking around trying to find any sign of Bea. Then, looking up he saw his faint outline in the buttresses and beams of the ceiling. His eyes were wide and Juan saw him give a mischievous wink as he effortlessly and silently swung down. But Mortis stopped and was looking at where Bea had just landed. Could he have seen him? No, he was staring at the stained glass window and hadn't noticed the outline of Bea, who was thankfully standing as still as a statue with closed eyes. If Juan hadn't been looking for him he was sure he wouldn't have noticed him either.

As Mortis turned and seemed to be about to berate the group of girls playing cards, Bea sped to the end of the hall where Juan was, now looking exhausted and panting.

'Up the next flight of stairs, down the corridor on your left and it's the first door on your right. The map is on the wall in a locked glass case. You can't miss it. I'll follow *you* this time,' said Juan.

Bea bounced up the stairs out of sight, pursued by Juan, his coat dragging behind him on the dusty stairs. A memory flashed in and out of his mind's eye of running up the same stairs only the day before.

He reached the top and saw his mud stained reflection in the glass cabinet, containing all those trophies he had never won. And next to his face in the glass he saw Mortis bounding up the stairs next to him. What could he do? Mortis would certainly see him if he darted to the classroom. He would never make it. In a pathetic and hopeless reflex he fell to the floor and rolled up into a ball, clenching his whole body up hard, and tried to remain as still as possible.

He heard Mortis' heavy breathing above him and closed his eyes shut, pitifully hoping it would make him less visible. After a life of never really being noticed, he was now praying not to be. He didn't even flinch when he received a painful kick in the side.

But then he heard Mortis and the unmistakably shrill voice of Miss Owen chatting only a few feet off. He braved a quick look from underneath his coat. They seemed quite glazed in their own world and Juan, ever so cautiously, lifted himself up off the floor and tiptoed past them into the classroom.

He squeezed through the door, not wanting to swing it open too fast for fear of it squeaking, and walked into the middle of a very hushed but very frenetic argument.

The dull light of the clouded moon sneaked in through the windows and gave the whole room a macabre white light. Bea was standing at the far end holding the piece of bark with the map on in one hand and pointing threateningly at what looked to be a glowing purple flower hanging in the air with the other hand.

'Sophia, this doesn't concern you,' he rasped through gritted teeth. '*Mooinjer-veggey* should never pry into our matters.'

'Don't call me that Bea, you obstinate fur ball, this concerns all of us,' said the flower. Juan's jaw dropped as he noticed a pair of purple petals, fluttering madly like wings. He stumbled backwards when the flower turned around and he could clearly see that it had a face and a body. It was a girl, all in purple, her body tightly wrapped in purple cloth and her purple hair elaborately braided and tied behind her tiny head. She looked Juan straight in the eye, put her hands on her hips and gave an obvious huff.

'So this is him, is it, the *key-per*? Can't say he's much to look at. Thought Manannin might have sent someone with a bit more grit.' She sounded most impatient.

Why he was so surprised by the sight of her he didn't know, especially after all that had been revealed to him in the last day. But to see what could only be a Fairy, a real Fairy, just seemed so very, well, stupid.

'You're a f… a f… a Fairy.'

'I prefer Sophia. But yes I am a Fairy, a *themself*, a *mooinjer-veggey*, whatever you want to call me,' she said sourly. 'Now Bea, seeing that you can't decide what to do, maybe we should let the great *key-per* himself decide for us.'

Juan shook himself out of his stupor and reluctantly cut in before Bea could object.

'Let's just get out of here first, Mr. Mortis is right outside,' he whispered, madly pointing at the door.

Bea didn't even need another second to think it through, but grabbed Juan again and ran to the window. He put one hand over his mouth and jumped straight out into the air. Juan's scream was muffled and they softly landed on the bed of earth directly beneath the window several storeys up. Juan looked up and saw a purple glow flash through the window just as the light of the classroom came on.

Mortis had walked through the open door and flicked the light on. He then stumbled, let out a shriek, and fell backwards into Olivia, who dropped her books again and began cursing under her breath as she bent down to pick them up once more.

'It's gone!' he yelled, 'the map is gone!' And indeed all that was left of the map was a faded outline inside the frame, which was still intact and locked. 'No, it can't be gone, it can't be!'

Mortis' heart was racing and he tore over to his desk and began to scatter his books everywhere. Olivia looked over at him, her mouth open in horror at seeing this transformation from an awkward, bumbling, over-grown boy to the desperate, wild man she saw before her.

Mortis was throwing books in all directions, and letting desks and chairs fall and crash on the floor in the mad hope that the map might be lying there. It was useless he knew, but he had to do something. Many of the objects on the shelves were falling and breaking; glass jars shattered and old rusted blades snapped. He stopped and felt the freezing draft wafting in from the window chill the tears of panic streaming down his face.

'Oh God no, not the window.' He rushed over to the window and put his head through the frame. The night had become overcast and the silvery moon was now a shrouded grey smudge behind the clouds. So nearly out of view, leading down to the beach, something moved and caught his eye. It was the back of an old filthy woollen rug falling from his view towards the sea.

Everything went bleary with rage as he began to pull hard on his hair with clenched fists and Olivia ran from him in fear and shock as his scream echoed out from the upturned classroom.

EIGHT

'Why are you meddling here Sophia? *Themselves* have always kept to, well, themselves. You have your habits and that's that, you've never so much as glanced at what's happening around you.'

'Well, my hairy friend, the thing about habits is that they often change. You know me,' she replied acidly, brushing the purple strands of hair off her forehead.

'Not *mooinjer-veggey*, unless something has happened to you,' Bea pointed an accusatory finger at her, 'has something happened to you?'

She was biting her lip and gave an unconvincing shrug of denial, 'Maybe.'

'Sophia?' Bea asked slyly. 'Have you angered the elders again? Spreading rumours of floods or droughts or some such?'

She was holding her mouth shut as if the truth might pop out of her at any moment. Bea snatched into the air and grabbed one of her glowing wings between his thumb and forefinger and pulled her closer to his face.

'Come on Sophia, tell me what you've gone and done, but please for once do try and think before you speak.'

'I only spoke truths!' she called out like a martyr. 'And do you want to know the thanks I get for warning them about all this nonsense, I get cast out, grabbed by my wings and kicked in the rear. You are now looking at an exiled Fairy.'

Bea let go of her wing, and blinked, blankly. He had no retort to this. For a Fairy to be exiled was their most serious punishment. They knew that once they were banished from their folk, they would have little chance of survival in the world elsewhere. It was thought to be worse than death. They would often plead for death instead of being cut off from their kind, having everyone turn their back on them. They had nowhere else to go and no one else to turn to.

Sophia, ashamed, turned around and flew ahead, continuing along the boundaries of the forest at Cringle, flitting between the trees like a wisp of purple light. Bea followed her glow, and Juan struggled to keep up behind. He had asked to walk on his own a little way and give Bea a rest from his weight, but was now regretting it somewhat.

'The elders thought my "meddling" was unsettling.' Sophia spat, bitterly, a short way in front of them, her voice cracking in the still night air. 'I spoke honestly and told them what I'd overheard about this Reclamation, but as usual they refused to see past the ends of their big noses! And do you want to know another thing, I'm glad of it. It was inevitable after all, they all said it was, looking down their noses and saying "Sophia, *myr shegin dy ve, bee eh*, what must be, will be." I'm glad of it I tell you, I'm glad to see the back of them.'

'You can't blame them for not believing you Sophia,' said Bea, his feet gently crunching the dry pine needles on the forest bed. He turned around and gave Juan a small wink, as if to apologise for Sophia's fiery temper. Juan forced a brief smile through his growing fatigue.

'You've been on their wings ever since you escaped from the Bridge Fairies; warning them that man was going to spray every flower with poison thinking they were weeds. Or remember when you convinced the lot of them that there would be snow storms in the middle of summer and they began fighting with the sheep for extra wool supplies?'

Though reluctant, Sophia couldn't help smiling to herself at the memory of that prank.

'You surely can't be surprised that they don't trust you this time either. Have you never heard the story of the boy who cried wolf?'

'No,' she replied impulsively.

'Well, it's about you! If you tell too many lies, nobody is likely to believe you again. I can't understand you. You get thrown out from under the Bridge, and now the Forest as well.'

'But it's not a lie this time Bea, you know how much

Bugganes hate us and the flowers we grow with, they find beauty in weeds and dead earth. Once they have dealt with all of the man-folk on the island they will set to uprooting us next, I know it. I must ask the stones what to do; it's the only hope we have.'

'Excuse me?' Juan said, lifting his arm as though to ask a question in class. 'Would it be fine if we stopped for a bit, and we could continue to talk then?'

'Of course Juan, we'll go further into the forest and you can rest there,' replied Bea. Sophia hovered in front of him, her wings a blur of colour, staring down at him, scowling.

'If you two go on ahead, I'll catch you up,' he said quickly.

'Alright,' said Bea and Juan smiled his thanks, although he could see Sophia mumbling something under her breath behind Bea's back. 'We'll be through there then, waiting.' He pointed down towards a small clearing through the dense trees with a stump at its centre, and patting Juan on the back, left him where he was.

Once they were out of sight and Juan could no longer see the fluttering glow of Sophia, he took a look around.

The forest shimmered in the dark. It was only a few hours before dawn and the trees seemed to be waiting restlessly before the onset of another day. The gentle rustle of the branches in the cold air sounded like secret whispers of long forgotten tales. Juan liked this secret time. If he couldn't sleep, or woke up especially early, he would reach down onto the floor of his bedroom and retrieve any book not propping up a bit of furniture and read it in the low light of his bedside lamp. He tried not to dwell on this too much; it wasn't so bad outside at this time after all and his sheepskins were a comforting protection against the night air. He listened again to the whispers of the pines, only to jump when he heard definite voices whisper back at him.

'…and since both the Bridge Fairies and the Forest Fairies have thrown you out, you have nowhere left to go, right? You're finally on your own, just like you always wanted. But don't think that I'm going to let you go and ask the stones on your own, we will both go. Not that either of us knows what to do as I don't think anyone has posed a single question to the stones in a considerably long time.'

Juan peered around the large trunk of a tree and looked down to the clearing. It was Bea, sitting cross-legged, holding his hands out together in front of him, and Sophia sitting in his palms, also cross-legged.

'Then we must hope that they are feeling chatty, mustn't we?' said Sophia. Bea grunted a reply.

'And the boy, what's his story.'

Juan, used to eavesdropping, leant closer and cupped his hand over his ear to hear as much as was possible.

'Ever since I was of an age of awareness I have watched man-folk,' Bea began, 'watching them from the dark corners of the island, and never in so many moons have I seen such a boy.'

Juan swallowed hard at hearing his words.

'He accepted my very existence with the heart of one far beyond his years. Who else could have done so, but the *key-per*? You shouldn't give him such looks. He's also an outcast from his people and his family, just like you Sophia, yet still he loves them and I believe would go a long way to try and save them. And he's curious too, with a question always hanging on his lips.' Bea paused and looked into the distance as though gazing at somewhere far off. 'He reminds me so much of…'

'Céa?' said Sophia, and Bea slowly nodded in agreement. 'I'm so sorry Bea. You know I am. I was more fond of Céa than you can imagine, but this boy isn't your brother.' She looked down at the scars lining his palms and sighed. 'Your scars run deep Bea, but they will heel if you let them. In the meantime we could do with finding out what message this boy bears from Manannin, and take heed of it.'

A small twig broke under Juan's foot and the snap alerted Bea and Sophia, who both spun around, ready to either attack or flee. Juan casually walked down, pretending he hadn't heard a word of what they had uttered, and they both relaxed once more.

Juan joined them and sat on the opposite side of the felled tree stump in the silence, unsure of what to say. He curiously looked over to Sophia, and she in turn glared back at him. Bea thought they were sizing each other up for some sort of argument.

'So,' Juan broke the quiet. 'Fairies as well, I guess there's not much else for me to see now, is there.'

'I wouldn't count on it Juan,' said Bea, with a wry grin.

'Let me see,' Juan squinted, staring at Sophia. 'The books had it most definitely wrong with you. You look like you're descended from some sort of flower, heather by the looks of things. Which probably means there are Fairies of all the flowers on the island, right?'

'Not bad!' she exclaimed, looking back at Bea, 'but just a few corrections. We are not descended from flowers, we have grown alongside them, with them. Only in the wilder places mind you. You won't find us in any old garden or hanging basket. In turn for their keep and protection, they offer us our food and…'

'Your wings!' said Juan, and Sophia couldn't help but open them up in display. Bea smiled at her showing off, and leant back on his elbows in the rough earth. It calmed him to sit and talk, as old friends would, and laugh at one of Sophia's ancient stories.

'To cut a very long and very boring story short,' she started in earnest, 'during the old wars, Fairies separated into two bands, the Bridge Fairies and the Forest Fairies, or as I like to call the selfish toads, *themselves*. They decided to settle their arguments by avoiding each other, and everyone else for that matter, altogether. But since I've now been booted out of both of them, it looks like you two are stuck with me.'

The thick smell of dried pine filled the air in the clearing, and Bea and Juan watched Sophia spin and dance through the trees like some wild butterfly. Juan tried to study her flickering form further. It was curious, he thought, she wore clothes of the finest linen, wrapped tightly around her, which wouldn't have looked wholly out of place on the main streets of the island. She had sun-blanched skin, which gave off light from every pore like a torch, and though she wore no jewellery, the nails of her fingers and toes were painted her uniform purple. She was slight of figure, but curvaceous, with pretty round features and thick pouting lips, and her hair was so complicatedly tied with bits sticking up in all directions that Juan thought she may well have been a follower of the latest fashions. But there was something else about her that struck him as somehow familiar, as though he had met her or at least seen her before, which of course couldn't be possible, but the feeling didn't leave him. It was something in her eyes. He thought hard about it, but couldn't remember and soon gave up trying.

He glanced over at Bea, who was still leaning back on his elbows in the dry brittle earth, and although smiling, looked drowsy and tired. It was an uncomfortable sight seeing Bea weary with fatigue.

'Maybe we should try and find something to eat?' he suggested. 'I could certainly do with a little something.'

'He's got a point,' said Sophia in mid-spin, hovering upside down. 'I for one am starving, why don't I head into the forest and see if I can find us any pine juice, and I could collect some sweet barks. That ought to do the trick.'

Bea sat up in protest. 'I am not having any of your forest foods. We all need to be able to think straight and be in our right minds, Fairy foods will only numb our spirits.'

'What do you mean? I would never try and make something that would have such an effect! You know that's one of the reasons I left the Bridge in the first place – all the nectar! And besides, at least I *can* cook!' shouted Sophia, flying right in front of Bea's face.

'You call that cooking! It's more like gardening. I saw a house about half a mile back along the path, I'll go and see what I can find.'

'You mean STEAL!'

Juan thought they might start striking each other at any moment, they were like two temperamental siblings; laughing and joking one minute and jumping down each others throats the next. He pushed his way between them and held up his hands.

'I'll go, I'll go!' he belted over the din. Two sets of angry eyes fell down to him standing between them. 'Bea, you can't go into that house, there was a fire lit downstairs, I saw it, which means there is probably someone up and about already and you would definitely be seen. So I'll go instead.'

'But how will you be able to get anything?' Bea asked, still hot from the argument.

'Manners Bea, just old fashioned manners.' And with that he began walking off to rejoin the path and left Bea and Sophia staring after him, silent and dumbfounded.

They sat there quietly for a few moments, huffing until their tempers settled. A light breeze had picked up and was dancing through the trees of the forest, stroking and rustling all of the branches it passed. The moon had sunk lower, its glowing white rays now shining out from the breaks in the ghostly clouds, and the long shadows seemed to be walking between the trees like many children playing some schoolyard game.

Bea watched the movement of the forest. It reminded him of the slow, heavy breathing of his father asleep on the cave floor under a pile of woollen rugs. He remembered how warm it was there as his fur stood firm against his skin, trapping any warmth and keeping it close. Sophia, though wearing relatively little, didn't even shiver; Fairies didn't feel the cold so much.

'Is it still summer?' Bea asked, his breath steaming in the cold air. 'Under the Bridge I mean.'

'It's always summer under the Fairy Bridge,' answered Sophia wistfully.

'I'd like to see it sometime...'

'No you wouldn't.' Sophia cut in sharply, rising in the air from the tree stump. 'The eternal summer blinds them. The whole lot of them bask in the sunshine all day and sip on cocktails of pansies and clover. They numb themselves into idleness, and waste away the time admiring their own reflections in the babbling brooks and streams. You're worth more than that Bea, you and I both.' Though angry, Sophia sounded hurt and sad uttering such truths. The Bridge Fairies had mostly been lost to the island in their drugged lethargy, choosing to ignore any life outside their own. Those who had escaped the tempting clutches of their ethereal existence, like Sophia, were treated with great scorn and defiance.

'Tell me again how your eyes were opened and you saw the wrongs of the Fairies.'

'Bea! I've told you nearly every time the moon has risen.' she protested.

'You know you enjoy telling it as much as I do listening to it,' he pleaded, sitting up like an eager, insistent child. Sophia sighed through her smile and gave a small elegant nod of feigned reluctance and cleared her throat.

'It was the briefest of moments that changed me. I was resting in the pastures of moss above the chasms, you know the place, where the wind is strong but the sea is calm. And out on the ocean I saw a prism of colours, under the sea. I blinked, not trusting my own eyes, but before I could look again I was hit by the sound, the music.'

'*Sheen-ny-Feaynid*?' asked Bea, his eyes wide with wonder and excitement.

'Yes, the Sounds of Infinity,' Sophia nodded, 'the music of the sea. It seemed to sing in the winds and make my blood dance, telling me to open my eyes and see the true beauty of the world.'

'What else, what else did it say?'

'I think it told me that we are all a little something of everything, or at least that's what it sounded like, it was hard to tell. It was as though it said that we are no more important than the rock we stand on, the air we breathe, the water we drink and the wool that clothes us. No better and no worse.'

'Do you believe it was a message from her, from Téeval?'

'I didn't see her, but now I believe the Princess of the Ocean watches us, and spoke to me.'

Bea broke into applause, beaming, and Sophia flipped through the air and gave a deep bow of thanks. Bea gave a long sigh and fell back onto his elbows once more.

'Oh, how I long to look upon Téeval, her words would surely be of help to us.'

'Maybe they would, but I don't think they would save all the Fairies or the boy's folk for that matter,' she shrugged, settling down on the ground.

'Who's words?' they span around again in shock, only to be faced with Juan plodding down towards them from the path once more. He was smiling and carrying an armful of food, clutched close to his chest.

'Oh…no one,' Bea answered hastily, and chuckled at the sight of Juan's successful hunt. 'What feast have you brought us?'

'Well,' said Juan. 'Mr. Seer, that's the man at the house, anyway, he certainly seemed surprised to meet anyone at this hour, he said he thought he was the only person ever up at this time. I told him I was camping in the forest with a few friends overnight, only my mum forgot to pack us any breakfast and I was only wondering if he might be able to help us out. Very nice man he was, very old and blind. He was wearing these funny old glasses with black glass in them, and behind them his eyes were all scarred, but he walked around his house as if he could see everything as clear as day. He was only too glad to be of help, so he ran off to the kitchen and I waited in the porch, and then…' he sucked in a big breath and continued, 'after about a minute or so, he came back and gave me all this, I've got bread, jam, cheese, milk and some fruit too.' And he opened his arms and let it all fall onto the forest floor. Sophia's mouth fell open.

'And you got all this with good manners?' Juan proudly nodded his head. 'I've got to get myself some of those things, they sound handy.'

They used the felled tree stump as a table, sat round it and ate in silence. Juan looked up once or twice and smiled at the sight of Bea and Sophia scoffing down everything with great relish. Sophia caught crumbs off the bread Bea was eating, dipped them into the jam and shoved them into her small mouth, sighing with pleasure.

The meal was keeping their spirits floating above the ground, instead of settling and turning to thoughts of their families, their loved ones and the impending trouble that was likely to ensue. The pain was still with them, like a pebble in a shoe, but they all knew that, for the moment, to dwell on it would do them, and the problem, no good.

It didn't take them long to finish all the food and before they knew it they had washed down all the fresh cold milk and were patting their full stomachs with satisfaction. Bea brushed the tree stump clean, and gently placed on it the bark of Manannin's Map. They all moved closer and looked down to it.

Juan, so familiar with the map, put a finger on it and drew it over the various coloured circles. The surface felt coarse and fragile, as though it could be reduced to dust if only blown on, and the colours were faded and barely recognisable.

'It's so simple,' said Bea with relief, 'look, next to this green colour here it says *ansoor*, which means answer.'

'Which means the circle we need to go to is here, at Braaid!' said Sophia, landing in the centre of the circle that matched the green colour on the key.

'You mean you can read those symbols?' asked Juan, excitedly.

'It's only the old Manx tongue. Few of your people speak it anymore, but we hear it often. It is Manannin's language, and to speak it is to honour him,' replied Sophia.

'Yes, but my markings are sort of like that, so why can't you read them?' Juan sounded both hopeful and frustrated.

'It's a form I don't recognise Juan,' said Bea, 'it's all back to front and muddled up or something. I've tried to make sense of it, but it's somehow incomplete.'

Juan sighed. He felt he was never going to find out what they meant. Maybe they didn't mean anything. Maybe he wasn't the *key-per* at all. He had always thought he had a talent to answer any puzzle that was put in front of him. He had always been able to do so in the past, but now he had never felt more hopeless and ignorant.

'So where is this message anyway?' asked Sophia. 'Did Manannin leave it lying around somewhere for you to find?'

Juan didn't feel like talking, and again lifted up his jumper to show the markings all over his skin.

'Wow!' exclaimed Sophia. 'That's some way of delivering a message.' But as she was flying over to Juan she froze in mid air and hovered as stiff as a board in front of him. Juan could see the blood rushing from her cheeks.

'What's wrong?'

'*Jee saue mee voish cloon ny moyrn.*' Sophia whispered. Bea also froze. He seemed not to even dare look around him.

'What is it…?' Juan was now scared and followed suite, not moving a muscle. Bea whispered through clenched teeth,

'Juan, we are being watched by some particularly nasty Forest Fairies. They must have been checking every forest in the hope of finding Sophia. When I say so, we need to get to the edge of the forest as quickly as we can.'

'I'm so sorry you two. It's me they're angry with. I never thought they'd be near here. Maybe I should just stay and pay the consequences.' Sophia's eyes were watering with fear.

'They'll tear you apart. In any case, you'll be able to help us.' She looked greatly relieved by this.

'Ready?'

Juan was suddenly aware of his sweating palms and his pulse quickening inside his head. He'd never even considered that some Fairies might be aggressors.

'Now!'

Bea grabbed the map in one hand and Juan's wrist in the other and began to bolt up the clearing. Juan saw that Sophia's purple glow was already ahead of them as he heard a loud percussive buzzing coming from all around him. Trying to keep up with Bea, he tripped up over his small legs, which had no hope of carrying him at such speed, and fell flat on his face in between two enormous pines. As soon as Bea's grasp abandoned him, he felt himself being picked up again. But he was being grabbed from every part of his body and was suddenly dangling several feet in the air.

'SOPHIA!' came a surprisingly loud shout next to his ear. 'Come back here at once, or this boy gets it!'

Juan looked up, and at first thought the forest had come alive and taken him hostage, but then saw an entire army of Fairies dashing in front of his eyes. Males and females in equal measure were speeding past him, hundreds of them, all well disguised in the muddy greens and browns of the forest, carrying tiny bows with quivers of pine needles. He tried to shake wildly to free himself of their hold, but there was no escaping from his captors; those that were holding him were holding on hard.

'Bea!' he screamed, his voice hardly rising above the furious buzzing of the army. Ahead of him he saw a wave of dark red splash over the fur of Bea's body and, seeing the danger Juan was in, the Fynoderee began to lash out.

Bea flung his arms through the air, and caught about twenty Fairies with one swipe. They were all thrown into the nearest trees and fell to the ground like flies, unconscious. Bea, growling loudly, was picked up off the ground by several of them, but spun in the air and kicked out at the fools who dared to tackle him, knocking them in all directions. Once free, he ran towards Juan and grabbed two handfuls of the little people and threw them back into the forest like mere balls. He caught Juan as he fell towards him and began making a dash back towards the forest's edge, leaving the map trodden and broken on the ground behind him.

As he was running through the trees, branches snagging on his face and body, Juan looked behind him and saw a mist of winged Fairies speeding up close behind, drawing their bows and furiously firing pine needles in their direction. Juan felt many of them piercing his woollen jacket and stinging him. Sophia's glow was just ahead of them beyond the trees, and as they reached her Bea turned around, and looked back at the army still hurtling towards them. What was he doing? They'll get us.

'They can't get us out here,' said Bea, panting, as if he knew what Juan was thinking.

And sure enough, as the army sped closer and reached the very edge of the forest, they all came to a most sudden and dead stop as though they had hit some invisible barrier, a wall denying them exit from their constrained territory.

'SOPHIA! Get back in here!' screamed an especially fearsome looking Fairy at the front of the troop, his beard, like a collection of stiff twigs, shaking with his raging fit.

'I think not Braker,' said Sophia calmly. 'Why don't you put your wings between your legs and shuffle off back to your overgrown garden?'

Many of the Fairies flew into an uproar and began beating their fists, and firing pine needles, which ricocheted back at them off the open air. After his original fear, Juan actually found this sight quiet funny, and began chuckling out loud.

'Poor boys and girls,' sneered Sophia, 'it's all backfiring on you now isn't it?'

'What do you mean?' wheezed Braker, getting gradually redder in the face. He was looking far too much like a bruised tomato for Juan to contain himself.

'I heard that it was you who wove the webs around the trees, to stop any of us who disobeyed you leaving the boundaries, but you forgot one thing.'

She hovered right in front of Braker, with only the impenetrable wall parting them, and lowered her voice to a scarcely audible gruff whisper.

'It is my disobedience that is the very thing that frees me. As soon as I began to see your world for what it was, a sham, I was free of your shackles and trickery. If you would only cease drinking that nectar, your eyes would be opened to the truth.'

'What truth?' All the other Fairies had stopped their pointless onslaught and were now panting as one, their bows by their sides and listening. It was as though the forest itself was listening. Perhaps it was, thought Juan.

'All of you, all of this, everything, every living thing, whether you hold it dear or not, is under threat. The Bugganes are coming over ground, and at the first chance they get, they will plough you all into dust. They do not care for life, only revenge.'

'Fallacies! They are too few. They wouldn't dare reveal themselves to man-folk. It would be suicide for them all.'

'They are prepared for that, if that is the cost of their needs,' added Bea, calmly. Everyone could clearly see the stern sincerity in his green eyes.

'Lies! You are all blind,' yelled Braker.

'It's you who are blind. All of you.' Sophia gave a small smile to herself. 'Selfish crows, you live up to your name so well; you are the perfect *themselves*, never thinking about anyone or anything but yourselves. May Manannin's scowl haunt your daydreams and curse your nightmares.'

With that Sophia turned her back on her people, as she had done many times before, and headed out north, away from the forest.

Juan and Bea stood together at the boundary of the forest and watched the hundreds of Fairies disappear, like the stars at dawn, into the shelter and seclusion of the trees, before turning and heading not only to catch up with Sophia, but also, they hoped, towards some answers.

NINE

The sun was tentative to rise in the east of the island that morning. Its dull light was grey and cold and it seemed anxious and wary to announce the onset of another day, as though fearful of what it might bring. The great water wheel, Lady Isabella, stayed shrouded in the dawn's mist and all the villagers of Laxey pulled themselves tight into their beds.

Derrick Kermode was tucked up in his bed in his house in South Barrule. He was happily dreaming of vast libraries and endless rows of old and dusty books. His wife Joyce, grunting next to him, was dreaming of ice cream on Peel beach in the thick of winter with the sand blowing at her feet like a haze of gold. And Duke, wound up in his blanket in his basket downstairs, twitched and dribbled as he dreamt of the fridge in the pantry, and the handle only inches too high for him to reach and nudge open.

Mr. Boyde dreamt of skies and rolling clouds of deep blue and mauve, and hoped the morning's sky would be such a painting. He saw himself conducting the colours like an orchestra of wild weather. His son Ewan dreamt of clocks; carriage clocks and fob watches, grandfather clocks that reached the ceiling and even grander ones that towered far above him, ticking down the minutes to the early morning and making him shudder.

Mrs. Quilliam of Port Erin was dreaming of the finest high tea imaginable, cakes with marzipan and the lightest smoked salmon sandwiches, with the crusts cut off of course, all presented on polished silver platters, stacked high with a doily on every plate. She smiled broadly at the tight, hidden expressions of jealousy on all her guest's faces. Her husband, Hugh, dreamt up excuses for not being there.

Stuart Skelly dreamt of every girl that he had ever kissed before he turned twenty-one. He was at a ball, and each girl was there, swooning before him and asking him to dance and the fiddle and drum were loud in his mind. He knew how handsome

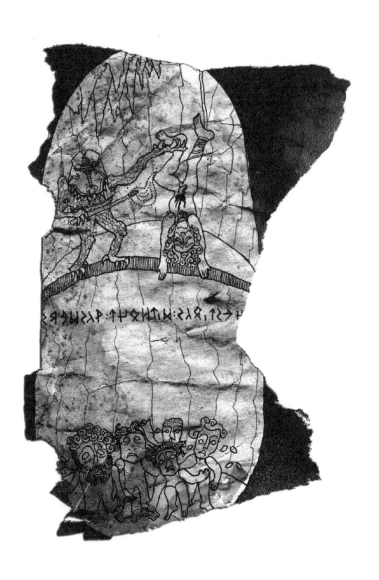

he looked and swaggered around the room like a peacock displaying his feathers. Through the misty maelstrom of the dance he could see Gene, the beauty of the village, quietly playing cards at a table with friends. She looked up, aware that someone was gazing at her, turned to Stuart and coquettishly smiled.

She however was dreaming of deserts, camels, nomadic tents of many colours and a young Stuart on horseback, like a mirage, riding towards her through the glare of the beating sun, his deep tan glistening.

Mrs. Cowley dreamt of a classroom of cupids; all angelically smiling and hovering above their desks, nodding in conscientious agreement of every word she uttered before handing in their homework, on time.

Richard Gill dreamt of being six feet tall and scoring the winning goal in the inter-school championships, and Johnny dreamt of Sarah and Sarah dreamt of Johnny, and all was quiet and warm and safe.

Outside all was cold, and bleak. Even Sophia shrank back against the icy wind whipping across the edge of the trees, and flew right behind Bea, protecting herself behind his furry bulk. The chill was also beginning to penetrate Juan's coat and he walked holding the collar tight around his neck and shoulders, his teeth chattering. Any gust of wind that got through his sheepskins sliced like a razor across his bare skin.

Juan trudged on behind Bea, his thighs burning from the uphill struggle through the hills of Sulbrick, and his knees jarring against the downhill stone paths round Chibbanagh. His muscles had been aching for what felt like hours before sunrise, but he knew the only way past the pain was to walk through it to the other side. Fortunately his feet didn't hurt, they had been numb for hours and were now mechanically taking each step, one in front of the other. Juan feared that when the time came, his feet might not want to stop and he would have to walk around in a circle until they realised they didn't have to go on.

Bea had thought it wisest to head into the forest of Chibbanagh from the south-west, avoiding the main towns nearer the east of the coast, and but for the occasional hum of a motorcar on some nearby road they were well hidden in the nature of the island. Bea seemed to know exactly which path to take to avoid being near any farm, or cottage, or road, and was able to casually walk at the head of the group, undisguised and undetected.

Over time, Juan grew suspicious of Bea's silence. He hadn't spoken much since he had saved him from the Forest Fairies of Cringle, but walked on at a steady pace in front of him and only occasionally turned around and nodded to check if he was managing. Juan felt guilty that he had had to call for his help when the Fairies had attacked him and worried that Bea thought him a burden, just extra weight holding him back. As he scuffed his feet through the stony path, kicking small chips of ice that had collected in the crags of water, he made a pact with himself. He would deal with everything that he was going to face as best he could, not relying on Bea alone but on some strength, which he was certain he had somewhere.

It was quite exposed where they walked and the great hills to the north-east glared down at them, their barely white peaks masked in the overcast morning sky. The long grass lay beaten flat from the wind, as if cowering at the raised hand of the blowing gales and frost had settled in on the higher paths around them. The patchwork landscape of fields and dales was now littered with sheet white blankets of ice.

Juan stepped over a clump of dead branches, like a worn skeleton at his feet, and cautiously walked down to the turnstile at the bottom, wary so not to slip on the thin black ice on the path.

Bea climbed over the stile and called out behind him, without turning around.

'The winds are blowing in fear of what is to come; their howling is a call for help. We can't have much time left, we must hurry now.'

Juan blew air out of his nose and looked down to the tracks at his feet. He could easily make out dog tracks and shoe prints in the hard mud, and before the stile was a large imprint of Bea's foot. It was a deep print and he could clearly see his toes and the heel even more impacted within the path. Juan stepped into it and wondered at how dwarfed his own foot was within its shape. He sighed at the sight and suddenly felt so small the world could swallow him up.

Barely a few inches beneath the mud, hard from the cold, was a brief layer of shale and beneath that, solid rock, descending for many miles. The hard rock sediment was the flesh and bone of the earth, its crust, which would, in many other parts of the island, continue straight down nearly twenty miles towards the boiling molten metal mantle of the earth. But exactly where Juan stood, only a few miles down, it opened out into a broken chamber of fire and ore, and confused screams of pain filling the whole space and falling on deaf ears.

Gavan Clague had only been able to hear the sound of blood pounding through his head for what felt like a long time. But what did he know? His concept of time had rapidly disintegrated since his interrogation began. He couldn't hear his own screams any more, he wasn't even aware he was screaming. His ankles were chaffing from the rope tied around them and he went to bend down and rub the sores, having forgotten that he was hanging from them upside down and let himself fall limp once more.

Every time the hot irons, red like the eyes of the beasts, branded his already blistered skin, memories hit his mind's eye; memories of the creatures smashing into his house, many of them breaking through and splintering the doors; the confused panic and bleats of his three children as they were taken, the endless tunnels they were dragged down and the stinking pit they had been in for days. He felt like he was spinning in and out of consciousness. The questions that they had been screaming at him for what felt like an eternity made no sense in his mashed mind. Something about wanting to know where a man is weakest and where they would most freely bleed. He thought at first they were merely tormenting him, but something deeper in his mind told him they needed this knowledge for some darker purpose. He remembered feeling a great desire to tell them anything, but held back, he wished now that he hadn't, he wished he could speak and give them everything they desired, if they would only stop burning him. He coughed and spat out more blood onto the congealed red puddle on the stone floor.

Gavan could see two of the creatures in front of his eyes, upside down to his perspective. They appeared to be shouting at him and threateningly pointing at their blazing pikes, but he couldn't properly tell any longer. Their jaws were opening and closing and they bared their rotting spiked teeth but he couldn't hear a word they were saying. He had become deaf with pain, and could feel himself drowning in it like plunging into a swamp. When they came closer and placed the steaming metal on his skin once more, he still couldn't hear them, but could see in their eyes that they were smiling and taking pleasure in his pain.

The skin on his stomach had become so blistered it cracked and blood streamed down his chest. His body lurched out in reflex; he tried to reach round and grab the wound, but his hands were so tightly bound behind his back that he heard a loud crack and pop as his shoulder came out of its socket and the bone snapped under the pressure. His eyes rolled into the back of his head and he began to froth at the mouth as he tried to hold back another scream, knowing that it would only give them more rapture. He had nearly bitten through his own tongue before the sound burst forth, pleading for the injustice of it all, begging for his meagre life, begging for the lives of his children, begging for the pain to stop.

He tried to stay focused, but the colours and shapes were distant and messy, as though gauze had been wrapped around his eyes. He could make out that the two creatures had sharply retreated from him as another one he hadn't seen before came closer. This one was more thick set, and had some sort of dark bone helmet covering his head and one half of his face, making him look even more like a living corpse than the other two. From this and the complex plated armour he had welded onto his form, Gavan could only assume that this was someone of high standing amongst them all, someone who had requested this action to be taken against him. The creature moved forward until they were face to face, and as Gavan faded out of consciousness he felt himself drift into the fires that were burning brightly in the beast's eyes.

Brother Ordo saw the man splutter as he faded into another realm and turned towards the Brother and Sister who had been conducting the questioning.

'Sister Anik, report the results of the questioning. I sincerely hope, for your sakes, they have been more fruitful than the last session.'

Sister Anik, a stooped, hunchbacked Buggane with a spine protruding from her back like some other creature trying to get out, lifted her face and glowered at him. She was not known for her tolerance, given the task because of her talent to keep victims on the brink of sanity, and was usually appointed by Mother to deal with the misfits within the family. She flung her hissing pike down onto the stone floor.

'Brother Ordo, with the greatest of respect, all we have found out is the surprising resilience that these men have to our methods. This one here has coped with more pain than any Brother or Sister I have ever worked on.'

'He looks suitably worn down to me,' said Brother Ordo, glancing over the welts and cuts across Gavan's bruised skin.

'No Brother, I don't mean the resilience of his body, but that of his mind. Why, Brother Hemi and I have created such wounds and sores on him that they demand pride and remembrance, and still he has told us nothing of any worth whatsoever.'

The mute Brother Hemi by her side vigorously shook his head in agreement. He was taller than both Brother Ordo and Sister Anik and his bulbous, shell like belly hung low around his body. He had no lower jaw and the teeth that remained jutted out from his face and dripped with saliva. Brother Ordo had never liked to look on Brother Hemi and avoided his gaze whenever he could.

'As their bodies grow weaker, their minds lock themselves shut like some impenetrable chest. The harder we try to pry the lock open the further they retreat.'

Brother Ordo grabbed onto one of the many chains hanging from the top of the chamber to take his weight and sighed heavily in frustration. The chains swayed and hit each other, jangling and echoing throughout the cave, each shining in the glow of the torches burning from the walls. He had so little time to get any results, and Mother would not be pleased with the lack of answers they had so far.

'You are sure you have asked all the questions? Did he tell you nothing of the workings of their bodies, how quick they are on foot, where they are most vulnerable? This one should know these things.' His teeth were clenched in impatience.

'Just look for yourself Brother, look how quickly he has stopped bleeding and his body begins to heal, it weeps only briefly before tending to itself. Its strength is not in attack but in defence.' Brother Ordo looked closer at Gavan's skin and how the blood had already congealed to form black scabs over the wounds and blisters.

'In short Brother, he told us nothing that you required. And I should hate to be the one to tell that to Mother.'

'Thank you Sister Anik, I will have you know that Mother thinks very highly of me. She understands my importance to the family, and besides, I can handle her.' He swallowed back his own fear for he knew this indeed would not please her. 'It was just like this with the other man,' he continued, 'exactly the same thing, not one word from either of them that will help us. I guarantee that if we were to subject all of them to this we would still be standing right here where we started, only with more blood staining the floor. If you want my opinion this whole scheme of Mother's is flawed.'

Brother Hemi and Sister Anik stared straight down at the floor; his words shocked and frightened them both. They had never heard someone speak out against Mother's choices. It had never even entered into their minds that it was possible to do such a thing. They gave nothing but thanks for the life that she gave them and the gentle embrace she held them in.

'She should show trust in me. After all, it is I who knows more about the over ground than any other member of the family. If you really want to know what I think about the whole thing…what?' Brother Hemi and Sister Anik were now staring wide-eyed straight at him as though they had some dark news to speak of but had both sworn to absolute secrecy.

'What? What is it? Surely you are not shaken by my words.' Their eyes grew wider and more insistent. 'I would not believe you if you told me you thought this a good idea.' He then heard the lightest slap of the flesh of a foot against the stone floor and knew that Mother was standing directly behind him. He didn't know how he knew, it was something to do with the feeling in chest, like being out of breath, or unable to swallow. He didn't know how long she had been standing there and how much she overheard and so slowly turned around to face her with his most innocent smile spread across the unmasked half of his face. As she thrust out and snatched his throat and he felt her claws pierce the unprotected flesh of his neck he saw how beautiful she was in her anger. He was always surprised by her beauty, which shone out like burning pitch. He suddenly felt not fear, but regret. What kind of a son was he to speak out against his Mother?

He didn't struggle as she reached for one of the hanging chains, whipped it round his neck like a noose and hoisted him up off the floor until he was dangling helplessly. He knew that to struggle would displease her more. Instead, he let her take complete control and became passive and limp, as was his duty as a son.

Mother stood away from him and let him swing back and forth for a few moments, listening to the melody of the chains, quite calm, and as he came to a stop, only then did she begin to speak.

'You, Brother Ordo, believe that our reclamation is a bad idea. You believe that I am deluded and that even if we were to get over ground then man-folk overseas would surely spy us, no matter what. You believe that it is nothing more than suicide to satisfy a long held vendetta against people who have usurped our island. Am I wrong?'

Brother Ordo couldn't speak, but knew that Mother didn't expect her questions answered. She began to slowly walk towards him, the closer she got the more hushed her voice became.

'It may be true that these man-folk have given us less fact than we had anticipated, but what does it matter? What does it matter if those across the sea see us? What does it matter if every one of us should perish in the battle, so long as we have reclaimed what is ours?' Brother Ordo's eyes widened as he saw the pure madness in Mothers words. 'This island is mine, and I will go to every length to ensure its return. If that means there are casualties along the way then that is a small price. Ownership is one of the few things worth dying for, don't you agree my son?'

She then did something he wasn't expecting. She moved even closer to him, circled her hands around his masked face and kissed him. He held himself stiff as she lingered on his mouth, and their sharp teeth collided. As vulnerable as he was, hanging there by his tense neck, he couldn't help but take pleasure in her affections and felt himself return the kiss as strongly as it was given. As they parted, she gently cupped his face.

'You would die for me, wouldn't you my child?' Her words were tender, warm and full of promise. Though nearly paralysed, he managed to nod his head a fraction within the slack of the noose. Mother swiped a nail through the chain, and with a spark Brother Ordo fell to his knees, sucking in huge breaths of stinking dull air.

'Good,' came her voice from the entrance. He looked up but she had already gone.

'You were right about one thing Brother Ordo,' said Sister Anik, stooped in the shadows of the chamber, holding back a leering smile.

'What?' he croaked.

'She does think very highly of you.' Brother Hemi couldn't laugh, but his shoulders were shaking up and down to compensate for his hysteria.

Brother Ordo, in his embarrassment, didn't reply to Sister Anik but pulled himself off the floor and ran out of the chamber into the tunnel to catch up with Mother.

They walked side by side in silence, back and forth down many tunnels. Brother Ordo dared not speak until Mother had broken the quiet and obediently kept his mouth shut until she stopped not far from the pit where the man-folk were being held and turned to face him.

Within the gloom of the pit, Eamon Kerruish had managed to climb several feet up the vertical wall and was clinging on with all of his strength. His toe holes were wide apart and his legs were splayed as far as they would go. Jamming his pocket knife into a crag in the wall, he held on with both hands, trying desperately to balance his weight so as not to break the blade. Though he knew there was little hope of reaching the top of the pit, and even if he could he had no idea what he would do, from this slight vantage point he could clearly make out voices coming from the tunnels above. His palms were sweating and greasy, and his knuckles and finger tips were torn and bleeding from the climb, but still he gripped tightly onto the small handle of the knife. He held himself close to the rock face and listened to the voices coming from the spark of light above them. For what felt like far too long, he had heard nothing but strange talk of shifting younglings, and several prayers to some mother or other, but nothing that had made any clear sense.

Just as his hands began to shake under the pressure and he thought about giving up and trying to climb down without falling, he heard a deeper more authoritative voice come closer to the entrance of the pit. All the background muttering had ceased, so Eamon knew that this voice must hold some charge over the others.

'…but you know, Mother, that we are getting no co-operation from these man-folk, even if we ply all of them for everything they know, they will tell us nothing of any use.'

'Then they will be the first to be sacrificed and our reclamation will have begun,' said a second voice, feminine but with a deep resonant rumble of masculine ruthlessness underneath it. Eamon held himself tense and still as the voices paused. He looked down and saw Grayse's worried face beneath him. His eyes had grown quickly adept to the dark, as had everyone's, and his world was now one of greys and colourless outlines. Grayse was holding Aalin close to her chest and stroking her hair. She seemed to know that something was wrong. She could see it in Eamon's eyes. He could never hide anything from her.

'But we must find that painted boy, the one the Watcher called Kerruish, I believe there are few ways our plans can be thwarted but I guarantee Manannin has scribbled one of them all over that boy.'

'We could…ask the boy's mother and father?'

Eamon knew by the word 'ask' that the voice meant much more than that, and remembered what state Markys Dawson came back in after his questioning. He shuddered at the thought, but couldn't grasp what they meant about Juan and why he was so important. They spoke about Manannin and plans being thwarted and it threw him into even more of a jumble than before.

'Perhaps,' said the female voice, 'but I think we know they would never answer our questions. We will ask the Watcher when he returns with the map. If he takes much longer we should send out a small pack of guards to usher him along, four ought to do it.'

'Yes Mother, and thank you for clearing my vision to the path ahead.'

'Most actions my child, after enough time, evaporate into nothing. But we will transcend the barriers of history, and even legend. Our actions shall outlive our memory. Now hurry, I expect everything to be ready by the next moonrise.'

Eamon hadn't taken a breath since the female voice had begun speaking and exhaled as both voices faded into the distance of the tunnels. A great cavern of terror had opened up in his mind, only to be filled with thoughts of his son, Juan, and his apparent purpose in this most horrible business. He felt queasy and dizzy as he found a finger hold just beneath the pocket knife, and began to retrace the same route down as he had taken before. The rocks that jutted out from the pit wall were so small he could barely grip his fingernails on them let alone his whole hand, so he took his time in case he should fall. Grayse ran over with Aalin to greet him as his feet touched the bottom, and they both embraced him. Eamon could plainly see the severe relief and worry etched all over Grayse's face.

'What is it? What did you hear?' she asked, taking a handkerchief from her pocket and wrapping it round one of Eamon's bloodied hands.

'Nothing, it's nothing,' he replied, unable to bring himself to tell her that an entire colony of torturous beasts were hunting down their only son, and that they may be sacrificed before the dawn of another day. He knew that she didn't believe him but couldn't yet bring himself to speak of what he had just heard.

In the far end of the pit base, opposite from where Eamon and Grayse stood, Markys Dawson was being tended to by several of the others. A busy huddle had formed around him and his quiet weary groans floated like a sad lament through the cave. Concerned, Eamon walked over to the group.

'How is he doing?' he asked.

'Much the same as before,' answered his elder daughter, Caren, mopping his wet brow with the sleeve of her torn blouse. 'If we're not careful he could fall into a fever.' Her voice was gently shaking with suppressed panic.

Eamon looked over the shoulders of the group at Markys lying on his back, a clump of jackets under his head as a pillow. He had no shirt on and his wounds covered most of his upper body. The burns weren't too deep but the skin was pink and raw and Eamon winced at the sight.

'Maybe you could use my sticky tape and some material to make some plasters for his sores?'

'All of our clothes are filthy and dust ridden.'

'They are all we've got,' said Eamon more firmly. 'You should cover them, it might lessen the chance of infection.'

'He's right Caren,' said Markys' youngest daughter, Breeda,

nearly sobbing with worry, 'we've got to do something, and Mr. Kerruish probably knows what he's on about.' She took the tape from Eamon, thanking him and began to rip off strands of her skirt to use as bandages.

In another cranny of the pit, Gavan Clague's three children sat huddled together, their arms wrapped around one another. Eamon wanted so much to walk over to them and put his arms around them and tell them that everything was going to be all right. To tell them that they didn't need to worry about their father and he was strong enough to look after himself, but he couldn't. He knew he would be lying. They all looked so helpless, like lambs lost on the cliffside, their shepherd out of sight. If only he could find words of comfort to give them. Robyn, the eldest son, a strong young man with curly mousy blonde hair, looked up and saw Eamon standing there, several paces from where they sat.

'Did you hear anything Mr. Kerruish? Anything about dad, or what's happening or why we're down here or anything? Anything at all?' His words sounded so desperate Eamon wanted to cry for him.

'No Robyn, I didn't hear a thing, I'm sorry.' He hated lying to them, but knew that the truth would do them more unwanted harm. He was just about to speak to Robyn further, offer him words of encouragement and strength, when Grayse tugged him by the arm into a darker recess, where no one would be able to hear them if they whispered. Eamon looked into her insistent hazel eyes; she pulled her auburn hair away from her face, which was still encrusted with dried mud, and stared hard back at him.

'You're lying Eamon, you've got the same expression as…I don't know, as when you've eaten some cake without asking for it.' She couldn't think of another more serious comparison but Eamon nonetheless smiled at her gentle words, they were of great relief. 'What is it that you've heard? You can tell me.'

He sighed, of course he could tell Grayse, but he didn't think this problem shared would lessen its enormity.

'They want Juan, Grayse, I don't quite know why, but I think we've all been taken for some reason, not randomly, but for some purpose or knowledge that they think we might have. And they said Juan has some plan that may stop them. No, he was given a plan that may stop them, yes that's it.'

'Given a plan, by who?' she asked, it all sounded like madness to her ears.

'This is where it all got even stranger, they said by…by Manannin.'

'What?'

'I know, I know it sounds stupid, but they made it sound so real, you would never have thought that it wasn't from how they spoke of it.' Grayse didn't stop to think but continued pressing him further.

'And what's this plan they have that Juan can stop, did they speak of that?'

'Something about a reclamation of some sort, that's all they said.' Eamon didn't say what he thought this might be, but Grayse could see his fear. She could feel it coming off him like steam. She didn't want to ask further but couldn't stop herself, not out of curiosity but from somewhere darker within, where all her terror resided.

'And what about all of us, did they mention us?' Eamon put his hands over Aalin's ears, even though she was asleep in her mother's arms he wanted to save her from his words.

'They only said one thing…sacrifice.' Grayse embraced him tightly, her eyes filling with tears.

As they held each other in the dark, they failed to notice that Reverend Godfrey had been sitting with them in the shadows all the time and rose up out of the dark like a crow at night and walked into the centre of the pit.

'It is as I said it would be!' he exclaimed to the whole room. Everyone turned to him. All the muddy faces knelt down eager for his prayers of saviour.

'Eamon here heard them. We are to be sacrificed, punished for our sins. Isn't that so Eamon?'

Every face turned his way. They were a room of eyes wide with absolute horror.

'I heard no such thing Dermot,' said Eamon, trying to keep calm by forcing all his anger into his clenched fists by his side.

'Our judgement day is here, just like the great flood and the ark. The sinful world will be laid to ruin, and built again.' Revered Godfrey was red faced, his habit in shreds and his eyes wild with danger.

Josie and Mona Clague began to cry, Colum and Cara Watterson stood up hand in hand in protest, their smart suits in tatters, as did Patrick Tooly.

'Keep quiet man!' shouted Eamon. 'Get a grip on yourself, can't you see you're scaring the children. I suggest you go and sit back where you came from and keep yourself to yourself until you've calmed down.' Eamon spoke as steadfastly as he could, and by the looks of everyone upstanding, he had spoken their sentiments too.

Reverend Godfrey turned on the spot, looking at all the defiant faces etched out in the dark, the faces of the sinful world to his mind, and slowly shrank back into the darkest corners of the cave, brooding.

Grayse's reassuring hand lifted up and touched Eamon on the shoulder. Aalin silently stretched her arms out and Eamon took her in his and held her close to him.

'How long have we got?' Grayse asked, her voice weary with the effort.

'A day, if we're lucky,' Eamon replied, feeling empty and hollow. Both of their thoughts turned back to their son, hunted out in the cold, and as another scream escaped from Gavan Clague and ran through the tunnels until it reached them at the bottom of the pit, Eamon closed his eyes and prayed to Manannin that Juan was not alone.

TEN

Bea, Sophia and Juan were standing together in a field, barely a hundred paces away from the nearest road. The road ran adjacent to the dense Chibbanagh forest and, though wary, they had had no trouble crossing it, for the signs of life so early in the morning were minimal. Sophia took the lead and flew into the middle of the road with abandon, hovering there and listening for any noise before darting over to the cattle fence on the far side, perching on it whilst waiting for the other two to catch up.

They had walked down the closest muddied path leading to Braaid, their feet crunching and scraping under the dry frozen earth, and then headed out into the open pastures. Besides the curious sheep, their coats thick with wool, coolly chewing their cud and indifferently looking their way, they were alone, to do as they would. One particular sheep bounced over to Juan and nuzzled its face into his side, stroking its black cheeks against the wool of his jacket and bleating. Juan gave the sheep a hard scratch under its chin and smiled. Bea spotted the sheep.

'You're probably wearing part of his grandmother.'

Juan smiled weakly. It was the first proper thing Bea had said to him in several hours.

From where they stood, on high ground, they could look down into the basin of the valley, embraced by the mountains, and see a small parish church and a village just waking up. Solitary lights were appearing amidst the grey mist and flock of roofs. The cold wind burnt Sophia's nose as she inhaled a great gulp of air and stared down at all the houses, so peculiar to her.

Juan looked up to the brightening morning clouds and realised he had absolutely no idea what time it was, or for that matter, even what day it was. Any recollection had walked out of his memory. But thinking further on it, what did it matter? From what Bea had told him about the reclamation, they must have barely a day left to prevent what they saw before them from

becoming a vista of fire and smoke and ash.

Past the turnstile, the field stretched out in front of them as they trudged through the grass, wild and uncut, straining up past their calves. It was only as they got closer that they noticed the stones come into view. A random cluster of mossy aged rocks revealed themselves and, once they were surrounded, it was clear they were the remnants of some sort of settlement. Juan could easily discern the shapes of a parlour, an out-house and a larger communal space in between the two. Sophia seemed less interested and landed briefly on one of the rocks, but flew up and chose to perch on Juan's shoulder instead, complaining that it was too cold. Bea rested a hand on one of the rocks, feeling its cool moss under his leathery skin, and gently closed his eyes.

'What can you feel?' Sophia called out over the growing low howl of the wind.

'It's old, that I can tell. But not so old that it lends itself to another age. This was a place of great shelter, of comfort, laughter and song. I can still feel the music of the pipe and the drum, even now. But there it stops, this is not what we seek, there is nothing deeper in these stones. Dear Manannin let us not have come here for nothing.'

Bea seemed distant and tired as Juan passed him further into the field. His great shoulders were slumped forward, and his back arched in fatigue. Juan blinked as his hair blew across his face and listened to the bleats of the sheep carry in the wind.

'Don't you worry yourself about him,' Sophia whispered in his ear. 'If you ask me, he carries too much weight on those shoulders of his. Believe me I've tried helping him, many times. Manannin knows how hard I've tried, and we've been friends for ages, but I doubt he'll let either of us bear that load of his.'

Juan bit down hard on his lip, he hated admitting to eavesdropping but as usual couldn't restrain himself. It was easier to think that it was for Bea's sake and not merely his own curiosity.

'What happened to his brother, Céa was it?' Sophia looked at him, and smiled that warm smile that Juan had already come to appreciate after such a short time. He knew she didn't mind his listening, he even suspected it was one of her talents as well.

'Céa, yes that was his brother's name, dear Céa, and poor Céa, perhaps it's best if you ask him yourself.' Juan felt he shouldn't press her further, and let the matter pass.

'Wait just a moment!' Sophia suddenly yelled out, leaping off Juan's shoulder, speeding over the top of the grass and then rising up several feet before abruptly stopping above their heads. 'Bea, get your hairy self over here right now!'

Bea slowly looked up and took a few heavy steps over to where they stood.

'What is it?' he asked, and Juan was wondering the same thing as he watched Sophia hovering above them. They both turned, looking around them and then saw what Sophia saw: that they were standing in the exact centre of a perfect circle of stones. Some were virtually invisible under the overgrown land, covered in mats of grass and soil, and were no bigger than a person lying low to the earth, but a perfect circle nonetheless. Every one looked so gnarled with decay that they could only belong to a much older age, a much deeper age, than those of the settlement. Juan instantly knew he had seen the place before, not where he stood, but in his dreams. And now it was all around him in the waking world.

'*Kiarkil voish Ansoor!*' Bea called out hopefully and ran to the edge of the circle putting his palm down on the nearest stone.

Juan saw that Bea didn't seem to close his eyes. They looked to be forced shut against his will, and he curled over as though the inside of his stomach was being squeezed. He looked like he may be sick. His hand fell away from the stone as Juan and Sophia raced over to him and he knelt up, panting but with a look of both alarm and excitement.

'These must be them. It was like falling right into the earth, without seeing any bottom, just falling straight down. I have a feeling these rocks weren't even put here, I think they just grew out of the earth like this.' Even in the cold he was wiping sweat from his brow.

'Great!' blasted Sophia. 'So they grew out of the earth, big deal. How do they work?'

'I don't know how they work,' said Bea, defensively. 'I thought you said you knew.'

'I said no such thing, I thought you knew.'

'Well, I don't.'

'Well, I don't either.'

'What can we do then?!' blurted Juan over the two of them, once again finding himself in the middle of their bickering. With every light that flickered on in the village beneath them in the corner of his eye, he felt his heart quicken with a frantic urgency.

'Why don't we just try something, anything?' Bea looked down to Juan, then back at Sophia and held her gaze as he placed his hand back on the stone and his eyes shut as if in a trance.

'What should I ask it?' he breathed, his voice was low and intense.

'Something, anything, ask it where your parents are.'

Bea took a deep breath and asked his question with a firm authority.

'*C'raad t'ad my ayr as moir?*'

Nothing appeared to change. They didn't even know what should change, what should happen, but whatever it was it was quite apparent that it hadn't. Bea called out again, his mane of hair blowing back off his face.

'*Ta mee geearee cooney vooyd.*'

'What was that?' Juan whispered to Sophia, back resting on his shoulder, she whispered back in his ear.

'He's calling on them for help.'

'*Insh dou my sailt! C'raad t'ad my ayr as moir?*'

'He's asking them again isn't he?' Sophia nodded. 'Why aren't they answering him?' she had no reply to this.

'*Ansoor gyn kialg. Red erbee!*' Bea now sounded desperate, his jaw was tense with frustration and he seemed to be pleading through his clenched teeth.

'*Cur taitnys da!*' Juan couldn't understand what he was shouting, but knew that Bea was giving up, there was no use, the stones weren't answering. He pulled his hand away from the surface and let forth a roar of anger. His whole body seemed to expand as the terrifying blood red flowed over his fur with the wind. Juan held himself, frightened of Bea's rage, though it was the look in his eyes that really got to him, a maddening green glazed with tortured frustration. A small flock of sheep at the further end of the field ran off and crowded into a corner near the stone walls.

Juan didn't know why he felt the need to try; whether it was just to prove that they may have been in the wrong place, or a need to feel in some way worthwhile, but before he even realised it, he was walking towards the edge of the circle.

'What are you doing Juan?' asked Sophia, flying off his shoulder to face him.

'I don't know,' he answered. And he didn't know. He didn't know why he knelt down and placed his hand on the stone, mimicking Bea, all he knew was that he felt impelled to do it.

The stone felt grainy and wet under his fingers. He didn't need to ask Sophia the words for the question he felt he should ask, they were just there inside his head, as though they always had been there, and were waiting for this moment to appear and be used.

'*Cooin lhien,*' he whispered, the words feeling unnatural inside his mouth. And just as had happened with Bea, he felt his eyes closing. He tried to hold them open but it was no use, they slammed shut and he began to fall.

There was no wind. His hair didn't blow about or his fleece billow. That surprised him. There was only blackness and weight. He felt so heavy. Though there were no walls to see flash by or cliff faces to see pass, he knew he must have been travelling very fast, further and further into the deep light-less space. He became unaware of time. He could have been falling for days and not have noticed. He liked it. He looked at the tips of his fingers and wondered at how hard they had become and at all the dirt and grit under his nails. It made him want to laugh. He imagined birds taking this much pleasure every time they soared through the skies, but couldn't remember what the sky looked like, everything was so black. He was lost in the plummet.

He hardly noticed when he began to fall through water. He had felt no splash and continued straight down through the green sea like a dead weight until he came to rest on the bed of the sea. Was he dreaming? He couldn't tell. It looked just like his dream, and felt just like his dream. The current of the water swathed past him as he blinked, looking into the endless distance. He wasn't cold or wet and it felt good to not be walking or hiking through the forests and glens. As before, he found himself holding a globe in his hand, but this time it was different. The sphere was entirely black, no sign of land or sea upon it, but as black as the darkest winter night, so black it was as if it was feeding off the light surrounding it. Juan had seen it before, not in a dream but somewhere else, he couldn't think where. His memory was a blur, like a ghost in candlelight.

The current began to carry a sound his way, a chime of music, which flowed towards him. It was like nothing he had heard before, but somehow seemed in harmony with the water as though they belonged together. He wanted to hear where it was coming from, and stood up, his clothes feeling heavy around him.

'Come to me,' spoke a voice through the water. Juan fell back down to the seabed in fright. It was the voice of his mother.

'Come to me *key-per*. I am whom you seek.'

'Mum, where are you, Mum, I miss you, please,' he called out, but his voice sounded pitiful and weak and the current pulled it away into the wide expanse beyond.

'You must come, for all our sakes.' She sounded so gentle and loving. He had never felt so alone.

'Mum!' he called out again, reaching in front of him and stretching through the water hoping she would reach back to him. A hand emerged, through the currents speeding past him. It was familiar: large, strong and scarred. He clung on to it, wrapping his fingers around its thick wrist as it pulled him upwards with tremendous force, towards the surface of the water. He had to close his eyes to the rushing wind of sea, clawing at him like a wanton beggar, and felt the surface getting quickly closer. As he knew he had emerged from the water, he gasped and caught his breath, choking and coughing. Opening his eyes, stinging in the low light, he found himself back on his knees clinging onto the grass of the field beneath his fingers and gripping onto Bea's wrist by his side.

'*Dy gooin jee lhien*! Juan, you looked like you were drowning, what happened?' he said, shaking him, and slapping his back, trying to bring him back from his ordeal.

Juan spluttered, and felt the sickening salty taste of seawater in his mouth. He now indeed felt like he had been rescued from the murky depths. But the voice, where was it? He madly looked around him, trying to find a sign of his mother's voice that had beckoned him from so far away.

'Mum?' he spluttered. 'I heard my mum, in the sea, deep down in the sea: it was definitely her. I heard her.'

He spat out each word as though with every second that passed she flowed further away.

'I was in the sea Bea, and I heard some sound, like music but different somehow, I don't know why, and then I heard my mum's voice, she said "come to me, you need to come".'

Juan pleadingly held on to Bea, and looked up into his wide green eyes, but Bea was staring at Sophia. They shared a look full of silent voices, and unspoken words.

'What, what is it?' asked Juan, still catching his breath.

Sophia looked down at him, and quietly spoke a single word, which couldn't be swept away by the wind.

'Téeval.'

'Téeval, what does that mean? I've never heard that word before, what's Téeval?'

'Not *what* Juan, *who* is Téeval. She is…'

'The Princess of the Ocean,' finished Bea, softly placing his hand on Juan's shoulder. It wasn't the voice of your mother you heard Juan, I'm sorry. It was the voice of Téeval. Every word you hear that she speaks is as though it comes from the lips of your own mother.'

'But I heard her, it was her.'

'It was Téeval Juan, believe me. And you say she said, "come to me", then that is precisely what we must do. She will help us. She will know what to do.'

Juan couldn't think straight, he could only picture his mother, and his home and his bed. He felt so tired, he wanted to just curl up where he knelt, sleep and let the world around him solve its own troubles.

'So it wasn't my mum?'

'No Juan, I'm sorry. But remember what I told you, do you still feel her near you, right there?' And he pointed a finger to the centre of Juan's chest. Juan put his hand there, and felt the calming beat of his own heart.

'I think so, yes, I think I do.'

'Then that's what you must hold on to, and don't let go.'

Juan walked away from them, his feet feeling heavy and dragging along the earth. He had begun to see that their journey was far from over. There was still a thick veil between him and the truth.

'I can see her, my mum,' he spoke, half to himself, half to the others. 'I'm walking down the stairs and it's morning, just like today. There's the smell of breakfast cooking as I reach the kitchen. She gives me a cup of tea and tells me to watch out for the slippery floor, Aalin's been playing with the paints again, and she doesn't want me to fall. None of the washing-up has been done, and I tell her not to worry and that I'll do it after school. Dad comes in through the back door in his boots and stamps big muddy footprints over the floor. Mum shouts at him but he only laughs, and gives Aalin a little wink. She blows a raspberry back at him. She's sitting on the kitchen table surrounded by finger paintings she's been doing since dawn, and I have to clear a space for dad and me to eat at. Dad pulls off his boots, messes my hair with his dirty hand, then straightens my tie and sits down with me to eat. And best of all, we don't talk much about anything that's happened, because we all know and understand and nothing needs to be said.

'That's what all this is about for me. Waking up there again, and for all of this to be like a story from some silly book I read before falling asleep.'

'Who are you talking to?' someone asked from behind him, not Bea or Sophia, but someone else. Juan spun around, startled. It was Doona Kelly, right there, in the fields of Braaid, in front of him. She was wearing her school uniform and a thick duffel coat with its collar turned up around her neck.

Juan was so taken aback. He turned on the spot looking around the fields and headland but couldn't see any sign of his friends. He was so dumbfounded he didn't know what to say.

Doona Kelly had never been particularly nice to him, she would either ignore him entirely or when she was with her gang of chums, glance his way then return to her huddle where they would all giggle like a pack of animals. Though he never let this get to him too much, he couldn't deny how pretty he thought she was. Behind her haughty expression and nasty remarks was something cheeky he liked, which usually meant that anything funny he thought to say to her got stuck in his throat.

Doona's thick, curly, raven black hair blew across her face hiding the freckles on either side of her small button nose and Juan tried to speak but nothing wanted to come out. She looked at him the way a teacher looks at the class troublemaker.

'Juan, what *are* you doing out here?'

'N...n...nothing,' he managed to mumble.

'It doesn't look like "nothing" to me. And what are you wearing? You look like a two legged sheep.'

Juan pulled his sheep skin protectively around him and held his cold hands under his arms. 'Well, why are you out here?' he sneered back at her. 'Shouldn't you be at school asleep or something?'

'I've been up all night coughing my little heart out I'll have you know,' she said, making sure she had a small burst of impressive coughs afterwards. 'Mum was afraid I'd got the measles, or mumps or whooping cough or something. She's like so paranoid, so she insisted on picking me up and bringing me home. I'll probably be off school for the next few days, even longer if I can help it.' Again she broke out into violent coughs. 'And where were you yesterday, I don't think you've missed a day of school in your life?'

'How do you know?' he said, defensively.

'I…just know,' she replied a little shyly, digging her hands deep into her pockets. She seemed to have become fascinated by her shoes, and was staring at the ground with surprising concentration, scuffing her feet into the mud, whilst Juan desperately thought of something to say.

'I've been sick too,' he said, over-enthusiastically. Doona looked at him suspiciously.

'Yes that's it, I've been sick. There must be some sort of bug going round.' He knew he didn't sound in any way convincing, but now he'd started so he had to go on. He was still looking all around him trying to catch a glimpse of Bea anywhere, if only to remind himself that he wasn't going mad. 'Mum decided I'd better stay away from school as well, what with all those germs floating about, she's well paranoid.' This was good, he thought, she looked like she believed him.

'You're lucky, its been totally crazy, everyone's freaked out over all this "people disappearing into thin air" stuff. Not just the pupils, but the teachers as well. Mr. Mortis was found screaming his head off in his classroom, books everywhere, like he was having some sort of weird episode or something.'

'Yeah, I know,' he said, but knew he'd made a mistake as soon as the words left his mouth, and tried his hardest to look cool and casual as Doona stared at him quizzically.

'What do you mean you know? You weren't there.'

'I…I mean, I know everyone's being going nuts, I bet some people even thought I'd disappeared like the other ones, right?' he garbled, trying to cover his tracks.

'No, nobody really noticed you weren't there.'

'Oh,' he said, not really surprised.

Doona hung on the silence a moment longer, pulling a loose lock of black curls from her eyes and tucking it behind an ear.

'Are you sure you're not doing some bizarre geography experiment or something, I wouldn't put it past you.' He looked up and saw the grass directly behind her shimmer, as though an unseen flash of sun had just passed over it, but there were no breaks in the morning clouds, and as it settled he could clearly make out Bea's familiar silhouette. He tried hard not to show any reaction, but couldn't help laughing a little with relief.

'No, I'm sure I'm not doing any experiments. I just like it up here that's all. It's nice isn't it?'

'I guess,' she said, looking down into the deep valley. 'You're weird you know.'

'Yeah, so you've told me.'

A call came from up towards the road, Juan followed the sound, and in the distance saw Doona's mum, Mrs. Kelly, shivering and madly waving her arms in the air.

'Come on Doona, you'll catch your death!'

'I told you she was paranoid,' she laughed. Juan laughed too, as she did look very foolish.

'You know, I'm sorry about all those things that I've said. You've got to look like you hate something when you're with my mates, and you were just…'

'An easy target?'

'I guess. I'm sorry. You're not all that bad you know?' she said lightly thumping him in the arm. He suddenly felt much warmer.

'I think you're quite cool actually, and as for that thing you're wearing,' she said prodding his fleece, 'it kind of suits you.' He knew his cheeks must be glowing bright red by now, and could only just manage to say, 'Thanks.'

'Doona, would you come on!' Her mum was now erratically waving her arms as though she was swatting a swarm of bees.

'I'd better go then,' she said.

'Yeah sure.'

She went to leave, then stopped, quickly turned around, bent down and gave Juan the smallest, briefest kiss on the cheek, like the brushing of a damp leaf, and ran off back towards the road. She called out, without turning around, 'See you back at school!'

144

Juan put his hand up to his cheek and held it there as he watched the motorcar drive off, and the lights fade over the lip of the hill.

As the grey morning returned to Juan's heart, from the hazy outline only a few paces away, came a raucous sniggering. The grass seemed to whither and fell into shadow around the shape as Bea resumed his natural state, and Sophia flew up from behind him. She spun around in such hysterics that Bea feared she might fly headfirst into the stones around them.

'Stop it you two,' Juan protested, feeling suddenly self-conscious, and swatted at Sophia whizzing past his ear. 'You were lucky she didn't see you.'

'We haven't been seen for a considerably long time, and I refuse to have our secret broken by some…frizzy haired school girl.' She let out another shriek as she flew high above him.

'What can I say, I can't help it if she likes me.' Bea smiled at him broadly.

'Good for you Juan.'

Sophia was gradually calming down, wiping the tears from her eyes with her sleeve and came to hover between the two of them. Something of the morning's weight had been lifted away and though still bitterly cold, their spirits at least felt lighter. It was as though they had woken up from a short but heavy, dreamless sleep. They all felt it, Bea especially, and he pounced on the energy like a cat.

'Now, we have someone to see. Sophia you know far better than I, where would be the best place to call her, where did you last hear the *Sheen-ny-Feaynid*?'

'Over the bay, near the chasms,' she said, having resigned herself to the more serious matters in hand. 'But that is too near Port St. Mary, it's too open. We can't risk calling upon Téeval, when there will be the fear of being seen looming over us. We need somewhere no one ventures in these late seasons of the year.' She rested her face in her hands, as she thought hard.

'What about the Bay of Dhoon, out near Glau Wooar,' said Juan, ready to be told what a miserable idea it was. Bea and Sophia looked down at him.

'Not bad,' said Sophia, clearly impressed. 'We can take the path down following the river and waterfall; it is far too steep for any people to want to amble down at this time of year.'

'We would, my family I mean. That's why I mentioned it. We like going down there, and it's always so quiet, you could imagine you were the only people in the whole world.'

'Then that's settled. If Téeval wants a word with you, there is no better place. But we must hurry, all this meandering is costing us time, the one thing we don't have. And we must now travel in daylight, for all to see. I fear the journey will take too long.' Juan hadn't thought of that, the sky was getting brighter all the time, and he was aware that they were quite openly exposed to the world around them. There were no shadows of night to hide in any longer.

'I'm sorry I can't keep up with you, I wish I could run faster, but my legs just won't do it.'

'Don't worry, I'll carry you again, if you'll let me, I have strength enough.' Bea could sense how much Juan wanted to make the journey himself, without his help, but every moment they saved the closer they would get to some dank dirty caves underneath them where their mothers and fathers lay, confused and frightened.

'We'll need to take a quicker route, we can't afford to waste our time hiding in the undergrowth.'

Sophia looked shocked, and was about to interrupt. Bea could tell this and raised his hand to stop her. 'Nobody will understand what they've seen Sophia, they'll forget us soon enough. It is for their sakes after all. If someone does see us, and speaks of it, I'm sure nobody would believe them. We've become bedtime stories, just like Juan said, we're hardly even legend anymore.'

'Then let's go,' she said, resigned. 'You always said you wanted to meet her, now is your chance. We should reach her by the time the sun is at its highest.' She had already sped up to the stone wall, right next to the road, her face strong with a newly found determination. Juan ran up to join her, he knew the Glen of Dhoon well, and the quickest roads to take, if they dared.

'Come on you great oaf!' Sophia called down to Bea. 'What are you waiting for?'

'One moment!' Bea yelled back. Juan looked his way and could clearly see Bea walk over to one of the stones and place his palm down onto its flat face. He was asking something, though Juan couldn't make out what over the whistling of the wind as it played within the forest behind him.

Bea wasn't there long, and shortly ran up the slope to join them. He seemed calm and expressionless as he knelt down for Juan to reach around his shoulders and get a good hold of him.

'What was all that about?' asked Sophia, flying in front of Bea's face with her hands on her hips.

He let the smallest crack of a smile break onto one side of his lips before answering, 'Nothing.'

Slyly he stood up to his full height, with Juan, now so used to it, clinging on behind him.

'Which way Juan?' he asked, and Juan pointed.

'North-east,' he said, and for the first time Bea began running along the boundary of the roadside, heading down towards places he had avoided his whole life, towards the frightening mass of lights and noise and people in the towns before them.

ELEVEN

The steady and even drumming of Mother's nails against the armrest of her stone dais was the only sound to be heard over the incessant chanting of her children, reaching into every tunnel.

'*We worship you. We cower before your glory, Mother, Queen, giver of life and death. Our lives are yours.*'

Throughout the entire nest patience was waning. She feared the map wasn't on its way to her grasp, in fact she knew it wasn't. Maybe she knew before Mortis had even left her sight, but was too weak to realise it, her view shadowed by such foolish temptation. It hurt to have so sweet a chance come into her sight only to be stolen away so quickly. How pathetic, she thought, she must have been becoming as feeble as the man himself. That would never do. She could hardly believe she was still sitting there, waiting, in the hope that he might return. Hope was for the weak, for those who didn't get, but were only left wanting. It was an uncommon feeling. She had never had to hope before. But she knew the Fynoderee and the boy must be found. She was well aware that a single pebble, no matter how small, could start an entire avalanche that would block her path. Who knew what powers they could muster to stand in her way? It made her palms sweat just to think on it.

Too long had they been in the depths of the world. They would see the next dawn over ground at whatever cost.

'*We worship you. We cower before your glory, Mother, Queen, giver of life and death. Our lives are yours.*'

Mother sat there listening to the chants and quietly dwelled on the frequent news that had been brought to her, of outbreaks and fighting between her children. Older and stronger Brothers and Sisters had ganged up and attacked the young and infirm, cornering and devouring whoever came in their way, feeding on the newborn and feeble, quenching their thirst on their blood. She smiled with pride. Her army was ready.

To one side of her, Brother Ordo stood awkwardly, waiting for instruction. He shifted his weight uncomfortably from one foot to another and tampered with his hands, not knowing where to put them. He had never for a moment put his trust in Mortis, the Watcher. He had been impressed to see such devotion to Mother coming from a man, but he suspected a quick change when the heat finally struck. Men were like that; if a safer avenue loomed, away from harm, they would inevitably take it, instead of facing the heat head on. If he had it his way, Mortis would be down in the pit with the others, or even better, he would let Brother Hemi and Sister Anik work their wonders on him. That would teach him a worthwhile lesson. But Brother Ordo had learnt the hard way to keep his thoughts to himself, deep down where even Mother couldn't see them.

'We worship you. We cower before your glory, Mother, Queen, giver of life and death. Our lives are yours.'

Four guards stood behind Brother Ordo, motionless and broad in the half-light. Disguised in the smoke of the walls it was impossible to tell them apart and they resembled nothing more than boulders lying on the stone floor. Their arms were thick and rough and their hands hung low down in front of their squat legs, so large they could crush trees.

Mother was especially proud of her guards. They had been bred using the stronger Bugganes in the nest. Being mute and particularly docile shielded them from such weaknesses as fear and doubt. What they lacked in their heads they made up for tenfold in their strength.

'Mother?'

'Don't speak my child. I know what you would ask, for it is

also in my mind. That map is very important to me. It is the only way I can see to get to Bea, that infernal Fynoderee, who I believe may be the fallen tree in our road,' she spoke in a light clipped voice, hiding her growing frustrations.

'But what can one Fynoderee do against us? His odds are thousands to one.'

Mother slowly turned to face him. The power of her gaze was so strong Brother Ordo felt like he had been struck across the face. He reached up and fingered the fresh wound around his throat, from the chain he had hung from the night before. It hadn't stopped stinging and had yet begun to heal.

'For all we know he may have found the boy. For all we know Manannin may have sent him a message to thwart our goals. For all we know these plans may have already been instigated and we may never see the light of day, ever.'

Brother Ordo could tell she was having more and more trouble remaining calm and shuffled back a step. He wished he hadn't spoken.

'It was said Manannin would only return when needed, and I can see no greater time of need than when we have the heads of man-folk in our hands and are squeezing the life from them. Am I wrong?'

Brother Ordo had never seen her like this.

'You are surely not nervous Mother? We are prepared. Our army will engulf the island like poison through a body. If you want Mortis, send out the guards. They are fast and will find him quicker than we could wish for.'

'They will be seen. I want tomorrow to be a big surprise,' she moaned, banging her hands down on her throne. Brother Ordo hoped she didn't know he thought she looked like a spoilt infant.

'*We worship you. We cower in your glory, Mother, Queen, giver of life and death. Our lives are yours.*'

'The guards are swift Mother, they will not be seen. They…' He suddenly stopped, thinking something had changed. He listened. Something *had* changed. It took him only a moment to notice, but the chanting emanating from the tunnels was different.

'*We have betrayed every Brother and every Sister and no longer deserve our place in this family. Use us as you will.*'

It was more obvious now. The chanting thumped alongside the hard beat of feet against stone. The wet fleshy screech of thousands of voices calling out as one turned Mothers heart to ice. Every Brother and Sister knew the supplication. It was only to be spoken before death, as proof that every beat of their heart was only there so that they may please their Mother, that they may honour and worship her; the giver of life and death. She had heard it countless times, but only ever from the craggy lips of a single Brother or Sister at any one time, that is how it had always been. She had heard it so often its meaning had been lost to her, weighed down under the droning tone. But now, with so many thousands of voices calling out as one body, the words were revived as if they had been uttered for the first time.

'Why are they doing that?' she whispered, staring out towards the dark smoggy entrance of her chamber.

Brother Ordo knew why. He felt it himself. It wasn't an instinctive feeling, but something baser, in his gut and through his blood. No matter if he often disagreed with Mother, or his own thoughts of the reclamation, he would still follow her to the ends of the earth. He would follow her for the good of the family. His life was hers and she could do with it whatever she chose to. If this pleased her then he had done his duty.

'They chant the supplication of death because they are willing to die for you Mother. We are all willing to die for you and the family. We will follow you wherever you go, even into the very clutches of death's embrace.' A grunt of agreement came from the four guards behind him.

Again she had always known this, but now it felt different, more imminent. Each and every one of them would lie down on spikes and make a floor for her to walk over should she wish it.

She gripped her chair tightly as her racing heart slowed to a pace of slow resolve. She had no other options left. Every time she imagined the open sky and the ashen smell of victory, the boy with painted skin flashed into her mind's eye like a bolt of lightening ripping through the night.

'Send out the guards.'

Brother Ordo lifted his arm and the four oak sized Bugganes disappeared into the smoke of the room without hesitation.

'Remember my child, they mustn't be seen, I don't want to hear of any disruptions, I only want the map. I would hate to have to tie you up again should anything go wrong.'

Brother Ordo bowed his head and also disappeared through the smoke, walking backwards and still facing her until he was sure he was out of sight. Mother called into the wall of smog as she was left alone.

'Make Mortis sorry for his failings.'

TWELVE

The old, beamed windows of Mortis' cold classroom clattered in their frames from the wind outside beating against them. Sitting there, he feared that if the wind sneaked inside, through a small gap in the sill, it would attack him, and he shrank even lower into his seat. He wanted to get up out of his chair and check that the locks were firmly shut but felt too heavy to walk over to them. He felt nailed down and hadn't left the room since he saw what could have only been the last Fynoderee on the island speeding off the school grounds faster than a hurricane.

The Fynoderee had taken his map.

He had tried to stop and explain his behaviour to Olivia, who had seemed so shocked and more concerned with the children laughing nearby. She said that he shouldn't raise his voice so, and that it didn't become him. She said she had obviously mistaken him for someone else, and that they shouldn't see so much of each other. He thought she would have understood, of anyone he thought she would have understood. He had tried to hold her, just so she wouldn't run away and he would have a chance to explain himself properly, but she had started shouting back at him. He had started shaking her, just so she would come to her senses and listen to what he had to say, but this only frightened her even more and she had slapped him hard across the face and run off down the stairs. He could still feel the sting on his cheek. It made his eyes water.

The night had passed slowly as he sat there doing little else but staring at the blank wall and the grubby marks where the map had safely hung inside the cabinet earlier that day. He had thought about many things as the hours crawled by; about Olivia and the time they would have spent together alone on the island, about Mother and her reaction if she knew he had lost the map, but most of all he thought about his father.

He hadn't noticed that an entire class had come in and sat down, ready for their first lesson of the day. They might have been noisy rearranging desks and chairs that had been turned over and knocked around the room. They might have been chattering, whispering and even gasping at the mess around them: papers everywhere, shelves collapsed and rusted antiques spilt across the floor. He hadn't noticed. Someone had even loudly suggested that he had 'lost the plot' and should be left alone, but everyone else was far too interested to leave. The sight of his back towards them, still as a statue, was far too intriguing.

Once everyone got bored of chatting away to each other, they sat in silence for several minutes, waiting for some sign of life to slip out of their teacher. That was until Turner spat out a small ball of damp paper he'd been chewing on across the room, which slapped onto the back of Creer's long, bare neck. Creer knew it was wise not to accuse Turner of his crime and so blamed Coombs, the smallest and most non-aggressive boy in the class, punishing him with an onslaught of flicked elastic bands. Harper took offence at this false accusation and quickly began throwing missiles of blunt coloured pencils back at Creer, who shielded himself with someone else's briefcase. Gelling backed up Harper with a powerful offensive of rolled up paper bombs flung at everyone on the opposite side of the room. Coombs took this opportunity to retreat underneath his desk and let the larger ones battle it out in no man's land.

Soon it was pandemonium. Paper and pencils were raining down on both sides of the room. Neither side seemed able to gain the upper hand and screams came equally hard from each faction. Things got even more interesting when Turner pulled out a large catapult from inside his desk. The opposition quickly struck up their defence of thick textbooks just in time to save themselves from marbles being pelted hard and fast towards them.

Mortis had heard none of this. He continued to sit staring at the empty glass cabinet hanging on the wall. He saw his reflection staring back at him in the glass and wondered at how like his father he looked. The same deeply set, wide eyes, same beakish nose and gaunt, drawn cheeks. He remembered as a boy, wishing above everything to grow up to be like him. Every night he would lie in bed thinking just that as his father came into his room, sat on the end of his bed and asked him which story he wished to hear. Young Brendan had many favourites, but more often than not he wanted to hear about his family, about old Timothy the tailor and his battle against the evil Buggane at St. Trinian's Church, the tale of the broken church, *Keeil Vrisht*.

'But you know it by heart son, you could probably tell it right back to me standing on your head,' his father would mock him.

'But dad, you tell it better than me, you know you do.'

Brendan knew his father was only teasing him and was well aware that this was the story he most loved to tell. Sitting there in the chilly classroom he tried to recall exactly how his father told it.

'The gentle folk of Greeba,' he would always begin, in an enticing, wintry voice, 'found the most beautiful and perfect spot to build their church, in praise of St. Trinian, just off the high road of the mountain. They hoped it was a place that wouldn't disturb an evil Buggane they knew to dwell in the mountain.

'But the vile Buggane saw them building their church, and was furious, " How dare they build their ugly church here, I'll never have a moment's peace!" it shouted, and swore that it would never let the roof stay put for a single night.

'Indeed, on the very night the church was completed, what the quiet people of Greeba thought was a thunderstorm was in fact that nasty Buggane bashing on the roof of the church until it toppled right in on itself. "Nasty Buggane! Nasty Buggane!"' Mortis remembered shouting back at his father in excitement.

'Now the gentle people of Greeba,' his father continued, 'thinking it had only been a storm that had felled their fine church's roof, simply set to work again, and before long it was fully restored. They were such fine decent people after all, not at all like the monster in the mountain.

'But again, on the very night of its completion, everyone in their beds thought a great gale was blowing and thunder roaring.

And again, they all awoke to find the roof of their precious church had been destroyed.

'The people now knew it couldn't have been the weather that was destroying their simple place of worship and that it could only have been the spiteful Buggane, jealous of their civilised ways. So with greater zeal than before, they repaired the roof once more. They hoped for the final time.

'The people thought that if someone was brave enough, or stupid enough, to stay in the church for one whole night then the roof's curse would be lifted and forever it would stand. They put out a wager around the town to find someone, and soon enough brave Timothy, the local tailor, accepted the odds. In defiance of the Buggane, he said that not only would he stay the whole night long, but he would also make himself a fine new pair of trousers while he was at it, to celebrate the occasion.'

"Hooray!" Brendan would shout from the warmth of his bed.

'And so, on the night that the roof was restored, Timothy found himself inside the dark church hall, surrounded by candles, needle and thread in hand, working away on his trousers.

'Timothy may have been a brave man, but even he couldn't help but feel the haunting chill of the hall, and jump at the sight of sinister shadows cast on the stone walls "How silly," he said aloud, "there is nothing unnatural here. Maybe it was the storm after all, and not some daft Buggane."

'But no sooner had he uttered those very words than the ground beneath where he sat split open and the giant, monstrous Buggane heaved itself out of the earth. Timothy ran into a corner, stitching faster, still determined to win the town's wager. The Buggane chased him here and there, all over the church, screaming horrible insults at him, but Timothy refused to escape until his trousers were finished. He tried to ignore the grotesque Buggane, which only drove it into a wilder fury and it ran at him like a bull seeing red.

'Timothy sewed the final stitch of his trousers, and ran straight out the door. As he headed down the mountain he heard the roof of the doomed church cave in for the last time. Turning around to see, he was met by the sight of the Buggane chasing him down the path and out along the main road. Timothy was as fast as any prize hound and kept ahead of the Buggane for several miles, until he took cover behind a gravestone in a nearby church. The beast, in a frenzy, grabbed his own head with both his enormous hands, pulled it off his very shoulders and sent it flying after Timothy, before exploding into a thousand pieces, never to bother the gentle folk of Greeba again.

'Timothy won the wager for completing his trousers and was hailed a hero amongst the villagers. He vowed to rid the island of such monsters, so they could live in peace, without fear or threat. The church still stands in Greeba to this day, still without its roof, and that's where it gets its name *Keeil Vrisht*, the broken church.'

Mortis remembered cheering and clapping at Timothy's victory.

'What do we think of those nasty Bugganes son?' His father once asked him at the end of the tale.

'Evil.' Brendan would obediently reply.

'We don't want evil things around us do we, evil things that could chase me and mummy and you and your friends, and do nasty things and hurt us do we?'

'No, daddy,' he replied, shivering at the thought of it.

'What do you think we should do to them, before they get us?'

'Get rid of them, of course. Just like brave Timothy did.'

'Good boy son, you remember that. We should get rid of every last one of them, all of their world, before they get rid of us.'

Mortis hadn't thought of that in years. He had admired his father so much, walking out onto the coasts of the island with him, hunting. He had said it was the family tradition, its calling. He had looked so strong, holding his shotgun and burrowing into every cave with his flashlight, setting mantraps to ensnare the beasts. It seemed second nature to hunt them down, like stepping on a bug that's on the path and not thinking twice about it, it was just what they did. Was that so wrong? Was that evil?

Mortis rubbed his forehead hard. He was suddenly having

trouble deciphering who exactly the 'evil' was that his father had spoken about. Was it the Fynoderees trying to survive against the hatred and outcry of the people who had decided to take over their land? Or was it the Bugganes, out for revenge against a people who had forced them into the caves of the earth so long ago? Or was it the folk who had such a fear of what was different, igniting a vengeful anger within them and driving the creatures away? He was too confused to know, it made his head thump with a dull ache.

He kicked the wall and let his chair swivel round to face the classroom. For some reason he didn't find himself surprised by the scene in front of him. Everyone had frozen and was staring straight at him as the last remaining scraps of paper floated down and lay on the floor. There were boys standing on desks, girls hidden under desks and boys and girls cowering behind books. The room was even more of a mess than when he had finished with it. He stared back at them all. He wasn't mad. They were simply playing, just children enjoying themselves and having a laugh. They were harmless. And he knew what was to become of them all.

But he didn't solely dwell on the fate of the children in front of him. Thinking on it, he suddenly knew that without the map he was of no more use to Mother. He was just the same as them.

'Let me ask you something,' he said to the class gawping back at him, their mouths collectively open in apprehension in the pale morning light. 'Oh, and please don't stop what you're doing on my account.' They all slumped back into their chairs a little ashamed of themselves and Mortis jumped out of his chair and slid onto the top of his desk, knocking the remaining books onto the floor. Everyone was startled at how untidy he looked. Instead of his usual pristine appearance, he was truly filthy. His shoes, pink socks, and the bottom half of his tweed trousers were covered in crusty dried mud. His shirt was creased and unbuttoned, his tie was loose and shabby, he was unshaven with large black bags under his eyes, and his greasy black hair was sticking up in all directions. The class was too shocked to laugh. They had never seen him like this. It was an unnerving sight. His strict nasal voice had also gone, he now spoke quietly, with a concerned calm.

'If someone you knew had something of great value to you, like for instance your catapult Turner,' Turner realised he was still holding his catapult armed and ready with a conker, and quickly put it away in his desk, 'and they lost it, or worse it was taken from them before you could get it back,' Turner looked horrified by the very idea, 'or even worse still, it was taken by the one person in the world you didn't want to have it, like Coombs perhaps,' Turner stared over at Coombs and gave him a very dirty look that suggested he'd better not even think about taking his catapult, 'what would you do?'

'That's easy sir,' said Turner, standing up from his chair. Coombs slid further down into his chair and held his satchel close to his chest for comfort.

'First of all, I'd find my mate, the one who took this thing, or lost it or whatever,' he stood behind Coombs' chair, who now looked decidedly worried about the situation, 'and I'd grab him,' He lifted Coombs out of his chair, who gave a little yelp but nothing more. He was a dwarf compared to Turner, who was all shoulders and neck. 'And I'd grab his head, and I'd put my thumbs over his eyes and I'd push them back inside his head until…' Coombs was now screaming as Turner continued his demonstration. Harper and Doyle, two tough girls who'd earned their respect on the sports fields, jumped from their desks and tried to pull Turner off poor Coombs. The rest of the class began shouting 'Fight! Fight! Fight!'

Mortis didn't stop Turner, but stared in shock. Was this his fate? He could see no other. He knew he meant nothing to the Bugganes, to Mother. He was just another problem for them and would be dealt with no differently to how they dealt with any other problems. The same as how Turner would deal with a problem. How could he have been so stupid as to have thought the Bugganes would let him live? He had just been a puppet for Mother to play with, and now his strings were broken, he was useless. They would be after him, as they would be after everyone else. He wanted to run, but where he would go he had no idea, he couldn't escape from them. He had to keep calm. He had to settle himself, give himself time to think. He could surely get out of this, he just didn't yet know how.

The two girls had managed to pull Turner off Coombs, who gave him a hearty slap on the back for being such a good sport, and went and casually sat back down, as though it had all been a bit of a joke. Coombs rubbed his eyes hard and looked more than relieved that it was over and that he was still in one piece.

'Thank you for that… display…Turner, most enlightening,' said Mortis, and he sat back down on his chair, and once again turned his back away from the class.

This was most odd, the class seemed to think as one, and they all sat waiting for his next move.

He had to escape. Where would he go? There was no escape, they would be swarming over the landscape in less than a day. He had to get away. He looked at his watch. It was waterlogged and still told the time of the night before when he had emerged from the stream in Glen Maye waterfall. He tapped on it angrily. He could catch a boat maybe, or a plane, and get off the island, or hide somewhere they might never find him, in a cave perhaps. How ironic, he thought, this is exactly what the Bugganes must have felt like when men first invaded the island over a thousand years ago when they had to take shelter under the earth, away from danger's reach. He had to do something. He couldn't just sit there. He was wasting time. They might even be after him already. Mother must have expected him to bring her the map hours ago. She may have sent guards to seek him out by now. He had to run.

He spun the chair around and stood up sharply. The chair fell back and knocked the empty cabinet onto the floor. The glass shattered loudly, and everyone jumped. They now looked frightened. His eyes were wild. They were only children, they didn't stand a chance. A lump grew in his throat. They were all so innocent.

'I have…somewhere else I've got to be,' he stuttered.

'Where?' the class collectively grumbled.

'N…not here.'

His shoes crunched on the broken glass as he walked around the desks and briskly headed for the door. He looked at his classroom. What a shambles it was. The shelves were on the floor, all his precious antiques were everywhere but where they should have been. He couldn't see his beautiful black baubles anywhere…he should have liked to take them with him. But what did it matter, Mother had been right about how worthless it all was. None of it could be enjoyed in the grave.

He felt guilty for leaving the children all hanging there. They too would have nowhere to run when the time came.

'Er… consider this a study period,' he said, stepping over all the books and papers littering the old wooden floor.

'But you haven't set us any work sir,' protested Harper, who was more concerned that he stayed so they might find out what was wrong with him, not that they had no work to do.

Mortis reached the door and turned to them, again looking at their harmless expectant faces, faces that would haunt him forever.

'How about the apocalypse, that should come in handy. Do excuse me.'

He threw open the door, and exited into the corridor, only to bump into Charlie Colbourn, the Head of School, who had no doubt been sent to see what all the noise coming from his room was. Mortis didn't want to talk to anyone and quickly passed him, rushing down the hall to the stairwell before he had a chance to say anything. Heads were stuck out of every door along the corridor, eager to see what all the fuss was about. Mortis couldn't look at a single one of them. Their stares felt like they were burning into him, into the real shameful person beneath.

As he ran down the stairs towards the quad, a few words span round in his mind like a broken record:

'What have I done?'

THIRTEEN

'Head straight down the valley towards the main road, we'll have to cross it there somehow. It's bound to be busy at this time of the morning but it saves us going closer to the town, and I don't think we can afford to stray any further away.'

'You're right,' said Bea, pacing down the mountain and keeping close to the border of the field, which rose up a few feet from the ground. The light morning's frost was already beginning to thaw and Bea could feel how sodden the ground had become under the leathery souls of his feet. The air smelt of damp pine and the cold burnt inside his nostrils.

'Once we've reached the far side of the village, there's a footpath that leads up alongside a small river, I think it's well sheltered, we can follow that, that's best don't you think Bea?'

'I don't know Juan,' Bea admitted, 'I'm afraid I'm trusting you this time.'

Juan felt a small tremor swell in his stomach. Of course, he thought, it was likely Bea had never seen these places. He would have no reason to travel through these peopled villages, perhaps risking being seen. His life was in the solitude of the forests and the barren lonely coastline, not here, where every glance could mean trouble.

Juan closed his arms tighter around Bea's shoulders as they descended. He tried not to think of Téeval, who they were to call upon for help. He tried to force the thought of her as far back in his mind as he could. This was impossible. Would she have the answers? Could she return him to his family? He ground his teeth down hard. No, he said to himself, don't think about her, just look ahead and face what's before you, the answers will come when they are meant to, that's what Bea would say.

Sophia flew up and landed in the hood of Juan's fleece and pulled the wool around her as Bea slowed down and cautiously began to stoop. Juan could feel his heart quicken, and Bea's breaths became short and shallow as a motorcar sped past them, only a few feet away on the other side of the border.

The beginning of the journey was much the same, and painfully slower than they would have liked, stopping and waiting to pass through breaks in the hedgerows and crawling out of sight as anyone passed them. Though Bea and Sophia were both used to this, and could seemingly disappear into the greenery whenever they chose to, Juan felt particularly unusual hiding away from his own folk, as though he himself was a threat.

And still the time moved on.

Juan couldn't help looking up to the ever-rising sun – a blurred white disk behind the clouds – and feeling his nerves quicken as he wished their progress could be swifter.

As they passed through the haggard oak trees near an old disused campsite and came to the stone wall separating them from the main road they sat down and leant against it. It was nearing the height of the morning, and the hum and coughing of motorcars was ceaseless behind them. Juan looked over at Bea, who looked back at him just as blankly. Neither of them had any answer to offer the other, so they sat there on the hard ground in silence, tense and edgy.

It wasn't long before Sophia suddenly rose from her rest as fast as a dart, and Juan saw her eyes widen as she looked down the pathway adjacent to the road.

'Someone's coming,' she hissed. 'Three of them; a couple, and they've got a dog with them, it looks like a fierce one too.' Juan squinted and could make them out in the distance, a middle aged couple wrapped up with gloves and hats and scarves, being pulled along by a vicious white pit-bull terrier in front of them. The dog was frantically sniffing the ground, but as yet hadn't noticed them.

'We're trapped,' said Bea, looking around him hoping to find some form of shelter. 'If we move, they're bound to see us. It's too far to get to that clump of trees over there. We have to cross this road now. It's our only chance. That dog will pick up our scent at any moment.'

Right enough the dog's nose twitched and he sprung to attention, growling and foaming at the mouth. The man struggled with the lead, gripping it with both his gloved hands before the dog's strength overpowered him and he began to hurtle straight towards them. Bea looked over the wall, but saw only the big hunks of coloured metal flying past his eyes leaving a bitter stench of smoke and burnt rubber. He looked back at the dog, now only a hundred paces away from them.

Juan, panicking alongside him, patted his body, hoping that he might find something, anything, of use. He then reached into the pocket of his trousers and pulled out a small handful of conkers. He looked down at them, they were all he had. So, to both Bea's and Sophia's surprise, he stood up and threw the conkers as hard as he could over the passing motorcars to the far side of the road. The dog, seeing them, and not being a terribly bright creature, flew from his path towards them, leapt over the wall into the onslaught and whipped straight across the road to his prize on the far side. The woman shrieked as every motor screeched to a halt, some skidding and colliding with those in front of them, and the sound of brakes sharply whistled through the crisp air.

Bea didn't hesitate a moment for the opportunity to pass, and bounded over the wall and through the path left by the pile-up into the overgrowth on the far side. Juan followed as fast as he could, with Sophia curled up inside his hood. All the drivers seemed more concerned with hurling abuse, rolling down their windows and waving their arms at each other to notice them, and the pit-bull terrier strolled back past the havoc that he had caused, biting and cracking his jaw proudly, with a mouthful of Juan's conkers. Juan stared straight ahead, wide-eyed and stunned that it had worked, and was ever so thankful for Bea's look of surprised gratitude greeting him behind the wall on the other side.

'Well done boy,' whispered Sophia in his ear.

With his spirits immediately higher from the success of the ploy, Juan eagerly rose from behind the wall to continue on and up towards the nearby footpath, but Bea put a firm arm between him and his path and pulled him back down fast. Though they spoke no words, Juan realised his mistake and knew it was necessary to wait until fewer people were lingering behind them. A small crowd had gathered by the side of the road, and through the wind they could hear the muffled shouts and curses not ten paces away.

It was hard waiting there behind the wall. All three of them were twitching with eagerness to be on their way. Bea momentarily rose up as if to spring his way into the distance, but hesitated, thought better of it, and returned to his place. He felt the frustrating impatience growing in his chest, burning, and tried to swallow it back down and calm himself. Every time he blinked he saw his parents behind his eyes, and felt their cold, hunger and fear. He looked towards the sun. It was still rising on its morning ark, and wouldn't stop, ever, not even for him, however much he wished it. Time was unstoppable.

Slowly the crowd got bored and went on their way, and after Juan thought everything had returned to normal, he pointed out the path they were to follow and they set off once more.

Everything here was so unusual to Bea. The fields were smaller and the fences were tighter, everything had become clustered and muddled together, squashed in on itself, unlike the wild abandon of the coast he knew so well, where the grass grew freely. He felt more than thankful for Juan being with him and knew that without him he would be lost, as would Sophia. Ellan Vannin was small enough, but the pastures they inhabited were very different. As his father had taught him, these peopled places were avoided at all costs.

Soon they reached the simple well-worn footpath that ran nearby the narrow ambling river, and Juan insisted that he walk by himself alone, and in front of the others who were to keep out of sight.

He knew it was inconsequential whether he was seen by any passers-by, but he couldn't imagine that there would be many at this time of day. They were gradually walking up to higher ground and it was bound to be very blustery and unappealing where they were heading.

Sure enough, there was no one else around, and as Juan trudged upwards, pushing his hands against his knees to help him, he had to call out to feel safe that his friends were still with him.

'We're right here Juan, don't worry,' came Bea's deep soft voice in answer, barely a few paces from where he stood.

Juan looked around him, but couldn't see any sign of them, so he pulled his hood up over his head and marched on, with the wind pushing him faster on his way.

The island was now truly awake. It had rubbed the sleep from its eyes and had settled into the passage of another day. No doubt elsewhere, workers were working, scholars were schooling, money was being earned and bills were being paid and the wind blew on, just as it did here. It was practically forcing Juan into a run. He tried to resist it at first, but that seemed to take more strength than just accepting its aid and letting it take his weight. He felt its hands envelope him and push him on, and when looking down he saw that with every step he was covering at least three times the distance than was surely possible with a single leap. He looked around him but could still see no sign of Bea or Sophia. He called out again, but his voice was lost in the rushing air. He could only hope they were still with him as he sped on.

He reached the end of the footpath sooner than he could have imagined, and came to an abrupt halt in a trough just below the peaks of the highest mountains of the island. The wind was spinning in every direction and the whole landscape swayed to and fro, like an angry sea. As he turned around, Bea was there once more, directly behind him, his mane of hair swaying like the grass in the fields. He rested his hand down on Juan's shoulder, and Sophia flew over and clung to his fleece.

'There has to be a quicker way,' she protested, flying in front of them and hovering in her place, 'these fields stretch around for miles. We've wasted too much time crawling through the blessed undergrowth as it is. The sun's rising at every moment, can't you do something Bea?'

Bea looked back into her desperate eyes, and felt her need only too sharply. They couldn't keep straying off track from the journey to keep out of sight. There must be other avenues available to them.

Juan wiped the cold sweat from his forehead on the back of his sleeve. The long grass in front of them was dancing with the wind, and the ever-moving shades of green passed over it as the sun shone between the clouds overhead. Further down in the field four horses were playing and grazing on the long grass. The eldest was a large muscular thoroughbred, the chestnut colour of autumn leaves, with thickening fetlocks ready for the winter. He was looking over the mare, whose ears were stretching forward as she watched two fillies playing and rubbing their faces in each other's necks; one was black and one was piebald with a white muzzle down her face. The sight both cheered and saddened Juan.

'Look,' he said, pointing over to the pack. 'They look happy, don't they? They've got each other.'

Bea looked their way, and as soon as he saw them he knew what was to be done. He pursed his lips and let out the softest whistle, not a high piecing note, but more of a low chord, as though there were many notes in its one sound. Juan thought it was hardly a sound at all and would be far too quiet to catch the attention of the horses, but their ears immediately pricked up in unison, and they jointly cantered over to where they stood, their black eyes both expectant and concerned.

The older chestnut thoroughbred went straight to Bea and stretching his neck over his shoulder, reverentially embraced him. Bea returned the embrace and stroked him gently down his withers. Sophia hovered over the horse and scratched him behind his ear, making him neigh with pleasure.

The two fillies found Juan a curious thing, and sniffed his fleece and nudged him in his side. Juan was equally curious of them, but as his initial anxiety quickly left, he also stroked their necks and let them lick his cold hands. The filly with the white muzzle was especially eager to do this, and her rough, grainy tongue warmed and tickled Juan's palm.

Bea hunched over and whispered in his companion's ear. Juan tried to listen but couldn't make out any words that he understood. As Bea went on, the chestnut horse's ears moved far back and he nodded and shook his head in what looked to be great worry. He turned to the others, stamped a hoof on the ground and neighed, they then quickly gathered around him, sharing in the news that Bea gave them exchanging looks with their deep frowning black eyes.

Once Bea had finished, the horse threw his head back, making his mane quiver in the wind. Bea turned to Juan and Sophia.

'We are to follow them, it will be much quicker this way.'

'But we're right out in the open…'

'We are to follow them,' Bea repeated, cutting Sophia off short. 'I promise you, it will be much quicker this way.'

As they walked out behind the mare, who had chosen to lead the way, the other three horses crowded around them, in a tight diamond. Bea crouched down below the smaller of the two fillies, and Sophia exclaimed 'I get it!'

Juan did the same, and as their pace quickened he knew they were invisible within the shape. Any one who saw them from a distance would see only the family of horses running together.

Juan struggled to keep up at first, but he soon got used to the pace, and as he looked to the side of him, he was almost certain the filly with the white muzzle winked at him. He stole a glance from Sophia, who looked just as bewildered as he was. But they were finally making headway, and Bea felt the relief of not crawling through the thorns and hedges. At this rate they would reach the Bay of Dhoon before the sun reached the top of its journey. They had to. The choices left to them were dwindling, as though their eyes were being blinkered to one path alone: the journey ahead of them.

The speed of the horses grew and grew, and though it took Juan a heave of momentum to catch up with them, it then seemed to become surprisingly easier, like having a firm hand at the base of his back urging him and helping him along. He could hardly believe the speed he was running by himself. His legs weren't even burning anymore. His eyes were watering with the wind against them and his chest felt tight but he didn't feel any weariness or need to pause for breath. He felt like he could go on like this for hours. He was a feather caught on a gust of wind and blown on its way.

Several places he recognised passed by them as they ran; the valleys and restful farmland near Close Mooar and the quiet path down the hills dwarfed under Snaefell, the highest mountain on Ellan Vannin, but there was no time to pause.

They leapt over the old tramline, which lead the way up to the top of the mountain and all the while the only sound to be heard was the drumming of the hard hooves of the horses ceaselessly beating out their rhythm across the land.

The male horse to the side of them threw his head back and whinnied loudly against the wind, his large teeth gleaming white in the light of the day. Bea shouted to the others over the din.

'They will be leaving us just ahead, where those trees make a break in the path. When they do, we'll be shot out like a pebble from a catapult. Don't try to stop yourself or your legs will be likely to break from under you, just keep running until you're sure you're in control of yourself again.'

Juan swallowed and nodded as he saw the trees rushing closer towards him, like a wall of sharp bark and a web of branches. He shielded his face with his hands, and as he closed his eyes, they hit it.

He couldn't equate the feeling of leaving the horses to anything else, possibly being shot from a cannon, he thought, as he lurched forward with an unimaginable force. His legs suddenly couldn't keep up with the pace he was going, and began to crumble beneath him, all the breath left his lungs and he choked as he tried to bring air back to his buckling body. Everything hurt in an instant and he fell forward. The branches and twigs snagged at the bare backs of his hands and face, and he yelped at the smarting pain as he rolled forward and span into the dirt of the clearing on the other side and came to a stop, winding himself on his knees.

Breath returned to his body, like bursting out of water and he coughed and spat out the dried mud inside his mouth. He looked back through the trees, but could see no sign of the horses on the other side. Nearby Bea, lying on his back, pushed himself up on his elbows with what looked to be a great deal of effort and discomfort. Juan scrabbled to his feet and ran over to his side.

'Are you all right Bea, do you need to rest?'

'I'm fine,' he answered, biting down against the pain. Juan could clearly see that he wasn't. He had fortunately fared better than the Fynoderee in the fall.

'Juan's right,' said Sophia, flying out from the hood of his fleece, a little disarranged, her hair freed from its locks and dangling down over her tiny shoulders, but otherwise looking uninjured. 'We all need at least some rest to catch our breath, it'll do us no good running until we collapse.'

Bea reluctantly fell down onto his back, breathing heavily. He knew Sophia was right. What use would he be if he couldn't even stand? He felt a burning wetness on his arm, and reached over to grab it.

'You're hurt Bea.'

'I'm fine,' he said again, curtly. 'You're cut as well.'

Juan cautiously put his fingers to his face, and felt a sharp sting along his cheek. He looked down to his hand and saw the shockingly bright red droplets of blood on his fingertips. He was startled by its redness, as though he was expecting it to be dark and syrupy and rubbed his thumb and fingers until it disappeared into his skin.

'I'll try and find some dock leaves to stop the bleeding. You stay there,' said Sophia, forcefully pushing at Bea's chest. He lifted himself up and wearily propped up against a tree behind him. Raking his fingers back through his matted hair he let both his arms drop to the ground and his head lean back. Juan looked over at the cut on Bea's arm, a deep but clean slice running the whole length of his shoulder, opening up like a devilish smile.

'Don't let him move whilst I go and see what I can find, Juan. Talk to him.' And Sophia flew off into the trees, until Juan could no longer see her glow in the still low light.

Juan watched the wound on Bea's shoulder, as it appeared to

close up before his eyes, the smile turning into a grimace and the hair around it seemingly dissolving into a white powder and falling to the floor.

'Why does it do that Bea?' Bea looked to the cut, unconcerned.

'Like I said before, it's just different,' he said, unwilling to go on further.

'But why?'

Bea sighed, looked over at Juan and smiled a weak but warm smile. 'You don't give up do you?' he said, propping himself up further into the seat of the base of the tree.

'I don't know if my kind is any older than yours. We've never known that. But I do know that we were walking upon Ellan Vannin long before your kind ventured here on boats of timber from the east, as though you had sailed out of the sun itself, with your weapons and tools of iron and flint. We grew as the island grew. As the winters grew colder, our hair grew thicker, and as the trees grew higher we became stronger.' He sat and wondered how he could explain it easily to Juan without confusing him too much.

'There is a bird that feeds on a particular worm that only inhabits the weeds and marshes a little north of here, but the mud in these marshes is quick and deep, and gets more so with every passing year. Now the bird doesn't want to have to go elsewhere for its meal, it likes it as it is, and so its feet have grown long and wide so it doesn't sink and can feed on the worm without fear of being sucked down into the depths of the marsh. This took more time than you can think of, but still that bird adjusted and grew to survive and endure. It was the same with us; we changed and moved with the current of nature until we were in harmony with its tune.' Bea looked over at Juan, getting all his attention before continuing.

'Whereas man-folk define themselves by constantly and obsessively striving to better the environment around them, to make it easier or more pleasing, sometimes with success and sometimes without, we were simply another part of nature, not standing above it, but slowly moving in its current.

'When we pass on and leave the island for different shores, in thanks, our bodies fall and nourish the soil and earth that has been our home for our mortal life. It is said that the better life we have led and the happier we are at the moment we leave our bodies, the greater good we will do to the land that has provided us with warmth, shelter, food and company. We will become a very part of the land that our children will walk on.'

Juan let the cold grass run through his fingers and marvelled at Bea's words, and what would become of him. He watched as Bea flicked the hair off his face in the breeze, his skin was thick and taut from the sea breeze and the tales of his life had already made their mark in the fine lines of his features.

Bea saw Juan's hand in the grass and pulled out a tuft himself, holding it up and letting the torn strands blow from his hand and be carried away by the wind.

'If you were to halve everything down, over and over, enough times, I expect you would at some point, and after a very, very long time, be left with the same base matter: earth, air, water and fire and I don't know what. And if that's the case, surely everything is connected in a way much stronger than we know.' He lay his hand back down on the grass.

'The way I see it is there isn't any space between any of us, we are all connected to everything in some way, throughout everything.'

Juan was struggling to grasp Bea's meaning, it sounded like something that wasn't meant to be read from a dusty book somewhere but passed on and told just as Bea was doing, spoken quietly and thoughtfully down through time. But who had Bea to tell it to now?

'Bea?' he asked, sitting up onto his haunches, and pulling his fleece tight around him. 'What will happen now? You said you were the last one left, that there were no more like you.'

'That's what I thought, but the stones said that perhaps that wasn't so. No, truthfully, they didn't say anything. But when my eyes were closed it was as though I could still see, and in the distance where the hills met, I glimpsed a figure, like me, running through the pastures towards the forest.'

Juan looked at him intently, his eyes aglow.

'It was only a glimpse mind you, like remembering a dream during the day. I don't even know what the vision means, but for that moment my heart didn't feel alone.'

Juan quickly moved and knelt beside him, eager to catch the giving mood he was in.

'And what about…'

'I believe nothing would satisfy your curiosity!' Bea broke in, feigning frustration. 'If you saw a piece of glass at the bottom of the ocean, you would have to swim all the way down there just to check that it wasn't a diamond.'

Juan apologetically shrugged as a big smile spread across Bea's face. 'You are so like…' he suddenly cut himself short and fell silent, aware that he had said too much.

'Céa, your brother?' Bea looked over to Juan, his green eyes instantly wet with memory.

'Yes,' he answered softly, combing his hair back from his face once more. 'You really don't miss a thing do you?'

'Would you tell me about him Bea?'

Bea paused, taking a slow and deep breath to settle himself.

'Please?' Bea shifted his weight and turned his body towards Juan.

'Céa was my younger brother, my only brother. He was very curious, always asking questions, even from me, thinking that if he didn't know the answer it was more likely that I would.' He let out a small laugh as the memories returned to his mind. 'He would never leave any subject untended until he'd soaked up everything there was to know about it. He was hungry to know everything about life and the lives of man-folk especially. He would get as close to your people as he could, always risking being seen. He enjoyed watching you all so much. He used to rush back to Fleshwick Rock and tell us all about what he'd learnt that day. About your funny habits of having neat and tidy patches of land behind your houses so you can feel you have a touch of control over nature, or all the absurd clothes you dress yourselves in to show that you are better than one another.' Juan smiled at the thought of him. 'He made us all laugh. That's what I remember the most; laughing around the table in the hall, the fire roaring in the corner. You may pity us for our simple ways, but there is no need, we had happiness and light in our lives.

'But Céa came back one night and spoke of rumours and whispers in dark corners, of the Buggane's plans to reclaim the land for their own. He started to follow the whispers. Father told him not to, warning him that if he got too close to the fire he was likely to get burnt. But Céa was reckless and paid no heed to him. He began going out at night searching for any Brothers and Sisters, just to overhear their plans. Each night he would tempt the fire and get closer and closer to them, becoming arrogant, thinking that he would never be seen. Father, in turn, became more worried and told me to follow him. I asked "What can I do?" and he just replied, "Protect him." I felt terrible following my own brother and watching him without his knowing, but I considered Father's wishes above my own displeasure.' Bea paused and took several more calming breaths before continuing.

'One night, a cloudless night when every star shone out as clearly as if they were jewels in the palm of your hand, and the moon was full and bright, I followed him, knowing it would be a hard night to keep to the shadows. It wasn't too far from Fleshwick that Céa discovered three Bugganes up where the rocks jut out like an arched spine. I made sure I kept well back out of sight, but I could still see Céa shifting with the colours of night and the land, and walking directly behind them, listening. Though in *arraghey*, one of the Bugganes saw him well enough, as though his disguise went entirely unnoticed, and like a crack of a whip, her arm span out and caught him by the throat. I ran towards them and saw that it was Atta, their Queen, right there out in the open, as if she owned the land she walked upon. She seemed delighted by her catch, as were Brother Ivor and Brother Steele, and you know their faces.'

Juan saw the craggy gargoyle-like faces flash through his mind, a memory from only two nights ago, that still made him shudder. Bea seemed to be struggling even more with his words and clenched his fists tight, not looking at Juan as he spoke but down at the dirty ground. He hadn't noticed that Sophia had returned with the leaves in her grasp and was sitting on a branch only a few paces away, quietly listening.

'Queen Atta's wants and needs jar with the true nature of the island. She is very much separate from it. She believes through the entire length of her body that this land is hers.' He picked up a handful of earth and let it crumble in his fingers. 'This land is not hers as much as it is not ours. My father always said that we are guests here, and should behave as such.' He knew he was straying off the point, and quickly corrected himself.

'A Fynoderee does not fight to attack, it is not our way, we would only raise our fists to defend. But our defence was slow, and they had swiftly backed us up to the edge of the precipice. I remember what that wicked Atta said, she looked on us with those grotesque flaming red eyes of hers and said, "To think we are family!" and laughed. Why she said that I don't know, but she ran laughing at us, and kicked us both off the cliff and down towards the sea.

'As we fell, I caught Céa by the hand, my other scraping along the edge of the rock face until my grip caught on a small ledge of sharp rock which dug into my palm like a knife. Blood leaked out and spread down my arm as I looked down to Céa. He was so helpless, with such fear in his eyes. He stared at me and cried "Don't let me fall Bea, please don't let me fall." It was the final thing he said. As the moon glared down on us, he slipped from my hand into the clutches of the rocks and to his grave in the waves below.' He stared down at his shaking hands and fingered the scars along his palm, refusing to let any more tears fall from his eyes.

Sophia flew over and landed in his empty palm. He closed his fingers gently around her and cradled her to him, forcing a smile, though she could clearly see the bare pain in his eyes.

'Let's take a look at this wound then shall we?' she said gently, flying round to his shoulder. Bea silently leant back against the tree once more, 'it has had time to bleed a little, so it'll heal soon enough.' Bea knew she was speaking about more than the cut on his shoulder, but he didn't mention it. Though it bruised to speak about Céa, it also felt easier, as though the baggage of his memory was being tended to by more than his own weakening shoulders. He looked over to Juan, who sat quietly staring at the ground. He reached out to him and patted his leg.

'But all of this doesn't mean my love for the Bugganes ceases.'

'Love? For them? How can you love them, they've murdered your brother and stolen your family? Those beasts don't deserve you love.' Juan felt himself getting hot and angry.

'You may be right, but I love them all the same. They show me what is good and what is not. This is deserving of my love. How else would I know?' Juan couldn't summon a reply to this.

'When I see the Bugganes and hear of their actions I know them to be wicked and harmful as certainly as I know night to be night and day to be day. This brings me clarity and love for them.

'It is the same with a young child. When it first rises onto its two feet and stumbles it knows the feeling to be pain and it cries. How does it know this pain to be a bad thing, to be the opposite of when its mother cradles it in her arms? It just does.' Bea's eyes grew wide and his voice lowered. 'But this doesn't mean that I won't stand in the Bugganes' way when the time comes.'

Juan gulped, but didn't feel like talking anymore. There had been enough words and questions spoken and asked. He felt his worries and troubles paled when he thought of Bea's pain and loss. How dare he have such worries after what Bea had been through? The Fynoderee looked over to him.

'Never think that Juan, ever,' he said firmly. Juan was surprised at how Bea seemed to know what he was thinking. 'We'll get them back, don't you worry. You'll be back with them soon enough and all this will seem like some ghastly dream that you'll be able to laugh at before long. Aww!' he yelled, as Sophia squashed bits of chewed dock leaf into his cut.

'Be quiet you great oaf! Don't be such a baby,' she ordered, taking more of the sodden chewed leaf from her mouth and forcing it into the wound. 'We cannot leave our past, we can only hope that one day it might leave us.'

'Well if you'd be a little more careful…'

'Oh, stop it! A big Fynoderee like you, whinging over a nick like that, whatever next?' Sophia rolled through the windy air, her untangled hair flowing with her graceful movements, and fluttered in front of them.

'Now if I'm not mistaken we still have an appointment to keep. By my watch…' She pointed up to the sky and the sun was still partially hidden behind the clouds, 'it is just about midday, and I hear it is very rude to keep Téeval waiting. We still have a lot to do, if all this wretched business is to be dealt with. So once you are quite ready…'

'All right, all right,' protested Bea, heaving himself up to standing and smiling a genuine smile. Juan lifted himself up also. He was more than a little relieved at Sophia's mocking tone, and felt ready to go on. Sophia was right; they couldn't be late for the Princess of the Ocean.

'Juan, if you could lead the way, we'll follow like before. I doubt there'll be anyone about on a day like this, I'll bet they are all sensibly indoors burning a good fire. I know where I'd rather be. But be that as it may, this duty has fallen into our hands, for some reason known only to Manannin himself, so we had better do it as best we can. Lead on.'

And so, in the shallow light of the end of the morning, Juan walked from the path, through the old gate, limp on its rusty hinges, and began the descent that would take them all the way down to Dhoon Bay, and a most unlikely meeting.

FOURTEEN

Juan stepped through the squeaking, fragile gate and closed it before beginning his descent. The gate banged behind him in the growing breeze of the late morning and he once again felt alone as he took his first few cautious steps down through the sticky muddy path, his shoes squelching beneath him. Though he couldn't see or feel any sort of presence nearby, he assured himself that both Bea and Sophia were indeed there. Whether it was behind the next tree he passed or further down past the rocks, they were somewhere very near, watching him.

The trees stretched high and their branches hung wide at the top of the path, like the splayed fingers of a hand ready to snatch a passer-by and the light wrestled with the branches to sift through and touch the floor. Juan had to slow his pace and jam his heels hard down with each step he took as the path became gradually steeper and the mud was more slippery underfoot. The air was moist and sweet from the spray of the thin waterfall running it's course towards the bay not far away. He knew he would soon be there once the path fell and crossed in front of the fall.

On more than one occasion he stepped down onto a smooth wet rock or a thick patch of slimy moss and his feet flew from beneath him and he landed hard down on his back, with his hands, back and hair newly caked in the mud from the path. The first time, a low, grunting snigger came from the overgrowth ahead of him, but when he snapped his head towards the sound, he caught no sight of anything but the rustling greenery.

The path snaked its way down the side of the coastline and the hissing of running water grew in Juan's ears. He held on hard to the weak rickety wooden fence that lined the path at its steepest turns, and took large, slow steps to prevent falling anymore. If he slipped another time he could, if he wasn't careful, fall into the rocky basin below.

The rocks became more slippery with every new step and everything began to shine with a silvery sheen as he emerged alongside the waterfall. Its refreshing mist sprayed out in all directions and droplets fell from the bracken, hanging onto the branches of every tree, like pearls.

Juan would usually splash his mother and father when they reached the waterfall, relishing in their screams as he kicked out waves of the cold water straight at them. He tried not to think too heavily on them as he saw an unfamiliar face staring right back at him from the wall of water toppling down from several feet above him. He jumped back and feebly raised his fists in front of him in protection. The figure copied him and raised his fists in exactly the same manner. He then stared closely at the filthy face, blood shot eyes and sunken cheeks of the strange boy staring straight back at him and realised he was sparring with his own reflection. He lifted his hand and waved at himself to make sure, and sure enough his other self did the same. He hardly recognised the boy in front of him, indeed it wasn't a boy but a young man, weary and hardened by his adventures, but stronger and more resolute than before. It might have been his imagination, but the round face that would always greet him in the mirror when he washed in the mornings seemed thinner, and was covered in layers of grime. He wasn't shocked or upset by what he saw, quite the contrary, he stood up tall and found himself impressed by the dirty mud stained wild figure in the water. This was someone the bullies Cairney and Creeses would no longer feel so comfortable confronting, they would hardly dare go near him he bet.

He pushed out his chest, turned his back on his new self and continued down with the flowing water gently lapping next to him, skipping faster as the path turned to pebbles and finally opened up onto Dhoon Bay.

The vista of the bay opened out like a mouth as he walked over the crunching stones. His path led directly into the centre of the cove and if he squinted his eyes, he could block out any visible sign of the coastline and be only able to see the dark green sea flooding out, as though that was all there was–nothing but the sea.

The scent of salt and seaweed was intoxicating and the spiking white waves seemed to be breathing their way closer into the shore. Juan looked over to his right. The rocks of the coast towered upwards like giants' fists raised in triumph, all gnarled and craggy, and the seagulls were hiding from the wind in the cracks all the way to the top. This was always a place of fun for him; of buckets and spades and hide and seek, where he would draw pictures of his parents and sister in the damp sand near the water's edge with his big toe, then watch them disappear as the tide came in.

Looking up, he could see that the sun was high now. It must be midday, he thought.

The wind was rapidly picking up and the dark low clouds were racing against each other overhead. The sea looked to be fighting against itself and the white horses of the crests of each wave were darting and leaping each and every way shooting spray up into the air.

'It's nearly time,' said Bea over Juan's shoulder. Juan didn't flinch. He had become very quickly used to his reappearances.

'You can feel it Juan, in the air, can't you?' said Sophia, who flew up and landed on his other shoulder, pulling herself into the wool of his fleece, and wiping the spray from her face.

'I think I can,' said Juan. 'It certainly feels very different from the last time I was here.' Maybe it was something in the smell of the air, something sharper and wilder, as though a storm could break out at any moment.

'It's Téeval,' said Bea. 'She's close by, and angry if I'm not mistaken. All we have to do is call her.'

'And how do we do that?' asked Juan. 'Just shout out her name, or whistle or something, like you did with the horses?'

'No, I think she still prefers to be summoned by the old method, and we don't want to get on the wrong side of her before we've even exchanged two words. Check your pockets would you Juan.'

Juan didn't see much point in that, he'd kept his cold hands buried deep inside them for miles and miles and he knew they were empty. But as he pushed his hands further down into them he suddenly felt two circular objects that he was certain weren't there before, like large baubles. Bemused, he pulled them out and there in his hands were two deathly black orbs. He instantly recognised them as those from the shelves of Mr. Mortis' classroom.

'But how did you…'

'I spotted them when we were looking for the map and swiped them. Thank Manannin I did see them, it was thought there were none left.'

'What are they?' Juan asked, looking down at them and the air around them like the night sky.

'They are old Calling Stones, etched out of rock taken from far below the seabed. All you've got to do is knock them together under the water, and up she comes…apparently…I think…though I've never seen it done.'

'What? You want *me* to…'

'She probably wants to talk to you most of all, you're the one she called, remember?' said Sophia shoving him forward closer towards the outstretched fingers of the water.

Juan span around to protest to Bea and Sophia, but was only met with their mocking, resilient expressions and Sophia hovering and flapping her hand as if to say 'get a move on.'

'Oh well, here goes,' whispered Juan to himself and he knelt down placing both the Stones in the water.

The cold stung his hands more than he expected and the Stones suddenly felt heavier. As instructed he gently knocked them together, and no sooner had he done so than he pulled back his hands, jumped away from the edge and put the Stones back in his pockets. The percussion had produced a piercing screech, like whale music, reverberating out of the sea and over the desolate headland. A flock of surprised gulls flew up into the air and fled from the sound and Sophia squashed her tiny hands against her tiny ears.

As the wail went on Bea looked down to the water in shock. It seemed to be turning black before his eyes, as though oil was appearing from somewhere and pushing the clearer water aside with its silt. It was the same black as the Stones, so dark it fed off the light around it. He closed his eyelids halfway to concentrate on the sight even more and saw that in fact no colour was spreading out, but the pebbles and sand of the seabed were falling away. The bed was falling so far it faded to a depth that no light could penetrate. Surely no light and no life could come from such a place.

The cry from the Stones ceased as quickly as it began, only to be filled with the sound of fast moving water. The pebbles had fallen into the shape of a large star and the black water was beginning to turn inside it at great speed.

'Look! There!' cried Sophia over the din of the swirling water and pointing at one of the points of the star. Colours were emerging out of the dark. Tiny flickering colours like the slivers of glass from Fleshwick Rock, each producing a glistening light from the unfathomable depths.

The colours were growing quickly, turning the black to an ever-moving rainbow inside the whirlpool. The flecks of light looked to be alive and moving, and each one giving off a different colour. The star was an undulating liquid of every shade imaginable.

The water was now steadily spinning its whirlpool and then began to rise out of the sea. Juan, Bea and Sophia gasped as the circle of water rose out of the waves and continued to grow until it was even taller than Bea himself.

All three of them stared at the spinning curtain and through its colours Juan could see the definite outline of a person, silhouetted within the circle. He could swear it was a woman, standing tall and proud. He could feel his heart beating like a broken clock inside his chest and he felt unable to take a breath. His lungs were refusing to work.

Then the circle of water dropped. A shower of coloured droplets cascaded and rained out as the water hit the sea and every sound had gone, hushed in reverence of the lady that remained standing.

Both Juan and Sophia fell to the surface of the shore onto their knees. The immediate sight of Téeval pulled them down to humble praise. But Bea couldn't fall. He couldn't do anything but stand, gaping at her form.

She was no taller than any woman he had seen, but she still seemed to tower over them, effortlessly. Her presence held her on some higher plane.

A light of age, wisdom and grace shone from every pore of her ageless self. Her hair wound down like a waterfall of sandy ringlets stroked in light green seaweed and fell over her shoulders concealing her chest. Her eyes were a pure brilliant white and the colours of the sea swam in and out of them as though she alone contained the wonders of the ocean. Her delicate arms moved like a breeze at her side giving the impression she was still moving within water, and down past her stomach, like a white desert encrusted with a single pearl, began the scales of her tail.

The scales of her fin began low on her hips, curving like waves. Every scale shone like a separate jewel of the most radiant silver, turquoise, opal and ruby and the tip of her tail slowly flicked back and forth, gently keeping her above the sea. Bea could see now that the ocean was indeed hers and as a tear of joy fell from his eye he wanted to thank her for every time he had gazed upon it and the solitary comfort it gave him so often. The sea was hers and she was the sea's. They were inseparable lovers for all time, unmoved by the endless changes on land.

'My three children!' She greeted them with open arms. 'Do not bow your heads so and please rise from your knees. I am not one for pompous ceremony.'

Juan slowly stood up and submissively raised his eye line to meet hers as Sophia returned to his shoulder. A lump stuck in his throat as the gentle breathy voice of his own mother passed from her lips, and he knew it would be so with the others. He missed her so much it nearly suffocated him.

'I know you miss her little one,' she spoke softly, resting her gaze down upon his with her pale eyes. Juan could see the waves continue to battle with one another in her stare.

187

'And that is why you shall see her again. If you want something hard enough, it is only inevitable that it shall come to pass in time.'

'But I don't think we have much time…your…majesty.'

Téeval let out a warm laugh and smiled broadly down at them, her arms still lightly waving by her side. Time seemed to have slowed down in her presence. All the gulls had quietly disappeared back into their nests on the cliff face and the sea was beginning to tame around her.

'There is no need for such titles either. I was not born into my responsibility surrounded by traditions or fears, there were none back then. The sea smells as sweetly bitter to me as it does to you, the fish look no different, the sun still rises and sets for me as it does for you. But all too suddenly time is the one thing we are jointly lacking. It can pass so quickly. I can often miss the brief flicker of a passing day above me. The moon's journey can be barely a blink to me.' She flowed softly closer towards them, and her voice shrank to an intense whisper.

'The weight of these troubles rests on the backs of every living thing that strives for happiness and prosperity. But it is down to us to keep their fears at bay, and let the island live.'

'But can't we raise an alarm? Tell someone about what's going to happen? Thousands of lives are at stake, they could surely do something.' Juan knew that his voice sounded desperate.

'None must be told. We must keep the wool covering their sight secure. If the old world is revealed we have sentenced it to death. In an attempt to save one world we will have inadvertently killed another. Ellan Vannin is such an enchanted rock where the old world can still continue to live un-noticed. There are too few left.' She shut her eyes for a moment and paused.

'Then what must we do?' asked Bea, tense and dutifully resigned to the next struggle.

'Always so quick to get to work dear Bea, that is one of your best qualities.'

Bea felt himself blush and looked to the shore beneath his feet, embarrassed.

'Each of you has a new path ahead, and each of you will walk this path alone. As we cannot slow the falling of the sun then this is the price we must pay.' The voice of their separate mothers softened the blow of her news as a break in the overcast sky revealed a sword of sunlight cutting through the air and reflecting off her skin.

'Bea, since you are so eager to get started and you saved the life of our boy here, I leave it to you to save those who have been taken and are held in the snare of the Bugganes.'

'If I knew how to I would have got to them, and my parents, as soon as I could.' He was struck with an immediate panic that he wouldn't be able to help. 'But we, none of us, know how to get to them, or where their caves and tunnels are.'

'You are wrong Bea. There is one person who knows how to get inside, one person who can help you get to them, a man who has held a lifelong grudge against our world. This man's grudge led him to make an allegiance with the Bugganes, even after what they did to his kin centuries ago. They warned him of a boy who would bear strange markings on his skin and bade him find that boy. And find him he did, but you saved him Bea. An obsessive gentleman he is, steeped in the old lore of the island…'

'Mortis!' Juan shouted out. 'You mean Mr. Mortis don't you?! He must be the Watcher, Bea. The swine, I knew he wasn't acting like himself. I should have realised he knew something of this business. He was the teacher who had the map all along Bea. But why does he hate your world so much?'

'A long held vendetta and nothing more. Some people cannot forgive so easily. You must seek the help you need Bea from one who fears and hates you most. You must free those people before they become the first sacrifice.'

Juan's whole body shuddered at the very thought of it as Bea bowed his head in acceptance of his task.

'You, too, Sophia must seek the help of those who hate you most. You know of whom I speak.'

'You can't possibly mean the Forest Fairies, *mooinjer-veggey*! They'll pull off my wings as soon as I enter into the forest!'

'You have ingenuity in abundance little one. What you lack in ideas, you make up for with that bold mouth of yours. I believe you could talk your way out of anything. But remember, you have two ears and only one mouth; you should listen twice as much as you speak.'

Sophia swallowed and shrugged her shoulders apologetically.

'You must all act as the bait, the worm to the bird, and lure the Bugganes.'

'Lure them?...To where?' Sophia asked, regaining her composure.

'To me.' Téeval spoke with a soft, remorseless passion. Sophia couldn't help but smile and nod at Téeval's determination and brutal resilience. 'Join together at the slopes by Eairnyerey at sundown (you know that ground well Bea) and we shall endeavour to put an end to all of this nonsense.' She waited for a moment. 'Well, hurry along now, you have much to do. Juan will be safe enough.'

Bea squeezed Juan's shoulder, and Sophia flew up and gave him a small kiss on his cheek.

'See you at sundown,' she said, licking her hand and rubbing off the tiny purple lip marks she'd left on his face.

'Don't be late,' said Bea as they both left him and headed back up towards the trees and the path. Juan felt as though he could have burst into tears as he watched the backs of his new friends move further away and disappear, it was like having the little strength left in his muscles dragged out of him.

'Seek help from those who hate me? Impossible!' grumbled Sophia, as she caught up with Bea clambering uphill. 'They are meant to be my brothers and sisters, but I see no likeness between the *mooinjer-veggey* and me. I feel no bond or kinship to them.'

'But now you must plead for their help.'

'Only out of necessity, if we have no other possible allies, then we have no other possible choices. But it's only because she pulled my arm behind my back.' Bea could clearly sense her unease, and he gave her a sympathetic smile.

'As a youngster, not so soon after we met, Bea, I'd often fly and play in the forests and valleys on my own, where I was free to imagine I was someone else. I could think myself into a different form, because you can do that when you're alone, just close your eyes and think yourself into whatever you want to be. I would sleep and dream myself out of this form and into another, one that was faster, and stronger and kinder.'

Bea stopped and turned to her. 'You've never told me that before. What other form? Surely not man?'

'No,' Sophia answered softly and held Bea's gaze with her almond shaped eyes. She looked into his deep green eyes and her lips parted as if to speak, but no words came. Finally, after several moments that seemed to stretch out like a summer's evening, she looked away and shook herself before resting down into the palm of Bea's hand.

'I must go to where no light breaks,' she said.

'Yes, but you will still glow out, as you always do,' replied Bea, 'and you will be a light for those trapped in the dark.' He closed his palm gently, to embrace her on her way. 'Safe flight.' And so they turned and went their separate ways.

'Worry is a burden you can do without, dear one,' said Téeval down to Juan, her multicoloured tail still flicking majestically above the water. 'You must look to the task in your own hands.'

'What must I do?' he asked humbly, tensing his own body so she might not notice his quivering fear.

'That is not for me to tell you, you have already been told. All you must do is take a long hard look at yourself.'

'What?' he asked, taken aback by her words.

She spoke more pronouncedly this time and began slowly to move away from the shoreline, towards the centre of the star carved out by the fallen pebbles of the seabed. 'Take a long hard look at yourself.' And with a warm but wry smile she was gone, back down into the sea with barely a ripple to say she was ever there, the waves enveloping any sign of her existence.

Juan stood there agog, helpless and simply not knowing what to do. His heart was racing and he began to panic.

"Take a long hard look at yourself" he whispered in confusion. What did *that* mean? Bea and Sophia were the only people who might know. I should ask them, he thought.

He ran away from the coast and up the path as quick as he could to catch up with his friends. They were certain to know what Téeval meant.

'Bea?! Sophia?!' he yelled, scrambling upwards, slipping with every step, and practically running on all fours. No answer came and he ran on, still calling out at the top of his voice. What if he couldn't find them? What was he to do? It was just like those silly stories he was told when the one character you needed to tell the simple truth was the one character who happened to speak in mindless riddles.

'BEA?! SOPHIA?!' Where are you?!' he hopelessly shouted out again, and listened hard for any possible reply that he was afraid would never come. He was alone.

He had reached the waterfall and kicked out hard at the water in the small rock pool, sending a splash of droplets into the wall of the rock. He wanted to scream out in frustration, it just wasn't fair. He dug his nails hard into the palms of his hands and stared at his miserable looking reflection.

'What are you looking at?' he shouted at himself. 'You can't do anything right, can you?! " Take a long hard look at yourself" indeed! Well now I'm looking at myself, and all I can see is…'

He stopped. Something was different. What was it? He stared hard at himself. Something slight. He looked down at his dirty palms, turned them over and looked at the markings on the back.

They looked the same to him, but then he looked at them in the reflection of the water. They suddenly looked less like random markings, but somehow more legible.

'NOOOOOO!' he shouted out at the top of his voice. 'THEY'RE IN MIRROR IMAGE!' He hit himself across the face. How could he have been so stupid! He pulled off his fleece as fast as he could and threw it over onto the bank. Hurriedly he pulled his woollen sweater over his head and threw it aside as well, and then, as Téeval had said, he took a long hard look at himself.

The markings ran up the length of his arms and he had to hold them out to make straight lines of the symbols which now ran parallel to each other all down the top of his torso. In the reflection, the symbols were exactly like those from the map, so he was able to make sense of them quick enough. Nervously he began to read, starting at his left wrist:

Juan my boy, you are probably standing stripped to the waist in front of some looking glass somewhere. My sincerest apologies for this strange form of communication. I could have spoken to you in your dreams, but I was afraid you may have ignored me, after all, your dreams have been less than normal of late. No doubt you are wondering why you are here. To be brief, when I was still walking upon Ellan Vannin my affections fell upon a mortal, of course this was forbidden, but my love for her was too great, as was hers for me. She was a kind and simple woman who had survived a shipwreck, a true survivor. In her village she would later be known as just that, survivor, or in the old tongue, Kerruish. In short Juan, we are kin. And as I can't be with you in person I'm asking a little favour of you.

The only way the island can be saved is if all those from the old world want it to be saved. There are those who couldn't care less, and you must make them care. You must head to the Fairy Bridge and make them care again. They must want to save themselves. Otherwise we are lost. That is all. But Juan, do not be tempted by them, it is all shallow and meaningless. Do not be tempted.

Manannin.

On the back of his right hand, in much smaller symbols so that the message was fighting with itself for space, the words read.

Remember the Stones.

And on the back of his left hand the faint lines of unfinished symbols lay beneath the surface of his skin, hiding. He rubbed them with his thumb but there was no encouraging them just yet, they would appear when it was time.

These certainly had been a strange few days, thought Juan, dragging his wet hands through his hair. The relief was immense. He could have fallen down right there and slept in the shallow stream. The mist of the water clung to his goose-bumped skin and the beads rolled down over the letters on his body. He looked at himself once more. He had his task. That was all he knew. That was all he could think on. The Fairy Bridge. The tiny little stone bridge on a back road of the island. A bridge he had crossed twice everyday on the school bus for years, where he would look out and say 'Hello Fairies' along with every other person on the island who crossed it. He didn't think on Bea, or Sophia, or his mum or dad, or Aalin. His mind only had room enough for the bridge.

He waded out of the rock pool and threw on his sweater and fleece over his damp cold skin. His mouth felt dry, he wanted to drink and quench his thirst, but it would have to wait. He had his task, and it alone was what mattered.

FIFTEEN

'I am *not* going down there,' insisted Brother Fellick, stretching over the lip of the pit and holding his torch out into the abyss with his one remaining arm. The ash from the burning pitch fell like snow from the torch into the depths, where he could just make out two grey figures huddled close together. He turned away from the sight and stared firmly at Sister Nidor.

'Don't look at me, I'm certainly not going down there,' she spat indignantly, pushing Brother Fellick back against the wall of the tunnel, her paper-thin skin flapping loosely off her spindly arms. She glared at him with a face that had shrunken so much with hunger that barely her skull remained and her red eyes shone angrily from deep within their sockets. Brother Fellick lifted up the stump of his arm, wrapped in sodden black cloth still weeping at the tip, and cowered beneath Sister Nidor.

'I've already snapped off part of you,' she said, raising her hand as if to strike him, 'and believe me, I wouldn't be afraid to finish off the rest of you. It's been ages since I've had a good meal.' She didn't look like she was joking, and Brother Fellick was about to fend her off with his torch when the squat form of Brother Erle came between them.

'Cut it out you two! Sister Nidor, we're all starving, you know that, but it's less than a day until you can feed on as much flesh as your belly can take.'

She hissed at them both but seemed pacified for the moment and shoved Brother Erle out of the way. 'Well one of us has to go down,' she muttered, not so much under her breath that the others couldn't hear.

'Then why don't *you* go down, seeing as you're so eager?' leered Brother Erle, leaning back against the stone, biting off a long yellow nail and spitting it out onto the floor. The light from the torch flickered across the flat broken features of his round face. He too felt wary towards Sister Nidor, who was the cause of

196

196

196

his cracked nose, whilst she was in one of her more rash moods, but he would rather risk another fight than give her the satisfaction that he did what she told him to. His pride was too great to stand that.

'Oh shut up!' Sister Fellick threatened impatiently. 'I've already said that I'm not, and that's that. I don't know what happened to Sister Litch when she went down there, but by the sound of her screaming it didn't seem like she was enjoying herself.'

'One of us has to go. Brother Ordo made it perfectly clear we had to find where the final Fynoderee may be hiding…by any means necessary.' Brother Fellick now had a hint of desperation to his already raspy voice. 'To tell you the truth, I'd almost prefer to face what's down there than the sharp edge of Ordo's wrath.'

'That's decided then,' said Sister Nidor, grabbing him by the scruff of the neck and dragging him over to the edge of the mouth of the pit, his feet scrabbling for any grip in the dust. He just managed to knock her away with his stump before being thrown over and fell down onto his side, barely keeping hold of the torch.

'But Brother Ordo's not here, is he. I hear he's out with some guards looking for some map or other that Mother's after. So for the time being, I'm looking after number one,' he said, prodding his chest and scuttling back towards the short but tough Brother Erle. Sister Nidor eyed them both suspiciously.

'You seem to know a lot about what's going on,' she said, whilst itching the sore looking raw skin across her stomach. 'What else have you heard?'

'I've heard that Mother's frightened!' cried Brother Erle, eager to join in and play his part in the gossip.

'Mother frightened? What utter filth! Our Queen is frightened of nothing.'

'That's not true,' he persisted, rubbing his hands together and grinning a toothless grin. 'I've heard whispers around the tunnels that they've heard her screaming out in her sleep, screaming about some boy, some little boy from above ground. And that's not all,' he said, excited by the dangerous thrill of spreading rumours further, 'she's terrified of the Fynoderees, especially the one they call Bea. They say she only sleeps in short bursts because of worrying about him and what he could do. That's why we're here. We've got to find out from those two down there where their son is.' Brother Erle spoke in hushed tones, and although they were in the deepest tunnel in the colony, he still couldn't help tentatively glancing around him, afraid of being overheard. He knew the words he spoke were treason, and no punishment was too severe for that crime.

'I can't possibly believe Mother is frightened of one lousy Fynoderee,' scoffed Sister Nidor. 'And as for being frightened of a boy, that's just plain laughable.' She didn't suppress her chuckling.

'I'm only telling you what I heard. Besides, you saw what a state Brother Ivor and Brother Steele came back in. They looked like Sister Anik had been allowed to practice her skills on them for several hours,' said Brother Erle, shuddering at the thought of it.

Sister Nidor glared at them again. 'Let's talk about something else. You two are giving me the creeps.' She walked away from them to look into the darkness of the pit once more, trying to catch a glimpse of the ageing Fynoderees.

'Looking forward to tomorrow then?' asked Brother Fellick, casually, trying to bring things round to more exciting matters.

'I can't wait,' whispered Sister Nidor, half to herself. 'The thought of all that fresh meat makes me tickle all over. I can practically smell all that burning oak and pine. You just wait. Ash and smoke will fill the air alongside the music of tens of thousands of cries for help. It will be the finest day we have ever witnessed.'

She hadn't noticed that behind her back Brother Fellick and Brother Erle had exchanged brief glances of understanding. They had both been on the end of Sister Nidor's anger and come out the worse off, and since neither of them had any intention of venturing into the bottom of the pit, it seemed only fair that she should be the one to bear the duty. They had spotted their chance.

It was too easy. Only the slightest push was needed for Sister Nidor to loose her footing and fall face first downwards and out of sight. A short roar and a loud crack followed quickly afterwards. Brother Fellick and Brother Erle winced and looked at each other wide-eyed.

'How about we tell Brother Ordo that the Fynoderee's uncompromising behaviour continues?' asked Brother Fellick.

'I think that's a fine idea,' agreed Brother Erle, stroking the rim of the mouth until the rock's seam rejoined, and it was closed once more.

Sister Nidor scraped her hands and feet down the side of the pit as she tumbled and spiralled closer to the bottom, hoping there may be some imperfection in the rock that she could cling on to. There was none. The face of the pit was as smooth as polished marble.

She was caught at the bottom by a large leathery pair of hands which quickly grabbed her face to stun her, and wrung her neck like a chicken's, until it easily snapped out of joint and ended her life.

'If they keep on sending them down like this, we might be able to make a considerable difference to the size of their force,' said Bea's father, Dane, in his rumbling gruff voice, drolly tossing the limp body of the Buggane into a far corner, where the rest of her kin who had visited them lay.

'Don't speak like that Dane. I doubt it will be long now,' said Bea's mother, Méa, blinking hard. Her eyes had quickly got used to having the smallest speck of light above them and she was now trying to readjust to the total darkness once more. She reached out her hand into the dark until she found Dane's shoulder and pulled him close towards her. 'Once they realise they'll get nothing they want, they'll be sending down many more to deal with us.'

'Then we'll just have to defend ourselves,' said Dane tensely.

'Against so many? It will be hopeless, even you know that,' she said weakly, her breath wheezing heavily. 'We may not even have enough strength left to *arraghey*. I mean look at us, we're fading with every passing moment.'

She was right. Their fur was turning from its healthy bristling dark brown to a weak ashen grey. They both knew that once it had turned to white they would barely be able to lift themselves off the ground, besides defend themselves against some form of an attack. Méa was already surprised that Dane was able to deal with the last Buggane so swiftly.

He placed a consoling hand onto Méa's soft cheek, feeling her skin wrinkle under his palm as she smiled at his touch.

'Bea may be with us before we have to face any more…problems.'

'Bea may already be dead,' snapped Méa, pulling his hand away.

'Don't speak like that,' he said, holding her firmly by the shoulders and pulling her into an embrace. 'You know we'd feel something if that were the case. We taught Bea better than to go and rush headlong into the eye of the storm.'

'I know. I'm sorry,' sighed Méa. 'It's just that every time I close my eyes I can see Céa falling, and I want to reach out and catch him, but I can't, he just slips out of reach. And if something happened to Bea…' she began to sob uncontrollably into Dane's shoulder, gripping his fur in her fists. He so wanted to join her in the grief of loosing their youngest son. He so wanted to cry with her. But he forced his tears away. He had to be strong for both of them. He had to keep their hope alight. For that was all they had left: hope.

'Shh now,' he said calmly, brushing his hand down her hair. 'Try not to think about it, we need our remaining strength; you spoke truths. We may have to *arraghey* before the end. It'll be all right, you'll see. Who knows, by this time tomorrow we could be on the headlands near Fleshwick, feasting on fresh water and berries with all the smells of autumn brushing our nostrils.' Méa sniffed back a tear and groaned at how wonderful and yet how distant it all sounded. 'We can curl up into a bed of fresh hay, pulling the sheepskins up tight over us and listen to the crackling of the fire as it dies down while only the cinders remain to keep us warm for the rest of the night.' Méa imagined it all and smiled.

'And I can shout at Bea and Sophia to stop their bickering in the main hall and settle down,' laughed Méa.

'That's it,' said Dane, 'and we can sleep long into the day.'

Feeling her spirits lighten, Méa let go of Dane's embrace and looked into his lined face, brushing his mane away from his green eyes. Eyes Bea had inherited.

'It's strange,' she began, 'however hard I try to picture what the island might look like after the Bugganes have reclaimed it, every tree felled and every flower uprooted, I simply cannot see it…'

'That's because it won't happen,' said Dane surely. 'I can't see it like that either. That's because it will never be like that. Manannin loves his island too much to let it be taken from him. You just wait, you'll see.'

'But maybe all this is supposed to happen, maybe in some bigger picture this change is supposed to occur, just like those stories we heard when we were young about man first coming to the island in their ships and driving us all underground. Maybe it's just the next step in history. The Bugganes will wipe the slate clean for another to come and paint his view.'

'Don't talk like that Méa. That's just what they want you to think; that all this is meant to happen, and that it's simply a new course in nature. If you think that then they've as good as won.' Dane raised his voice in a way that Méa hadn't heard before and she shrunk back. 'They want us to go quietly and not stand in their way, to lie down and let them tread all over us like they always have. They've always thought the island was here solely to provide for them, that they somehow walked above it. But you know that's not true, don't you? Please tell me you know that's not true!' she nodded, frightened by his desperation.

Dane strode away and pounded the face of the rock with his fists, letting out a tremendous roar that echoed around them like thunder. The pit seemed to shake from the strike and a shower of dust fell down onto them. He fell onto his knees and held his bleeding hands up to his chest, panting with pain.

'I won't let them,' he growled. 'They are a plague, and I won't let them infect the island, I won't!' he sounded hysterical, but Méa bent down towards him, and cupped his wounded hands in hers.

'You're right Dane, I'm sorry, everything you've said is right,' she pleaded. 'It's just this place. I can't stand being locked up like this. Please keep strong for me, I can't do this alone.'

Dane looked up to her, and saw new tears collect in the corners of her eyes. He squeezed her hands hard, blood curling round their knuckles.

Another echo of his strike resounded round the cramped space and shook deep in their stomachs. Though it couldn't have been another echo, they seemed to think at the same time as they looked at each other. It was a separate noise, breaking into the deathly quiet of the pit.

'That wasn't you was it?' asked Méa, whispering in the hope of hearing it again. Dane shook his head. The sound didn't seem to be coming from above them, from the mouth of the well, but through the rock from somewhere nearby. They both held themselves as still as possible, not wanting to disrupt any further discord in the silence, and listened.

Just as they were about to give up it came again, a large thump through hollow rock. Dane leapt up and put his ear hard against the face of the pit, in the direction the sound had come from.

'It must mean there's another pit like this, not far from here. There are certainly no more tunnels this far down.'

'Maybe it's Bea,' said Méa, panicking. 'Maybe they've already got him, and put him into another cave.'

'No, they would have told us if they had caught their prize. They would have loved to see us squirm with that news. That would be just like them. No, they must have some man-folk trapped down here; it's the only answer. But what in Manannin's name do they want with man-folk if they intend to kill them all anyway?'

'I don't know. But they're probably either trying to break their way out or find out if there is anybody else down here,' answered Méa.

'So maybe we should answer their question,' said Dane, walking over to the small pile of Bugganes' corpses in the far corner. He pulled up the most recent body and jamming his foot on it's neck, tugged hard and yanked it's already loose head clean off with a dull pop. He shook it until the syrupy blood had ceased to spill from it's neck and walked back to the wall, wiping his wet, stained hands on his thighs.

'They've got very tough skulls,' he said knocking on the Buggane's head, in answer to Méa's disgusted look. He took a firm grip of the head by the emaciated jawbone, banged it hard against the rock twice and waited for a reply.

'Wait, wait!' Did you hear that?' whispered Eamon Kerruish, waving his arms for everyone to be as quiet as they could.

'Hear what?' asked Patrick Tooly, rising from the ground where his wife was resting.

'Two knocks, from over here, I could have sworn I heard knocks.'

'You've been trying for ages, it's probably nothing,' Patrick said, quickly dismissing it.

'No, no, I'm telling you I definitely heard something...'

'Maybe there *is* someone else down here,' said Robyn Clague, hopefully, jumping up to his feet and rushing over to the dark outline of Eamon on the far side, away from his injured father, Gavan, lying on top of his own bloodied rags.

'Robyn, pass me that burnt out torch over there would you.'

Robyn picked up the dead wooden torch and passed it to Eamon, who immediately banged one end of it hard against the rock floor and knelt down to listen. All he could hear was the low haunting groans of pain from Robyn's father and Markys Dawson lying next to him. It was a most horrible sound that nagged and tugged on everyone's already crippled spirits, but he needed quiet if he had a chance of hearing anything.

'I'm sorry,' he announced to the dark room, 'but we're going to need to be a bit quieter for a moment if we want to hear something.'

Though he hated asking, they were all co-operative. Caren Dawson quickly put a cold bit of torn dress on her father's forehead and stroked his face until he fell back into sleep. And though Gavan Clague was too wide awake with pain, he knew what was being asked of him and clenched his jaw to try to suppress his weeping.

Once they had settled down, Eamon raised the torch and banged it against the rock once more, and waited, holding his breath. Two knocks came quickly back, and he exhaled excitedly, looking over to Grayse, who was sitting with Aalin near the two injured men. Eamon then knocked three times and was answered instantly with three knocks. He knocked four times and four came back.

'There are definitely other people down here!' he exclaimed.

'Maybe they've come to rescue us,' cried Caren, full of desperate hope.

'Yes!' shouted Betty Loony, pushing herself slowly up with a great effort. 'Maybe they can get to us in here.' She paced over to the wall and started banging her fists madly against it. 'Help! Help!' she shrieked. 'We're in here!'

Caren also ran over and began banging and shouting, possessed by her longing to be free. Before long, everyone that could stand was on their feet yelling and screaming for help.

Through the madness Eamon looked over to Grayse, holding her hands over Aalin's ears and, even in the dark, saw the worry drawn over her face. This wasn't good. The hysteria would do nothing except ignite further fury from the creatures.

'Please stop, everyone!' he tried to shout over the racket. 'You'll make them come back again.' No one seemed to have noticed him as they were all too caught up in their plea for rescue.

'Please stop, it'll only cause more trouble!' Still there was no other sound but for the mindless cries of the desperate.

'For heavens sake, BE QUIET!' he screamed, raising his arms in the air. He could feel his head swell with blood as everyone's shocked faces fell silent and turned to him.

'Listen to me, please. Making such a clamour will do nothing but enrage those things even more. If there are other people down here with us, then they are probably trapped just like we are.'

'No, they're here to save us, they must be!' pleaded Betty Loony, still clinging to her prayers.

'If they are, then they *will* find us, but I don't think we should be drawing too much attention to ourselves at the moment.'

'He's right,' said Grayse, walking over to her husband's side and taking hold of his hand, surprised at how much he was shaking. 'If they come down here again they'll only take more of us away for questions and we'll come back like them.' She pointed at the figures of Markys Dawson and Gavan Clague lying on the floor shivering. 'By the looks of it they are getting better at it each time.'

Gavan's arm was in a makeshift splint, but the burns across his chest were unbearable to look at and the whole space smelt of dried blood. The two of them had been slipping in and out of consciousness for what seemed like several hours. If anything could be a warning to them all, it was the sight of what the creatures were capable of.

Everybody, wheezing in the dull air and exhausted from their shouting, let the new light of possibility fade away and slumped back down onto the hard floor.

'I suggest,' Eamon said calmly, clinging onto Grayse's hand as though he might fall, 'we wait a little while longer and see whether or not the noises coming from the rock are people trying to get to us.'

'Who cares what you suggest?' whined the hollow voice of Reverend Godfrey, stepping out of a corner into the middle of the chamber, his eyes still managing to look wild with danger in the darkness. 'If we wait, we die. If we shout out, we die. If we dance and skip about to our hearts content, we die,' he said, skipping up and down on the spot like a marionette, laughing out madly. Eamon could see sweat teeming off him and sense everyone's unease at his disposition.

'Get a grip on yourself, you're speaking like a madman,' he said through gritted teeth, feeling anger rise up inside of him like steam.

'Well maybe I am a madman!' The Reverend laughed, his eyes now as big as plates. 'Maybe we're all mad, and them, those creatures up there, or whatever they are,' he said pointing to the mouth of the pit far above him, 'maybe they're the ones with the right idea; punish all the sinners. Maybe they're the sane ones.' The whole while he was laughing and skipping in circles, and the younger children hid behind the older ones, afraid of the clown.

'If you keep going on like that, then you are as bad as they are,' said Eamon, now boiling, but still trying to keep control of himself.

'I think you're wrong, I think they are the righteous ones!'

Eamon couldn't help it, he released his anger for barely a moment, but in that moment he struck out and hit the Reverend across the cheek, knocking him instantly to the floor. He clutched his face as he hit the ground and Patrick Tooly jumped up and held Eamon back by the shoulders, shaking him as if to bring him back from a trance. Most people moved away from them afraid of being too involved.

'I'm sorry Dermot, I really am, but you can't speak like that, it's the last thing we need. Now why don't you go back to your corner and keep yourself to yourself.'

'He's right Dermot, that was out of order, you better go back there,' repeated Patrick.

The stooped Reverend shrunk back into the darkness, his torn habit dragging behind him, silent in shock. Eamon looked around at everyone else's faces, but they all tried to avoid his gaze, fearful of causing another outburst in their direction.

'Don't worry, you were right,' whispered Patrick in his ear.

'I'm sorry,' he said again, walking away from the group to join Grayse and Aalin.

'You were right,' said Grayse, putting an arm around his as he sat down, flinching against his aching muscles, 'don't think that you weren't. But you probably didn't need to thump him. You boys never grow beyond schoolyard scrapping do you?' she joked, trying to lighten his mood.

'What Dermot was saying, he was wrong. We can't start thinking like that. It's hard enough for all of us as it is,' he said defensively, wishing his anger would ebb away quicker than it was doing.

'I know, I know.'

'Sorry, I don't mean to shout at you. It's just that for a moment I wondered whether they'd got Juan as well, and he was alone in there. You know, from what they were saying it seemed like he was so important. Why, I simply can't fathom.'

'J…Juan,' squeaked Aalin, crawling into her father's lap, squeezing her arms around his waist and putting her head underneath his worn jacket. Maybe it all seemed like a game to Aalin, Eamon thought, a fun little adventure to break the monotony of hand painting and making a mess of the kitchen.

'That's right Aalin, Juan, we're worried about him, that's all,' he said, stroking her soft curly blonde hair.

'J…Juan…fine,' she chuckled to herself, chewing on her father's jumper. Eamon smiled.

'Thanks for that, I'm glad you're keeping an eye on him for us.'

Grayse let herself smile as well, just a small smile through her fear and gripped Eamon's hand so hard she could break it. 'It will be all right, won't it?' she asked, blindly seeking reassurance she knew wasn't there.

'Yes,' replied Eamon instantly, though he hated lying to her, and neither of them believed it anyway. 'We'll be home before you know it.'

He held Grayse close to him and felt her and Aalin relax as they drifted into an uneasy sleep, trying to block out the dull moans nearby and again prayed that hundreds of paces above them Juan knew what he was doing.

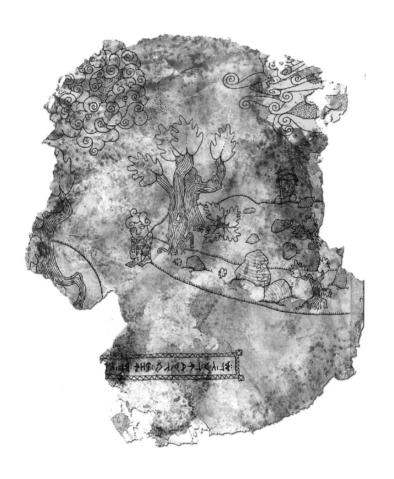

SIXTEEN

I don't know what I'm doing, thought Juan sourly, looking out across the road from the top of the path. He glanced over to the clearing out of which he had hurtled barely any time ago and his eyes glazed over, partly with fatigue and partly with muddle. He knew he needed to get to the Fairy Bridge, that much was clear, and he knew where the Fairy Bridge was, so that problem was also solved, but how was he ever going to get there without the speed of Bea to catapult him on his way? He doubted he could ever walk that distance in an entire day being on the north-east of the island, the Fairy Bridge was much further towards the south, not too far from his school.

He felt annoyed and deflated that he didn't think about it in time to ask Bea and Sophia for any help, or maybe even Téeval (though he doubted he would be able to make head nor tail out of what she spoke). She may have sounded like his mum but that was where any likeness ended; mum had no need for riddles and such nonsense.

He puffed out his cheeks and blew out a cloud of cold air as he sighed at the unpleasant feeling of being so suddenly alone. Although he hadn't thought about it up until now, being so preoccupied with meeting the Princess of the Ocean and finally deciphering the meaning of the markings that had been disfiguring his skin for days, he really was awfully hungry. His stomach croaked its agreement. He was also terribly thirsty. If he had only drunk some of the fresh water from the stream he wouldn't have the vile sticky taste at the back of his dry mouth. But he had no time to go back or stand there dithering for that matter. He had to get going.

As he stood away from the roadside several motorcars passed in each direction, speeding through the wide corner in the growing wind. Should he just start walking and see what happens, see whether or not the wind would take him as it did before? Or should he at least get as far as Laxey village to try to catch a bus from there? He didn't like the idea of walking around in the middle of the afternoon looking like a tramp who was searching for a comfortable doorway to sleep in. He stamped his feet down onto the hard earth trying to warm them and encourage his mind to think faster. He was just wasting time standing there doing nothing; it wasn't a time for thinking it was a time for doing. So he huffed and did the first thing that jumped into his head, the only idea that seemed in any way the quickest, though certainly not the most sensible; he walked over to the roadside and stuck out his thumb to hitch a lift.

No sooner had he done so than he heard the rather antique parping of an old horn coming from round the corner to his right. At first there was no vehicle to belong to the sound and he figured it was the calling of a strange bird. Then the sound blew out again and was finally joined by a weary looking red tractor trundling round the corner towards him, with a small queue of motorcars behind it. The motors overtook it at the first chance and raced away, leaving it on its own, chugging nearer. Once closer, he saw that the tractor wasn't red at all but was entirely covered in rust, like a bad rash.

Juan bit his lip hard, he was afraid it would be too slow as it was hardly going much faster than he could walk. He lowered his arm and turned away from the road trying to look as unassuming as possible and hoped that the tractor would simply pass him by without stopping. But the driver must have seen that he had his thumb out, as when it came alongside him it screeched to a halt, sending a shiver down Juan's spine as he tried as hard as he could to look as though he was inspecting the view over the headland.

'Get in boy,' came a low, nasal voice from behind him.

'No it's all right thank you very much, I'm not looking for a lift, I was just…erm…admiring the view, it's wonderful isn't it?' said Juan, trying to sound as polite as he could whilst keeping his back to the tractor and still concentrating on looking out to sea.

'I said get in boy,' said the voice again, only this time a little stronger. 'This may be your last chance and don't worry, I think

I'll be going past the Fairy Bridge.'

Juan span around, utterly startled by what the voice had said and saw that the tractor was being driven by Mr. Seer, the old man who lived in the cottage near Cringle. Mr. Seer stared straight ahead of him, his dark glasses perched high up on his crooked nose. Juan recalled that he couldn't possibly be staring straight ahead of him, he couldn't be staring in any direction at all: he was blind.

'You couldn't really expect me to…'

'Don't worry, I know these roads better than you know your own back yard,' Mr. Seer said, far too calmly for Juan's liking. 'Now don't just stand there staring at me like a fool, hop in. It's about to rain, and it looks to me as though you're wet enough as it is,' he said slyly smirking to himself.

Juan looked down at his soggy trousers and feet. How on earth did he know that? He looked one way down the road, then the other. There was no one else to be seen.

'There won't be anyone along for a little while,' Mr. Seer told him, appearing to know exactly what Juan was thinking about.

It seemed he was right. This may be his only chance and so he put his foot up onto the large tyre of the tractor and heaved himself up into the seat next to Mr. Seer.

'Right choice,' said Mr. Seer, jerkily pulling away from the edge of the track and heading down the coast road towards Laxey. As they descended, he began to hum what Juan thought was a jaunty folk tune whilst clutching hard onto the steering wheel.

They speeded up on the downhill road, but still not fast enough for Juan to relax, and he sat impatient and tense in his seat.

After a few awkward moments of sitting in silence whilst Mr. Seer contentedly hummed away, the sky, that looked but moments ago to be clearing up with the gusts of wind, suddenly closed up and let loose a downpour of fat, heavy rain.

'Told you,' Mr. Seer muttered knowingly, shaking his head. Juan groaned in agreement as a howl of wind blew round the tractor followed by an angry roar of thunder bellowing through the air. He tightly crossed his arms into his fleece to keep his hands warm and the rain beat hard down on the roof of the tractor, trying to break in.

On any other day it would seem slightly less than ordinary to be driven by a blind man and Juan was still having some trouble believing it as he looked over at Mr. Seer clutching the steering wheel and apparently concentrating on what was in front of him. He was wearing four tatty old jumpers one on top of the other with a thick tartan scarf wrapped tightly around his neck and stuffed inside his collar, and a pair of grey finger-less woollen gloves with his craggy, weathered fingers protruding from the ends. The few strands of long white hair that he had left blew back in the wind and his unshaven face was so lined that it was impossible to tell what he may have looked like when he was younger. The contours of his earthy skin gave the impression that a whole lifetime of hard work had been mapped onto his face.

'What are you looking at?' he suddenly garbled, still staring blindly straight ahead of him as he slowly edged around a sharp corner. Juan looked away embarrassed and held his breath until they were heading in a straight line once more.

'It's just that, well, you're…'

'Go on, spit it out,' Mr. Seer said gingerly.

'You're, well…you're blind.' Juan was nearly thrown out of his seat as Mr. Seer swerved out of the way of a small rabbit happily sitting in the road unaware of the danger around him.

'How did you…?'

'There's not a lot that passes me by.'

'How do you know…?'

'I know a lot more about you than just your name.'

'How could you…?'

'Ask me no questions and I'll tell you no lies.'

'What's that supposed to…?'

'It means I'm not going to tell you,' said Mr. Seer with a smile growing around the corners of his mouth. He turned away from the road to face Juan, still steering perfectly across a junction to the great bemusement of the drivers on the far side, whose mouths fell open.

'I'll only tell you this,' he said, lowering his voice as if people might be listening in. Juan only nodded his head wishing he would turn back to the road. 'There's not much that passes me by and up until now you've done a grand job Juan, you really have. Not many could have coped with everything as well as you have, believe me. But don't think it's the easy roll down the hill from here, you've barely started your climb, and I suspect it's about to get a whole lot steeper.'

'Thanks,' said Juan, still nodding his head like a broken jack-in-the-box. 'But I think I'd feel a bit better if you kept you eyes, sorry, I mean if you faced the road Mr. Seer, if you don't mind.' He tried hard not to sound as though he was meaning any offence.

'Oh right, of course,' replied Mr. Seer turning away and humming again.

They began to climb the steep winding hill leading away from Laxey village, leaving the giant water wheel, the Lady Isabella, behind them. Passing the small stone terraced houses and simple uncluttered shop fronts the tractor was struggling so much with the climb it had assumed the pace of an unwilling schoolboy heading to detention. As another motorcar pulled out and passed them, honking its horn, Juan felt his urgency take hold of him once more.

'Can't we go any…?'

'There's no rush.'

'But…?'

'You'll have all the time in the world when you get there, trust me, so cease your worrying and probing, it's all wasted. I'm surprised Bea didn't lose his patience with you more often, you're intolerable!'

Juan was just about to blurt out 'YOU KNOW BEA!' but Mr. Seer had already raised his hand to stop him from asking and he fell back into his seat defeated.

'Now there's a small box under your seat with some food in it, just sandwiches and stuff mind you, but I thought you'd be needing some by now so I made sure I packed it. Now to look at you, I think maybe I should have brought some more.' Juan turned to him, not even bothering to ask his question this time. 'I'm only joking,' he said laughing and lifting his hands off the steering wheel, waving them for what felt to Juan like a painfully long time.

Juan didn't think to question him again. He was far too hungry to let his confusion lead him elsewhere, so he quickly found the suitably rusted tin lunchbox beneath his seat, laid it on his lap and opened it.

He immediately started to wolf down the sandwiches inside and was delighted, if not a touch surprised, to find that they were delicious. There was also some fruit and even some chocolate.

'Thank you,' he tried to say, his mouth swollen with food, and continued to eat, rolling his eyes with pleasure.

Another motor passed them, again honking its horn in annoyance and Mr. Seer advised Juan to put up his hood. 'We don't want anyone noticing you,' he said, tapping his nose with his wiry forefinger.

Who would want to notice me now, he thought. But then his mind began to wander, maybe he was thought to have gone missing, or moved away like the others. What would people think if they saw someone who they had only just read about having left for a new life somewhere else? Maybe, for all he knew, there was a manhunt on for him, who could say? He knew he couldn't afford to be stopped and questioned, that was certain and so he lifted his hood up and over his head, pulling it as far down his face as it would go, trying to conceal himself totally.

He doubted whether he had ever been missed before. Doona Kelly had noticed he hadn't been at school though. He hadn't had a moment to think about her, and now that he did it felt like snakes were winding their way through his insides. She had even said that she thought he was cool and she just acted weird because her friends would think she was stupid otherwise. He hoped she wouldn't mention that she saw him to anyone, though she'd probably be too busy skipping off school, he concluded, smiling.

He touched the spot on his cheek exactly where she had kissed him, feeling warmer and better than he had done all day.

Once he had thrown the core of his apple out into a passing hedgerow and licked his fingers clean of all the chocolate, the rain stopped as suddenly as it had started, although the clouds still looked grim and heavy and the strong wind still blew through the tractor.

'Strange day,' mumbled Mr. Seer, ceasing his humming to speak, 'like all four seasons at once.'

'No different from normal for this time of year,' said Juan dryly, looking up to the sky, but he became quickly aware at how quickly the clouds overheard were travelling, low clouds the size of mountains chasing each other across the sky as if thrown by the titans themselves.

'Like they're trying to fight with each other or something,' said Mr. Seer, grinning to himself. 'Don't think I've ever seen a day like this before.'

'Mr. Seer?' Juan asked cautiously, dusting the crumbs off his legs and returning the tin box under his chair.

'Mmmm?' he murmured suspiciously.

'I was just wondering how you, well, how you lost…?'

'My eyes?' Juan nodded as if he could see him. 'Born like that I was. Popped out with them just like they are now. Upset my poor folks terribly. My mother used to tease me and say that when I was born I saw a goddess naked and she punished me by making me blind, but I can't really remember seeing any goddess. I think that would be something I'd remember,' he laughed, 'but over time I came to realise that you can't really miss what you don't really know, not really. Though I'd sure like to see a weeping willow tree, or a honey suckle bush in blossom, I hear they're mighty beautiful.'

'Yes. Yes they are,' Juan agreed.

'And my wife, I would have liked to have seen Mrs. Seer just once, though I know she was still the most beautiful bride this side of Barrule.' He laughed louder still, elbowing Juan in the ribs.

'Oh, and the sea! I'd love to look out on the sea, I bet that's quite something,' he sighed, 'though fortunately I've never had to look at a building site. I hear they're as ugly as sin.'

'They are!' Juan agreed again, laughing. 'You're not missing much there.'

'Yep, never seen a single colour. You can tell me the sky is blue and an orange is, well, orange, but it means nothing to me. Gives everything a different value it does. Like what's the value of gold if you can't see it? Huh? Makes things a lot less fussy if you ask me.'

He had a point, thought Juan as they passed a stone house in Baldrine, where a lady was hanging out her washing to dry, trying to catch the brief clear spell. She yelped loudly and saving her underwear from the line, dashed back inside as the sky opened again and now began to spit down hail onto them. Tiny sharp stalactites of ice fell down and shattered like glass on the road.

Yet another motorcar honked as it passed and even another tractor overtook them, the driver waving his hand in a most unpleasant gesture, and Juan felt his anxiety return. It started at his feet, twitching and unable to keep still, moving up through his legs and into a sick feeling in his stomach. He was afraid he couldn't keep his food down. It made him feel horribly guilty as he was very much enjoying Mr. Seer's company and the last thing he wanted to do was appear ungrateful for his great kindness.

He wished he could tell what time it was, to put his mind at ease, but the sun was entirely concealed behind a curtain of dark clouds drawn across the sky. The clouds were so dark he could easily assume it was evening. This thought didn't make him feel any better and he took several long, slow, deep breaths to calm himself down. Worrying will do no good, he told himself, worrying will do no good.

'Don't fret yourself boy,' Mr. Seer said, no doubt sensing his mood. 'If you rush through everything then you're only bound to trip up somewhere along the line. And we don't want that,' he added as an after-thought, elbowing him gently in the ribs another time.

Juan rubbed his side. He was beginning to find it rather

antagonising that Mr. Seer had an answer for every question. He thought that if he was just to think of anything Mr. Seer was likely to finish the sentence for him.

'That's probably right,' said Mr. Seer out of nowhere.

'What's probably...?'

'I'll probably finish your sentences for you, it's a bad habit of mine. It used to drive Mrs. Seer up the wall it did!' he laughed, banging the steering wheel with both hands.

'You're quite scary you know,' Juan confided.

As they continued alongside the tracks of the old electric railway, heading away from the coastline and down towards Douglas, Juan felt his head becoming heavier, as though a hand was beckoning it to droop onto his chest. What with the gentle and even bouncing of the tractor, the rhythm of the rain, the soft embrace of his fleece and the low tuneful humming of Mr. Seer he felt inclined, against his will, to close his eyes. He'd close them for only a short while, simply because they felt heavy, he told himself. He certainly had no intention of sleeping. In fact, he was determined not to. The thought of dreaming he was at the bottom of some cold wet ocean was not a happy one. Instead he put his mind towards the Fairy Bridge.

They must want to save themselves. He touched the place on his stomach where those very words were marked. He thought that didn't sound too difficult, but he'd quickly learnt not to take everything at face value. He was sure things would become clearer once he got there. How he was going to find them, however, he had no idea.

'You just greet them like you always have Juan, then leave the rest up to them.'

Juan opened his eyes, and looking out around him he sat bolt upright. They were already well past Douglas and were heading in towards the smaller, winding roads near their destination. He had only closed his eyes, he was sure. He hadn't fallen asleep.

'I didn't fall...?'

'Nope, not as far as I noticed.'

'Then how did we...?'

'Must have been the wind I suppose, does strange things when you turn your back on it,' said Mr. Seer chuckling away.

Again Juan began to ask a question and again Mr. Seer had already raised his hand to stop him.

They were now on the road that Juan took everyday to school. It felt very peculiar to be taking it now, as if it was for the first time again. Going somewhere strange, like his first day at his new school, worrying if they would like him or if he would make any friends. He bit his lip and hoped he would have more success with the Fairies than with his fellow classmates, otherwise everything was done for.

The tractor came to a slow bumpy stop not twenty paces from the small bridge, where the trees hung over the road like spiders' legs. Mr. Seer turned to him and Juan felt his dark glasses boring right into him.

'This is where you get out boy. There's not much that I can tell you that you don't already know, you're a bright lad, but…keep you wits about you, they're not what they seem.'

Juan climbed down onto the roadside and was about to thank him for the food, both this time and at the time before at Cringle, as Mr. Seer smiled and said 'You're welcome,' before he had the chance.

'Goodbye Juan Kerruish, see you soon,' he said, pulling out and bursting into hysterics. 'I love that one, *see* you soon. Ha!' His tractor moved off from the curb and began crawling away, Mr. Seer humming his merry tune once again. Juan watched him go until the rusty shape was out of sight.

He stepped off the road and down towards the small rise in the road that was known as the Fairy Bridge. He couldn't help feeling a little silly as he climbed over the fallen trees and hoped that no one would pass and see him wading into the narrow stream that flowed underneath. Although he was standing right next to it, the bridge, if it could be called a bridge at all, came up no further than his waist and was densely overgrown with unattractive weeds. Worrying will do no good, Juan told himself again. That's what Bea would say, worrying will do no good.

He stood there for a moment, his feet cold and soaked again in the stream and remembered what Mr. Seer had said. Then he opened his mouth and spoke the words that he, and everyone else for that matter, spoke as they daily passed over the bridge and waited for an answer.

'Hello Fairies?'

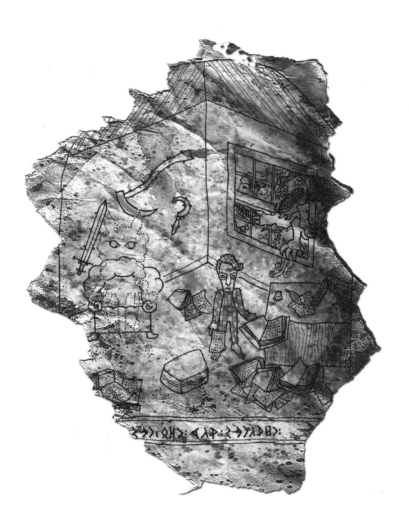

SEVENTEEN

The school cook, Maureen Brew, was a short-sighted woman at the best of times but she still refused to wear her glasses even when working in the kitchens. She had left her newly baked tray of hot pies to cool by a window and, on her return, hadn't noticed that nearly half of them had disappeared. She hadn't noticed the large hand come in through the window and she hadn't noticed the large hand filch the pies from under her nose. Later, she would hardly even notice Mr. Corkish, the head cook, shouting at her for her incompetence. She was known for little else other than her short-sightedness.

Bea had eased the window of the school kitchens open far enough to reach inside and swipe as many of the pies left on the side as he could. Much time had passed since he had last eaten and the smell of the food wafting out from the window had made his mouth wet and his stomach grumble. He couldn't help himself, and as he heard the footsteps of the cook walk away he took his chance.

Bea blew on the pies to cool them before wolfing each one down, barely giving himself any time to enjoy them. He crouched beneath the windows of the kitchens with his knees pulled up tight into his chest, and though thankful for the meal, couldn't take his mind off what was happening to Juan. He felt somehow responsible for his new friend's welfare and the thought that he would be struggling all alone made him shiver more than the brisk wind that was speeding across the bottom of the school. The worry that sat deep in the pit of his stomach only fuelled the fire of anger he felt towards Mortis; the Watcher. How could any man ever think that some good would come from forming an allegiance with the Bugganes? And what grudge could be handed down through so many generations? He had no answers to the questions nagging him, but knew that Queen Atta would certainly have been ecstatic to have her own little puppet to manipulate at her will, her own little toy. The Watcher's actions bordered on the wrong side of madness. He wanted to tear him apart, not bleat for his help like some desperate, hurt lamb.

'Our lives are not to be shared with the man-folk,' his father had told him time and time again, and now he had to go against those very words and plead with a man who had spent his life hunting them. If his task had come from anyone other than Téeval he may have ignored it altogether. He shook himself and rubbed his face, 'worrying will do no good,' he said under his breath. Worrying will do no good.

Though Bea knew it was only the early afternoon, every light inside the building had been switched on and the crumbling grey stone glowed with an orange sheen under the oppressive dark clouds. He licked his fingers clean of the meat and gravy and let his head rest against the stone, only a hair's breadth under the kitchen windowsill. He was so tired. He'd never known such fatigue, as though sleep was aggressively holding him down and claiming him for itself. He could forget it all in sleep. There would be no Bugganes. There would be no task. There would be no problem. It sounded blissful to have it all lifted from him for just a short while and let his eyes shut into unfeeling, unthinking darkness.

Just as he felt himself slow and his worries uncurl something hard hit him across the face. He flinched and sprang up onto all fours ready to pounce. But there was no one there. He quickly looked all around him, but still saw no one. He listened but heard nothing except the moaning and shouting of the school children inside. Then it happened again, a hard strike across his face, like a slap, that sent him toppling over onto his back. He growled, and as he was about to heave himself up a low whistle blew out from everywhere. He felt his fur sweep all around him as a hundred unseen hands circled and lifted him up to standing. He huffed as he realised it was the wind forcing him on his way and he felt a spike of guilt at his selfish need for rest. There was much to do that out-weighed his need for sleep. The wind swept behind his back urging him to take a step forward. He couldn't help impatiently whispering through his teeth 'I know', and tried to brush the wind away as he crept along the side of the building to find an open door.

Whilst winding his way closer to the ominous stone buildings of the school, he had caught sight of Mortis passing a window in a room high up on the top floor. The Watcher had been running backwards and forwards, pulling on his hair and waving his arms in the air like some crazed animal caged behind bars. Maybe he was mad, thought Bea, but regardless, that was where he was heading.

He sneaked his way silently through several doorways until he came to the first stairwell. His feet gently tapped against the cold wooden floor of the steps as he hopped up onto the landing. He stopped at the top and, standing flat against the wall, held his breath and shifted into *arraghey* as two giggling girls strode past him, one, unbeknownst to her, brushing his fur with her sleeve.

He found it increasingly hard to concentrate enough to *arraghey*, and as soon as the girls were out of earshot, he let go of the tension in his mind and his gut and ascended the next flight of stairs undisguised.

He may not have known his way around the maze of musty corridors and dingy doorways, but Mortis was high up, so if he climbed every staircase he came across he was bound to be on the right track.

He paused momentarily as he passed a door that was slightly open and, cautiously peering inside, saw a class of young children with their noses obediently down in their books, surveyed by a grim looking woman with a long black dress buttoned right up to her throat. He looked in at another classroom next door where a riot was building to a great momentum and a gentle harmless looking man in the corner looked to be on the brink of tears, pleading for them to stop. Céa would have loved this, he thought as he ran on.

Reaching the top of yet another staircase, he heard a sudden curse coming from nearby, and knew Mortis must be close. He took a slow breath through his nose, suppressing his twitching rage, and followed the noise to the end of the narrow, empty corridor. The walls on either side of him were lined with dusty browned photographs of old men staring right at him with austere expressions, not so different from the statues in the Great Hall of Fleshwick Rock. He pressed his ear against the last door and, from the racket going on behind it, he was certain it was Mortis. He took hold of the brass door handle, gently turned it and let himself in.

'Damn this weather!' cursed Mortis under his breath as he stepped over a pile of clothes and suitcases spread over the floor and slammed the door shut.

Bea stepped over the tip, in *arraghey*, careful not to disturb anything, and went and sat down in a large worn green leather armchair in the corner, watching Mortis bumbling past him like a headless chicken.

His study was much the same as his classroom. The walls were covered with maps of the island, from very primitive sketches through to elaborate paintings with every possible detail. There was a cabinet next to him displaying a host of ancient weapons and tools: scythes, axe heads blunt with time, spear heads and blades that looked as though they would crumble to dust if he blew on them. On the wall nearest his desk was a framed drawing of a vicious wild beast with blood on its hands and murder in its eyes. Bea knew it must have been a representation of a Fynoderee, or at least what Mortis thought a Fynoderee looked like, and he had to suppress a snort of laughter.

The windows clattered violently in their frames as the wind outside picked up and hail began to beat down against them. Mortis was throwing crumpled papers and dusty books from his shelves across the room into suitcases and trunks on the floor and then sitting on top of them as he tried to close them.

Resting back in the chair, Bea felt far more comfortable sitting and watching Mortis about his business than actually speaking to him. He was still afraid that anger would take its grip and he would lash out, doing something he would regret later. He could feel himself glow with heat at the thought of this flimsy man doing anything to endanger Juan. But he thought of Téeval and her words; he thought of his mother's voice and how calming it sounded. This was the only way if ever he was to see his family again.

He let go of the tension and shifted back from *arraghey*, feeling his fur return to its natural state and waited for Mortis to see him.

However Mortis continued to fluster about, opening drawers and scattering clothes about the floor, not noticing that he had a new guest in the room. He even looked straight past Bea at one point, who sat there quite silent, gripping the arms of the chair. This was ludicrous.

'Going somewhere?' Bea grunted.

Mortis span round to where the voice had come from and looked Bea directly in the eyes. Bea saw his face turn from surprise, to recognition, to absolute horror.

Mortis stifled a scream, it caught in his throat, and he stumbled backwards, tripping up over all the mess on the floor and fell, hitting his head on his desk. Bea, slowly and calmly, stood up.

Mortis scrambled to his feet, his mouth still wide in shock, and there they stood for several moments, facing each other in silence. Mortis' eyes fluttered to his right and saw his old, rusted sword hanging up on the wall in its leather scabbard. Bea knew his intention immediately, and when Mortis leapt over to it, Bea was already there with his hand firmly gripped on the weapon's handle, preventing him from pulling it free.

'Believe me, you don't want to do that,' he whispered, so close to Mortis' face he could smell the fear on his breath. 'Sit,' he quietly commanded him. Mortis, without taking his eyes from Bea's, obeyed and staggered over to his desk where he sat down, as stiff as a board of wood.

'W…w…w…' Mortis stuttered, trying to get a hold of himself. 'W…what…do you want with me?' he managed to get out.

Bea also found the words difficult to say. He didn't want to say them. He would rather have grabbed Mortis' throat and squeezed with all his might.

'I want your help,' he said grudgingly.

'If you want to kill me, then you might as well do it now monster,' hissed Mortis. 'Heaven knows, I deserve it.'

'I may want to kill you, and yes, you do deserve it, probably more than you realise, but against my will I am sent to bid for your help.' Bea still hadn't unclenched his jaw.

'Why on earth do you want my help? Haven't I caused enough trouble already?! I'm sure it's better for everyone if I just left and didn't come back.' Mortis face was glistening with sweat.

'I *also* am sure that would be best. But I'm afraid what *we* think is neither here nor there. Mistakes have been made. Those mistakes must be rectified before the innocent ones, and not the guilty, suffer. And since a great deal of this rests on you,' he paused letting the judgement sink in, 'it is only right that you play your part in putting it all right.' Bea, still tense, spoke slowly and clearly, sensing a regret in Mortis' voice that he wasn't expecting.

'What can I do? All I've caused is carnage. I deserve to perish alongside everyone else on this cursed island. There is nothing I can do. You haven't seen them. You haven't seen all of them like I have, seen them in their tunnels growing in numbers by the day. They are too perfect to be stopped. All they know is hate, to them it's like love; they strive for it and hunger for it and at dawn tomorrow, they will unleash it on everything.' Mortis shook with panic, wringing his damp hands together.

'I can't let them do that,' said Bea, simply.

'Oh, and what are you going to do, one Fynoderee against such an army! You beasts were always so arrogant. My father was right about you. We should have killed all of your world whilst we had the chance. There is no room for legends anymore.'

Bea snatched Mortis' tie from around his neck and lifted him from his seat, holding him a foot above the ground, the tie choking him and getting ever tighter the more he struggled. He brought Mortis' red gasping face close to his and spoke firmly.

'I have more reason to hate you than anyone you know. For no excuse but an ancient grudge and sport, you have striven to hunt us down, although we caused you no harm. If you want reasons I could take you to where my uncle, Grey, was caught in a mantrap and bled to death alone. Would that be enough to convince you of your madness?' Bea couldn't help but take satisfaction in the reddening form of Mortis shaking before him. 'And what's more, you have endangered Juan's life.' Mortis' eyes widened. 'Yes, I know Juan. I know what he is, and if anything happens to him, so much as a scratch, I will repay it on you ten-fold.' He let go of Mortis' tie and watched him fall to the floor, coughing and pulling it from his throat. Glaring down at his crumpled form, Bea wanted to hurt him more, but saw that he was shuddering and shivering.

Mortis was crying.

'It all got out of my hands,' he whimpered, looking up at Bea with wet eyes. 'It all happened too quickly for me to even think about. It was what my father would have wanted, and his father before him right back to where this began at the *Keeil Vrisht*. I just wanted to make him proud…'

'By setting in motion the murder of tens of thousands of innocent man-folk?!'

'I never thought of it like that. I only wanted to know that every Buggane and Fynoderee was dead, that it was I who had finished the vow made by our family so many hundreds of years ago, to rid the island of monsters like you so we could live in peace.'

'Do you not think we deserve peace?' asked Bea. Mortis couldn't answer, but only stared into his deep green eyes.

'And who do you think the monsters are now?'

Again Mortis couldn't answer, but wiped his eyes on the back of his sleeve.

'I always admired you man-folk so much, for your ability to love and forgive in abundance. Is there no trace of such a man left in you?' Bea sniffed. 'If you do not help, you will soon see what the Bugganes think of peace.'

With a slap of terror, Mortis suddenly remembered. 'They've probably been expecting me back since last night. I meant to take them the map. Mother won't be pleased. She may even have sent…'

He didn't have a chance to finish.

The old timber framed windows that looked out across the sports pitches and down towards the sea, imploded in a cloud of dust and glass. Splinters flew in all directions and as the mist settled, four armoured Bugganes stood as still as though they had been carved into that very spot years before.

Mortis instantly knew them to be Mother's guards. There was hardly a scar to tell them apart. They were several feet taller than the Fynoderee, with frames like bears. They were all muscle and sinew squeezed into their tight, dull greenish skin, and on their chests they wore charred plates of bone, perfectly carved to their form. Each one of them stared unblinking at Mortis, their red eyes far back from their high brows, which jutted forward giving them an expression of gormless rage.

Mortis fumbled his way further back into the room as the central guard flung the desk aside as if it was no more than an irritating insect. He found himself snatching out towards the Fynoderee for protection, but when his hands clutched only onto air he turned around and saw that the beast was no longer there. That wasn't possible. The monster had disappeared. He didn't have long to dwell on this as a thick webbed hand stretched round his face and he was plunged into a brief darkness. The rough mitten scratched his skin and smelt of fire. He was pulled forward, and could barely make out the one word the guard was grunting in his ear.

'Map.'

He tried to shout through the blackness that he didn't have the map, that it was stolen from him, that he prayed Mother would forgive him. The fingers clenched harder round his face, digging down into his temples, and the grunt came again.

'Map.'

He was afraid he would pass out.

Bea watched silently from the corner of the room. He had smelt the burnt odour of the Buggnes only a moment before they had crashed into the room and shifted into *arraghey* before either Mortis or the guards could notice him. For several breaths he watched Mortis receive what was coming to him from the very hands of those he chose to side with, and felt a sickly pleasure in his stomach. That'll teach him, he heard a bitter and twisted part of his mind shout out. But the feeling didn't last long. It was quickly eclipsed. He was more than the image of the monster that Mortis had framed on his wall. He also felt a need for compassion, survival and peace.

He had hardly noticed that he had taken the old rusted sword from its scabbard and cut the hand of the Buggane holding Mortis clean off just above the wrist. Time seemed to slow down and Bea felt himself fall into a fluid trance as the jagged tip of the blade broke through the brittle bone of the first Buggane's chest plate and pierced him cleanly through the middle. He pulled the sword out sideways, so that the guard toppled to the floor practically severed in two. The guard didn't scream, but his eyes rolled backwards into his skull with a visage of immediate shock.

Bea pushed Mortis towards the door and approached the three remaining guards.

He raised his sword arm to strike, but was caught at the wrist by the vice-like grip of one guard and as he lashed out with his other arm, it too was caught by another guard. They held on tight, and his erratic struggle didn't free him. The final guard threw his fist hard into Bea's centre, knocking all the wind out of him. He saw red dots float across his vision and shook his head against the pain when another blow came, harder than the first, and he fell to his knees fighting for breath. A bony foot came up and made swift contact with the bottom of his jaw, sending him crashing backwards, and he was pulled to standing by his long mane of hair.

His eyes tried hard to focus on what was in front of him, but everything was blurred. He saw the bleary faces of the guards directly in front him, and though the faces were well nigh expressionless, he thought they all wore smiles of snide pleasure. Sucking in a heavy breath, he threw his head into the face staring straight at him and heard an unpleasant crunch as the Buggane's nose broke. Momentarily released from their grip, he swung out with the blade once more. It cut gracefully through the air, like a scythe through corn, and didn't stop until it had passed through the necks of all three of the guards.

Each of their heads fell to the floor with dull thuds, followed by their bodies. Bea panted like a wolf, soaked in their dark blood, sticking to his fur, which already shone scarlet with rage, and turned back towards Mortis.

Mortis was panting as hard as Bea was. It had all happened so quickly. He leant against the wall by the door, and let it take his weight. He was acutely sure of one thing-the Fynoderee had saved his life-and inside that thought was a certainty of how precious life suddenly was, how each heartbeat was worth fighting for. His regret cut deep into him, but his new resolution cut deeper. He made to speak, but the door behind him swung open into his back, and the urgent voice of Charlie Colbourn came from outside his study.

'Sir? Are you all right sir? I heard a lot of noise from downstairs.'

Mortis quickly pushed the heavy door shut in the Head of School's face and looked into the room. There was gore and rubble everywhere. It looked like the sight of some monstrous battle.

'Er…I'm just spring cleaning, Colbourn. You know how it is, so much junk to throw out.'

'Could I possibly come in for a moment sir? Just to check you're all right, a few of the staff have been worried about you.'

Bea was too exhausted to *arraghey* and stared hard at Mortis, urging him not to let anyone enter the horrible scene.

'No, no, it's a frightful mess in here. I'd be far too embarrassed. You run along now Colbourn and I'll catch up with you shortly.' He tried to sound as carefree as he could. The pressure on the door ceased.

'Well as long as you are sure everything's all right sir.'

'Yes, yes, no worries here,' he said, spiritedly.

'See you shortly then,' said the deflated voice behind the door. Bea and Mortis listened as the footsteps walked away and descended the stairs at the end of the corridor. They both exhaled in relief. Mortis looked over at Bea with blood splattered all over him, the scarlet hue draining from his fur, and saw the need drawn into his face.

'What can I do?' Mortis asked, desperately. Bea closed his eyes in thanks.

'Simple,' he said, 'you know the way in, I don't. Go and get those man-folk out of there, the ones they took.'

'You want me to…'

'You're the Watcher, practically one of the family, they probably call you Brother,' Bea cut in. 'You are no doubt a man of reasonable intelligence, I'm sure you can slip in and out without being noticed.'

Mortis knew he had no choice; he hardly needed Bea to go on any further. He felt himself going cold with fear and the hairs on his arms and the back of his neck stood to attention. He nodded that he understood.

'There are two others like me, who will also need your help.' said Bea.

Two more Fynoderees, Mortis thought. What would they think of him if they knew what he had done?

Again he knew he had no choice if things were to be undone, and again he nodded that he understood.

Bea trod over the broken glass, wood and bodies scattered over the floor. The curtains billowed into the room.

'One more thing,' he said turning back into the room. Mortis looked at him, crippled and helpless.

'Yes?' he asked, weakly.

'I want you to tell them where I am.'

'But then they'll…'

'Come looking for me,' Bea finished. 'Exactly. That's what we want. I want you to tell them I'm hiding from them at Fleshwick Rock ..... and make it sound like a secret.'

'I will,' said Mortis, resigned to his task.

With the wind blowing ever harder over him, Bea was about to jump from the window when he saw the ugly drawing of the unrecognisable beast that was meant to be a Fynoderee, hanging on the wall near him. He pulled the drawing from its hanger.

'Oh,' he said, throwing it back into the room where it landed between the crumpled bodies, the glass shattering in its frame, 'and get rid of that will you.'

EIGHTEEN

Juan squinted against a sudden flash of sunlight and lifted his hand to his forehead, shielding his eyes from the glare shining down on him. Once the light had receded, he felt abruptly and wildly disorientated. He was facing a density of very tall reeds of grass as thick as his wrist, stretching up and bowing gracefully in a gentle breeze. His eyes traced a path upwards and he saw something even more unusual; a stalk of a flower, easing up next to the grass, extending upwards to well over his own height and an enormous unmistakable daisy head spreading out from its top. He turned back and looked to where he had stood the moment before, in the grey damp brook of the Fairy Bridge, but was again faced with only the dense forest of tall grass. He faltered and wondered for an instant whether he should turn back, but told himself that that wasn't even an option. Time was running away like water through a stream and his only path was to go onward. He stared at the grass briefly and quickly decided he needed a better view of where he was. He knew he had little time for shock or surprise: he should have realised by now that there were many strange places hidden away from the curious eyes of men.

He parted the long thick blades in front of him and saw a rise of rocks only a short walk away. He forced his way through the overgrowth, panting from the oppressive humidity, and stumbled closer. When he reached the clump of rocks he was again taken aback that they appeared to be more in the form of giant sized pebbles, stacked one on top of the other. Their surfaces were smooth and rounded and one wrong step would send them toppling down and easily crushing him beneath them. He took extra care when climbing to the top so as not to slip or upset the balance of the stones and, when he finally pushed down on his thighs and stood up, he gasped in awe at the view.

He was looking out towards what could only have been the land of the Fairies. He knew it as certainly as he knew his own

name, and now felt truly swallowed up by the Fairy Bridge.

He was standing at the top of a valley which spread out far and wide before him, its lush green pastures waltzing in the breeze. The stones he stood upon were near the bank of a slow moving stream, which smoothly made its way down into an enormous shimmering pool in the basin of the valley, glowing like a crystal. Juan could hear little else but the gurgling and bubbling of the stream as a wisp of dandelion as big as his fist floated past him.

The land undulated with small hills and in the breeze the waves of grass swayed against each other. A thousand man-sized yellow daisies and buttercups shone out from the green land, each one like its own sun. Magnolia trees, heavy with blossom, dotted his view down towards the pool where many willows yawned on its bank. The poolside was littered with trees; majestic alders, oaks and great black poplars, covering a good deal of it from sight.

Juan's nose was teased with intoxicatingly sweet perfumes of rose petal and honeysuckle, making his head spin in the summer light. His eyes felt like they were misting over from the scent, and his head felt as though it could float right off his body.

One sobering thought did unsettle him however, besides all the world in his eye line, he could see no other sign of life. The view was deserted, with no sound other than the whispers and sighs of nature.

He had at least expected to see a clan of Fairies arguing and roughing each other up, as he imagined Sophia and her kin would do, but there was no such sight.

He strained to hear the single call of a sparrow, click of a cricket or croak of a frog, but there was nothing. The loneliness felt suddenly unpleasant and he called out into the blue day.

'Hello?!' he shouted, and listened hopefully for a reply. Nothing. Then his echo weakly returned his call from within the empty valley.

'Is anyone here?!' he yelled out again.

He expected no answer, and dropped his heavy arms down to his sides, but then a solitary voice called back from out of nowhere.

'Yes,' it said. Juan took a defensive step back and nearly lost his footing on the unstable rocks. It was his own voice that had called back to him, he was certain of it. He swallowed and shouted back at himself.

'Where are you?'

'Everywhere,' his echo answered, sounding as if it was speaking through a broad smile. Juan still couldn't see any other sign of life.

'Over here,' his voice came, from far off on his right-hand side, towards a thicket of brambles and nettles. He spun around, but there was nothing.

'And here,' his voice said again, this time much closer on his left-hand side, just across the far side of the running stream. Again, nothing.

'I don't have time for games!' Juan stamped, quickly spreading his arms wide to regain his balance. His echo laughed.

'Oh, well in that case, you'd better go and check down by the pool,' his echo giggled, seemingly highly amused by the whole situation. Juan couldn't say it was a pleasant experience conversing with himself.

The grass rustled and the water lapped as he climbed carefully down from the rocks. Pushing through some thick yellow flag and purple ragged robin he found his way onto the shingle by the stream, which wound a clear path down to the pool.

His shoes beat like a snare drum on the shingle as he followed the meandering stream gradually downwards. It was thankfully cooler in the shade of the giant rushes and sedges, which bordered where he trod, and Juan found the movement of the water both calming and agreeable, though he was becoming increasingly anxious about facing his task.

Perhaps the Fairies were already waiting for him? Perhaps they knew what was happening and were only awaiting further instruction? Perhaps Sophia was right, and they shouldn't be meddled with? So many perhaps', Juan thought, *perhaps* I should just find them first and then see what happens.

When he turned a sharp bend in the stream's course it fell and ran down several rocks before steadying itself over a patch of giant circular lilies and was strained through a thick covering of peculiarly long silver shimmering flowers that looked beautiful but somehow unnatural. Whilst Juan took a moment to study them, he thought he heard the sound of laughter rising up out of the spray. This time the high laugh was certainly not his own; it came from the direction of the pool. He looked out but couldn't see anything for the trees, and so quickened his pace, breaking into a jog.

More sounds of life hit his ears the closer he got to the trees lining the pool, quiet shouts escaping through the branches and flowing on the fragrant air. Juan felt his heartbeat quicken. He wasn't anxious now, he was excited. With every step he felt himself getting closer to the arms of his family, reaching out to embrace him.

The laughter grew louder as he approached two wild oaks, as tall as towers, resting over each other to create an arched doorway into the pool. He passed through the overhang and was greeted with a sight matched only by the cheers of happiness and hoots of joy, which burst out from the other side.

Juan didn't know where to look first. There was an explosion of colour and play wherever his eyes rested.

A group of young girls, wrapped in material of vibrant reds, yellows, pinks and whites, were swinging from the golden leaves of a weeping willow and, tucking their transparent cobweb wings behind their backs, gracefully diving into the water, barely disturbing it. Others screamed and applauded from the branches as each girl slid into the water without so much as a ripple and, emerging, splashed every one in the crowd on the shore, who shrieked with delight.

Further round the pool, boys who looked to be the same age as Juan, were jumping from a far higher spindly branch of an alder tree and bombing into the water, making as much noise as they could. One boy, dressed only in loose lilac trousers, was hovering above them, his wings a blur, and laughing hysterically as he threatened to throw a giant crabapple down onto the swimmers.

Further on still, a group of mothers in yellow dresses were sitting up inside the heads of sunflowers, which leant down to a small cluster of mushrooms. Children were happily sitting down cross-legged on top of the mushrooms having their hair tied, bunched, plaited and spiked by the ladies behind them as they played at pat-a-cake with one another.

The children only stopped playing to shout at two older boys who were chasing each other over the middle of the pool. They sped so fast, one just behind the other, that it was hard to keep track of them.

On the far side, what first looked to be a cloud of multicoloured tulips were in fact many older Fairies playing at some fast paced mid-air game involving enormous oranges and pears.

A crowd of spectators lounged on the trodden grass or slept in the hammocks of forget-me-knots near by, only raising their heads to give a weak cheer or take a bite from the fresh, succulent fruit on hand.

Juan couldn't help but smile. Their laughter was infectious. This land was in absolute contrast to how Sophia spoke of it. Her attitude always became cold and abrupt when her home was mentioned. But in truth, it was so languid and alive and utterly divine! Why would Sophia ever want to leave such a place? These Fairies would surely be quick to help him once they knew of the plight that lay beyond the Bridge.

'Good neighbour,' spoke a voice from directly behind him, soft enough that it didn't startle him. Juan turned and was greeted by a boy who looked to be barely older than him. The boy had white blond hair sculptured upwards into many sharp points, making him much taller than he in fact was. He wore a linen apple-white shirt and a pair of loose trousers of the same colour. He was bare footed, bronze skinned and exuded a calm and polite manner. But the most noticeable thing about him was the large petal-like wings, which protruded from holes in the back of his shirt and rested all the way down his back to half way down his legs, moving and fluttering occasionally. He was face to face with a Fairy, and not only that, he was the same size as the Fairy. This was *too* different, he thought, this must be magic.

Standing there, he tried hard not to stare at the Fairy's wings for fear of being rude. The last thing he wanted was to be on their wrong side straight away.

'Won't you have some nectar?' the boy asked, his unblinking wide eyes not shifting from Juan's.

Juan looked down to the flower in the boy's hands, with its long, shimmering silver petals, just like those at the bend in the stream, filled with what seemed to be clear fresh water. With all his haste he had yet again failed to quench his thirst when the chances were there and became acutely aware of the dryness in his mouth once more. He looked up into the kind yet troubled face of the Fairy and though he couldn't be sure, the boy's smile looked somehow unreal. His face spoke of a boy who had lost something dear but was trying hard not to show it.

'What's your name?' he asked, figuring that once simple politeness was shared he could then enjoy their hospitality and have their trust.

'We do not like to be so personal as to know each other's names neighbour,' replied the boy, his voice never wavering with any emotion. Juan, embarrassed by his own candour, looked down at the earth floor.

'Don't look so,' came the smooth slow voice of the boy, and Juan was relieved to see that he had not upset him with his forward manner, 'you've come just in time, drink with us.'

Juan gratefully took the flower cup, but paused when he realised that all the music of screams and cheers had stopped. Every Fairy he could see had ceased their play and was either hovering above the pool or lining its banks, each one holding a flower in its hands just as he did. They raised their cups to their lips as one, and drank. Juan copied them.

The cold liquid touched his lips. It was sweater and thicker than he had expected, like the juice of elderflower berries, but cool and refreshing. As he sighed with pleasure at its taste, Manannin's words passed across his vision, '*do not be tempted by them, it is all shallow and meaningless. Do not be tempted.*' But before he could pay heed to the crippling warning seizing his heart, he had swallowed the nectar.

As the sweet juice passed through him, he felt the deep warning ebb away. Fear first took hold of him. He tried to think on why he was there; the task, Bea and Sophia, his family. But the thoughts of them were growing heavier, as though he couldn't keep a tight grip on them and they were falling from his hands. He thought he could see his mum, dad and sister in front of his eyes, he reached for them, but they were running into a soupy grey mist, out of sight. He felt panicked and afraid, but those feelings were also running into the mist. He tried to think hard on his family, but they had gone, disappeared. He tried to think why he was there, but couldn't remember. He concentrated hard; he was under the Fairy Bridge for some reason, he had a purpose, a task, but what it was eluded him, darted from his memory…some task…some…what was it? He paused. It mustn't be anything of great importance, he thought, if its need was so great he would surely remember it…surely…surely?

The mist in his vision parted and he once again saw the smiling face of the boy that had greeted him. What good folk these Fairies are, Juan thought to himself.

'I'm glad I am here neighbour,' he said to the boy.

'So are we.'

'I think I shall rest here some time, until I remember what it was I appear to have forgotten.'

'Some time then,' said the boy with a half smile. 'In the meantime let me show you a little of our home.' He led the way down to the banks of the pool.

As Juan walked on behind him, he felt an indescribable lightness. Every inch of his body was smiling. The sugary tunes of laughter had struck out once more and the endless stream of play had resumed. He felt a contentment and peace he had never known as he trod over the springy, mossy grass towards the water's edge. Not that he was aware of anything he had known before that moment. He tried to think about a time before being under the Bridge, a past time, but it made his head thump and he quickly stopped. What did it matter? He was where he was, and it was wonderful.

'This is the *Cochistey voish Shilley*, our Pool of Sight,' said the boy, flitting a few paces above the earth and waving his hand out over the pool. 'This is where we feast, drink, and, of course, play!'

'Is that all you do with your day, play?'

'Why, what else gives more pleasure than play?' asked the boy.

'True,' conceded Juan.

'......and what is life worth if not brimmed full of pleasure?'

Good point, thought Juan, nodding his head in agreement.

'There are the tulips diving from the willow.' He pointed at the girls who were again splashing the folk on the bank.

'The apple blossom making their usual mess.' He pointed over at the boisterous boys fighting and bombing from the alder tree.

'The ragwort playing at *troar-crig*.' Juan knew he meant the high-speed game on the far side, with the oranges and pears. 'They take that far too seriously they do,' huffed the boy.

'Oh, and of course the Asrais.'

'Where are they?' asked Juan, looking about for other coloured forms.

'Just look a little harder, that's all.'

Juan looked over the pool and the movement of the water and again saw the glistening shapes of even more Fairies darting to and fro, much faster than any of the others could move. Only the waves of water parting and fleeing from them revealed precisely where they flew. The beams of sunlight passed straight through them making them look like speeding shapes of clear silk.

'Water Fairies those ones, very shy.'

'What about those over there?' said Juan, pointing towards the ladies and children on the sunflowers and mushrooms.

'That's where you're heading actually, so you can ask them yourself. You need cleaning up a bit.'

Juan was gently lifted up by two of the girls he had seen diving earlier and flown over the surface of the pool towards the sunflowers.

'Thank you neighbours,' he called as the two girls rested him in the soft bed of the head of the tallest sunflower. They hung his fleece up on the nearest petal before they stopped beating their wings and fell giggling back down into the water.

Juan lay into the head of the sunflower, feeling the pollen squelch between his fingers, and looked up into the pebbled blue sky. He felt himself drift in and out of a half dreaming daze.

Well isn't this nice, he thought, as he found a ripe plum by his side and bit into it. It certainly was a good plum, though when he tried to remember what a bad plum might taste like his temples began to ache again and he had to stop. Instead he looked up and marvelled at the ever so blue sky, bluer than any sky had ever been. He couldn't take his eyes away from it in wonder.

'Perfect, isn't it?' said one of the older Fairies he had seen earlier, braiding the hair of the younger children. She had hovered over to behind where he lay and was now gently twisting his hair upwards into elaborate knots.

'Perfect,' Juan nodded, hazily, enjoying the pampering touch of the kind lady.

'Even better than the real thing, don't you think?' she said.

'What do you mean?' he asked, staring at it harder.

'Oh, I'm sorry, of course you don't know, how silly of me,' she laughed, leaning over and facing Juan, her face upside down from where he lay.

'You don't think the real sky could ever look so blue as ours, do you? If you follow the horizon you'll notice more clearly the line of the sky and how it curves. Can you see it?'

Juan leant up onto his elbows, the sunflower swaying with his movement, and looked out towards the top of the valley in the far distance. The horizon was a definite grey line, like a thin wall of stone that gradually faded into the piercing electric blue of the sky, where unmoving clouds hovered.

'It's the Bridge, isn't it, the underneath of the Bridge I mean?'

'That's right neighbour,' she smiled, 'the first of the Fairies that came here painted it, and they were even better artists than nature itself. Glow-worms hide in every nook and cranny of the stone work, lighting our world. You'll learn that much here is better than the world outside, everything here is as it should be.'

'But I can't remember what it was like outside. If I try to think about it, my head starts to hurt,' Juan said, lying back and letting the lady rub his temples. All he could think back to was drinking the sweet juice from the strange shimmering flower cups.

'Might I have some more nectar? It was ever so nice.'

'No,' she said in a simple unapologetic tone. 'We only drink the nectar when we congregate shortly after first light, or on very special occasions. We cannot abuse the nectar. It is our most valuable gift from our forebears. The nectar is as much a part of our life as the blood running through us. The nectar keeps us on our path of truth.'

'What truth?' Juan asked, drawn in by her soft voice and the gentle touch of her delicate hands.

'Nothing matters beyond the Bridge,' she spoke, looking deep into his eyes. 'All that matters and all you need is here. What has happened and what will happen is inconsequential, don't waste your time dwelling on it. Memory is a painful thing and the pain you feel when you try to remember is only your mind telling you that those times were evil and should be left well alone. Your life is here now, with us.'

Juan nodded again, feeling his eyes growing heavier.

'Now repeat after me;' the Fairy said, 'all I have is here, this is my life now and forevermore.'

'All I have is here, this is my life now and forevermore.' Juan obediently repeated, his eyes closing shut. He was happy to be under the Bridge, knowing he would remain there for the rest of his days and the kind Fairy's words ran though his mind, over and over again as he drifted off to sleep.

All I have is here, this is my life now and forevermore.

NINETEEN

Mortis ran down to the end of another tunnel. His heart was beating so fast he thought he might faint at any moment, but never had he felt so sure about any actions in his own life. This was his one chance to put it all right, not what his father thought was right or Queen Atta thought was right, but what he, in his own heart, knew to be right.

Turning a corner and rushing downwards he felt an unfamiliar quiet hidden underneath all his haste and panic, as though a lifetime of lies had been removed from his vision and he could see the truth for the first time. He didn't allow the regret he was feeling to well up in his chest, but ran on.

Outside it was still only mid-afternoon and the weak light had already begun to fade much earlier and stretch the shadows far beyond his liking. The sun had barely a chance to shine out through the wild sky, closing in like a curtain, as he had sped his way through the grey roads towards Glen Maye. He went the last mile to the inn on foot so he could travel without being noticed. The last thing he needed was to be stopped and questioned by any of the nosy locals. He was afraid he might tell them too much.

The water had been ice cold as he clambered through the waterfall, but he only pushed himself harder and faster, ignoring the weight of his sodden and ruined tweed suit.

The tunnel suddenly widened and continued sharply downwards, but split at each side of him in opposite directions, well lit by the torches burning at every corner. He was at a crossroads. He stopped and allowed himself a pause to catch his breath, leaning on his knees and panting. The sound of his heart seemed to echo around him, but there was another sound behind it, beating out a rhythm, a much larger, more visceral sound.

Though he knew it wasn't the way he should be going, the sound was drawing him towards it, like a moth to a flame. His steps were slow, as though his body was fighting his mind, pleading with it to go the other way, but still he followed the sound. The nearer he got the more definite a form it took, until he was close enough to make out the separate words resonating with a dreadful passion.

'We have betrayed every Brother and every Sister and no longer deserve our place in this family. Use us as you will.'

It made Mortis shiver and, as he reached the lip of the tunnel, he looked down into the cavernous main chamber below and his blood froze.

The entire expanse of the lofty cavern was shoulder to shoulder with Bugganes. There was not a space left unfilled by the hateful creatures. From where he was, high above them on a ledge, it looked like a thick rug of grotesque insects, alive and moving to the rhythm of their own chanting. There must have been tens of thousands of them.

He held his breath and leaned in against the side of the wall overlooking them all. How could anything stand up and survive against such an army? What chance did the island have against such thoughtless anger? It seemed hopeless for a moment as Mortis watched the hordes, mesmerised by their indomitable power, and held firmly onto the moulded bone handle of his ancient dagger, as if it might be of some protection.

At the farthest point away from him in the hall, but higher up still, he could see their Mother, the Queen Atta, on a dais, throned above her children. She was at her most impressive and hideous, wearing fresh jewellery of weeping flesh, with dark blood draining off the teeth of the skull hanging round her neck. She stared out at the sight of her family with little emotion, but Mortis could still see the dangerous madness flicker in and out of her burning red eyes. She sat there and took in the wonder of her family on the eve of their return to the daylight over-ground. Next to her stood Brother Ordo, grim and haggard, shifting uncomfortably from foot to foot. He was a Buggane bred for survival, not for the pomp that Mother so enjoyed.

Amongst the hordes, enormous staves of wood were jutting upwards, reaching high above them. Mortis counted over a dozen of them in all, each a different height and positioned into a horseshoe formation, like an uneven set of teeth. A number of Bugganes were free from the chanting and had begun to stack each pike with kindling, bark and thick branches at its base. Was this some elaborate ceremony before the slaughter of battle, or some sacrificial rite perhaps? Mortis paused, mid-thought. Sacrifice? It could mean only one thing: the captives had run out of time.

He had to hurry if he was to have any chance of helping them get out before they became the first results of Atta's vengeance. It could be the last thing he was ever to do, he knew that well, and he was determined to face it without fear. He ran back the way he came, continued straight over the crossroads and down, deep down, to where he knew the pit lay.

'There it is again,' hissed Betty Loony through cracked bleeding lips, 'it's something else, I'm sure of it.'

Patrick Tooly pushed himself up onto his feet and joined her in the centre of the pit, staring up into the darkness, listening for any sound other than the grumbling of the creatures. Betty had been right, there was another noise coming from above them that sounded like a busy clattering.

'Eamon, get over here,' he said. 'What do you think that is, that noise?' Eamon untied Aalin from her embrace and passed her to Grayse, who had begun to nod in and out of a sickly sleep.

Eamon stood listening, and was moments later joined by Caren and Breeda Dawson, and all three of the Clague children. They all strained their necks, staring and listening.

'Maybe that's it...' said Robyn, 'time's up. We're no good to

them any more, taking up too much room, like a child's first doll.'
He tried to swallow, but there was no wetness left in his dry
mouth.

Eamon put a firm hand on his shoulder and looked through
the dark into his sunken eyes.

'That's not true,' he spoke sincerely, 'I still have my first teddy
bear.'

Robyn smiled, and even laughed a little as Eamon slapped him
heartily on the back.

They stopped when the end of a thick old rope hit the pit
floor with a slap, not two paces from where they stood. They all
looked at it and followed its faint outline upwards until it went
out of sight. None of them could say a word, or even move, each
too afraid to believe in the sudden hopes that were fluttering in
their bellies.

A breathy voice came from above them, but though they
strained, none of them could make out any of the words.

'Say again!' shouted Eamon up into the blackness.

'Are you all down there?' came the voice, clearer now.

Everyone but Gavan Clague and Markys Dawson sprang to
their feet and ran to where the group was standing. They all stared
up towards the voice, which held every wish in its sound.

'We're all here!' yelled Betty Loony, her eyes welling up with
tears.

'I've come to get you out!'

The words echoed around them all like the sweetest music
they had ever heard. All the children began to jump up and down
cheering, 'We're going home! We're going home!' Cara Watterson
embraced her husband, Colum. Betty Loony closed her hands in
prayer and let tears of relief fall freely from her eyes. Patrick Tooly
ran over to tell Gavan and Markys the news, and Eamon and
Grayse held each other tightly, resting their heads on the other's
shoulders as Aalin clapped her hands in between them.

'We don't have long!' the voice shouted, halting everyone's
celebrations. They all stopped and listened, their hearts thumping
in their chests.

'I'm afraid it's only me here, so I need all of you who have the strength to climb up on your own to come first. If you can carry any of the children, all the better.'

A small panic set in. Colum and Cara Watterson were afraid that because they were elderly and didn't have the strength to climb, they would be left behind. Eamon quickly put their minds at ease, telling them that they would all be leaving, or they would all be staying, no one would be left behind.

He was the first to climb the rope, his muscles rejuvenated from all the excitement. Aalin was wrapped in a shirt, tied tightly around him, cradled to his chest. Patrick Tooly, with Breeda Dawson holding on around his shoulders, quickly followed Eamon. Caren Dawson managed on her own and Robyn Clague heaved upwards carrying both his sisters, Josie and Mona, who held onto him around his back and waist and pushed up from the wall whenever cracks appeared along its face. The rope creaked under the weight, but their enthusiasm seemed to bear their load.

Those who remained watched the others disappear as they ascended the rope, hand over hand. Their breathing sounded quick and shallow as they were left behind, unable to lift their own weight. Grayse, who had chosen to stay and help them up, walked around the group, offering kind words and a gentle smile.

'Grayse!' came Eamon's voice from high above them. 'Tie a large knot in the rope, then everyone can put it under their arms and we can pull each person up in turn.' Grayse didn't question him, she knew there wasn't time, and hurried to tie the rope, her hands were madly shaking.

Cara Watterson was the first to be slowly pulled up, followed by Colum, and then Betty Loony, who still hadn't stopped crying with relief and kissed Grayse gently on the cheek before rising upwards.

Markys Dawson, stifling a scream, had hoisted himself up to standing. His face had the blue sheen of a corpse and, as he staggered over to the rope, Grayse felt as though she was helping a spirit not a man. He gritted his teeth hard when the rope rubbed against his blistered skin, holding back his tears, and managed to give Grayse a little wink before he too disappeared into the dark.

She apologised over and over to Gavan Clague as she dragged his body over the pit floor to where the rope would fall, knowing the discomfort she was putting him through. He mumbled something she couldn't make out as she put the rope over his head and secured it under his arms. His eyes were tiny puffy slits and beads of cold sweat trickled down off his nose as he was pulled slowly to safety.

Grayse stood and watched him go, alone in the close silence of the pit, waiting for the rope to fall one last time, gulping down long breaths of stale air. She felt weak but clear-headed, too tired to feel any emotion. She span around when she heard a sound of more breathing behind her and realised she wasn't alone. They had all forgotten about Reverend Godfrey. He hadn't come out and joined them, but stayed hidden away in his corner.

'Dermot, where are you?' she called towards the wheezing sound.

The Reverend silently slithered out from the shadows. He looked a mess. His downcast eyes were bloodshot and had shrunk back into his skull. He stumbled towards her as though he walked on a rolling ship deck, with outstretched hands, seized up in half opened fists, and shivered from head to toe. He didn't say a word and only stared at the dusty floor.

'You can go up next Dermot, before me,' she said softly, hiding her fear of his battered form.

'I'm not going anywhere,' he whispered, his wide eyes still staring at the floor. 'I'm staying right here. This is my home now, with them. You run along and leave me to my thoughts.' There was a childish devilishness to his voice that made Grayse shudder.

'Don't be silly Dermot,' she said, in a tone she would usually save for Aalin when she wasn't behaving herself. 'You heard what Eamon said. I'm not leaving here without you, so come on.' The rope had fallen in between them.

'But my place is down here, with them,' he said, lifting his eyes to meet hers. She took a step back when she clearly saw that his eyes were glowing as red as the creatures did, a torch in the darkness. 'I can't go back up there with you. What will they all say about me? Evil things, evil!'

He showed his teeth like a wolf threatening its prey, and his hand lashed out towards her. But he stopped. Something held him back. There was confusion in his eyes, a child's confusion before telling its first lie.

Grayse slumped forward. She was too weary to fight with him. He seemed possessed. She wished she could grab him and force him into the loop of the rope, but she could hardly stand upright her legs were so tired. She looked back into his eyes.

'Don't you want to see it again Dermot, the island?' she said, hearing her husband's words running around her head; *we're all leaving or we're all staying.*

'I always think it looks its most beautiful at this time of year. The leaves will have turned bronze and gold and crunch under your feet, and the mornings will be as crisp as ice and as blue as the sea. I'll bet Maughould will be looking like a painting Dermot, the church will be covered with moss, and the grass will be shining with fresh dew.' Grayse's heart was aching as she spoke but she could see that she had begun a battle behind the Reverend's eyes. He had begun to shiver more violently, as though he was trying to free himself from chains that bound him. The light in his eyes faded for a moment before flaring out even brighter, igniting the dank pit. He screamed out and bit down against the pain, stamping his feet.

The fit didn't last long. His breathing settled and the fire in his eyes dimmed and finally went out. He looked up to Grayse, and she saw the soft, fragile features of the Dermot she knew once more. She reached out her hand to him.

'Come back to us. Don't stay down here in this wretched pit. You do want to see your home again, don't you?'

He weakly nodded his head and stepped towards her. Grayse took him by the hands and gently squeezed them, feeling no more threat. She held his hand until he went out of reach, jolting as the aged rope frayed yet more, and again waited, now truly alone in the dark. She smiled when she saw Aalin's tatty doll she had made her covered in dirt on the floor, it's grimy face still smiling, and she picked it up and put it in her pocket.

As she pulled herself up, a shrill twang sounded the breaking of the rope. She was now holding onto barely a few strands. Panicking, she sped up, fear giving her strength, and, only an arm's length from the lip of the pit, the rope finally gave in and snapped. She screamed and swung her arms helplessly upwards, and to her surprise caught onto a hand, which closed around her wrist with a vice-like grip. The hand pulled her up and over and she saw a face she was not expecting: Brendan Mortis, Juan's history teacher from school. Had this been the man who had come to save them, alone? Why, in Manannin's name, was he here?

Mortis could see the confused expression on her face and pre-empted her questions.

'I don't have time to explain,' he said to her, untying the rope from the torch bracket on the wall and gathering its length into his arms. 'Ask Juan, he'll be able to tell…'

'You've seen Juan! What's…'

'Not now! We don't have time. Listen to me all of you.' His eyes glistened in the burning torchlight. 'You mustn't tell anyone about what has happened to you. Come up with any story you can, but don't tell them anything that you've seen.'

'They wouldn't believe us anyway,' Breeda whispered to Caren.

'Be that as it may, it is more important than you can possibly realise. Every life on the island may depend upon your silence.' He waited until everyone had nodded and agreed before continuing.

'Go up any tunnel you can, never down or across, keep on going up and you'll find your way out.'

'There's other people down here,' Patrick Tooly remembered and blurted out, 'we heard them through the walls.'

'That's where I'm heading, but none of you can wait, you have to go at once.' He paused for them to make a move. 'Go!'

Eamon grabbed the flaming torch from the bracket on the wall, and went to shake Mortis' hand.

'We won't forget this,' he said. 'See you on the other side.'
Mortis only nodded, unable to express to him how unlikely that was.

Eamon rushed to the front of the group, hand in hand with Grayse, clutching Aalin close to him, and led them on their way home.

Mortis didn't watch them go, but turned on his heel and plunged deeper into the tunnel ahead of him.

The deeper he got the more the air changed into the foul stench of death. It was lifeless and sickening and he tried to take as shallow breaths as he could to stop the painful gagging.

The tunnel widened and dipped suddenly and the walls of green-flecked secretion stopped, leaving the bare rock, like raw skin, beneath it. He threw the torch to the ground and span around where he stood. Though he couldn't describe the feeling, he was certain he was in the right place. It couldn't be possible to get any deeper into the thick strata of the rock. His clothes were clinging to him from the heat and he peeled off his thick tweed jacket and discarded it. There was no sign of any opening in the rock, certainly no crack big enough for an ant to crawl through, let alone a fully-grown Fynoderee.

He began to feel panic rise up inside his chest. It wouldn't be long before some guard passed this way, he was sure. He fell down onto his knees and began to scrabble at the earth, desperately brushing dust away from the smooth rock floor.

'We don't want evil things around us do we, evil things that could chase me and mummy and you and your friends, and do nasty things and hurt us do we?'

His father's words splintered his mind.
'Open, please, open,' he said out loud, clearing away the dirt and finding a thin jagged seam in the rock.

'We should get rid of every last one of them, all of their world, before they get rid of us.'

'Damn you, OPEN!' he screamed, banging his fists hard down onto the floor. There was a loud crack as the seam stretched to the length of a man and the rock crunched its way open to form the wide open mouth of a well. Mortis hid back against the wall as the dust settled around him, before crawling to the edge of the mouth and peering down over the edge.

'Hello?' he tentatively called down.

'If you have come to humour us, I will break your neck like a blade of grass, just like I did to your Brothers and Sisters.' The voice of the Fynoderee rumbled through him. It held a weight and power he had never heard before. He had to grip down on the rock so as not to run away and forget them.

'I've c-come to help you,' he stuttered, 'to help you out of this hell.'

There was a silence then a distinctly female voice called up from the depths.

'And why should we trust you?'

'Because I am a man of my word,' Mortis quickly answered.

'Man!' boomed the male voice. 'We have always survived without your help, and today will be no exception. Go back to your comfortable home *man* and leave us in peace. These are not matters that concern you.'

'Your son sent me!' he shouted, the words echoing out. 'I am here on your son's words and I believe that if you do not accept my help you will certainly never see him again.'

As he let his words rest in the quiet, a webbed hand reached out and grabbed him by the shoulder, spun him around and pulled him up harshly. The red eyed Buggane looked into Mortis' face with a mask of dismay. Mortis looked down to the creature's belly and saw the serrated rusty blade of his own dagger protruding from its gut. The Buggane coughed once before its eyes rolled back into its skull and it fell forwards, toppling over the rim of the well, and limply falling into the abyss. It was several moments before the sound of breaking bones arose from the bottom.

Hundreds of paces away in the main chamber, Queen Atta

flinched. She had felt the death of the Sister and leant over to Brother Ordo, whispering in his ear, she then closed her eyes and clenched the stone arm of her dais.

'Now do you believe I'm here to help you?' Mortis called down, shaking with shock. 'Atta will have sensed that. There is no more time for decisions, I'm throwing down a rope.'

As Mortis turned his back on the well and began to uncoil the remnants of the rope from around his waist, a loud cry of cracking rock sounded all around him. He spun back and saw that the entire well was closing in on itself.

In the depths, the walls of the cave were shrinking closer towards Dane and Méa, like a pool filling with water. The rock would crush their bones until they were nothing more than powder.

'Quickly!' beckoned Dane, forcing his back against the moving walls. They both jammed their feet against the opposite side and, pushing out, chimneyed upwards. Their backs tore against the uneven wall, cutting and slicing their skin, and their knees were moving closer into their chests as the rock sealed together. They weren't going to make it. They were going to be crushed.

'Grab my hand!' shouted Dane. Méa reached out and took hold of him. As soon as she did so, Dane threw her the final way before scraping up and over himself as the mouth closed up and tore out only a few strands of his fur.

Mortis faced the two Fynoderees. One was a faded golden colour and slight of frame with soft delicate features, and the other was a deep grey, flecked with black and of a strong build with wide shoulders and a square jaw. They both lay there breathing heavily and watching him like he was a dangerous wild animal.

The male Fynoderee slowly stood up and walked over to him, sniffing the air around him and looking directly into his eyes.

'Strange,' he said, 'I'm certain I know you from somewhere.'

'My actions in the past have no bearing on my actions today.' Mortis replied, trying to return the stare without his own guilt crushing him.

'Well,' said the Fynoderee, backing away from him, 'your actions today have proved you a worthy man. Will you lead us out of this maze?'

'My business is not yet finished here, there is one thing I've left to do, and it must be done alone.'

'Don't be a fool, you'll be offering yourself as a snack to the Bugganes. Come with us,' said the female Fynoderee, reaching out her hand. Mortis so wanted to take it, to take the hand of those he had tried to destroy, but stood firmly against her words.

'No. There are many tomes left of your story, mine has mere pages remaining, but I intend to use them wisely.'

'Then we part here man. May the luck of Manannin walk alongside you,' and the two Fynoderees began to rush up the tunnel.

'Wait!' called Mortis after them. 'Will you be able to find your way out?'

'We'll manage,' said the female Fynoderee, a half smile breaking across her lips. 'Do we have strength enough?' she asked the male Fynoderee by her side.

'We'll see,' he replied, taking her hand.

As Mortis watched them, they became the darkness and the rock before his eyes, and as the tapping sound of many webbed feet running his way grew in the tunnel, they were gone.

TWENTY

Juan awoke to the smell of lavender and rosehip, and let out a long, slow breath. He knew he had been under the Bridge for many days, perhaps it had even been many months. He tried not to think back further in case his head began to ache again, so perhaps it had even been years. He was sure he hadn't been there forever. He was sure there had been something and somewhere before all the play and idleness had begun. He couldn't think what or where, but he was still sure, as sure as he had hands and feet and a voice to speak.

Time had elapsed into senselessness. It had congealed into a mess that didn't come from anywhere or go to anywhere, but floated somewhere in between. Juan had spoken to his neighbours about it early on, but they were quick to put his concerned mind to rest.

Whilst walking barefoot along the banks of the pool, feeling the cool water between his toes, two young Asrais, flitting by his side, were so excited to tell him, they span around him inside out and upside down.

'That's the best part about being under the Bridge,' they chirped, speeding through his legs and nearly throwing him to the ground, 'we can enjoy being children for ages.' Juan stopped and stood where he was.

'What do you mean?' he asked.

'We can enjoy being children for ages,' repeated one of the Asrais, hovering upside down in front of his face. 'You see, when our elders brought us here, they wanted to give us a present that we could enjoy for a long, long time. They said the best present anyone could ever have is childhood, and so they wove a web, a really special web, around the Bridge. The web is so special and so tightly woven that time can hardly escape, it's practically trapped inside.'

'Like a spider in a bottle!' shouted the other Asrais, scampering

on the ground in her best impression of a spider.

'That's right neighbour,' said the first. 'So we get to enjoy the best time of our lives…for a long time to come!' They both burst out laughing and flew out spinning into the centre of the pool, light passing through them, until they were too difficult to see.

How nice, thought Juan, watching them fade into the light. Although he felt a moment of sadness that he may never get the chance to grow up, the feeling quickly passed and he continued to paddle through the *Cochistey voish Shilley*.

Every new day brought the same pleasures as the day before. Every Fairy congregated around the pool at first light to jointly drink their nectar and exchange complements with one another. The sunflower mothers had given Juan fresh clothes, after they spent an eternity scrubbing the grime off him. He now wore loose woven purple trousers, tied at the waist and a purple top, which kept him cool in the lazy hazy days. The sunflower mothers had told him that the colour purple suited him perfectly, and though he lacked any wings he should still fit in well enough. Juan blushed at this, and cheerless as he was to hang up his fleece on the petals of a honeysuckle, he soon forgot about it. He had even formed his own team that rivalled the older ragwort at the game of *troar-crig*. Two Fairies had to hold Juan up and be his wings for the duration of the match, but he did have a good strong arm and could throw a pear as far as anyone under the Bridge. Indeed, he was hardly aware that he was in any way different to his neighbours, they had welcomed him with such warmth. He often reminded himself that he wasn't some relative or old friend that had returned from a long trip elsewhere, but if he pondered on it for too long he only confused himself again.

He had quickly become quite a swimmer and spent most of the days basking in the light down by the pool. He took part in diving contests with the tulip Fairies, who always cheered and whistled as he climbed higher up the willows and dived or bombed into the water from such a height. He could even beat several of the apple blossom boys in races along the length of the pool and would splash them and laugh as they came in after him.

He had asked the names of his new friends many times, but was always berated and given the same answer.

'We do not like to be so personal as to know each other's names neighbour.'

Why? He thought that they were all friends and it stung him that they couldn't speak as friends did, as he had done with…someone sometime before here.

He still enjoyed their company however, and especially relished sharing the sweet juice, though he felt peculiar for a short time afterwards and his mind had trouble resting on anything for more than a matter of moments.

Many of the Fairies spent the rest of each day idling away their time, lounging in the meadows and brooks or admiring their own reflections in the stream and poolside. Groups of violets would gather together and paint each other's toenails, sorrels would plait the hair of pansies, and orchids would argue with roses over who was the fairest. Juan was free to walk where he wanted, through the valleys and up to the edge of the Bridge, spending much time marvelling at the paintwork of the Fairies. Even close up it was easy to mistake the stone face as sky, although when Juan reached out to touch it and confirm the illusion, a tearing and razor-like pain cut through him, making him fall and run back down towards the safer pastures near the pool.

There was no dawn or dusk under the Bridge, and no morning or noon. The glow worms ignited to announce the break of day and their light ceased at the close of each day. Everyday it was the same, beautiful golden light shining down from the pale blue heavens onto the pea green valleys. Everyday the same.

'Why did you come here neighbour?' Juan asked his apple blossom friend who had first greeted him.

'It's so long ago I try not to remember neighbour,' he began, in the smooth slow voice that Juan found so comforting. 'The elders say it was because we had had enough of fighting and hiding or some such,' he said, swinging Juan up onto a high branch of an alder tree and hovering, thinking in front of him.

'That's it,' he called out, 'they said the land beyond the Bridge had so many troubles and was changing so fast that they decided it was best to leave it to take care of itself and take solace where we could find peace, harmony, and...' he span through the air, somersaulting a dozen times before falling headfirst into the water, 'room enough to spread our wings!'

He flew back up, laughing, and sat next to Juan on the same branch, letting the warmth of the day dry him. They both swung their legs back and forth and Juan threw a fresh crab apple into a group of tulips, busy dying and braiding their hair.

As the shouts of the tulips quietened, the blond haired boy looked all around him before sitting up in the branch and facing Juan.

'I know we're not supposed to talk about it, but...do you think you might be able to tell me about what it's like beyond the Bridge? I don't try to remember very often, but when I do I get this horrible feeling that someone has put a hand inside my head and is squeezing it into a fist, so I stop.'

'It's the same with me,' Juan admitted in a hushed voice. 'I would swear to you that I know I came here for some reason, but I can't think what. It's as though a dark cloth has been dropped over that part of my mind and I can't lift it to look what's underneath.'

'Perhaps if you gritted your teeth and thought really, really hard, you might be able to find something under there.'

Juan looked around one more time, just to check that nobody was paying them any attention. 'I could give it a go I suppose,' he said, closing his eyes and settling back down on the branch.

He had no trouble remembering back as far as waking up in the head of his sunflower, leaning in the breeze, on his first morning under the Bridge. But then he tried to push himself further back, to lift the dark cloth covering his mind. He had travelled for some reason. He saw a blind man, and the sea. There was something he had to do. He felt the familiar burning behind his eyes begin again, hot and needle sharp. He tried to lift the cloth higher. Something was important, some task. He clenched his teeth against the pain. Heat upon heat upon heat. People he knew were in trouble. People he loved. His eyes began to water. The pain sliced through him. Family. He felt faint. Bea. Darkness was coming over him. The cloth was too heavy. *They must want to save themselves*. He retched, and fell forward into his friend.

'What? What was it?!' said the boy, catching him before he fell.

Juan let the pain quickly subside with relief. 'I…I don't know, but it hurt that's for sure.'

They both looked down towards the tulip girls, who were now whispering to each other and pointing up at them.

'I'm sorry, that was my fault, I shouldn't have asked you to do that. Maybe we shouldn't try it again.'

'But it's so silly,' said Juan, standing up and balancing with his toes curled around the rough wood. 'We shouldn't have secrets like that from each other. I mean, you are a friend aren't you?'

'Of course,' answered the boy, though he was beginning to look worried.

'But I don't even know your name.'

'That's because…I can't remember it,' he said sadly. 'Every time I try, I feel like you just did, as though I could pass out with pain.' He looked down towards the girls once more before turning back to Juan and whispering.

'What's *your* name?'

That was easy, Juan thought. Nobody and nothing could take that away from him.

'Juan Kerruish.'

As soon as he had spoken, his stomach shrank, his head splintered a thousand times and he fell from the branch.

When he came to, he was back in the head of his sunflower. He sat up, but felt queasy and weak, and so lay back down to rest amongst the soft pollen again.

'What happened?' he wheezed.

'You broke a rule,' said a sunflower mother, smoothing his brow with a damp dock leaf. 'You break a rule, and you feel it. I suggest you don't do it again.' She left the cool dock leaf on his forehead and flew off, leaving him weary and restless.

After an uneasy sleep, much of his strength had returned and he climbed from his bed, sliding down the stem, and joined everyone down by the poolside just in time for nectar.

But something had changed.

Whilst walking barefoot over the cool spongy grass, he found that he was not thirsty. He found he had no desire for the sweet juice. In fact, he didn't want to have it at all.

As he was passed his flower cup, brimmed with its translucent liquid, he accepted it graciously, smiling at the Fairy as he always had. But he already knew he wasn't going to swallow one sip.

Every Fairy circling the pool, not a space between them for its entire circumference, raised their cups. Juan did likewise, but when they drank he cautiously poured every drop of his nectar onto the earth and watched it as it drained into the warm and thirsty soil.

By the time the light of the glow worms ceased for another day, and every Fairy had fallen into their own slumber, Juan lay still, wide eyed and awake. His head no longer hurt and there was no dark cloth shrouding his mind.

He had begun to remember.

TWENTY-ONE

Mortis sniffed the air. The odours of burning peat and kindling drifted past him. The scents made his drowsy body smile in the unforgiving darkness. It was all that he could sense. He tried to move his legs but he could feel nothing. He tried to lift a finger to scratch, but it was as though there was no finger to lift. All he could do was breathe and let the timeless smells lift his spirits.

He knew now why they stirred such longings in him. How amazing he thought it was that they could arouse such memories. He was suddenly a child again in his front room, sitting by the hearthside watching the flames and smoke of the fire skip up the chimney. He sat back on his ankles gazing, mesmerised by the colours, as he carefully put another lump of coal on the fierce heat and wiped his black, sooty hands on his trousers. He loved watching the hypnotic movement of the flames, one moment they were playing, the next they were fighting. Though he knew it would only be moments before his father would come in and tell him that it was time for bed, he couldn't pull himself away. He was ready to put on his saddest and most sorrowful face, pleading to stay just until the fire had died down.

'Please Dad, it won't be much longer!' he would whinge.

'Brendan, you know if your mother were still here she wouldn't approve. If you're very good and go to bed now, without any fuss, you might get a story.'

He hated it when his father used his mother's words to make him feel guilty. It was unfair and mean of him. She'd been gone for so long he could hardly keep a clear picture of her in his mind, which made him feel even worse, as though forgetting her would be some sort of betrayal. And no, he didn't want a story, he wanted to watch the fire, and listen to its chatter, crackling and popping.

He breathed in the hot, sweet scent once more, but the smell had altered. As the room in his mind faded, bleeding into darkness once more, the smell became a stench, unwholesome and putrid, reminding him all too cruelly of where he was. The burning caught in the back of his dry throat, tickling it with sharp talons, making him cough and feel nauseous. His eyes began to sting and when he went to open them they seemed swollen shut, like trying to pry open a rusted lock. He wanted to rub them and scratch his face, but his hands still wouldn't work. He couldn't even twitch a little finger.

As his body gradually awoke, so too did the excruciating pain. There was a hard, dull cramp in both his shoulder blades, making them tense and uncomfortable and his arms were also immovable down by his side. Slowly he realised he had been stripped of all his clothes and was sitting upright on some cold stone chair. When he tried to wriggle free a tearing sensation split over every part of him, scraping and pulling until he ceased.

He wasn't surprised that it was like this. It couldn't be any other way. He knew that when he watched the two Fynoderees disappear in front of his eyes and the pack of Bugganes running towards him, he would likely end up here, trapped and enslaved to their mercy. He hadn't struggled against them as they tackled him in the deepest tunnel and threw punch after punch until he couldn't feel them any more. He was relieved he was alive; there was still more to do. To fail after getting this far would be a fine thing.

The pain came in stronger more visceral waves, shuddering through him, as his senses regained more life. He wanted his body to give in to the waves and crash into the blackness where pain could be forgotten, where mistakes were forgiven and it would all be a memory, but not yet, his mind screamed at him.

With great effort he pried his eyelids open. They were so puffed up that he could barely see through the slits, though it was enough to focus without the dense smoke making them water too much and he then saw where he was.

He was in the centre of Atta's main chamber, circled by a thick wall of smoke. His neck was too stiff and his head was too heavy to lift and see properly, but as he listened a single shrill voice became more distinct, it was an unmistakable voice Mortis knew immediately, the only voice he needed to hear, the voice of Queen Atta herself.

'It is wasteful fussing over them Brother Ordo, they're gone. Who knows, you may have your chance to find them once more as soon as the moon sets and the sun rises. I consider it my fault that I didn't anticipate the possibility of this happening. I did not see clearly, I admit that, but what does it matter, we learnt so little from them that we didn't already know.'

Mortis quelled a laugh. It hurt to even smile, his lips were so chapped and dry, but he had done it. The people had got out.

'But they will talk Mother, they could prepare…'

'They will not talk!' Atta cut in on the husky, phlegm-ridden voice of Brother Ordo. Mortis could now see their red eyes shining though the fog. 'They do not know what they have seen. They have nothing to say that other man-folk will not scoff at. We are myth, a fairy story, and nobody believes in fairy stories anymore. Am I wrong?'

There was a silence. Mortis knew that silence. He had felt that silence. He willed them to come closer still, so he could see them more clearly.

'But Mother, changes were happening, just like you said they would.'

'What kind of changes?'

'One of them showed signs of the first stages of change. It is just like you said; squeeze hard enough and they will turn.'

'One of the man-folk that Sister Anik and Brother Hemi were working on?' she inquired hastily.

'No Mother, that is what is most surprising. Sister Anik and Brother Hemi's work only made their wills stronger. It was one of the others, a man battling with his own faith, unsure of which fairytale to believe in, Godfrey or something. He was vulnerable and the turning had begun.'

'We cannot dwell on this now. My concerns lie solely on the painted boy and that beast of a Fynoderee. I can feel their very shadows laughing at me. I must have them before the moon sets. I refuse to have them getting in our way any longer. The boy will be with the beast, but where the beast is Manannin only knows.'

This was good, thought Mortis. This was what he had been waiting for. Now all he needed was to get their attention. He winced against the pain as he tried to move, and again couldn't. His skin was somehow welded onto the dais where he sat. Deep thin wounds across the underside of his body had been blended into the rock, inseparable from his bare, pale flesh. If he were to pull himself free, he wouldn't be taking his skin with him. A high price to pay for freedom, he thought, leaning back and wheezing. He tried to shout out, but the words wouldn't escape his throat, now sickly sweet with the taste of his own blood. All he could manage was a weak splutter, as he nearly choked. But it did the trick. Several sets of flame-red eyes quickly turned his way and floated through the grey mist towards him.

'He's awake Mother,' said the raspy voice of the deathly thin Buggane, now staring down at him and lifting his head by the jaw to look him in the eyes. Mortis could see she was an ugly creature, with a spine that jutted harshly out behind her and a smile that widened at his discomfort.

'I can see that Sister Anik,' said Atta, swiping her hand away so Mortis' head fell back down onto his chest. He flinched at the tightness of the skin on the back of his neck, where it had bonded with the stone. Mother grabbed his hair in her webbed fist and yanked his head sharply back. Mortis inhaled in shock, until their eyes met, and behind all the anger and hate, he could clearly see the hurt buried deep within her, the hurt he had caused her by his treason.

He stared back defiant, refusing to let Mother see back into his own mind. He couldn't let her see he was concealing a secret. He had to keep it hidden for as long as he could. If he revealed where the Fynoderee was hiding too soon, Mother would surely suspect foul play. She would know she was being drawn out of the earth like a splinter and she would know the snare that Bea had set in Mortis' mind. She would smell it on his breath and in his words. He had to let her draw it out of him, to make her believe she had pried the words from his mind herself. She squeezed his hair tighter, pulling him closer and he felt the skin on his back begin to tear and weep.

'Where are they?' she growled through clenched teeth. Mortis wanted to laugh in her face, or spit in her eye, but he couldn't. Mocking her would only rouse her suspicions. Instead he creased his brow and feigned absolute ignorance as best he could.

Mother threw his head back against the dais and immediately pulled him forward again. Mortis struggled to keep conscious and coughed on the bile rising in his throat, but he kept focused on Mother's eyes, and continued to stare steadfastly. He must let her take him to the brink of his own sanity, the edge of his own life, before he spoke. Only then would she think it was a secret not to be spoken, a true secret not for her ears.

'Where are they?' she asked again. Mortis answered with an expression of both confusion and dismay.

As his head hit the rock for another time and he blacked out for a moment, it was only then that he truly realised he would never see the light of day again. Maybe he had known all along, but now it struck him with a new definition. There would be no morning sky, no lazy faces of Gelling, Creer, Turner and Coombs staring at him from behind their desks in his classroom, and no Olivia Owen, blushing as she played with a loose strand of hair that had escaped from her bun.

As the red eyes of Atta came back into view, he knew it was time. He coughed and opened his mouth to speak.

'I...I know w...where they are...the boy...and the F...Fynoderee.' He caught his breath and tried to look as helpless as he could, to make Mother believe he was truly terrified and didn't want to speak. She didn't frighten him anymore. 'It's them you w...want isn't it?'

It had worked. Mother held his face with both her hands and pulled him even closer, his back peeling from the rock. Mortis couldn't help it and he screamed. It felt good to release the pain surging up like steam inside him.

'Come now my child,' she said, stroking her greasy hand down the side of his face. 'Tell your Mother what she wants to know, and I promise I'll save you any more…discomfort.'

Mortis allowed himself to smile. He could see the desperate hope in her hideously beautiful face. She would have to work for her prize. This was good.

'Tell me!' she yelled, smashing his head once more. Mortis felt a wound open up on the back of his skull and the cool blood slide down his shoulders. This was perfect. Once more and she would truly think it was a secret. He could take it once more. He had to.

'N…never,' he grunted through the dark.

Again she threw his head back. He felt himself start to sink, drowning in the blackness.

He couldn't go yet.

Not yet.

He swam towards the light, for Laxey wheel in the morning and Castletown in the evening, and for Olivia. He wouldn't let them get to her. His cracked lips quivered to make the shapes of the words as he looked through the cloudy, fading light into Atta's eyes.

'F…F…Fleshwick Rock.'

Queen Atta's face instantly lit up as all the fear fell from her expression. She almost looked like a child with the great grotesque smile spreading across her charred face, like an open wound.

He had done it.

Mother let Mortis' face drop and leapt from the dais.

'So foolish of me!' she laughed, running towards Brother Ordo. 'I should have guessed it when I killed the beast's pathetic little brother that they wouldn't have dared stray too far from where they dwelt.'

'Mother?'

'Fleshwick Rock Ordo, Fleshwick Rock! That's where we'll find them. We must go there at once.'

'But Mother…'

'AT ONCE!' Her scream shook the very foundations of the

tunnel. 'They must be destroyed before anything else, I know it, I will not have them laugh at me in my dreams any longer. I will not let them watch me fall.'

Brother Ordo stepped back and watched her. He had never seen her so distracted; it unnerved him.

'I want all the Brothers and Sisters who were preparing the fire stakes for the sacrifices. They will be hungry for meat and thirsty for blood.'

The Fynoderee could not have asked for more, thought Mortis, as everything drifted away from him. The splinter would be drawn from the ground for Bea to discard.

'But Mother, that is nearly ten-fold, no more than two or three have ever been out at one time since before the days of the tunnels.'

'And what do you think would be happening at the next rise of the sun?' she scoffed.

'That is different Mother,' Brother Ordo persisted. 'We have plans. If you do not want an alarm to be raised, then I suggest...'

'I will take as many as I need to ensure that the job is done properly. I want them all armoured, and have my own armour laid out for me while you're at it.'

'But Mother, you are not possibly...'

'I should not need to repeat myself so often Ordo. I will be leading my family to Fleshwick Rock as soon as the moon begins its rise. Now go and prepare my armour, and find me a good weapon.'

'Mother...'

'ORDO?!' Dust fell from above them, and even the torchlight seemed to flicker with fear.

'Yes Mother?' he squeaked.

'Do you have your own weapon on you?'

'Why yes Mother, it is a hand-spike. I carved it myself, but if we could get back to...'

'May I see it my child?'

'Of course,' he said and obediently brought out the spike from behind him. It was perfectly smooth and curved to half the length of his arm with a simple, moulded handle that fit snugly into his webbed palm. He had been very proud of his craftsmanship of the weapon and was pleased to show it to Mother. She took the spike and passed it from one hand to another, feeling its weight and the sharpness of its point.

'This is a fine piece of work my child.'

'Thank you Mother, I too am satisfied with it. But if we could...'

'You know you have always been a favourite of mine Ordo,' she told him wistfully, still studying the weapon.

'I am blessed by your attentions Mother.'

'Nonsense, you deserve them. You are a fine member of the family. I have even thought of taking you as a mate, but sadly I cannot abide you any longer,' she spoke in a cold, off-hand manner.

'Mother...?'

'I cannot abide you child.'

With that she thrust the tip of the spike into Brother Ordo's stomach, and shuddered at his pain. He didn't look shocked, just saddened, as he went to speak but the words failed him and he slowly retreated backwards, fading, and disappeared through the wall of smoke.

Mortis smiled. There was nothing stopping Atta now and he knew the Fynoderee would be waiting for her and she *would* fall. He was numb all over and finally ready to welcome the mysterious dark looming over him as all the eyes turned to go.

'Mother?' hissed Sister Anik.

'What?!' she squealed impatiently.

'What about him?' she said, pointing towards Mortis' twisted, naked, bloody shape on the dais.

'He was to be the one man-folk to remain,' Atta said. 'Now he shall be the first to go. Oh, how irony does tickle me,' she smiled.

Sister Anik and the bulbous Brother Hemi by her side looked at her, puzzled.

'Finish him...in whatever fashion suits you,' she dismissed with a nonchalant wave of her hand, before she also disappeared through the wall of dense smoke.

As the faces of the two Bugganes bared their teeth and ran through the smoggy air towards him, Mortis felt the dark close in. He no longer had to swim for the light. He saw Olivia's face in his mind, smiled, and sank into peace.

TWENTY-TWO

'Wake up…oh, do wake up,' whispered Juan, nudging his blond haired friend once more, whilst grappling onto the stem of the sunflower with his legs crossed tightly round it.

'Oh come on, wake up will you,' he hissed.

'W…what? What is it?' said the boy in a groggy voice, opening his eyes. Once he saw that it was Juan he sat up. 'What's the matter?'

'You've got to come with me, now,' Juan didn't stop looking around him whilst he spoke, checking that everyone was still asleep.

'Why, what is it? It's the middle of the dark, can't it wait until light, I'm half asleep.' He rested back down, but Juan shook him again until he reluctantly sat back up.

'You said you wanted to know what it's like beyond the Bridge.'

'Yes…?' said the boy, warily.

'I can show you,' said Juan. 'You've just got to come with me first. There's something you've got to see.' His legs were starting to shake, and he held onto the petal of the flower to keep his head in view. The sunflower swayed with the added weight and leaned over to one side.

'You know you can't do anything.' The boy insisted, trying hard not to raise his voice. 'Look what happened to you when you even thought about it. If we try any harder we could really hurt ourselves. A tulip girl asked too many questions and tried to get out some time ago, but the damage she caused herself sent her mad, barking mad. They found her soon afterwards drowned in the pool. Go back to sleep, you'll get us both in trouble.'

But Juan wasn't ready to give in so easily.

'Well I've got a friend who did get out. She saw what was wrong here and she refused to be controlled any longer. Do you know how I know that? I remember it. Look, what I've found will mean you won't get hurt anymore, you'll be able to remember and think about anything without ever having to worry again, I promise. So stop whining and climb down.'

The boy was surprised by Juan's brusque manner. He wasn't used to seeing anyone like this, and after huffing and stretching, he soon followed Juan and climbed down the stem after him, dropping quietly onto the soft mossy earth.

Everything was asleep and the quiet was absolute but for the slight sound of the stream running its course down to the pool.

'Where are we going?' whispered the boy, looking around him at all the silhouettes of the sleeping Fairies. Some were lying in the branches of the trees, some in the heads of flowers and some in the lilies floating casually over the surface of the pool. He'd never seen his world like this, and though it was peaceful, he had an unsettling anxiety in his gut. He knew he was doing wrong.

'Just hurry up and you'll see,' Juan told him, running quietly through the bowing, overhanging trees that formed the gate of the pool and up alongside the path of the stream. The hard soles of their feet crunched on the pebbles next to the water, and still Juan ran on. The boy spread his apple white wings wide, hovering a foot or so above the stream's edge and flew gracefully over to catch up with Juan. He had never had any reason to come up this way and it was all very new to him. He stopped in mid-air, his wings beating steadily behind him, and put his hands in the cold water to splash his face and wash the sleep from his eyes.

'Hurry up will you, we're nearly there,' called Juan, risking raising his voice above a whisper. They were bound to be out of earshot from the other Fairies by now. The boy huffed at Juan's bullying and sped up to join him.

They rounded a bend in the stream and in front of them was the mesh of strange tall flowers, their unnatural shimmering silver heads reflecting the undulating water beneath them in what little light there was.

'There,' said Juan, pointing over at them. 'That's why you can't remember anything. That's how they've trapped you here.'

'What do you mean trapped us here? They're just the nectar flowers, they turn the water into our juice, that's all.'

'Exactly,' stressed Juan, waving his arms in exclamation. 'It's the nectar that keeps you here!'

'Don't be so silly neighbour, the nectar only reminds us that all we need is here.'

'I'm not being silly *neighbour*, it blinds you, it makes you forget everything, every memory you've ever had before you were here. It turns you into nothing more than a slave and I don't know about you, but I think that's just not on.'

The boy was scared by Juan's words and quickly looked over his shoulder. They shouldn't be here, talking like this.

'I stopped drinking it days ago,' Juan admitted.

'You stopped drinking the nectar!'

The boy was shocked, that was the highest of insults to the other Fairies, the very idea of it was terrible, and the thought of not enjoying the sweet juice ever again upset him.

'I just woke up one morning and didn't want it, so when everyone was drinking around the pool and I was sure no one was watching, I poured it away.' How rude, the boy thought, no one had the right to waste the precious juice.

'The first day or two was really hard,' Juan continued. 'I was confused and my mind was all in a muddle. I really wanted to drink it again. I wanted the nectar so much I would break into a sweat and shake all over, it was horrible. But I still didn't have any, it was like something inside of me was telling me not to. If I were thirsty, I would come up here and drink from the water further up stream, before it had drained through the flowers. I don't think anybody noticed. You didn't, did you?' The boy shook his head, amazed by Juan's story and waited for him to go on.

'Eventually, I felt I didn't want it anymore, in fact the very idea of drinking it now makes me feel sick.'

'But that doesn't prove anything.'

'I haven't finished yet,' said Juan, impatiently. 'I said that I was all in a muddle before, well it was as though I was having the strangest dreams, even when I was wide awake. Weird and scary pictures kept on popping in and out of my head all the time, pictures that I couldn't recognise or attach to anything. But, as they took a clearer form and joined together, I realised that they weren't dreams at all, they were memories. I remembered everything, who I am, where I've come from, why I'm here, everything.'

The boy was really scared now and couldn't think of anything to say to Juan. He sat down on the pebbles, his wings folding up behind him, and tried to think it all through. He tried to think up some argument to prove that Juan must be wrong, that he must be mistaken, but his mind was blank. A flutter in his heart and the look in Juan's eyes made him know that his friend was telling the truth, however much he didn't like to hear it. He felt stupid, and tricked and deceived. He felt like shouting and crying.

'I can't even remember my own name.'

'You will,' said Juan, sitting down next to him, throwing a pebble into the stream and watching the circles spread out as it plopped into the water, 'and, you'll remember the thick forests, the endless sky and the sea.' The boy rubbed his temples, which throbbed as he tried to imagine a world beyond the Bridge.

'But we've got to let everyone else remember as well.'

The boy turned to him. 'What do you mean?'

'We've got to free everyone. You're all shackled in here. You may not think you are, but trust me I know you are. If you're left here like this, then you'll all die.'

The boy shuddered, he knew Juan meant what he said. He looked up to the sky, nothing but a painted fallacy of night, and wondered what was beyond it and what could want to destroy them.

'But what can we do?' he asked. 'Nobody will want to stop drinking the nectar, and if you try and force them, they'll probably end up doing something mean and nasty to you.'

'We can't change their minds to stop drinking the nectar, but we can take it away from them.'

'And how do you suppose we do that?'

Juan stood up and waded into the middle of the stream. He

strode into the cold current where the water rose up to his waist and headed into the middle of the morass. Reaching down into the water, he firmly grabbed onto a thick sticky stem of one of the flowers and, heaving, pulled it out of the stream's bed, roots and all. The boy gasped.

'You can't do…'

'Yes I can,' insisted Juan, throwing the whole length of the flower onto the bank, 'and you can either sit there and watch, or make this job twice as quick and lend me a hand.' He held onto another stem and yanked it out. The boy watched Juan struggle with a third before he made up his mind to stride out into the cold water and help him. He wanted to remember and he wanted to see the world beyond what he knew.

The current was strong and the rocks were slippery, but they stood their ground and pulled each and every stem out of the bed, one after another after another, until their palms bled and their arms seized up. But with every flower gone, the boy felt the dawn of new mysteries and adventures rising and they laughed against the pain as they did their job.

There were far more flowers than they had expected, a thick covering of them stretched for several feet up stream, and as they continued Juan told the boy his story. He told him of how his family was taken, of Bea and the Fynoderees, of Teéval, and of the Bugganes planning to take their vengeance over ground. With every word that Juan uttered the boy shook his head in amazement, but he believed everything. Juan even showed him the markings over his skin, hidden underneath his shirt and the boy nervously giggled at the madness of it all.

As they pulled up the last remaining flowers and scrambled to the water's edge, they collapsed onto the pebbles, wet and exhausted, but elated.

'That's that then,' said the boy, catching his breath and leaning onto his elbows. 'I guess we've just got to wait and see what happens.'

'Not quite yet,' said Juan. 'We've got to get rid of the evidence first, we've got to burn that lot.' He pointed over at the piles of the dead flowers.

'Burn? What's that word? I don't know what that means.'

'We've got to set them on fire so nobody can do anything with them,' Juan spelt out.

'Fire, what is fire? Do you mean hide them where nobody can find them, because I know a great place we could bury them.'

'You mean you've never…? I mean get rid of them so there will be nothing left at all.' The boy looked at him, puzzled, and Juan knew that there was no other way of explaining.

'Come on, I'll show you.'

'Oh no, I'm too tired, can't we rest a bit, I can hardly move my arms.' Juan stared at him, his jaw locked tight, and the boy knew it was a look not to be questioned and slowly pushed himself back onto his feet.

The boy took Juan's lead and grabbed the largest armful of flowers he could carry and followed him further upstream.

They both made several journeys and dumped the flowers in a large pile behind the rise of pebbles that Juan had stood on when he first arrived under the Bridge. They were close to the boundary, surrounded by reeds of grass as tall as they were, and the boy's head burned, but he worked through it and kept up with Juan.

When they were finished, Juan asked the boy to collect a pile of twigs and branches, and a handful of the driest moss he could find. He did so obediently and returned with a clump of arm-length branches of birch. Juan picked out two stronger pieces and put the rest as kindling underneath the stack of flowers. The boy watched, spellbound, as Juan took a rock and threw it down onto the floor, breaking it in two to make a sharp blade and began cutting a small hole into a piece of wood as much like a flat plank as he could find.

'What are you going to do with that?' he asked.

'Trying a little trick I saw my dad do when we were out camping one time. He'd normally use matches, but this'll have to do. I'm going to try and make fire.'

The boy didn't understand a thing Juan had said, but decided not to question him any longer, he could see that he needed to concentrate. He watched Juan impatiently look for something, give up, then have an idea and pull on the woven cord from his trousers. He wound the cord tightly onto both ends of one of the branches he had chosen to create a makeshift bow.

'Sharpen one end of that would you,' Juan said, handing him another branch and the bladed stone. The boy did so as best he could, though he found it difficult, he wasn't used to such things as sweat and hard work.

When they were both done, Juan wrapped the bowstring onto the middle of the sharpened branch and placed its point into the hole he had cut into the plank. He then took some of the dry moss and placed it into the palm of a dock leaf. He put this nest under the hole of the plank and then took hold of the bow.

'Right,' he said, 'if I've done this like my dad then all we have to do is make the branch spin very fast so that we create enough heat to light the moss, and then we'll have fire.'

'This must be some sort of magic,' said the boy.

'Not magic,' smiled Juan, 'just different.'

They both pushed and pulled the bow making the sharp branch spin and Juan held the stone on top of it forcing it down into the hole. The boy didn't know what he was doing but it was wonderfully exciting. They made the sharp branch spin faster and faster until a light wisp of smoke started appearing, together with the sharp smell of burning wood.

'Keep going,' Juan ordered, and soon enough the moss ignited and the boy nearly fell backwards at seeing the fire sparking from the tiny nest.

Juan acted quickly and delicately took the dock leaf in his cupped hands and put it down into the kindling under the flowers, blowing on it to coax the flames to life.

The sticks and twigs caught alight and what began as a spark turned into a blaze, consuming the flowers in its gold and red lapping tongues. It was the most dangerous and most beautiful thing the boy had ever seen, as attractive as it was frightening. They both clasped hands and laughed as the tall flowers smoked and turned to ash before their eyes.

Whether they liked it or not, the Fairies were going to wake up and face a new beginning.

There was no noise or movement as they quietly returned to the edges of the pool, so no one had either seen or heard their misadventures (although Juan didn't care either way, he saw no other way of bringing them out of their stupor). Before long they had returned to their beds and Juan lay down, restless with excitement and danger.

It happened slowly to begin with. Everyone convened around the pool at first light to drink the nectar, as they always did. Juan joined them and carefully watched. He exchanged looks with the boy on the far bank and drank the juice from his cup. The flavour was sweet and honeyed and for a moment he feared that his plan hadn't worked and he had been mistaken, but as the liquid passed through him there was no numbing of his spirit or senses and he breathed out his relief. None of the Fairies registered any change with one another and politely smiled as usual, but Juan could already see in their eyes that they had felt some difference. He'd seen the same look before, when his parents had tried to convince him that the supper he had cooked for them was delicious, when he honestly knew that it was fairly terrible. They were lying to themselves that everything was as it had been.

The daily routines continued as they had done every day he had been under the Bridge, but the change came quick enough. The lilies dived from the top of alder branches, but soon became bored and argumentative, like petulant children, and flew off in every direction. Asrais chased each other over the surface of the water, but quickly tired and became melancholy, sitting on the banks of the pool and kicking the muddy floor. Other Fairies whispered and pointed at their unnatural behaviour and Juan kept his distance, watching from the edges. Even the heated games of *troar-crig* slowed and became sloppy, each player becoming angry and shoving anyone who flew too near them, or else flying away to sleep elsewhere.

By halfway through the light, an unpleasant weariness hung in the air. No Fairy was talking to another, or if they were, they were arguing or scrapping. It was uncomfortable to watch and made Juan tense as he stood behind the drooping green tears of an enormous weeping willow. But he told himself to be patient and hoped that the memories that would be returning to them would be happy ones.

'I can't do it,' said a voice behind him. A quick hand landed on his shoulder and spun him around. It was the boy, now noticeably paler and covered with a glistening sheen of cold sweat. Juan didn't know what to say to him.

'I can't do it,' he repeated. Juan looked down and saw that his friend's hands were shivering, he couldn't keep still and was rubbing his palms as though they were covered in deeply stained dirt.

'We have to undo what we did, it was wrong of us, I feel all torn up inside.'

'It'll be all right,' said Juan, putting a supportive hand on his shoulder, which the boy immediately shrugged off.

'No it won't, it was wrong. I want the nectar. I can't think straight. I keep on seeing horrible things, trees on fire just like those flowers, Fairies being hurt in awful ways, screaming as their wings are torn off their backs, horrible things. I want the nectar. It's all wrong.' The soft weeping of lilacs began further away as the boy continued to rave.

'What's happening to me Juan?'

'You're remembering neighbour.'

'Don't call me that. Why can't I remember my name, it's just a name but it's so clouded in my mind that I can't reach it. I know that's a tree, and this is earth,' he said picking up a clump of dried mud and crumbling it between his fingers as it fell to the ground, 'but I can't even remember my own name.'

'You will, it'll take a bit of time, that's all. Everything will come back to you, good and bad, and you'll be free. The Fairies that brought you here took your name and your life from you, but now you can have them back, and you won't rely on anything. You won't need the nectar.'

'But I miss it!' he snapped, with a frightened look in his blue eyes. 'You must get it back for me, I'm suffocating.'

Juan grabbed him by both his shoulders and shook him.

'Get a hold of yourself. I can't do this alone. I'm too small for all of this. You know this is the right and only path we can take. Please be strong, if not for yourself, then for me.'

The boy closed his eyes tightly as his breathing steadied and he calmed down.

'You're right, of course you're right,' he said, clenching his fists at his side. 'But I don't like what I can see in my mind, it's all so ugly.'

'It's what they did to you and your people,' Juan realised. 'It's what happened before you were brought here. I'm so sorry. But it is all going to change, and it will be for the best.' He turned and looked over the pool and many figures of drooping and mournful Fairies locked in their own thoughts. 'It has to be,' he whispered to himself.

The sad songs of weeping continued long after the light was extinguished for another day, and throughout the majority of the dark. Juan couldn't sleep in the head of his own sunflower, he wanted to avoid being seen for the moment and after he found and retrieved his woollen fleece hanging nearby, he spent his time wandering aimlessly over the valley beyond the pool. He tried to find somewhere with peace and quiet, away from the incessant and haunting sobs of the Fairies. He imagined what sort of an island the Fairies had fled from and how different it was from his own. He lay down and put his hands over his ears and pretended he was at home in his own soft bed reading a story of dangers where everything turned out well in the end. The hard, uneven ground jabbed into his back, but soon the heaviness took him over and he fell asleep.

The immediate shine of light woke him suddenly and he sat up, groggy and sore all over and looked around the green pastures where he had lain. The first thing that struck him as he stretched and rubbed the sleep from his eyes was the quiet. The weeping had stopped. He stood up and rushed down towards the pool, hoping to get there in time for the congregation at first light.

As he passed through the overhanging trees he was greeted with a sight that stopped him in his tracks. Many more Fairies than he had ever seen under the Bridge at one time now surrounded the pool, from the very young held in the arms of mothers, to the very old gripping onto sticks for support. Every one of them looked heavy eyed and weary, and every one of them was looking straight at him.

Juan swallowed his fear, he knew this was inevitable, though he hadn't wished for it so soon. He knew at some point he would be expected to speak. He felt the weight of Téeval's and Manannin's words rest on him as he slowly walked forward, and he let the thought of Bea help his burden. He would think what his friend would do. He refused to let any feelings of guilt settle on him and he stood as tall as he could in the silence. He looked around the edges of the pool, trying to catch sight of the boy, but couldn't see him anywhere amongst the crowd. He was alone in his task.

An elder Fairy all clad in burgundy robes, with his wings limp and motionless behind him, stepped forward away from the crowd with the help of two younger Fairies on either side of him. Juan had never seen anyone who had looked so old, his skin was weathered like crumpled paper, but there was still a spirited fire blazing within his bright eyes and Juan had to struggle not to pull himself away from his stare.

'So the wingless boy has dared to come before us after what he has done.' The elder's voice was husky and harsh in the early light and he coughed brutishly into his hand. Several Fairies murmured their agreement with what he had said, but Juan still didn't take his eyes from him.

'What you have done cannot be undone; you have released a knot that cannot be retied. You have wrenched us from the shelter we made for ourselves, with neither right nor reason. You have forced those of us who were there, to remember the malicious and callous world that you so casually walked in from. You do not know of the nightmares that we have experienced, you have not seen the thoughts in our minds, the memories of such grisly cruelty afflicted on our kin, and yet you still think your actions were justified.'

More jeers shot out from the crowds. A few Fairies even took to the air to hail down their curses upon Juan. He wanted to run, or at least lower his head in shame, but that was not what Bea would have done. Bea would stand fast, never waver and keep his eyes fixed on the elder. So that was what Juan did.

'You have no idea how long the Bridge took to prepare, a place where we could come and be happy and free at last, a place where we no longer had to hide and live in constant fear. All those that first came here consented. None were forced against their will. Others who came later were generously welcomed, such as you, and this is how you repay us?!'

As the elder railed on, Juan pulled his eyes from him and looked out over the throng. Sure there were many that glared at him with nothing but disdain, murmuring curses under their breath, but there were equally as many with confused and sad faces, looking at him with sorrowful eyes. It was these faces that Juan clung to, these faces that were his hope. He could see that they longed for simple freedom, without the trappings of the Bridge and the nectar. It was these Fairies that he would speak to.

'Yes there were those who wished to remain,' the elder continued, becoming more passionate with every passing word. 'But they fled to the forests, where they more than likely still dwell. We knew we deserved better lives than we had, we deserved nothing less than happiness and beauty forevermore.'

Juan understood the elder's words, but what was happiness and beauty without truth? A lie and nothing more.

'And you, a boy, have come here and ruined it!'

That was it, anger burst out from many of the Fairies like the cork from a bottle.

'It was perfect, and you ruined it!'

'How dare you come here, and take what was ours!'

'The wingless one doesn't know what it was like!'

'The wingless one hasn't seen our dreams!'

'Make them stop!'

'I miss the nectar!'

'I want the nectar!'

'I need the nectar!'

Juan didn't shift from where he stood, but continued to do just as Bea would have done and stood his ground. He watched all the troubled faces and listened to the screams.

Soon the shouts took more order and bled into one strong voice, speaking the words that he too had once spoken and believed.

'All I have is here, this is my life now and forevermore. All I have is here, this is my life now and forevermore.'

The volume grew and grew and many more joined in, those who believed the words, those whose belief hung by a thin thread, and even those who merely followed like confused lambs to the slaughter. Fairies were waving their arms, stamping their feet and jumping several feet in the air and viciously pointing Juan's way. He knew that if he couldn't get a word in, the Fairies would continue until he left, many were too frightened to even listen. His time to speak had come.

Juan reached down into the deep pockets of his fleece and felt for the two fist sized Calling Stones resting at the bottom. He pulled them out and raised them above his head. All the light around his hands seemed to be extinguished, sucked into the blacker than black orbs. With one swift action he brought his hands together and the Calling Stones let forth their wail.

The piercingly beautiful call echoed around the Bridge. It was so loud that Juan shut his eyes against the pain and many Fairies fell and put their hands over their ears. The Stones' lyrical song lingered over the pool for many long breaths before ending with an equal abruptness. The silence it left was almost as strong as the call itself, and Juan's ears rang loudly. But now was the moment, now he had their attention and now it was his time to be heard. He stepped forward to the edge of the water, feeling the coolness of it lapping at his toes, and opened his mouth to speak.

'Do not think you can goad us with your cheap and ancient trickery!' the elder shouted out, refusing to let Juan utter a single word.

'Oh, would you just SHUT UP!!' yelled another furious voice from the crowd. Every head spun around to see where it had come from and who had dared speak to the elder with such impertinence. A small figure rose up into the air and hovered above them all, a figure with scruffy blonde hair dressed in apple white. It was Juan's friend, the boy.

'You are such an old windbag!' shouted the boy, straight at the elder. Several Fairies tried, unsuccessfully, to repress their laughter, and the elder stumbled back into his entourage with shock.

'Why don't you just let Juan speak, you're surely not afraid of what he might say, are you?'

'Juan, what do you mean by Juan?' the elder muttered through clenched teeth.

'That's the boy's name, Juan,' the boy called out. Gasps went out over the perimeter of the *Cochistey voish Shilley*, at the mention of someone's individual name.

'Oh please!' mocked the boy. 'Pick your jaws off the floor, it's not that amazing, it's just a name, everyone has one.' Juan joined in with the chuckling of a good many more Fairies.

'You know we are not so personal as to call each other by our names...neighbour.' The elder was going a distinctly brighter shade of red and broke into another heavy fit of coughing.

'That's because you took them from us. When you brought us here, and offered us salvation, you may have told many of us what we were going to gain, but you didn't tell any of us what we were going to lose.'

'What do you know about it?' coughed the elder, holding on to the two worried looking Fairies on either side of him.

'I'll tell you what I do know,' said the boy, flying into the centre of the pool so that every Fairy could see him, many of whom rose off the ground to get a view of the one who dared speak out against the elders.

'My name is Aedan, not *neighbour*, but Aedan, and I helped my friend Juan destroy the nectar flowers. Over there is Feena.' He pointed to a young lilac girl who blushed at the mention of her name.

'There's Niall and Peddyr,' he said, pointing at two ragwort Fairies that Juan knew from playing *troar-crig*. 'And there's Greeba.' Greeba waved as many turned her way then made a very rude gesture in the direction of the elder and those around her cheered.

'My name's Reina,' called out a proud Asrais Fairy, speeding into the centre of the pool to join Aedan. 'And I agree with Aedan, you are an old windbag!'

'My name's Donachan,' said an older brown-clad Fairy.

'My name's Creena,' called out the sunflower mother that Juan had met on his first day under the Bridge, 'and this is Ina.' The child in her arms clapped her hands together and made a gurgling noise that Juan thought must be a laugh.

'You see,' said Aedan, 'many of us are remembering what you took from us. So I think you should let Juan speak, and we should all listen to what he has to say.'

More cheers than Juan could have imagined burst out into the air. All of a sudden the mood of disdain had turned on its head to one of expectation. Juan exchanged a smile with Aedan and jumped on the mood (as Bea would have done), and this time, without interruption, he spoke into the silence.

'Though I know the purpose of your webs, I believe we have little, if any, time left, so I must be quick.

'I know what you ran from when you came to the Bridge, I know what you are hiding from, and I know that I'm as frightened as you are. But the time for fear has passed. If you run today all you will find is that there is nowhere left to hide. All this will be gone, that's for certain.' He waved his hand out over the pool and the surrounding pastures, so beautiful and fragile.

'Today is not a day to hide, but to face what we fear head on.' Every face in the crowd was held still by what he said, but to him it was as though the words had been in his mind ready to be released all along, as though they didn't come from him at all.

'Something's coming, something bad. I'm leaving now to face it with my friends, if I can find them, but if you don't join me you may as well say goodbye to me, and your friends, and your family and all of Ellan Vannin, because everything will be gone,' he sighed a desperate sigh.

'My mum and dad always told me that one of the worst things you could ever do was tell a lie, and that it would always come back and bite you. All I can offer you is the truth, nothing more or less, but surely that beats hiding under the Bridge and denying what you are?

'I wish there was some spell I could perform to make all the problems disappear so we could all go back home, but there's no such thing. I can't make your minds up for you. I've made my choice, now it's your turn.'

Juan then stood quietly and waited for some reaction, but none came. Even the babbling stream and flowing grass seemed to have hushed at his words, as if they were sharing the indecision of the Fairies. There wasn't a word to be heard under the whole Bridge. He had done what he had been sent to do and now all that he could do was wait for them to choose their own fate.

Wait in the silence.

TWENTY-THREE

The rolling groan of thunder echoed in the sky and the clawing waves broke against the rocks of Maughold Head, shooting spray into the evening air. The heavy swelling clouds, the colour of slate, wove into one another, concealing even the light of the evening, and the mists floated upwards where they froze into sharp hail and fell to settle on the cold earth.

Mr. Boyde drew the curtains in the kitchen and told his son, Ewan, of how he had only once before seen such weather, and that back then it brought nothing but ill news. Mrs. Quilliam had cancelled her dinner in the village of Port Erin and her husband, Hugh, now had to sit with her as she baked scones. Stuart Skelly dared not venture out of doors to brave the storm, and so reluctantly let his wife, Gene, give him his first lesson in cards. Mrs. Cowley had a hot bath, tucked herself into bed and left marking her class's homework until morning. Derrick Kermode checked every window and door in the house for drafts and patted his dog Duke, who hadn't stopped whining for hours. Richard Gill moaned to his parents when they wouldn't let him go out into the yard and splash in the rain, and Johnny stared out of his bedroom window and Sarah stared out of hers, each wondering what the wind was bringing and worrying about the other.

In Fleshwick, Bea had beaten his fists against the mouth of rock that led down to the Great Hall and his home for the last time. The rock had refused to part at his touch, time after time and try after try. As he had pressed his palm down hard against the cold surface where the opening would usually be, he felt a great confusion and mistrust course through him. The very land had curled up like a hedgehog to protect itself, and so denied him entry. The falling hail had begun to settle on his damp fur, and no matter how many blows of frustration he landed on the door, it was to no avail, he was left out in the wicked open.

Bea took hold of fistfuls of the long wet grass and climbed up the slope until he reached the headland. What lay before him, leading up towards Eairnyrey, was moderately barren land, with tufts of aged gorse bushes dotted around the fields, that after the flat pasture in front of him, reached high up at a steep climb. In the distance, the faint glow of a solitary cottage more inland died as its lights were switched off for the coming of night. Bea looked back to the hill in the pale light. If Mortis had succeeded and the Bugganes were coming for him, he knew where he would see them first.

The winds whistled all around him as he knelt down on the earth to conserve his strength. The thick grass swayed in unusual and possessed ways on every side of him as he closed his eyes and blocked out the sting of the icy hail now beginning to beat down on him with yet more purpose. He let his mind calm and settle in a place of cheerful memories, memories of comfort and peace with his mother and father, and of time spent chattering with his dear Sophia, and of pushing and teasing his brother, Céa, with whom time was seldom without laughter.

He rested in his thoughts for a while, where the whipping gale and pin pricks of the hail couldn't reach him, and let the warmth of his memories suffuse his spirits. Though surrounded by emptiness, he felt no loneliness here, he knew now that he was never truly alone. If he should fall, he was certain Céa would be pleased to see him on the far away island from where no one could return. But as much as he missed his younger brother, he had no desire to be rejoined with him so soon – he would try and hold off that meeting until later days. If he did take that journey to the far off place, he would be sure to drag Atta with him.

As his thoughts slipped away from his brother and on to his meeting with Mortis, doubt crept into his mind. But the distant and definite drumming of feet on the highland, the drumming of many feet, joined the sound of the howling wind. Bea sniffed and caught the stench of rotting flesh in the air. His doubts were immediately sated.

They were coming for him.

Bea felt the vibrations of the pounding feet through the ground where he knelt. So many Bugganes hadn't ventured over ground for countless centuries, and now he could already smell their putrid breath on the wind. It repulsed him. Though he said he loved them, the Bugganes still repulsed him. Everything about them made him want to retch. They were the scourge of the island, which was all natural and good but for their rank presence.

The thoughts of them brought forth an untameable anger within him, swelling outwards from beneath his chest. Anger upon anger grew like a dry forest fire that began with a single flame and consumed him until an inferno raged. A deep, penetrating red spread over his whole mane of hair until he was like the fire himself, blazing in the darkening light. He stood up and opened his eyes, ready for whatever came his way, and saw the mottled forms of the Bugganes crash over the top of Eairnyrey, like a wave of death.

There must have been at least fifty of them, Bea thought to himself, as they tore through the hail and began their descent. There were Brothers and Sisters of every shape, size and strength, from Bugganes no taller than his waist but broader than a man with breast plates and pikes, to Bugganes even taller than him with wiry frames and sharp lances held out in front of them. Each and every one of the mob had improvised their arms and armour, which were all carved and chipped out of charred bone. Some wore masks to shield their vile faces, some wore vicious elbow spikes, and some wore shoes out of bone, turning their feet into deadly stabbing weapons. None were unarmed. Bea had nothing but his empty hands.

The black wall of Bugganes had seen him and descended apace, eerily silent but for the pounding of their callused webbed feet. Bea remained unmoved and frantically looked around to catch sight of Queen Atta.

'Dear Manannin let her be somewhere,' he whispered, still searching for her in the tightly packed mass of trampling creatures tearing ever closer down on him.

He glanced around the empty headland, but it was useless, Atta wasn't there and his friends weren't coming to stand with him. Maybe they had failed in their tasks. Maybe they were dead. It was too horrible to think about.

The grass continued to sway in its possessed way as Bea rubbed his palms together and felt the deep scars running along them, scars marking the day of Céa's death: the death the Bugganes brought upon him, those abductors and murderers. Another swell of fire and anger beat through him, and he screamed out to his enemy.

'Do not think you will take me easily!'

With that he let the wind take him and ran head on to join them in battle.

The wind catapulted Bea up and into the onslaught and he hit the first line of the Bugganes like a rock splintering brittle wood. Brothers and Sisters scattered in all directions on his impact, many knocking down others alongside them and tumbling head first down the slope.

Bea fell to the ground, dazed from the initial strike, but bounded back onto his feet and found himself in the middle of the chaos. No sooner had he regained his balance than he caught a webbed fist speeding towards him. He crushed the fist in his and twisted the arm until the creature jerked over with a sickening crack, then kicked him into several others darting his way.

A Sister with a horribly pummelled face leapt past her kin from the higher ground down towards him, baring nails sharpened into fierce talons. Bea ducked and seized her by the throat and the waist and held her aloft as she screamed and writhed, trying to free herself from his grasp. He swiftly brought her down onto his bent knee and she snapped like kindling. The surrounding Bugganes suddenly gave him a wider berth, and began to slowly circle him on the slope. Bea stared back mercilessly at their red eyes and unsightly faces as they laughed and mocked him.

'The odds are against you, beast,' spat one.

'Why make it hard on yourself?' spat another.

'We'll feast on your flesh!' spat a third.

Bea was having none of their games, he had no time for patience and his fiery anger needed satisfaction. He jumped uphill with both his arms outstretched and his fists struck the chests of the two Brothers directly in front of him, knocking the wind out of them. A Sister took her chance and kicked out at him with a spiked boot, but Bea blocked it just in time and struck his assailant in the throat, who then fell backwards, choking for air. Bea quickly grabbed one of the Brothers he had winded by the scruff of the neck and spun him around to use as a shield. The Brother threw up his hands in protest, but the other creatures were too dim-witted and slow and had already begun their beating before realising what they had done. When they paused in surprise, staring at the standing yet unconscious Brother in front of them, Bea used the limp arm of the creature to lash out at the others, making them trip and topple downwards.

As Bea let them roll past him, a heavy kick landed behind his knees, which was followed by a hard blow to the back of his skull, flooring him. He spat out the mud of the earth as he turned over onto his back and saw the dark shape of a foot coming down at his face. He shoved the foot aside and kicked the remaining leg the Brother was standing on out from under him. The ground had become so sodden and slippery in the hail that the Brother tried to scramble to his feet, but instead slid down, tearing at the grass as he went.

Bea pushed himself up, still pulsing with uncontrollable rage, as a Sister with a long black blade, extending like a sword from her hand, swiped out at him. He tried to pull back and avoid it, but it was too late and he felt the cold bone cut across his stomach and the wetness of his own blood stream down his front. The Sister hooted with laughter and dragged her rough tongue along the length of the blade, savouring the taste of his blood, before swinging again to finish her kill. Bea locked the pain away and lunged forward, forcing her wrist away from him and back at her. It happened so quickly that she didn't have time to scream before her severed head hit the earth and rolled away. Bea removed her blade and beckoned for the others to come and test him. He could see that their arrogant surety was waning as they paced more anxiously around him. Their grunts and curses misted in the cold air and their skins glistened as a rare ray of moonlight broke through the thickly woven clouds.

Bea grimaced and shook his head, throwing out a shower of water from his mane and held the blade out as the creatures continued to circle him. As he nudged forward in attack, they nudged back in defence, but he knew that they were still too many. He paused, realising how fast his breath was and passed his finger over the clean cut on his abdomen, which fortunately wasn't deep and closed at his touch.

He continued to fend off each Buggane that was stupid enough to leave the group and try to attack him. No matter where they came from, whether from either side or even directly behind him, they were that much slower than him that he could predict their next move. He cut and slashed all who came near. But he was getting tired. The cold hail was beginning to quench the heat of his rage and his muscles were feeling the fatigue of every block and hack. By far the worst of all was that he hadn't seemed to have done much damage. The creature's numbers were still many. He couldn't keep this up for long.

As the tension of the fight began to weigh heavily on his spirit, the Bugganes suddenly stopped in their circling and taunting and looked up towards the peak of the headland. Bea, taken aback but still keeping his guard high, heard more noise and was hopeful that Sophia, or Juan, or anyone was coming to his aid. The sound got closer and as the dark shadows emerged over the tip of Eainyrey, Bea's heart sank to its lowest depths. It wasn't help that had come, but another wave of Bugganes, as big and daunting as the first. At its head was the face he had been praying to see, the face of Queen Atta herself, smiling down at him. She was more fearsomely dressed than the last time he had seen her, at Céa's death. Her knotted hair was tied back tightly against her scalp with red strings of flesh, sharpening her already piercing eyes, and her body was clothed from top to toe in finely carved bone armour. Each plate perfectly fitted her feminine form and was stained a dark red, much the same as Bea himself had become, the colour of war.

Though panting, the sight of Atta on top of the hill invited a renewed wrath within Bea. He ran into the circle surrounding him and hit out to get closer to her, but with each Buggane he shouldered, two took its place, and those two by another four, and so on. He could make no headway, and Atta remained where she was, flanked by her children, her smile growing as Bea's fatigue grew.

He fought on without gaining so much as a clear foot fall closer, but still didn't take his eyes from hers. He reached out into the dark sky towards her, clawing at nothing but air, and a heavy but fast Brother slammed into his gut and they both crashed to the floor. As soon as he touched the ground, Buggane after Buggane piled down on top of him, and what light there was left his sight as everything went as black as deep sleep. He tried to lash out, but with all the weight squashing him down, it was futile. He thought he was lying in the mud and earth that he would give his body to. He couldn't move, he could barely breathe and the last breath in his lungs was quickly being crushed out of him.

It was just as he felt a calm peace flow within himself, ready to accept his fate, that several miraculous things happened at the same time.

In the dark Bea could make out many noises, first there was the grunting and yelling of innumerable Bugganes on top of him, then a humming and buzzing of such volume that the ground where he lay shook, and then cries of terror and pain as the crushing weight lessened and he found he could move again. He quickly pushed aside the last of the screaming Bugganes and lifted himself up, only for the air in his lungs to leave him again.

The land around the whole slope was shifting and shaking. The strangely swaying grass was now more pronounced than when Bea last noticed it. At first he thought the earth had come alive at his feet, but as the misty carpet of greens and browns of every shade surged upwards, and the deafening buzz increased yet more, Bea's heart leapt at the unmistakable sight of the Forest

Fairies, the *mooinjer-veggey*, filling the air.

Amidst the clatter of a thousand tiny arrows of pine needles shooting through the air, Bea, in his confusion, could hear the small but powerful battle cry of the Fairy Braker, that only days ago he himself had attacked.

The arrows, like sheet rain, showered down on the Bugganes, who ran, swiping at the air in all directions. Bea grabbed hold of two of the creatures running his way and mashed their heads together. As they fell in a heap, he saw a light in the near distance to the east that made him blink in astonishment.

A rainbow of colours was shining out through the dark and coming his way. He stumbled back in fear at the sight. The lights came closer, at the speed of the wind and with them more screams of battle. These were miracles indeed. The Bridge Fairies had come.

The Forest Fairies let out cheers of joy as they were reunited with their kin after so long; reunited against a common foe. They were no longer Forest Fairies and Bridge Fairies. They were united once more. If this wasn't enough, what Bea saw next truly made him gasp and rub his eyes in disbelief. Leading the rainbow was Juan.

Bea's young friend, the *key-per*, was being carried by many of the small Fairies, all holding onto his fleece, keeping him only a foot above the ground. But this was not the Juan Bea remembered leaving on the shore of Dhoon Bay. The Juan he saw now was lithe and determined, bare footed and strong faced in the dress of the Fairies. The boy had changed into a young man, and what was more he had done what none had been able to, he had succeeded when all others had failed, he had freed the Fairies from their hazy prison.

Bea's attention was brought back as he heard a familiar voice shout his name. He swung around, but couldn't catch sight of the one who had called him.

'Bea!' It came again, nearer this time. A Sister, with a build similar to his and a mask with a long spiked snout, dived at him, but was met by his forearm swinging into her side. Her knees landed in the mud, and then Bea saw who had called him. It was Sophia. She flew around and before the Sister could rise to her feet, hovered in front of her face and struck her as hard as she could between the eyes. The Sister fell face first into the mud.

'I've been waiting a long time to do that,' she said, clapping her hands together in pride.

'You took your time,' said Bea, stepping over the body towards her. 'I thought for a moment you'd all left me to get the job done myself.'

Sophia gave him the smile that she saved just for him. 'What can I say? I missed you, you great fur ball.' She ducked out of the way of a snatching hand that Bea immediately caught and threw back. The Buggane looked more stunned by being hit by his own hand than by the hit itself.

'How did you pull this one off? You sounded so worried I didn't think you'd manage it.'

'Are you kidding me! Once they tied me up they finally decided to let me argue my case for coming to them, so I just told them that the last Fynoderee was going out on his own to face an army of Bugganes. You should have seen them. They fell about hooting like madmen. So I said I could prove it, and if I did, they would have to help us. Naturally they agreed. The Forest Fairies never want to miss a good scrap and they knew this was something they would have to see to believe. We've been waiting around for a little while. I was afraid you might notice us in the grass but you obviously didn't. All they wanted was to wait and see just how crazy you are.'

Without flinching, Bea lifted his elbow to catch the jaw of another sinewy Buggane running up behind him.

'I think you gave them what they came for,' said Sophia, flatly. Bea gave her a small smile and wanted to tell her how happy he was to see her safe, but quickly spun on his heel, ready to strike another blow, when he felt someone behind him. He lowered his arm and relaxed when he looked down and saw that it was Juan, dropped down in front of him by the Bridge Fairies. Bea threw his bone blade to the ground and swept Juan up into his arms and embraced him with delight. They both laughed, though Juan had to plea for him to stop squeezing him so tightly.

'How in Manannin's name did you…?'

'I only did what you would have done Bea, I only told them the truth.'

'But…I…you…me…' Bea couldn't say anything else-he was speechless.

'I thought it was touch and go whether they'd make the right choice for a while. That would have been plain embarrassing, leaving the Bridge without them. But enough had made up their minds to come with me and they helped convince the others that leaving was the right thing to do. Before I knew it, they were all flying out of there with the elders left screaming behind them. Jolly weird coming out, I can tell you that for nothing. Not only were all the Fairies small again, or I was large, or something like that, but only an hour or two had passed out here, talk about lucky! I thought I was under there for months, maybe even longer.'

'Juan I'm so sorry,' said Sophia, flying into the open palms of his hands. 'I should have warned you about the Bridge, it was stupid of me not to have done.' Although she was upset, she still looked pleased to see that he was safe.

'Don't worry about it, Manannin warned me.'

'What?!'

'Yeah, turns out you were right Bea, he was some sort of relation of mine, it was all in the markings. When I finally figured out how to read them they told me about the Fairies and the nectar and what I had to do, well not quite as straightforward as that but they pushed me in the right direction.'

Sophia flew up and planted a sloppy wet kiss on his cheek. 'You are a rare lad indeed, you did what I never could have done. You brought the Fairies together again.'

'Just in time by the looks of it,' said Juan staring around at the dark sight of action around them. Everywhere he looked there were arrows and fists flying, though it was unclear which side had the upper hand. Juan couldn't help but feel a little frightened, even with everything he had been through, and he stood behind Bea for protection.

Bea rested his hand on Juan's shoulder. 'Stay by me, you understand. Don't leave my side. Our work is far from over. Look up there.'

Bea pointed up to the top of the slope and Juan followed his finger. With a flash of lightening he saw where Bea was directing his stare. He saw Queen Atta for the first time, illuminated by the blue-white fork ripping the night apart. He knew it was her, he felt it, though she wasn't what he had been expecting. She was indeed terrible, but she was also beautiful and powerful, as a Queen should be. Juan couldn't take his eyes from her.

'I think she's as shocked as I am that you all showed up,' said Bea, relishing in seeing her squirm and shrink back from joining her children beneath her.

Juan watched Sophia fly from his side, with a surprisingly savage cry, and join a mist of other Fairies bringing down a Brother with a long length of twine. The Brother jerked and panicked as though he had upset a bee's nest, and as he fell Juan saw his friend Aedan swoop in with a makeshift sling and a handful of small rocks, stunning as many of the creatures as he could. Seeing Aedan in action made Juan suddenly eager to join the fray and do his part, but Bea could sense this and kept a firm hand on his shoulder.

Reluctantly Juan stayed as Bea knocked several more of the Bugganes into the firing line of the arrows, but as another fork of lightening tore through the sky he decided that it was wiser to stay put. There was madness all around them.

The Bridge Fairies, much easier to spot in the dark with their brightly coloured dress, were no natural warriors, their idling had relieved them of that, but what they lacked in skill they made up for in heart. Many threw themselves at the Bugganes with a wild and unleashed fury, especially the near transparent Asrais, who dashed in and out of the creatures so quickly they became dizzy and fell to the floor without encouragement.

'Look at them,' shouted Bea over the din. 'They're nothing

more than a rabble without *her*. That's why Mortis had to bring her here.'

'You mean Mr. Mortis told her…'

'That's right.'

'Then you mean to…'

'That's right.'

'Right.'

It was all becoming clearer to Juan. Without their Mother the Bugganes would be leaderless and alone, with no one to will them over ground. They would remain in their tunnels and the island would endure.

'But how can we…?'

Bea had hardly had his back turned for a moment, than a sly Sister had taken her opportunity and scooped up Juan from his side. When he turned it was as though he had never been there. His heart tightened in his chest and he called out to him, but no answer came. What's more, the Bugganes had clearly taken the advantage. A number of them were throwing poorly woven nets through the air, and though many of the Fairies freed themselves from the webs, just as many found themselves trapped and trampled under heavy feet.

The Sister, though skinny with armour loosely jangling around her frame, was still stronger than Juan and restrained his thrashing as she dashed away from the action. Juan spluttered as she covered his mouth with her stinking webbed hand and lay on top of him, forcing his face down into the soaking mud. As he felt the cold hail hit his cheeks he was briefly reminded of having his head forced down a toilet by Cairney and Creeses. What he would give to be back there now!

'Are you what Mother was afraid of?' grunted the Sister, spittle falling from her sharp yellow teeth. 'She'll reward me generously if I take her your corpse, you'd like that wouldn't you?'

Juan madly looked around for anything that could help him. He spotted a fist-sized stone embedded in the mud not an arm's length away. He reached for it, his nails scraping along its slippery side, and looked back into the hideous face of the Sister crushing him. As his fingers curled around the rock he was aware that it was not what he had reached for. It seemed to fit perfectly into the palm of his hands as though it was shaped for that very purpose. He pulled his eyes away from the Sister's and saw that he was holding a pristine blade of a dull grey hue curved like hay in the breeze. Without another hesitation, and with all his might, Juan brought the blade back in a great arc and thrust it deep into the neck of the Sister.

It took Juan only a moment to realise that he was making hysterical gasping noises as he pushed the creature's body from on top of his and he gritted his teeth down hard to still himself.

Dazed and wide-eyed, he wiped the thick dark blood from the blade on the sleeve of his fleece, and saw the words *Remember the Stones* on the back of his right hand. The weapon had such a delicate balance and as he inspected it further he was certain that the entire object was hewn from stone, but that was hardly possible. He turned it over, admiring its blade and moulded hilt, but as he did so his attention was once again drawn to the back of his left hand and his breath caught in his throat. The markings that had as yet been incomplete and incomprehensible had now settled into a finished form. They were ready to be read.

The script was still in mirror image so it took Juan a few moments to decipher its meaning, but once he had done, that which he hoped would become clear remained in riddles. He was baffled.

Bring the stars down upon them.

He wanted to scream in frustration. He looked up to the sky but couldn't see a single star shinning through the dense clouds. Bring down the stars indeed! He began to push himself up, but as he rose a squat Brother with a broken nose came out of nowhere and tackled him around the middle. They both tumbled to the ground and slid a short way down the slope. The blade was knocked from Juan's hand as he fell and so he was left with no other option but to try to grapple with his assailant. He gripped what he thought were his ears, though they could have been tufts of stiff hair, and shook his head back and forth. This only made the Brother more infuriated than before and he leant over, opening his mouth to bite down on Juan's neck. Juan held him off, pushing his square jaw away from him and called out to Bea.

Bea had already seen him and was running through the frenzy head on, flattening any in his way, until he was tripped and keeled over onto his front. Again the creatures threw themselves on top of him, restraining his every move. He could feel the red of his fur fade fast as the acrid stink of the Bugganes overwhelmed him. Juan saw him mouth an apology as their arms stretched out towards each other from where they lay. The terrifying endless dark closed in around them once more and the final thing Bea saw was Juan's helpless face.

He had failed him.

'You haven't failed anyone Bea,' came a voice in his ear.

Time suddenly ceased to matter and slowed to the pace of a lazy morning. Bea cut short his struggle and listened.

'You have never failed anyone, least of all Juan.' He tried to turn his head to see where the voice had come from, but still couldn't move. It was his mother, Méa, calling to him. Mortis must have failed to save her. She must have passed onto the other island and was beckoning him to join her.

'You know that's not true my child. You can still feel her, can't you?' The voice was right. He could still feel his mother with him, and like light in a darkened room the truth came to him, bright and definite.

'That's right Bea.'

'Téeval,' he whispered.

'Always so quick my child, you never were one to hang about, even under…pressure.' The Princess spoke through a smile. Bea wanted to smile with her. In the cold blackness her voice was warmth to him.

'If you are not careful, the worry you lay on yourself will give you lines on that soft face of yours, and I doubt that would please Sophia's eyes.' Bea could hardly believe what she had said and felt himself blush.

'I am sorry. I do not mean to jest with you, especially when you are in no position to retaliate. But remember, that which you love makes you stronger, and you will need that strength before the end.

'Many may not follow me, if that is so, Juan will know what is best to do with them; he has been well advised.'

'*Follow* you?' Bea croaked. 'What do you mean, what are you going to do?'

Téeval spoke one more word in the soft gentle voice of Méa. 'Wonders.'

Bea held himself rigid, ready but anxious for her next move. The voice he then heard in his ear was not that of his mother, or some all knowing voice that he imagined Téeval might have, it was the voice of Atta, shouting out over the whole headland.

'Come to me my children, I need you!'

The weight of the creatures suddenly lifted and Bea felt the sea air fill his lungs. The Bugganes stood up off him, and moved slowly away. Bea saw that they had done the same to Juan. They caught each other's eyes and shared a look of confusion. All had gone silent but for the wind and the drone of the Fairies' wings. Every Buggane in the first wave moved together into the centre of the slope, each walking with slow dead steps. Bea looked up to the top of the slope, where Atta and the second wave of Bugganes stood and saw true horror painted on the Queen's face. He then saw why, for her voice screamed out across Eairnyrey once more, but it didn't come from her lips.

'Come to me my children. I am here. I need you. Come to me.'

The voice came from beyond the cliff, from the sea.

The voice came from Téeval.

Bea sprung to his feet and ran over to Juan, who had also realised what was happening, and he gave him an enormous grin.

'She said she'd come, didn't she?'

'That she did Juan, that she did.'

The voice called out once more, strict and harsh.

'Don't just stand there my children. Come to me!'

Without another pause, the entire first wave of Bugganes ran as one towards the cliff. They ran with such eagerness and obedience, and never stopped until they fell like pebbles tossed over the edge into the violent sea below.

The true voice of Queen Atta pierced the night, full of pain and malice.

'You fools! I am here. It is fallacy, nothing more than a trick. You foolish children!' She fell to the floor and writhed in agony as her children perished. But there was no stopping them, each one ran until they fell and were claimed by the jagged rocks and crushing waves. Téeval had kept her word.

A great cheer from the Fairies echoed over the headland and they all darted back and forth, embracing one another in flight. Juan watched them above him in the star-less sky and then looked up to the second wave of Bugganes and the wasted form of Atta on the floor in front of them, and rubbed the back of his hand. *Bring the stars down upon them.* He sighed. Manannin surely didn't mean what he said. But if he didn't mean the stars, then what did he mean? What other *stars* were there?

Bea watched Atta being helped to her feet, ragged and fuming. She pushed the Brothers away from her and stood tall on her own and with a great cry she gave the order for the second wave to charge. All the Fairies stopped in their celebrations and quickly regrouped.

Juan's mind couldn't move fast enough. He thought of all the night skies he had ever gazed on and still couldn't make sense of the message. But then, without a prompt, an image glowed in his mind's eye of a night sky underground and a constellation of stars that had never hung in space, and the answer came to him.

'Bea, listen to me,' he said, tugging on the Fynoderee's arm to get his attention. 'I know what we've got to do.'

'What's that?' asked Bea, his voice tired and hoarse. He didn't pull his gaze away from the oncoming Bugganes but stared at them, exhausted.

'We've got to get them inside Fleshwick Rock.'

'What good will that do? Besides, I can't even open it, the door has sealed itself shut and refuses my touch.'

'Bea we've got to.' Juan couldn't believe that he was refusing. He yanked harder on Bea's fur, who winced and looked down to him. Juan lifted up his hand and showed him the markings. 'We've got to bring the stars down on their heads.' Bea looked puzzled.

'I don't think we can do that,' he said wryly.

'Please trust me Bea, it's the only way.'

'Journeys with only one direction will take you where you wish to go,' he said, half to himself, then looked into Juan's eyes. 'My father told me that. I do trust you Juan.'

The Bugganes were gaining speed on the slope.

'We can hold them off until you get there,' said the blood stained Sophia, swooping down to them.

'Yeah you listen to that one, he can do all sorts of crazy stuff,' said Aedan joining her and pointing over to Juan. 'Now get going.' Juan smiled at his friend, and looked up to Bea.

'You'd better know what you're doing,' he said, reaching to grab Juan and swinging him onto his back. Juan held off his hand.

'Thanks, but I can carry myself from now on.'

Without saying farewell to his friends Juan ran down the muddy slope and headed for the horseshoe alcove of Fleshwick Rock. Bea nodded to Aedan, winked to Sophia and headed after him. Sophia spun around, wiping the blood from her face, and beckoned Aedan to follow her as they joined the swarms of Fairies flying headlong into the enemy.

TWENTY-FOUR

'I told you it doesn't open. It's as though the whole island has closed in on itself.'

'Can I try?' asked Juan, hastily, through chattering teeth. Water was dripping off the end of his nose and he had begun to shiver in his damp clothes.

'*You* want to try? This rock knows that it is only ever to part at the touch of a Fynoderee's hand. It has known only that since Fynoderees first came to these caves hundreds of years ago. I don't think it would do any good.'

'Please Bea, what harm can it do? I mean if I am this damned *key-per* I must be able to open something. Why have a key if it has no lock to open, it's like a house without a roof… pointless.'

Bea combed his hand through his wet mane trying to think of a riposte. When he couldn't he stood aside and ushered Juan up to face the flat stone, away from the hail beating down on them.

'All you have to do is drag your forefinger gently…'

Juan had already ignored his advice and put his whole palm flat against the rough cold rock and closed his eyes. At first an unpleasant dread, deep like a well in his stomach, soaked through him. He immediately wanted to pull his hand away but forced himself to keep it there and tried to tame the feeling inside. The dread turned into a longing so extreme that he could have cried out. As stupid as it may have sounded in his own head, he tried to quell the sensation, offering the rock words of assurance, much as he might a hurt animal. He told it that they needed help and needed to get inside. For everyone's sake they needed to get inside. He mouthed the words over again, until the feelings flowing through him gradually shifted from fear and withdrawal, to trust and willingness.

He opened his eyes to see a thin break, no thicker than a strand of hair, tear its way down the length of the face and the rock silently parted, revealing the opening to the stairway and the Great Hall below.

'Well I'll be...You're proving to be quite useful, *key-per*,' said Bea, ruffling Juan's wet hair and making his way into the entrance. Juan held out a hand to stop him.

'Wait, they've got to see us first. They've got to see us go inside or else they'll never follow us.'

Bea nodded and they both stood where they were most open to the slope of Eairnyrey, watching the Fairies continue their defence.

Their winged friends valiantly fought off the Bugganes' assault, breaking the wave apart and keeping them clearly away from Fleshwick. Bea could see Sophia keeping a close eye on their progress as she whirled around in the wind, avoiding the snatching hands of the creatures and looking like she was having more fun than words could describe. Ten or twenty Fairies of every colour and breed swooped in on each Buggane, beating them to the ground or luring them to the edge of the cliff side. Though many Bugganes still held their ground, jumping in the air, swiping at their flying foes, catching hold of their prize and throwing them into the mud to be squashed, or smashing them together in their hands.

Bea and Juan could see Sophia and Aedan call out to the Fairies that they had reached the rocks, and directly they flew higher into the swirling wind, out of reach of the Bugganes, and giving them a clear path down to Fleshwick. But some didn't rise. Some stayed where they were and in the heat of battle continued to fight, hurling rocks and peppering arrows of pine down on them as though they were battling the very fear that had kept them in hiding for all those years.

The Asrais, hardly visible in the savage downpour, dared to fly up close to the faces of the beasts and blinded them with handfuls of earth. But this didn't stop the Bugganes attacking. They swiped madly through the air with their blades of bone and inevitably knocked some of them out of the sky, laughing madly as they did so, as if it was sport.

Sophia and Aedan flew back down into the swirl of the creatures to call up those who had stayed, but they refused to move they were so possessed with blood lust. Bea called out to them to leave, but his words were lost in the wind and still they sped between the creatures.

Bea knew it was dangerous for them, they could only be so lucky and they were too few against the reckless might of Atta's family. He called out again, and again they didn't hear him. He wanted to return to the slope and help them, but knew he had to trust Juan and stay by the rocks.

Atta yelled for her children to forget the Fairies and head towards Fleshwick. The painted boy and the last Fynoderee were all that mattered to her. If it took half her family to ensure their fate she would have gladly paid the price. The Brothers and Sisters obeyed her words, though as they moved on down the slope, slipping and sliding like fish out of water, they still lashed out at the remaining Fairies when they could.

As Bea watched Sophia glide through the wind and hail, as happy as she could be, a cold breath of fear passed over him. He saw it happen all too quickly. One Brother, near the cliff side, caught her around her ankles as she flew by him. She bit down on his hand and wildly tried to wriggle herself free but this only made him tighten his grip and bring him closer to the edge. Bea shouted out, but the Brother had already lost his footing in the mud and fell out of sight, keeping his deathly grip and taking Sophia with him. Bea reached out, as though it might help, but she was gone. One moment she was there and the next she wasn't. He felt his eyes sting and a gaping empty space open up inside of him. He could see the Bugganes closing the distance between them with every passing moment, but he no longer felt that it mattered. If he could have done so, he would have lain down on the rock where he stood and surrendered. He would have happily given in. But Juan wasn't going to let that happen.

He had also seen what had happened. He had seen Sophia dragged over the edge and not return and had waited beside Bea, expecting her to fly back into view, hurling abuse and somersaulting through the air, but she didn't come. He wanted to wait some more, but his attention was hauled back when the

312

Bugganes had reached the flat plains before the final descent into Fleshwick, their heavy breath misting in the cold air. There was no more time to wait and he pulled on Bea's arm.

'We've got to go inside now Bea, they're coming.' Bea didn't seem to hear him. He just continued to stare out at the spot where Sophia had fallen.

'Come on now, she'll be all right. She knows how to look after herself. Come on, we've got to go.' He tugged on his arm again, a little harder, and pulled him out of the hail into the entrance of the cave. It was like pulling a reluctant child, but Juan still felt the urgency of the approaching Bugganes, even if he had to feel it for both of them.

It was as black as coal inside the cave and Juan couldn't even see the beginning of the stairwell making its arc down to the hall. They made their way further in and Juan kept hold of Bea's arm, afraid that he would wander back outside.

'Bea, we've got to hide somewhere, out of sight, just for a while. Do you understand? Where can we hide?'

Bea continued to stare out of the cave's entrance at the wild night sky. There was something horribly empty about him, thought Juan. That was the only word that came to him: empty.

'...painted illusion...' he muttered to himself, his voice slow and weary as though the very act of speaking was crushing him. Juan didn't know what he meant. All he knew was that he needed him there alongside him.

'Bea!' he raised his voice. The name echoed through the cavernous space and the wind blew inside and shrieked around them, jangling the glass hanging from the ceiling. Bea looked down to him. In the dark Juan could still make out his green eyes, wet with tears. He took hold of his hand. 'We've got to hide,' he said softly.

'If you can open it,' Bea whispered, 'there is a space behind here.' He loosely gestured at the wall nearest to them, next to the stairs. Juan ran over to the wall, raising his hands, but even before he could touch it, it had silently parted. Inside was a space big enough for them both to stand in. He pulled Bea over to it and once they were inside the thin wall closed them in.

'…nothing more…' Bea continued to mutter, and there they stood, Bea's green eyes the only light in the darkness, until the drumming of feet came from overhead. He then went worryingly quiet. Juan squeezed his limp hand sympathetically. That Bea had lost his brother, Céa, was toll enough, but now Sophia as well…it didn't seem fair.

'What can we do Juan?…What can *we* do against such hate? Maybe there's no chance, maybe we should give ourselves up.'

'To that harpy? You must be joking. If you think I'm going to let us fail, after everything we've done, after everything we've seen, you've got another thing coming. This can be done. I don't know about you, but I intend to sleep in my own bed tonight.'

If he had the strength, Bea would have laughed.

'But what can we do?'

'I told you, it's simple. We've got to bring the stars down on them.'

'That doesn't sound very simple to me.'

'That's because you're thinking about it all wrong. There's a clear sky full of the brightest stars right here in the cave.'

Bea's ears pricked up in sudden comprehension.

'You don't mean…'

'You know that's what I mean.'

'That's a tall order.'

'The tallest I don't doubt. But that's what we have to do nonetheless.'

Bea paused. The sound of trampling feet was getting closer. 'You are right,' he growled. 'This can be done.' He said nothing else. Nothing else needed to be said.

They weren't there long before the Bugganes began to rush by them, barely two paces away on the other side of the wall. The sounds of feet went past, cautiously feeling their way down the spiral stairs and into the Great Hall. Bea and Juan held their breath and waited until no more came through.

'There is nowhere else for you to run!' shouted the guttural voice of Queen Atta. It was the most unmusical noise Juan had ever heard, like someone clearing her throat. 'I have both of you all to myself, after that my children can have you, and believe me when I say they are mightily hungry. Am I wrong?' She laughed out loud and all the Brothers and Sisters laughed with her. The dreadful noise echoed around them, and the glass still jangled.

'It is time,' Bea whispered. 'Let's finish this.'

Juan put his hands to the wall and it slid aside. They slowly walked out into the open. Bea knelt down to the ground and felt for the strongest pebble he could find, one that wouldn't crush when he squeezed it in the palm of his hand, just as he had done countless times before. He pointed out into the dark, tossed the pebble lightly in his hand and then flung it into the cave.

With a startling blue flash, the pebble scraped along the wall, shooting a spark into the wood at the far end. The fire awoke and illuminated the Great Hall. Again, its beauty staggered Juan. A myriad of colours danced over every surface, and the sculpted Fynoderees of ages past, terrifyingly real and alive, stared down at the hall full of unwelcome guests.

The Bugganes didn't know which way to turn and the stony faces of authority on the statues hushed them into silence. In their tunnels they had never seen such splendour and decoration, it was outlawed, and now they saw how one race celebrated its great forefathers and it frightened them. They huddled together and clung onto each other, staring around them at the ominous figures, until they finally caught sight of Bea and Juan at the top of the winding staircase. Their fear instantly evaporated and, jeering, they became mere beasts once more, darting back across the hall.

Bea didn't let them get any further.

He put a hand to Juan, moving him back. Juan saw a look in his eyes that he could only liken to an oppressive sky before a storm unleashes. It unwittingly scared him and he promptly moved out of his way. Bea turned back to the cave and with a motion as swift as wind, leapt high into the air. His back arched, his arms lifted high with clenched fists and waves of many colours swept over his fur. He seemed to hover there for a moment, his roar filling the hall, and then, with all the strength, love, pain and loss left in him, threw his body down onto the floor. His fists smashed into the rock with a deafening crack that sent splinters flying and all around them the cave shook.

Dust fell from the ceiling. Many of the Bugganes began to cough in the fog of it or lost their balance and fell. There was only panic amongst them in the shaking tomb. The jangling glass threw patterns of light everywhere. But then the glass, the stars of the cave, dropped down upon them. The thousands of sharp shards left the ceiling and cut like blades through the air until they met the Bugganes and tore them asunder. The rain of stars, sparkling gold, silver, blue and red sliced through the flesh and bone of every creature with ease. Screams bounced off the walls but were cut short by the downpour, which only lasted two or three quick breaths. Then the colours had stopped their dance, the screams were silenced and the dust rested over the gore remaining in the Great Hall.

Bea collapsed onto his back, his chest painfully heaving in and out. He may have passed out for a while, he was unsure, it felt like too much effort to lift his eyelids and the darkness in his mind was dreamless and absolute. His ears were ringing and his hands throbbed, but still he lay there, just breathing and nothing more.

'Is it over?' he eventually croaked. No answer came, though his ears were ringing so loudly that perhaps he was unable to hear one. He asked again. This time he was answered with a muffled whimper. He grimaced as he leant up onto his elbows.

'Juan, is it over?'

'It's over,' came the reply, but it wasn't Juan's voice that had spoken. He slowly turned his head to look and was staring into the bloodied eyes of Queen Atta. She clenched her webbed hand around his mane and dragged him over the dusty floor into the open. Bea was too weak to struggle and could do nothing but look to his other side and see that she was also pulling Juan behind her, her hand covering his mouth. They reached out to each other and took hands, but were nearly wrenched apart as Atta swung around with surprising agility and threw them over the precipice.

As they both tumbled down, the wind swept them away from the sea and hard back into the cliff face. Bea, keeping Juan's hand locked firmly within his own, took the brunt of the impact on his side. It knocked the air from him, yet still he found a tooth of protruding rock and clung on tight with his remaining hand. He had found his hold in the jagged razor sharp shale, which cut down deep into his palm and opened his scars anew. The blood spat forth from his old wounds and trickled down the length of his arm, dripping red tears towards the sea. He was carrying both his own and Juan's weight on his one weak grip and his muscles tightened and shook in protest. He looked down to Juan and saw the very same face of terror and helplessness as he had seen in his own brother's the moment before their hands slipped from each other and Céa had plummeted to his watery grave.

Hanging there against the cliff, the rock gnarling as it began to crack under the pressure of their weight, a solitary ray of moonlight sneaked through a break in the clouds and shone down on them.

'Don't let me fall Bea, please don't let me fall,' Céa's final words coming from Juan's lips.

The frenzied wind threw them back and forth and still they held on. Bea bit down against the pain as he felt his muscles tear with weariness.

The welcoming sight of Céa laughing passed through his mind. How easy it would be to let go, to join him and be done with such struggles. But he looked into Juan's face and knew that wasn't going to be his fate.

The gusts flew in and about them every way they could and the slippery blood was making Bea's grip tenuous; he wouldn't be able to hold on for much longer. He had nothing left to do but to put his trust into the hollow hands of an old friend.

'Juan, I'm going to let go!' he bellowed down to him, over the din of the storm. Juan's jaw fell open and his face turned ashen white.

'Are you out of your mind?!'

'Trust *me* this time.'

'Don't do it Bea, don't...'

Bea let go of his hold on the rock and, with both feet, kicked out from the cliff face into the wind. Juan shut his eyes and waited for the fall, bracing himself for the impact of the waves, which never came. As they bounded away from the rock, they were ensnared by a great gust of wind that cradled them in its powerful hands. The billow lifted its burden and carried them up and over the edge, dumping them onto the safety of the ridge.

Juan opened his eyes and couldn't help but laugh hysterically, pressing his face down into the wet pebbles, wanting to kiss the flat land.

Bea, as though possessed by an untamed spirit, didn't rest. He stood and raced for Atta, who had barely turned her back on them. She howled in shock as Bea snapped her head back by her wiry black hair and took her by the throat. His hand was still bleeding freely and it oozed down and was lost on her red stained armour. She reached out to tackle him, but he was too quick for her. Before she knew where she was, she was hanging over the same precipice she had thrown Bea and Juan over only moments ago. Her face contorted into a painting of fear as her feet dangled out over nothing but the drop towards the sea.

The crashing waves beneath her suddenly calmed, and from the flat water Juan could see the mesmerising image of Téeval rise from the depths, her multicoloured tail flicking gracefully against the gentle current. Her golden locks of hair and seaweed wavered in the wind and her eyes were now a bottomless black.

She was waiting for Atta.

'No, no, no, you are being too hasty my child. The fastest runner often stumbles.'

'There is nothing you can say that will make me change my mind Atta, you are a murderer. Read my eyes if you wish, all you will see is your own end.'

'I see far more than that my child. I see ignorance cut through those big green eyes of yours like a fault in a jewel.'

Bea tightened his grip. Atta spluttered on her words. Now he looked on her, she was a wreck, adorned with a thousand bruises and wounds, her eyes puffed up and her face swollen and battered. The demise of her children had cost her dearly. She tried again to speak, and although Bea's patience had long gone, he felt inclined to listen and lessened his hold around her throat.

'To…to think that we are…family.'

Bea hesitated. He had heard her utter those words before. They sent a chill running right through him.

'What do you mean by that?' he barked, bringing her face closer to his.

'Oh how sweet it is!' she smiled through chipped teeth and bleeding gums, before glaring at him with such a piercing intensity that Bea trembled and had to force himself not to turn from her.

'We are kin you and I.'

'KIN?! There is nothing that joins us, save for my hand around your neck.'

'You know when a lie is spoken, I grant you that Fynoderee. So look now into my eyes and you will see only truth in the words that I speak. Were you never told the bedtime stories of the birth of Ellan Vannin, of Finn Mac Cooil and the giants?' Atta spoke quickly, taking short sharp breaths whenever she could.

'Of course I have, but what has this got to do with us?' He so wanted to let go. It was only some thread of curiosity keeping its hold that was saving Atta now.

'Suppose they were more than just stories,' she began, in a dark whisper. 'Suppose that when the island was born there were only two families of men upon it, and even then the land wasn't big enough for both of them. The two families bickered and fought ceaselessly, often with fatal consequences, and their disputes over land and laws were never resolved. Suppose they fought until there was only one solution left, only one path left to take. They would create boundaries and live apart, just like those winged friends of yours. And then suppose that over time, over more time than history could ever trace, they changed and grew and evolved into what they have now become…you and I.'

Bea's eyes lit up. He couldn't be hearing her right and yet he knew that she was speaking truths.

'You mean…you and I…we…are…'

'Just like them: people, man-folk, one and the same, like that little boy there. We are all the same, men and women who have simply taken different paths through time to end up here.'

Bea's mind was reeling with confusion. They were all one and the same, they were all connected, and they were all family. He had to steady himself in the wind and hail. Atta's loathsome grin widened.

'Now you wouldn't hurt your Mother would you?'

'Don't say that! You are not my mother.'

'I might as well be. We are all one big happy family, and this island is ours Bea, yours and mine, and together we can take it back from those thieves. Don't you want that, to walk in the free air whenever you wish? You and I alone are stronger than they are. We can do it together. Join with me and we can reclaim the island for our own. It is ours.'

Bea's mind stopped spinning and he shook his head. He knew now what he was. He was a man like any other.

'*Dy juen yn hoilshaghey skeayley'n roig shak er geinnagh ny marrey.* We are guests here and should behave as such.' His father's words spoken through him. 'I hope on the other side you will have all the time you need to see this.'

Atta's narrow puffy eyes widened. Her dreams had escaped from her slumber and joined with her waking life. She could see herself fall. This was to be her end.

'Do you think this will be it Fynoderee?' she spat. 'Do you not think in time another Mother, another Queen, will rise and share my desires, in a time when you are gone from this land? It will never be over, never, am I wrong?!'

'You are wrong, you have always been wrong.'

Bea released his hold of her.

Her mouth opened into a silent scream and both he and Juan watched her tumble in the wind against the rocks and fall down towards the sea. Téeval opened her embrace and took her down into the blackest depths. The waves crashed over them and they were gone.

Bea, a dead weight, fell into Juan's side and they collapsed onto the rock of the precipice. His great bulk shivered in the cold and, for the first time, Juan saw something in the Fynoderee that told him he was barely out of childhood himself, that he too was hardly yet a man. He stroked off the water from his dull brown mane.

'Is it over?' he quietly asked him.

Bea turned and looked up at him. His eyes spoke a thousand words, but he could only manage one.

'Maybe.'

The hail continued to beat down on them, and as the wind whistled by, Bea's ears pricked up and he sniffed the air. He could hear no whispers in the wind and the only scent was that of the sharp salty sea. There they sat in silence, as brothers, holding each other in the cold for some time.

TWENTY-FIVE

The hail did gradually end and soon enough the wind parted the dense clouds, letting in the welcome light of the moon, before eventually dying down. The silver glow of night seemed to quickly fade and was usurped by the flame red dawn awakening the island to a new day. The morning sky was a clear, pale blue with wisps of high cloud lying stagnant in the firmament.

Mr. Boyde and his son, Ewan, had woken early and were breakfasting on kippers. Ewan was rushing his food, not wanting to be late and let down his father. Mr. Boyde was muttering that he always ate too fast and should get out of bed sooner. Not that he really minded. He was thankful for the company.

Derrick and Joyce Kermode took their dog, Duke, for an early morning walk up South Barrule. Derrick held his wife's hand as they trampled up the hard path and relished a full breath of the crisp air. Duke broke free from his lead, barged past them and ran on ahead, chasing a rabbit into the thicket.

The sun shone down over the whole island, thawing what frost lay on the highlands and reflecting emerald and gold off the sea. Curphey the fisherman pulled his nets up onto the deck and threw an old penny overboard in thanks for his fine catch.

Bea quietly sat on the headland of Eainyrey, away from the slopes where he could be seen in broad daylight, and looked down to the cliffs and the water below. He saw Sophia fall ten thousand times over in his mind, and whispered a goodbye at every one.

Not far away in Port Erin, Mrs. Quilliam was busy baking in the kitchen. Her husband, Hugh, rushed passed her, and as he stole a bite of a fresh cake she slapped his hand and berated him. The cake was for the guests. Hugh left quickly through the back door and made his escape towards the local bookshop.

At Marown Primary School, Mrs. Cowley asked the children

to work in pairs. Johnny and Sarah beamed as they rushed together and found a table where they could hold hands and not be seen. Once everyone had found a partner, Richard Gill remained alone at his table and scuffed his shoes on the floor at the back of the class.

The splendid light of the day was all too brief and the evening soon stepped in, bringing its shades over the land. Stuart Skelly met his friends in the local pub for a glass of ale and a game of dominoes, as they always did, and his wife, Gene, played cards at the farm next door and day-dreamed of sun-kissed beaches.

Manannin's thick cloak wrapped tightly around the island once more and all remained quiet and warm and safe.

The days gently rolled into one another, so quickly they were barely a flicker in the sky to some. Winter came and went and was soon followed by the season of the Fairies, the Spring, bringing a festival of colour and life.

Méa and Dane saw some life return to their son, but they knew something in him had died that night above Fleshwick. Though he spent much time with them in the Great Hall, once it was cleared, his company was quiet and thoughtful and he spoke little about their time apart.

Gavan Clague's wounds eventually healed, as did Markys Dawson's, but the scars they left remained. None of them spoke a word about what had happened over their few desperate days in the pits and tunnels of the earth, not even to each other, but many of them endured marks of the truth upon their bodies as proof, if only to themselves, that it was real. And Mr. Seer sat quite still in his old armchair, smiling.

One morning in a modest house on the coast outside of Peel, Juan Kerruish lay in bed only half awake and hit his hand down on the alarm clock for what may have been the fourth time. He had slept heavily and was so warm and cosy that the last thing he wanted to do was get up. He turned over and let his eyelids fall shut again. He'd rise in a moment or two, he told himself.

'Juan, hurry up would you. You don't want to miss the school bus. You've missed it once this week already and I can't take you in this morning,' his mum shouted up the stairs.

Juan grumbled under his breath and turned back over to look at his clock. That couldn't be the time, he gasped. He was late again. He hurriedly climbed out of bed and fumbled into his school uniform. Catching sight of his reflection in the mirror, he passed a finger over where his markings had faded away, as he did every morning, and ran out of the room still doing up his tie. He flew down the banister of the stairs, nearly fell when he landed and tripped over all the toys strewn across the hall.

Clomping into the kitchen in his unlaced shoes, he smiled at the smell of his breakfast cooking and sat down at the table, taking a big gulp of his tea. His dad passed him, ruffling his hair as he went, and sat down next to him, reading the morning paper and speaking through a mouthful of toast.

'Nothing in here about the bones they found over at Eainyrey. They must have forgotten about them already, or else they can't figure out what on earth they are.'

Juan shrugged as he tied his shoe laces, but smiled when his mum put down a full plate of breakfast in front of him. He heartily tucked into the food and looked up at the clock. He didn't have much time.

'So how's it going with that girl in your class?' his mum asked, leaning against the table with Aalin in her arms. 'What was her name, Doona something?'

Juan dropped his shoulders, trying to give the impression that he wasn't too bothered by her question. 'Fine,' he mumbled through his food.

'Fine?' his dad chuckled, closing the paper sharply. 'Just fine? That's not an answer. What about all of the gory details?'

Juan could feel himself going red. 'Dad, don't be weird.'

'You can invite her round for dinner one night next week if you want?' his mum suggested.

'We promise we'll behave ourselves,' his dad added, smirking.

'Maybe,' said Juan, coolly, swallowing down the last of his food.

'Well come on then, you better run, or you won't get to see

her today at all.'

Juan threw on his blazer, swung his satchel over his shoulder and jumped for the door, calling out as he ran, 'Love you Mum, love you Dad.'

'Me?!' bleated Aalin.

'And you!' laughed Juan, and the door slammed behind him.

That very same morning Bea had woken not much later than Juan and left Fleshwick Rock in *arraghey*, unnoticed by his parents, still sleeping in the Great Hall. He had finally decided that there were some things that needed answering and he resolved to go to the one place where he knew his questions would be heard, *Kiarkil voish Ansoor*, the Circle of Answers.

He ran the many miles to Braaid flat out, without stopping once to pause and rest, and when he arrived it was much the same as the last time he had been there with Juan. How strange that it already felt so long ago. The valley was dotted with sheep and the ground was thick with daisies, buttercups and dandelions. He stepped through the turnstile and walked down to the cluster of rocks, still covered in moss. He passed the settlement and walked on until the perfect circle of rocks surrounded him, every one as aged and decaying as the other. He ran to the edge of the circle, took a deep, calming breath and placed his hand down on the nearest rough stone.

Again he felt his eyes forced shut with a great weight and the overwhelming sensation of falling into darkness surge through him. As hard as he looked he saw no one and nothing, only the blackness of the unknown. There was no one waiting for him. He removed his hand and fell to his knees. There was nothing for him in the dark or in his own world. In the springtime sunshine, looking out to where the distant hills met, he only felt wintry cold. The grass swayed and lay flat in the early morning breeze, but then a movement caught his eye and he instantly dropped onto all fours and shifted back into *arraghey*.

Where he looked, the long grass wasn't swaying to the gentle hands of the breeze, it was moving in a possessed way that he recognized, as though touched by something invisible walking through it. He closely followed its pattern and shape and then nearly screamed aloud when he saw a tall slender figure shift in and out of sight right before his eyes. It was exactly like the vision that he'd had in that very spot all those moons ago; a female, like him, crossing his path. He shook himself to make sure he was indeed awake, when she appeared again further off towards the forest, running into the thick of the trees.

He ran after her, knocking back the branches so he could catch another glimpse. His heart was quickening in his chest and his forehead was moist with sweat. He was almost certain that his mind was playing tricks on him, yet the remaining edge of doubt impelled him on. He stood behind the thick trunk of a pine, slowly peered round and there she was, with her back to him. She had soft silky golden fur covering her delicate frame and a mane that stretched far down her shoulders, in every way like his painting on the wall of the Great Hall. She was by far the most beautiful thing he had ever seen. He wanted to call out to her, but the words stuck in his throat and he coughed. She turned and saw him from over her shoulder. For several moments they looked into each other's eyes.

Bea was dumbstruck.

He gazed deep into her almond shaped eyes and realised that he knew her. She gave him a broad smile as though it was saved just for him and ran on ahead. Bea chased after her and couldn't stop smiling. This was more than just different, he thought.

This was magic.